THE BEST AMERICAN

NONREQUIRED

READING

2015

WITHDRAWN

THE BEST AMERICAN

NONREQUIRED READING™

2015

∎

EDITED BY

ADAM JOHNSON

AND THE STUDENTS OF

826 NATIONAL

MANAGING EDITOR
DANIEL GUMBINER

A MARINER ORIGINAL
HOUGHTON MIFFLIN HARCOURT
BOSTON ▪ NEW YORK
2015

www.hmhco.com

ISSN: 1539-316x
ISBN: 978-0-544-56963-8

Printed in the United States of America
DOC 10 9 8 7 6 5 4 3 2 1

CONTENTS

Editors' Note

It is Monday night and *The Best American Nonrequired Reading* committee has assembled at the offices of McSweeney's Publishing in San Francisco. They have met here every Monday for the past year to read over every magazine and journal that was published in 2014 and decide which pieces to include in the book that you are currently holding. It is a cold night, this night, the whole city covered in a creamy layer of fog—but inside the publishing house it is warm and the light is soft and, miraculously, the committee's chief intern, Taylor Stephens, has brought cookies. It is probably around 7:30 and, at present, there is a great hubbub, mostly because of the cookies, but also because I have just told the committee that they must write an editors' note.

"To explain to the world how this process works," I say.

"I think we should tell them about the cookies, obviously," says Marco Ponce, a junior at George Washington High School.

"Yes," says Evelyn Pugh, a senior who has just found out she will attend Macalester College next year, "The cookies are certainly a very important part. And the gummy bears. They should know about that time Taylor brought gummy bears."

"And the smell of Zola's fries that she brings to class every day," says Kelly Lee, a first-year committee member.

"Man, those always smell so good," says Samantha Ng, a junior at June Jordan School for Equity.

"I think they want to know more about the content of the class," I insist. "What types of things we talked about, what we learned."

"Look, Daniel," says Juan Chicas, a senior at June Jordan, "Class is a very big, very juicy piece of meat. It's very hard to eat the whole thing in one bite, if you know what I'm saying."

There are many nods of affirmation. The committee knows what Juan is saying.

"You know what I would say," says Cynthia Van, a junior at George Washington. "I would say that the most important part of *BANR* is getting to share our opinions. I get to share my opinion and hear everyone else's opinions about everything we read. I don't have a single class in school that does that type of thing, and when I come here, everyone discusses everything and we all learn from each other."

"Discussion is sick, bro," says Juan.

"I would also say that we just pick the things we love," says Cosmo Comito-Steller, a junior at Lowell High School. "It's really not that much more complex than that."

"The complexity comes in when certain people love things that other people don't love," says Cosmo's brother, Milo, a junior at Balboa High.

"And that the whole process helps us with our own writing," says Isaac Schott-Rosenfield, who is just finishing up his first year on the committee. "I wrote a lot of stuff this year that was inspired by things we considered for the book. Sometimes I would even start writing stories on the backs of the print-outs we read in class."

"Yeah," says Zola Rosenfeld, a freshman at Jewish Community High School, "after you read through hundreds of literary magazines you really start to see things differently: you start to hone your taste."

There is a lull in the talking and the committee members seem immersed in thought, reflecting on the past year. Then from the corner, Cynthia speaks up,

"You just learn a lot, you know?" she muses. "Like, I didn't even know who Andre the Giant was before this class."

Everyone laughs. Thanks to Box Brown's graphic novel, an excerpt of which is featured on page 241, everyone is now a big fan of Andre the Giant. So much so that there has been talk of a *Princess Bride* viewing party.

In a half hour the committee will disband for the evening. Some students will be picked up by their parents, others will take the bus home across the city, or hop on trains to the East Bay. These brilliant young committee members are the latest iteration of a long line of committees that stretch back to 2002, when Dave Eggers first had the wonderful idea to let a group of high school students edit an anthology of writing. Today, Dave no longer edits the anthology, although his spirit and intuition still serve as a guiding force for the committee. The editorship now rotates on a yearly basis and this year, we were honored to have Pulitzer Prize-winning author Adam Johnson serve as our commander-in-chief. He visited the class and spoke to the students about writing and helped us select the stories that are included in this book. The committee was also aided by a group of students at 826 Michigan who met weekly, just like the San Francisco committee, and sent along excellent recommendations.

As a former member of the committee myself, I can tell you that it is a very challenging but incredibly empowering experience to be given the responsibility of putting together an anthology like this. Sophie Halperin, a senior on the committee, summed it up well when she wrote about *BANR* for her college application personal statement: "Oftentimes in school I am asked to analyze a work, but I am never asked what I think about it. That is because the pieces we are assigned to read are considered classics. It has already been decided that those pieces are worth reading. But this time, I'm the one who decides what value a work has." This is the uncommon and instructive challenge that students on the *BANR* committee face and, this year, as with years past, they have risen marvelously to the occasion. We have found value in every piece in this book and we sincerely hope you do as well. Thank you, thank you, thank you for reading.

DANIEL GUMBINER and the *BANR* Committee
San Francisco, June 2015

INTRODUCTION

IN HIGH SCHOOL, I read the standard-issue texts: *The Red Badge of Courage, Of Mice and Men, The Old Man and the Sea*. They were good books and they interested me, but when I read on my own, I reached for Stephen King or my Mom's James Clavell novels. My most literary commitment was a subscription to *Omni Magazine*. Unfortunately, I was the most bookish of my early '80s teen posse. We spent our free periods in the parking lot of a church across from school—in an effort to lure us in with their cool attitude, the pastors had declared the lot a hassle-free haven for clove smokers, metalheads and assorted hood sitters. Instead of meeting for a book club, we were the kind who took turns pulling each other on water skis down Arizona-hot irrigation canals with ropes attached to the roll bars of our pickups. We spent our free time souping up engines, shooting up the desert, and throwing keg parties in the basement of a decommissioned alcohol-rehabilitation facility where my buddy lived with his twenty-one siblings, half siblings and step siblings.

College is where I would discover literature, as if for the first time, and more importantly, it was where I would first know the deep satisfaction of writing. But I didn't go there directly. I spent a few years forming concrete on mid-rise buildings and industrial construction projects. I worked on bridges, tunnels, a couple corporate headquarters and even the parking structure at Fiesta Mall. It's hard to stay in a Hilton after you've built a couple of them. Looking back, though, I can see that during these years, stories and storytelling were a central part of my life. I witnessed many story worthy events. I saw a falling piece of lumber cleanly remove the ear of a man working next to me. I heard, but didn't see, the sound of a falling rat-tail file going through the bicep of a pipefitter I knew. I'll never forget the blinding, explosive light that resulted from a crane boom lowering into the high-power lines that fed downtown Phoenix. There were things I didn't witness yet were so vividly described to me by those who did that they worked into my mind forever, as when a worker on our Buckeye jobsite took his life with a worm-drive Skil saw.

I remember these episodes not as life that I lived, but as stories I recall in which I was a character. Some of the best stories were the simpler ones—a jug of hot urine that fell twelve stories, an exploding jar of mayonnaise, the crane operator who loved to drop Kentucky Fried Chicken bones a hundred feet down to our hardhats. Sometimes I became the subject of stories other people told—when a foreman foolishly allowed me to operate the Manitowoc crane, for example. (Its braking system was counterintuitive.) Or when I was foolishly allowed to operate the Cat 992D loader. (It was really hard to see around a twelve-yard bucket.)

If I felt like a character, the men I spent my shifts with truly were characters, like the millwright who kept a sawed-off, pistol-grip shotgun in his toolbox, each barrel of which was filled with a half roll of dimes. Or the cement finisher who tried to hide the fact that he was going blind. Or the patient, thoughtful carpenter who had two wives—they always packed him the best lunches! Of course there were the oddballs, addicts, ex-cons and preachers, guys who told stories that revolved around buried money, airport lockers, bad checks and women who were onto them. And then there were stories workers brought from other jobs and swapped like wampum. These were tall tales of lost lives, betrayals, epic heartaches, reversals of fortune, random fates and the ever popular revenge narratives.

I'll admit it's hard to keep straight which stories happened to me, which I witnessed, which I heard direct testimony about and which were communal lore. But keeping such things straight doesn't really interest me. I loved all those stories, their rightness and trueness, and it didn't matter to me if they were verifiable or not. I trust the vagaries of my own memory least of all, and as my identity has changed over the years (from a lost, yahoo of a young man to a professor at a fancy university) I fear my narrative keeps warping into alignment.

I wouldn't have taken a different path, and I wouldn't trade my time in the sun with guys who went by names like Grover and Nuggs and Doggy Bear. But I've always felt I missed some critical years of reading. Who would I have become if, rather than pulpy jobsite yarns, I'd been exposed to writers like Wells Tower, Rebecca Curtis or Daniel Alarcón? Who might any of us have become if as high school freshmen we were invited to read, discuss, debate and adjudicate literature in the most serious of terms. That question is at the heart of *The Best American Nonrequired Reading* project, set in motion by Dave Eggers.

There was nothing like *BANR* in my time. I like to think I would have been drawn to it, to the awesomeness of the project, to the adultness of the endeavor. So when an opportunity arose to edit an issue of *BANR*, I found the prospect immediately appealing. What was not to like? There'd be lots of good reading and discussions. There'd be burritos. And there'd be the inherent coolness of editing a book with teens. What would high-school sophomores make of Katie Coyle's "Fear Itself" or Victor Lodato's "Jack, July," I wondered? Lots, actually. A whole lot. More, I'm afraid, than I would have at such an age.

The young editors read widely and proposed interesting and often overlooked works to be devoured and discussed. Right away, I found a story I thought was heartfelt yet edgy, perfect for *BANR*'s panel of young editors. I attended the Monday night session when the editors read and discussed the piece I'd put forward. The discussions take place around chuck wagon tables in a storefront on Valencia Street in San Francisco's Mission District. The verdict on the piece I'd presented: rejection. I hadn't seen that coming. I was the editor, right? But the passion, thought, and seriousness with which the students engaged the work was all I'd hoped it would be.

The next story I put forward did pass muster, and I was an admirer of all the work the editors suggested and selected. And I could see in their passions and devotions the false analogy I'd created. As a construction worker, stories were all I had to help me get through long shifts and terrible working conditions with people you normally wouldn't sit next to at the DMV. There was no way to compare that to the experience of reading today's best works with our community's finest young minds. And I always forget the awful stories from my days as a construction worker. I once worked on a big job in Chandler, Arizona. One of the carpenters would bring books to read on his lunch breaks. Everyone teased him mercilessly about that. They started calling him "professor." I called him that, too. I wince to think of it now, and it reminds me that, even though I would have been drawn to an amazing project like *BANR*, I probably wasn't ready for it. Books had a lot to offer me back then, but I had little to return. Perhaps I had to learn what literature wasn't before I could appreciate what it was. Literature isn't about porta-potty disasters or people reading blueprints while intoxicated. It's about the most important examinations in life. In that regard, the young editors who bring you this anthology are leagues ahead of us.

ADAM JOHNSON

Adam Johnson *teaches creative writing at Stanford University. He is the author of* Fortune Smiles, Emporium, Parasites Likes Us, *and* The Orphan Master's Son, *which was awarded the Pulitzer Prize for fiction. He has received a Whiting Writers' Award and fellowships from the National Endowment for the Arts and the Guggenheim Foundation. His work has appeared in* Esquire, Harper's, Playboy, GQ, *the* Paris Review, Granta, Tin House, *the* New York Times, *and* The Best American Short Stories. *He lives in San Francisco.*

THE BEST AMERICAN

NONREQUIRED
READING
2015

WELLS TOWER

■

Who Wants to Shoot an Elephant?

FROM *GQ*

Chapter 1: The Huntress Seeks Her Trophy

It is just before dawn at a hunting camp in Botswana's game-rich northern savanna, and Robyn Waldrip is donning an ammunition belt that could double as a hernia girdle.

"You can't help but feel like sort of a badass when you strap this thing on," she says. Robyn, a Texan in her midthirties, seems to stand about six feet two, with piercing eyes of glacial blue shaded by about twelve swooping inches of eyelash. She's a competitive body-builder and does those tractor-tire and sledgehammer workouts, and there is no part of her body, from the look of it, that you couldn't crack a walnut on. In her audition video for a reality-television show called *Ammo & Attitude*, Robyn described herself as a stay-at-home mom whose "typical Friday-night date with [her] husband is going to the shooting range, burning through some ammo, smelling the gun-powder, going out for a rib-eye steak, and calling it a night."

Robyn Waldrip could kick my ass, and also your ass, hopping on one leg. Her extensive résumé of exotic kills includes a kudu, a zebra, a warthog, and a giraffe. But she has never shot a *Loxodonta africana*, or African elephant, so before she sets out, her American guide, a professional hunter named Jeff Rann, conducts a three-minute tuto-rial on the art of killing the world's largest land animal.

"You want to hit him on this line between his ear holes, four to six inches below his eyes," Jeff explains, indicating the lethal horizontal on a textbook illustration of an elephant's face. The ammo Robyn will be using is a .500 slug about the size of a Concord grape, propelled from a shell not quite as large as Shaquille O'Neal's middle finger. About three feet of bone and skin insulate the elephant's brain from the light of day, and it can take more than one head shot to effect a kill. "If he doesn't go down on your second shot, I'll break his hip and you can finish him off."

"Anything else I need to know?" Robyn asks.

"That's it," says Jeff.

"Just start shooting when they all come at us?"

"The main thing is, just stay with the guns," Jeff tells the rest of the party, which includes Robyn's husband, Will Waldrip, two trackers, this journalist, a videographer who chronicles Jeff's hunts for a television program, *Deadliest Hunts*, and a government game scout whose job it is to ensure that the hunt goes according to code. The bunch of us pile into the open bed of a Land Cruiser and set off into the savanna, the guides and the Waldrips peering into the lavender pre-dawn for an elephant to shoot.

If you are the sort of person who harbors prejudices against people who blow sums greater than America's median yearly income to shoot rare animals for sport, let me say that Will and Robyn Waldrip are very easy people to like. They didn't grow up doing this sort of thing. Robyn's dad was a fireman who took her squirrel hunting because it was a cheap source of fun and meat. Will's father was a park ranger. In his twenties, Will went into the architectural-steel business, and now he co-owns a company worth many millions of dollars. They look like models from a Cabela's catalog. They are companionable and jolly, and part of the pleasure of their company is the feeling that you've been welcomed into a kind of America where no one is ever fat or weak or ugly or gets sad about things.

The Waldrips arrived in Rann's camp on the eighth of July, and they've allotted ten days for the hunt. But it is unlikely to take that long to find their trophy. Botswana contains somewhere in the neighborhood of 154,000 elephants, most of them concentrated in this 4,000-square-mile stretch of northern bushland where the Kalahari Desert meets the Okavango Delta.

In addition to airfare, ammo, and equipment costs (the antique double-barreled Holland & Holland rifle Robyn bought for the trip typically sells for about $80,000), the Waldrips are paying Jeff Rann $60,000 for the privilege of shooting the animal, at least $10,000 of which goes to the Botswana government. In September 2013, a ban on elephant hunting goes into effect in Botswana, making the Waldrips' hunt one of the last legal kills. It is a precious, expensive experience, and Robyn wants to take her time to find big ivory, not to simply blast away at the first elephant that wanders past her sights.

Through the brightening dawn, the Land Cruiser bucks and rockets along miles of narrow trails socked in by spindly acacia trees, camellia-like mopani shrubs, and a malign species of thornbush abristle with nature's answer to the ice pick. No elephants are on view just yet, though a few other locals have come out to note our disturbance of the peace. Here is a wild dog, a demonic-looking animal whose coat is done up in a hectic slime-mold pattern. Wild dogs, among the world's most effective predators, are the biker gangs of Africa. They chase the gentle kudu to exhaustion in a merciless relay team. A soft-hearted or lazy dog who lets the prey escape can catch a serious ass-kicking from the rest of the heavies in the pack. What's that, Mr. Wild Dog? You're on the endangered-species list? Well, karma is a bitch. Let's move along.

Now here is a pair of water buffalo. Charming they are not. They scowl sullenly from beneath scabrous plates of unmajestic, drooping horn. "Hostile, illiterate" are the descriptors I jot on my notepad.

And there is the southern yellow-billed hornbill, and there the lilac-breasted roller, which, yes, are weird and beautiful to look upon, but if you had birds jabbering like that outside your window every morning, would you not spray them with a can of Raid?

Say what? I'm unfairly harshing the fauna? Yes, I know I am. I'm sorry. To the extent that I've discussed it with Jeff Rann and the Waldrips and other blood-sport folk I know, I believe that hunters are being sincere when they say they harbor no ill will toward the animals they shoot. Not being a hunter myself, I subscribe to an admittedly sissyish philosophy whereby I only wish brain-piercing bullets upon creatures I dislike. I've truthfully promised Jeff Rann that I'm not here to write an anti-hunting screed, merely to chronicle the hunt coolly and transparently. But the thing is, I'm a little worried that some unprofessional, bleeding-heart sympathies might fog my lens when the elephant gets his bullet. So I'm trying to muster up some prophylactic loathing for the animals out here. I want to be properly psyched when the elephant goes down.

Perhaps out of a kind of kindred impulse, Will and Robyn Waldrip are quick to point out the violences elephants have inflicted on the local landscape. And it's true, the *Loxodonta africana* isn't shy about destroying trees. We are standing in an acreage of bare earth ringing a watering hole Jeff Rann maintains. It looks like a feedlot on the moon. Where there is not a broken tree or a giant dooky bolus, there is a crater where an elephant started eating the earth.

"Man, [the elephants] have just destroyed the ecosystem," Will says. "People who oppose hunting ought to see this." Will is a bowhunter. Elephants aren't his bag. And while he has no reservations about Robyn shooting the elephant, he is doing, I think, some version of the hunt-justifying psych-up going on in my own head. He wants to feel like it's a good deed his wife is doing out here, a Lorax-ly hit in the name of the trees.

It's midafternoon before we spy a candidate for one of Robyn's Concord grapes. In the shade of a very large tree, a couple of hundred yards from the jeep trail, is something that does not at first register as an animal, more a form of gray weather. We dismount and huddle before setting off into the brush.

The elephant appears to be a trophy-caliber animal, but at this distance, it's hard to say for sure. "One thing," Jeff says to Robyn. "If it charges, we have to shoot him."

"If he charges, *I'm* gonna shoot him," Robyn says. The entourage begins a dainty heel-to-toe march into the spiky undergrowth. As it turns out, it is not one elephant but two. One is the big, old, shootable bull. The other is a younger male. Elephants never stop growing, a meliorative aspect of which (elephant-hunt-misgivings-wise) is that the mongo bulls that hunters most want to shoot also happen to be the oldest animals, usually within five or so years of mandatory retirement, when elephants lose their last set of molars and starve to death.

For the record, this detail does not soothe me as the guns make their way toward the elephants under the tree. I have not yet figured out how to dislike elephants enough to want to see one shot. In private treason against my hosts, I am thinking, *Not now, not now. Let it please not get shot today.*

We near the creatures. The big bull shifts its ears, and it is a significant event, like the hoisting of a schooner's rigging. Jeff lifts his binoculars. As it turns out, the bull is missing a tusk, probably broken off in a fight. So it will not be shot, its ultimate reward for the tusk-snapping tussle.

We creep back to the jeep. Robyn is electrified, breathing hard, her blue eyes luminous with adrenaline: "That was big!" she says to Will. "As soon as we got out of the truck, was your heart going?"

"Nah, but when he turned and his ears spread and he went from huge to massive? Yeah."

"Huge," says Robyn. "It could just mow us down."

"We'd be jelly," says Will. "But you wouldn't want to have shot him on your first day, anyway."

Chapter 2: Can You Save Thousands of Elephants by Shooting Just a Few?

Fair warning: An elephant *does* get shot in this story. It gets shot pretty soon. Maybe that upsets you, as it did 100 percent of the people (hunters and nonhunters) to whom I mentioned this assignment.

Elephants are obviously amazing, or rather, they are obvious receptacles for our amazement, because they seem to be a lot like us. They live about as long as we do. They understand it when we point at things, which our nearest living evolutionary relative, the chimpanzee, doesn't really. They can unlock locks with their trunks. They recognize themselves in mirrors. They are socially sophisticated. They stay with the same herds for life, or the cows do, anyway. They mourn their dead. They like getting drunk (and are known to loot village liquor stashes in Africa and India). When an elephant keels over, its friends sometimes break their tusks trying to get it to stand up again. They bury their dead. They bear grudges against people who've hurt them, and sometimes go on revenge campaigns. They cry.

So why would you want to put a bullet in one? Well, if we are to take hunters at their word, it is because the experience of shooting an animal yields a thrill, a high that humans have been getting off on since we clubbed our first cave bear. And if you go in for this sort of thing, then it arguably stands to reason that the bigger the beast, the bigger the thrill when it hits the ground.

On the subject of hunting's pleasures, Robyn Waldrip has this to say: "It kind of taps into your primal instincts. I think everybody has it in them."

But an elephant?

"It was on my bucket list of hunting. It's the largest land mammal, and just to go up against something that big, it's exciting. I ran into this mom at the grocery store and she was like, 'What are you doing for the summer?' and I said, 'I'm going to Africa to do an elephant hunt.' And she said, 'Why in the world would you wanna do that?' and I'm like, 'Why wouldn't you?'"

Jeff Rann has a similar take: "Hunting's almost like a drug to people that do it." In his thirty-eight-year career, Jeff has presided at the shootings of around 200 elephants, and he has never had a trophy get away from him. It is Jeff Rann whom King Juan Carlos I of Spain calls when he wants to shoot an elephant, as he did in April 2012. (King Juan Carlos likely will not get the hankering again. He broke his hip on the safari—in the shower, not on Rann's watch— and amid the general outrage sparked by leaked photos of the king posed alongside his kill, Juan Carlos was booted from the honorary presidency of the World Wildlife Fund and compelled to issue a public apology.)

Rann is the most perfect exemplar I have ever met of Hemingway's speak-softly-and-shoot-big-things-without-being-a-blowhard-about-it masculine ideal. He is lethally competent and incredibly understated and cool, even when he's telling swashbuckling stories, such as the time he nearly got killed by a leopard: "The leopard charged. I shot him. It was a bad shot. He jumped on me, and we just kind of looked at each other. I remember those yellow eyes staring back at me. He bit me twice and dropped to the ground. He also pissed all over me. For about a year, I'd wake up in the night and I'd smell that strong cat smell. But I don't think about it anymore." Or the time he led the Botswana Defence Force into a camp of poachers who'd been hunting in the land he leases from the government. "We went into camp, and there were two old guys and one kid about 16 years old. The agents just opened up on them. Killed the two old guys outright. The one they shot eleven times, the other they shot fourteen times. The kid took off running, but they shot him a couple of times in the back."

Q. So you, like, saw three guys get shot and killed?
A. Yeah.
Q. Whoa. Wow. What was that like?
A. Didn't bother me.
Q. Wow, really? Weird. Do you think that's because maybe you've seen so many animals killed over the years that seeing the poachers get shot, it's, you know, just another animal?
[Patient silence during which Rann seems to be restraining self from uttering the word "pussy" in conjunction with visiting journalist.]
A. I don't know. Hard to say. Those guys [illegally] killed a lot of animals. It pissed me off.

In addition to million-acre leases in Botswana, Rann has a hunting concession in Tanzania and a 5,500-acre rare-game ranch outside San Antonio. The economic downturn did not put much of a bite in Rann's business, a happy fact he credits to the addictive nature of hunting's elemental pleasures: "Our clients might not buy a new car as often, or buy a second or third home, but they're still going to go hunting." But this new hunting ban is poised to do to Rann's elephant-hunting business what economic calamity could not.

There's been a regulated hunting industry in Botswana since the 1960s. Before the ban took effect, the government was issuing roughly 400 elephant-bull tags per year, of which Jeff Rann was allowed to buy about forty. And counterintuitively, even in the presence of an active bullet-tourism industry, Botswana's elephant population has multiplied twentyfold, from a low point of 8,000 in 1960 to more than 154,000 today. These healthy numbers, as people like Rann are keen to mention, mirror elephant populations in other African countries where hunting is allowed. Despite a recent uptick in poaching problems, both Tanzania (with 105,000 elephants) and Zimbabwe (with 51,000) have seen similar patterns of population growth. Kenya, on the other hand, banned elephant hunting in 1973 and has seen its elephant population decimated, from 167,000 to 27,000 or so in 2013. Some experts predict that elephants will be extinct in Kenya within a decade.

As the pro-hunting side has it, elephant safaris assist conservation by pretty simple means: A bull killed on a legal hunt is, in theory, worth more to the local economy than an animal slaughtered by poachers. In the most far-flung parts of the Botswana bush, the hunting industry has been the chief employer, offering a paycheck to people in places where there simply is no other gainful work.

When locals' livelihoods are bound to the survival of the elephants, they're less likely to tolerate poachers, or to summarily shoot animals that wander into their crop fields. Furthermore, hunting concessions are uninviting to poachers. Hunters like Jeff Rann employ private security forces to patrol the remoter parts of the preserve.

Hunting's critics maintain that, in practice, the industry tends to fall short of these ideals. For every professional hunter who follows the rules, there are others who overshoot their quotas, or engage in illegal ivory tracking, or cheat their employees of a living wage. In countries more corruption-plagued than Botswana, crooked officials commonly siphon off safari profits before they reach the elephants' rural human neighbors on whose mercy and financial interest the fate of the species ultimately depends. And lately, in Tanzania and Zimbabwe (where last year 300 elephants were poisoned in a single massacre), the hunting industry has proven no antidote to poaching. Citing "questionable management" and "lack of effective law enforcement" in Zimbabwe and Tanzania, the U.S. Fish and Wildlife Service, in April 2014, suspended the import of elephant trophies from both nations.

But Satsumo, the Department of Wildlife and National Parks employee who's tagging along on the Waldrips' safari, believes that Botswana's hunting ban may ultimately turn out badly for the elephants. "There will be more poachers," she says. "More elephants will get out of the reserve. They will go to people's crop fields. The hunters pump the water for them, but now they will have to move to the villages to find it. It's a bad thing. It's a very bad thing."

Abhorrent as the practice is to most Western, Dumbo-adoring sensibilities, elephant hunting occupies an awkward, grayed-out space in the landscape of conservation policy. Some nonprofits such as the

World Wildlife Fund have quietly endorsed it as part of a conservation strategy but decline to discuss their position on record. The issue is such an emotional live wire, for people on both sides of the debate, and is so deeply laced with PR perils, that it's just about impossible to find a frank and disinterested expert opinion about hunting's efficacy as a means to help conserve the species. It's worth noting that I couldn't find anyone on the anti-hunting side who could convincingly answer this question: If hunting is so disastrous for the long-term survival of the species, why do the countries where it's legal to hunt elephants have so many more of them than those where the practice is banned?

With the next couple of tourist seasons, most of Botswana's elephant concessions will be converted to photographic-safari destinations, which many conservationists promote as an effective way to monetize the animals and thereby protect them. But according to Jeff Rann, photo safaris aren't all that difficult for poachers to work around. "[Photo tourists] are not armed. And they stick to a set, predictable routine, so the poachers just go kill animals in parts of the concessions where they know the photographers aren't going to go."

Obviously Rann's got a vested interest in this perspective. But looking at the case of Kenya, home to one of Africa's largest photo-safari sectors and a poaching problem of catastrophic proportions, you sort of have to give Rann his due. Of course, there's every possibility that some combination of public policy, private money, and anti-ivory market pressures will render hunting obsolete as a conservation instrument. But for now, if you are one of those people who chokes up at reports of poachers poisoning elephants by the herd, you may have to countenance the uncomfortable possibility that one solution to the survival of the species may involve people paying lots of money to shoot elephants for fun.

Chapter 3: The Killing

The hunt continues. We are not back in the truck ten minutes before the tracker calls for a halt. Robyn and Will linger in the Land Cruiser while Jeff and the tracker go off into the bush to investigate. On the heels of our run-in with the monotusker and his pal, it feels as though the day has already coughed up a full lode of potential prey.

So it registers as something of a surprise when Jeff returns with this news: "There's five bulls, all of 'em pretty good size." One of them is carrying at least sixty pounds of ivory, Jeff's threshold, I gather, for trophy viability. "It's a shooter," he says. "If we get a shot, we've gotta shoot it."

Robyn shoulders her rifle. Her eyes are incandescent. Off we troop over the sand.

The bush resounds with a din of timber destruction. The sun is making its descent, and perhaps a hundred yards off, through the brambles, tusks glow in the rich light. The animals are fanned out ahead of us, noisily munching. We come in closer, and the elephants begin to take note, though we register more as a mild irritant, not a mortal threat. The trophy animal is in a lane of dense shrubs, moon-ing us. Robyn could conceivably flank it and get an angle on its head, but in the thick undergrowth it would be a poor shot, and that first bullet might be all she'd get. There's a risk that she would only wound it and her $60,000 would sprint off into the weeds. Jeff and Robyn whisper tactically. The elephant's obliviousness is exasperat-ing. It seizes my lungs with a breathless frustration to watch the ele-phant foolishly grubbing salad while we stand within a stone's throw, plotting the proper method to put a bullet in its brain.

Not thirty feet from us, the elephant with the missing tusk, the same elephant we just ran into, suddenly appears, having made its approach way more stealthily than an animal the size of a bread truck ought to be capable of. The bull is pissed. It nods and snorts and tosses snoutfuls of sand our direction. *Okay, whatever you are, it's kind of annoying, so get the fuck out of here, please.*

I find the performance convincing. It keeps coming. Two more strides and the elephant could reach out and touch someone with its trunk. The elephant looks to be about twelve feet tall. The trunk weighs hundreds of pounds and is easily capable of breaking a hu-man spine.

Apologies if that sounds like sensationalistic inanities you've heard intoned sotto voce by Discovery Channel narrators trying to ramp up the drama of snorkeling with porpoises and such. But the elephant is about fifteen feet away, and I will now confess to being scared just about shitless. The elephant snorts and brandishes its vast head. Lunch goes to lava in my bowels. If not for my present state of sphincter-cinching terror, I would well be in the market for an adult diaper. This is an amazingly pure kind of fear. My arteries are suddenly capable of tasting my blood, which right now has the flavor of a nine-volt battery.

Jeff Rann is in dialogue with the elephant. This consists of whispering menacingly and jabbing his rifle around in the air. The elephant does its pissed-off little shuffle for perhaps a minute, probably less. And then the tape runs in slow reverse. The elephant retreats backward into the shrubs, eyeing us, curtsying hostilely as he goes.

"Wells, you good, buddy?" Robyn asks, grinning. Apparently I'm visibly, risibly freaked. I regain my bearings, and we resume our approach to the trophy bull.

It requires the same strategy. The target is in the middle of the fan of five. The elephants have arranged themselves such that it's kind of diffcult to get an angle on the prize without straying into the paths of the others. A disquiet, a shared unease, is taking hold among these fellows. The racket of salad consumption is tapering off. The elephants are beginning to push on. But, goddamn, these guys could use a coach. The interaction with the one-tusker notwithstanding, their defense pretty much sucks. They're moving, but it's not so much flight as a slow and cranky mosey.

The light is caramelizing. If Robyn can't get a shot in the next five or ten minutes, the sun will sink past the trees and it will be liono'clock out here. The sun, too, seems murderously slow in its descent. We move past one elephant, past another, until we are on the trophy beast. Again, its butt is to us. Nothing in the animal world tops an elephant's ass as an emblem of indifference and reproof.

Coyness is keeping the elephant alive. If he does not turn his head, the sun will set and the elephant will not be killed today.

And then he turns his head. His expression is wary, rueful. In his long-lashed bedroom eyes is the look of an old drag queen turning to regard an importunate suitor tugging at the hem of her dress.

Robyn raises her rifle. For the past few months, she's been rehearsing this moment in her bedroom closet in Texas, aiming, reloading, aiming again. She shoots.

The rifle's thunder is somehow insignificant. The shot catches the elephant in the appropriate place, at the bridge of its trunk. But an elephant brain is a big piece of equipment—it can weigh as much as twelve pounds. Robyn's bullet did not apparently sever enough vital neurons to kill the animal in a single shot. He shakes his head, as if to wag away the pain of a wasp's sting. There is a second shot that strikes him in the neck. He turns to flee, but his right foreleg has buckled. He strives to stand. The effect is of a cripple trying to pitch a broken circus tent. In the franticness of his movements, one can sense the elephant's surprise that his body, a machine that has served him well for over fifty years, has suddenly stopped accepting his commands. To see so large and powerful an animal vised in an even larger and more powerful inevitability is, for lack of a better word, intense.

The other elephants scatter. Robyn and Jeff jog toward the animal. In the fervor of the moment, Robyn has momentarily forgotten to put fresh rounds in her gun. "Reload, reload, reload," Jeff instructs. They advance to a distance of maybe twenty-five feet. "Okay, shoot him right in the hip." The gun fires twice. The tent sags right and seems to sort of sway and billow, as though surrendering to wind.

"Okay, come with me," Jeff says. He leads Robyn along the animal's left flank. At the sound of the hunters coming in close, the elephant struggles more direly to rise, but instead, he loses ground against gravity and settles closer to the earth. "Just watch his trunk. [Be sure] he doesn't hit you with it."

Jeff leads her to a position perhaps ten feet from the elephant's left temple. "Okay, hit him right in the ear hole." At this point there is little the elephant can do except to turn his face away. The last shot claps into the elephant's ear.

"Perfect," says Jeff Rann. "Brain shot. You brained him."

And the elephant, still swaying on its haunches, a slow faucet of blood trickling from his forehead, is no more.

Chapter 4: How It Felt to Watch an Elephant Die

So that is how the elephant got shot. Once in the forehead, once in the neck, twice in the hip, once in the ear. How it felt to watch the elephant get shot is something else. As I watched the elephant go down, what obtruded into my consciousness was a kind of a *thing*, a psychological sensation with a very particular shape and weight and texture, a geometry as discrete and seemingly physical as a house key or a tire iron, but which I don't have any useful language to describe. This thing, this mute-pseudo revelation, had something to do with adrenaline's power to catalyze time into taffy. Forty seconds elapsed between the first shot and the last, yet what happened in those forty seconds seemed to happen out of time. It was another kind of time in which a new understanding of death impressed itself upon me more rapidly than my cognition could accommodate.

The indescribable thought sensation was not this, but some tiny part of it was sort of like this: Before I saw the elephant get shot, I understood that there was life, and there was its cessation. But now I understand there is this other thing—dying, when death stops being an idea and becomes a thing that the body, if not the conscious mind, grasps in its full intensity. Watching the elephant die granted the illusory understanding of death's grammar and meaning, as with an alingual child who hears five words and thinks he knows a language. The first word went through the forehead, the second through the neck, the third and fourth through the hip, the fifth through the ear. The month before this trip, on another assignment for this magazine, for the first time in my life, I handled the corpse of a dead human being, and I learned nothing about death. I learned nothing about death, either, when Robyn Waldrip shot the elephant. But it left in my skull at least the languageless shadow of the indescribable thing: *Death is this. Death is the elephant taking the first shot in the forehead, and the second in its neck, slumping, listing right, taking two in the hip, struggling, sinking, turning, taking one through the ear and not moving anymore. As it was in the beginning, and as it always will be: one in the forehead, one in the neck, two in the hip, one in the ear, world without end.*

Sorry about all that. Useless, I know.

Chapter 5: The Strange Rush of Death

The dead elephant is leaking audibly. A substance resembling scrambled egg is spattered on its ear. I'm jotting notes and hoping Jeff

Rann or Robyn does not notice how badly my hand is shaking. But Robyn is off in her own intense moment. She is sort of hooting and jumping up and down, going "Oh, my God, oh, my God," and generally experiencing an order of ecstasy we tend to share only with our intimates. On either side of the animal, we are both of us breathing hard, massively doped with a storm of neurochemicals that, if you could synthesize in a smokable form, would make you very rich. But the manner in which we are riding our respective highs is a pretty good illustration of why, in high school, Robyn was almost certainly a more welcome and popular presence at parties than I was. While I am privately gibbering darkly and visibly whacked-out, she is pepped up, thrilled. We embrace her congratulatorily. She kisses her fingertips and touches the bull's trunk. Salt water, rather gratuitously, spills from the elephant's eyes.

Chapter 6: Breaking Down an Elephant

In the morning, the elephant is as we left it, unmolested by snacking carnivores. Today, the animal will be cleaned and butchered, its flesh shared out among the locals. The hide and other mementos will be packed up for the Waldrips. Though the tusks and the rest of it are, ostensibly, the prizes Robyn came to Africa to collect, the electricity has gone out of the safari. Returning to the animal has a cleaning-up-after-the-party sort of feel.

A team of a half-dozen Botswana men and women have turned out for the event. The equipment list includes an ax, a winch, and a bunch of cheap-looking plastic-handled boning knives. First order of business is a stropping orgy that lasts the better part of half an hour. While that's going on, the Waldrips' children—Lola, 6, and Will junior, 8—who have been back at the camp, play with the elephant, touch its trunk for its rough, lichenish feel, handle its ears.

"It's surreal, isn't it?" Will senior says, squinting at the creature.

"Yeah," says Robyn, a little dreamily. "I hope it stays that way for a long time."

I'm feeling it, too, the slightly spongy sense of dislocation emanating from the previous day, but this is why I will never be a hunter: She wants to savor it. I am ready for it to go away. Before the skinning commences, the tableau is beautified and made camera-ready. The elephant's tusks are scrubbed. One of Jeff's assistants takes an ax to a tree that is casting an unphotogenic shadow.

"Look how long it takes him to chop that down," Will observes. "An elephant would walk right over it."

Larry the videographer takes some footage of the children perched on the elephant's skull, though Jeff cautions him, "You might get shit if you put that in the show. You don't want to be seen as disrespecting the animal."

The children dismount, and the skinners move in.

The cleaning goes like this: First you take the ears. Each is the size of a manta ray. It is severed close to the head and laid in the dirt. Next, the trunk, the size of a middle-aged gator, is girdled at its bridge and then removed. Blood comes forth in an incredible tide, more of it than I've probably seen in aggregate over the course of my lifetime. Yet the flaying, surprisingly, inspires none of the mortal vertigo the killing did. As the knives flash, the animal becomes less extraordinary, less like the world's largest land mammal and more a bricolage of familiar butcher-shop hues. The trunk is stripped of its leather, and for a time it lies in the dirt, looking like an automobile transmission made of fresh raspberry sorbet.

Will is by the elephant's rear. He has taken up a knife, eager to do his share of the dismantlement. "I always tell my kids, anything you kill, you gotta clean it yourself. I know Jeff's got clients who come out here and kill five elephants. Shoot 'em and leave 'em. To me that's not right. Out of respect for the animal, you gotta do it yourself. I didn't kill this elephant, but even still."

A cut has been made along the spine. Will slashes away, pulling at the skin, revealing a goreless expanse of fibrous white fascia. The winch is applied to help peel the hide. The resistance is sufficient to pull the truck forward at first when the crank turns on.

Once the skin has been freed, Will and the skinners begin blocking out the meat. The sound is of hard, wet work. Up front, they are getting at the skull. The skin is gone from the elephant's cheeks, and the bare eye peering from the pale tissue is demonic. Below the eyes, the look of the tuskless head, still actively suppurating, recalls a cliff face after a strong rain. Then the head itself is cut off, into the arms of a pair of catchers. Later today or tomorrow, the skull will be buried for a period of ten days. Insects will attend to the finer details of cleaning the skull for its voyage to Texas.

When the head is removed, the elephant begins to speak in a morbid throat-flatus. Air escaping the trachea makes sounds of growls and shudders and sighs. This is not upsetting. By now, it is not elephant but a wrecked Volkswagen made of flesh.

The job wears on. How much of the creature, I ask Jeff Rann, do the skinners intend to take?

"Everything," he says. "This'll probably feed a hundred people."

The skinners cut away fire-hydrant-sized wads of meat and fling them heavily into a Land Cruiser's bed.

The carcass is winnowed to a pile of innards that calls to mind one of those inflatable-looking sports arenas. In the flawless blue above, a fleet of delighted buzzards has begun to wheel.

The work is mostly over. Will Waldrip can now retire from the job. He is abundantly daubed in blood and is exhausted, though chipper. "A little different than quartering out a whitetail," he says.

Amid the spare parts lying in the grass is the elephant's jaw, from which we can know the elephant's age. An elephant gets six sets of teeth in its lifetime. This one was on its final set, and judging from its condition it was probably about 53. The sand of the savanna is hard on an elephant's dentition. Five to seven more years and it'd have blown through this set and starved to death, assuming neither Jeff nor the poachers got him first.

Looking at this rummage sale of elephant flesh inspires an equally messy inventory of contradictory thoughts.

1. *Eww.*

2. *Then a sort of wordless, inner viola fugue that accompanies the sight of a magnificent organism that has been treading the savanna since the Kennedy administration, now scattered in pieces on the ground.*

3. *Then, this retort: Yeah, but wasn't the leather your wallet's made from once the property of a factory-raised cow whose sole field trip from the reeking, shrieking bedlam of the factory farm was a ter-*

rified excursion to the abattoir? And don't you gobble bacon and steaks whenever you get the chance? And aren't "hypocrite" and probably also "pantywaist" accurate words to describe a person who gets queasy at an animal being flayed but who eats meat and/or dons leather shoes?

4. Right, but elephants are so smart, and old.

5. A caged chicken once beat you at tic-tac-toe. I don't hear you crusading for the pearl mussel, which can live for over a century.

6. But elephants are so splendid to look at.

7. Unlike a ten-point buck?

8. No, but okay, look: We can assume that most people, for whatever totally arbitrary reason, have an affinity for elephants over chickens and pearl mussels. Sure, it's the same illogical pro-mammal bigotry that lets people mourn the slaughter of dolphins and not mind so much the squashing of an endangered spider. BUT? Isn't it a little bit fucked, when the average person looks at an elephant and goes, "Aww, what an amazing animal," to be the one guy in a thousand who goes, "Yeah, cool, I want to shoot it"?

9. So it's bad to shoot elephants because other Westerners arbitrarily sentimentalize them? Consider your fantasies of grenading the deer who eat your gardenias. Multiply that by about 10,000 and you've probably got a good approximation of the feelings of the Botswana farmer who wakes up to find that elephants have munched a full year's worth of crops.

10. No, I mean I guess I just don't really understand the impulse behind wanting to shoot this big amazing animal, or how, after shooting one, you'd want to jump up and down.

11. So what's she supposed to do? Cry and drop into the lotus position and sing a song in Navajo? It's not terribly hard to understand why people go hunting. They go hunting because they find it exciting. As Robyn herself put it, you get a primal thrill. And whether or not you want to admit it, you had the thrill, the neurochemical bongload that hit you when the elephant died. It made Robyn Waldrip

> *jump up and down and it made you go on a pompous, half-baked death trip, which is your version of jumping up and down. You were at the party, bro.*

12. *But I'm not the one who shot the elephant.*

13. *No, you're the one who came on this hunt so that you could ride the adrenaline high while at the same time reserving the right to be ethically fastidious about it. I mean, what really distinguishes your presence here from Jeff Rann's or the Waldrips'?*

14. *Maybe only this: Though the harrowing intensity of the elephant's death will, in time, denature into a fun story to tell at cocktail parties, right now I would trade all of it—the morbid high, the anecdote for my memoirs—to bring this particular elephant back to life.*

Chapter 7: The Buzzard in the Baobab Tree

The elephant's skull is buried. Its flesh has been hung out to dry. The Waldrips are booked at Jeff Rann's safari camp for eight more days, but these folk are hunters, and the notion of spending a week doing nothing but observing creatures of the wild holds little interest for them. So tomorrow, they will go to South Africa, because Will Waldrip Jr. wants to undertake something called a "springbok slam," which involves shooting one of each of that species' four subvarieties. Jeff has an extra elephant tag for his concession in Tanzania. He offers this to Will Sr., and Will declines.

Our last evening in camp, we go for sunset cocktails at a locally famous baobab tree. The tree is craggy, Gandalfian, and 1,000 years old. It has a crazed unruly spread of branches, which inspired the folk saying, Jeff tells us, that "God pulled the baobab out of the ground and stuck it upside down." A leopard sometimes hangs out in the man-sized cave in its trunk. The leopard isn't home. The only locals on the scene are a squadron of huge buzzards, resting in the baobab's branches. The camp dumps its hunting refuse not too far from here, and the buzzards, Jeff tells us, have likely spent the day gorging on the remains of Robyn's elephant. At our approach, they take grudging flight in a storm of black wings.

While Jeff's wife is arranging the cocktail table, the party moves in to have a look at the leopard hole. Suddenly the sounds of shrieking pierce the quiet of the dusk. My first thought is that the leopard was home after all and has mauled one of the children. But it turns out that one last buzzard had been hiding in the tree. The bird had gobbled so much of Robyn's elephant that it couldn't take off. So, to attain flight weight, the buzzard started puking on the safari group. Fran, the Waldrips' nanny, got the heftiest portion of Robyn's elephant, on her shoulders and hair, and Jeff Rann got speckled a bit. The elephant huntress herself dodged the vomit entirely as the bird set a course for the sun.

■

Jack, July

FROM *The New Yorker*

THE SUN WAS A WOLF. The fanged light had been trailing him for hours, tricky with clouds. As it emerged again from sheepskin, Jack looked down at the pavement, cursed. He'd been walking around since ten, temperature even then close to ninety. The shadow stubs of the telephone poles and his own midget silhouette now suggested noon. He had no hat, and he'd left his sunglasses somewhere, either at Jamie's or at The Wheel, or they might have slipped off his head. They did that sometimes, when he leaned down to tie his shoes or empty them of pebbles.

Pebbles?

Was that a word? He stopped to consider it, decided in the negative, and then marched on, flicking his thumb ceaselessly against his index like a Zippo. His nerves were shot, but unable to shut down. No off button now. He'd be zooming for hours, the crackle in his head exaggerated by the racket of birds rucked up in towers of palm, tossing the dry fronds. What were they doing? Ransacking sounds. Looking for nuts or dates, probably. Or bird sex. Possibly bird sex. Maybe he should walk to Rhonda's, ask her to settle him. Or unsettle him. Maybe he wanted more. *Share* was what she should do, if she had any. He always shared with her. Not always, but it could be argued.

Rhonda was a crusher, though, a big girl, always climbing on top. Her heft was no joke, and Jack was a reed. Still, he loved her. Ha! That was the tweak coming on. He'd never admit to such a thing when he was flat. Now his immortal brain understood. He wanted to marry Rhonda, haul her up the steps of her double-wide, pump out about fifty kids. In the fly-eye of his mind he saw them, curled up like caterpillars on Rhonda's bed.

Jack picked up the pace. The effect of his late-morning tokes was far from finished. Though he'd pulled nothing but dregs (the last of his stash), it was coming on strong, sparking his heart in unexpected ways.

So much gratitude. Jack made a fist and banged twice on his chest, thinking of Flaco, a school friend, now dead, who'd first turned him on to this stuff—a precious substance whose unadvertised charm was love. It was infuriating that no one ever mentioned this. The posters, the billboards, the P.S.A.s—all they talked about were skin lesions and rotten teeth. Kids, sadly, were not getting well-rounded information. If Jack hadn't lost his phone, he'd point it at his face right now and make a documentary.

Traffic, a lot of it. On Speedway now, a strip-mall jungle, which, according to his mother, used to be lined with palm trees and old adobes, tamale peddlers and mom-and-pop shops. Not that Jack's mother was nostalgic. She loved her Marts—the Dollar and the Quik and the Wal. "Cheaper, too," she said. She liked to buy in bulk, always had extra. Maybe he should go to her place, instead of Rhonda's, grab some granola bars, a few bottles of water for his pack. Sit on the old yellow couch under the swamp cooler, chew the fat. He hadn't seen her in weeks.

Weeks?

Again, the word proved thin, suspect. "Mama," he said, testing another—an utterance that stopped him in his tracks and caused his torso to jackknife forward. Laughed to spitting. He could picture her face, if he ever tried to call her that. She preferred Bertie. Only sixteen years his senior, she often reminded him. Bertie of the scorched hair, in her sparkle tops and toggle pants. "What's it short for?" he once asked of her name. She'd told him that his grandfather was a humongous piece of shit, that's what it was short for.

Of course, Jack had never met the famous piece of shit, had only heard stories. Supposedly he and Grandma Shit still lived in Tucson, might be anywhere, two of Jack's neighbors. He might have passed them on the street, or lent them an egg or a cup of sugar.

Jack tittered into his fist. What eggs? What sugar? There was fuck-all in the fridge. In fact, depending on his location, there might not even be a fridge.

Buses roared past, their burning flanks throwing cannonballs of heat at the sidewalk. Jack turned away, moved toward himself, a murkier version trapped in the black glass façade of a large building. Twenty-two—he looked that plus ten. Of course, a witch's mirror was no way to judge. The dark glass was spooked, not to be trusted. Hadn't Jamie said, only yesterday, in the lamplit corner of the guest bedroom, that Jack looked all of sixteen? "Beautiful," Jamie had whispered, touching Jack's cheek.

Beautiful. Like something stitched on a pillow, sentimental crap from some other era. The lamplit whisperings had made Jack restless, the dissolved crystal blowing him sideways like a blizzard.

To hell with Jamie! Last week, after partying all night, Jack had woken up to find Jamie lying beside him, the man's hand crawling like a snail across the crotch furrows of Jack's jeans. Half dead, in deep crash, Jack hadn't even been sure they *were* his jeans—the legs inside them looked too skinny, like a kid's. He'd watched the snail-hand for a good five minutes, feeling nothing—and then, with a gush, he'd felt too much. When he leaped from the bed, Jamie screeched, "Oh my gosh! Oh my gosh!"—apologizing profusely, claiming he'd flailed in his sleep.

"Why are you in my bed *at all?*" Jack had asked, storming into the bathroom with shame-bitten fury. He'd got into the shower, only to find a bar of soap as thin and sharp as a razor blade—scraped himself clean as best he could, until he smelled breakfast coming on hot from the kitchen. It had turned out to be silver-dollar pancakes with whipped cream and chocolate chips. Jack's favorite. Could the man stoop any lower?

Jamie just didn't add up. A bearded Mexican with a voice like a balloon losing air. Wore pleated slacks, but without a belt you could sometimes glimpse thongs. Didn't smoke, but blew invisible puffs for emphasis. And the name—Jamie—it sat uncomfortably on the fence, neutered, a child's name, wrong for anyone over thirty, which Jamie clearly was. Plus he was fat, which made his body indecisive, intricately layered with loose slabs of flesh—potbelly and mother-flaps. "Stay with me, why don't you?" he'd said, for no discernible reason, at the Chevron rest-room sink, where Jack had been rinsing his clotted pipe.

That had been a week ago, maybe two. They'd been strangers in that rest room, the obese man appearing out of the gloom of a shit stall. His words, *stay with me*, had seemed, to the boy, vaguely futuristic, a beam of light from a spaceship.

Jack should have known better.

The sun drilled the boy's head, looking for something. He closed his eyes and let the bit work its way to his belly, where the good stuff lived, where the miracle often happened: the black smoke reverting to pure white crystal. A snowflake, an angel. He smiled at himself in the dark glass. It was so easy to forgive those who betrayed you, effortless—like thinking of winter in the middle of July. It cost you nothing. Reflexively Jack scratched deep inside empty pockets, then licked his fingers. The bitch of it was this: forgiveness dissolved instantly on your tongue, there was no time to spit it out.

He'd have to remember to speak on this, when he made his documentary.

"Welcome to Presto's!"

The blond girl stood just inside the black door, her face gaily frozen, as if cut from the pages of a yearbook. Jack comprehended none of her words.

"Welcome," he replied, attempting a flawless imitation of her birdlike language. Jack was good with foreigners. Most of his school buds had been Chalupas.

The girl tilted her head; the smile wavered, but only briefly. Her mouth re-expanded with elastic lunacy.

"Ship or print?"

Jack was taken aback. Though it was true he needed to use the bathroom, he was disturbed by the girl's lack of delicacy in regard to bodily functions.

"Number one," he admitted quietly.

"Ship?" she persisted.

Jack felt dizzy. The girl's teeth were very large and very white. Jack could only assume they were fake. Keeping his own dental wreckage tucked under blistered lips, he lifted his hands in a gesture of spiritual peace. "I'm just going to make a quick run to the rest room."

"I'm sorry, they're only for customers."

"George Washington," Jack blurted, still fascinated by the girl's massive teeth.

"What's that?"

"Cherry tree," he continued associatively.

"Oh, like for the Fourth?" asked Blondie.

"Yes," Jack replied kindly, even though he knew she was confusing Presidents. Fourth of July would be Jefferson or Adams. Jack had always been sweet on History. In school, when he was miniature, he'd got nothing but A's. Again he sensed the expansiveness of his brain, a maze of rooms, many of which he'd never been in. It didn't matter that he hadn't finished high school, there was an Ivy League inside his head, libraries crammed with books. He just needed to pull them from between the folds of gray matter and read them. Close his eyes and get cracking. See, this was the other thing people never told you about meth. It was educational.

The girl informed him that there were no holiday specials, if that's what he was asking about.

Jack nodded and smiled, tapping his head in pretense of understanding her logic. As he moved quickly toward the bathroom, the girl skittered off in another direction, also quickly.

Perhaps she had to print, too. Or take a ship.

Jack giggled, and opened a door leading to a storage closet.

"Can I help you?"

"Yes," Jack said to the man inside the closet. "I understand what you're saying."

"What am I saying?" asked the man.

"Perfectly clear," said Jack. He held up his peace-hands, walked back through the room of humming and spitting machines, and exited the building—behind which he quickly peed, before resuming his trek down Speedway.

As soon as he knocked at the trailer door, he was aware of the emptiness in his hands. He should have brought flowers. Or a burrito. He knocked again. Sweat dripped from under his arms, making him feel strangely cold.

"I have flowers," he said to the door.

"Go away," said the door.

"I'm not talking to a door," said Jack. "I don't take orders from doors."

"You can't be here. Why are you here?" The voice was exhausted, cakey. Jack could picture the pipe.

"Baby," he said. "Come on. Why are you being stingy?"

"I'll call the police, I swear to God."

Jack was silent, but stood his ground. He scratched at the door like a cat. After a while, someone said, "Please." The word sounded funny, like a flute. Jack tried saying it again. Even worse. It almost sounded as if he were going to cry.

When the door opened, it did so only a few inches—most of Rhonda's mouth obscured by a chain.

"You cannot be here, Jack."

Jack, who was clearly there, only smiled.

"I'm okay," he assured her.

"You look like shit," said Rhonda.

"Sunburn," theorized Jack. "It's like a hundred and twenty out here." He could barely see the girl—or he could see her, just not recognize her. She seemed different, her hair and her clothes fussed up, neat. He smelled no smoke, only perfume. "What's going on?" he asked, flicking his thumb.

Rhonda made an irritated snort, half laugh, half fart. It seemed to come from her mouth.

Jack, confident he was at the peak of his charm, refused to be put off. "Can you just open the door, so that we can talk like humans, without the frickin' mustache?"

"The what?"

"The ..." Jack gestured swoopily toward the door. "The frickin' ..."

"Chain?" suggested Rhonda.

"All I want is, like, *hello*, okay? Like hello, whatever, a glass of water."

The girl grimaced dramatically, egging on Jack's own sense of tragedy.

"I am literally dying, Rhonda."

Jack pressed his face into the door crack, letting the cool air caress his skin. His eyes, blinded from sunlight, barely took in the fact that the girl was gone. After a moment, he heard water running in the sink, the clink of a glass being pulled from a cupboard. He closed his eyes, felt a stirring between his legs. Rhonda had always been so kind.

"I don't need ice," he called out.

"Good. Here you go."

At first Jack wasn't sure what it was. The water thrown in his face was cold. It dripped down his neck and into his shirt, slow trails across his belly. It lingered, drifted lower, like a kind of kiss. Jack licked his lips: the tap water salty, mixed with his sweat. Something was humming, too—the bones under his cheeks, near his eyes, vibrating like a tuning fork or an organ at the back of a church.

"Don't cry," he said to Rhonda, who said she wasn't.

"Why would I be crying after a fucking year?"

Jack said, "What year?"—to which Rhonda replied, "I thought you were dead."

She wasn't making a whole lot of sense. Jack asked if she was going fast.

"Are you insane?" said Rhonda. "Those were the worst two months of my life."

"Why don't I come in and we'll take a nap?" suggested Jack.

"Listen to me," the girl said. "You have to lose this address—do you hear me?"

Jack ran a hand over his wet face.

"Please," begged Rhonda. "You have to go. Eric will be home soon."

Jack wondered if she meant *Jack*, since the names were so similar. "Do you mean *me*?" he asked in earnest. He tried to find the girl's eyes—and when he did he saw that she wasn't a girl at all. She was old, practically as old as Bertie. What was more astonishing, though, was the look on her face. There was no love in it whatsoever.

"I don't know you," said Jack.

"Good," said Rhonda, shutting the door.

He stood on some gravel, and felt terrible. Even the little plank of shadow beside the cement wall held no appeal. Were he to lie there, he'd only get the jits.

Walking was what he needed, and to hell with the sun.

That's what people in his position did. They walked, they moved, they got things done. Sitting was no good. Talking was fine, if you had someone. Sex was primal. Jack's body knew the rules. There were any number of ways to keep one's brain from exploding.

People going fast rearranged the furniture, or crawled around looking for carpet crumbs. Anything that used your hands, which, compelled by the imaginative fervor of your mind, became tools in a breathless campaign to change the shape of the world. It was art, essentially. Jack wondered why more people going fast didn't do crafts. He suddenly wished for construction paper and Elmer's glue; glitter, cotton, clay. Once, when he was little, he'd made a kick-ass giraffe from a walnut and some toilet-paper tubes. The legs, ingeniously, had been chopsticks.

Bertie used to leave them for hours, on the days she attended her meetings. She'd always made sure there were coloring books and Play-Doh, carrot sticks and DVDs. Little notes saying *Love* and *Be back soon*. Jack and his sister had in no way been deprived.

His sister? *Fuck.* His sister. She came back to him like sheet lightning. He hadn't seen Lisa since she'd gone away. He clapped his hands, to banish the thought. It was almost funny how, at certain elevations, it was so easy to pretend you didn't know things you could never forget. Jack dug for his phone, to see if he had Lisa's number.

But, being that there was no phone, he pulled up only lint—which he quickly dismissed, into the air, with a puff. He watched it float for a moment, fluttering with indecision, before it drifted down, in a slow sashay, and landed on his shoe.

"Fine," said Jack. "Fine!" He picked up the gray fluff, and stuffed it back in his pocket.

Walked around the block to see if he could trick it. He'd done it before. Pull one over on time. Circle back and confuse it. Like one of those Aborigines. They were big walkers, too. Ugly fuckers, but the cool thing was they could walk a thousand miles, no problem— and they weren't trying to get to China or some shit like that. What they wanted was to get back to their ancestors—way the fuck past Grandma and Grandpa, all the way back to the lizards and the snakes.

Jack, of course, would have been satisfied with a smaller victory—finding his way back five, six years, to Bertie's crumbling adobe. "Star Trek" and pizza with Lisa. Hell, he'd be fine with getting back to just last year, to the old Rhonda, the Rhonda of the bra-welted back and the cream-cheese thighs, the sad girl he'd met at The Wheel, and whom he'd made happy with snowflakes and black clouds.

Had it really been a year? Jack felt nervous now, flicked his thumb even faster, sensed his shadow growing longer, trailing him like gum stuck to his shoe. Soon, he knew, the freak would come, the soul-suck, if he didn't get one of two things: more crystal or a sound sleep—both of which would require money, because sleep, at this point, wouldn't be free. It would cost a bottle of grain or a six-pack or a pill. Sometimes he wondered why a person couldn't just hit himself over the head with a rock.

He climbed on top of the gas meter and opened the window, as he'd done a million times before. A small, high window, facing the alley. Lisa's window, which Bertie never locked.

A tight fit, even for a skinny drink like Jack. Halfway through, he found himself stuck, but with a series of wriggling bitch-in-heat motions he managed to make it through, head first, onto the dusty shrine of his sister's neatly made bed. The friction of passing through the small opening, though, had pulled down his pants, as well as given him an erection. When he stood to hoist his jeans, a young woman in yoga tights entered the room, dropped a pear, and screamed.

Jack, thinking the pear was some sort of grenade, covered his head, leaving his erection exposed.

The woman moved quickly to the bureau and grabbed a bead-encrusted candlestick that Lisa had made in sixth grade. Jack, watching the drama through smoke-scented fingers, calmed, seeing the familiar prop. Plus, the grenade, bearing teeth marks, was obviously a ruse.

"I'm not here to hurt you," said Jack—a comment that, judging by the woman's anguished face, failed to impart the cordiality he wished to convey. The woman squealed and fled the room.

"I just want to see Bertie," Jack called out, pulling up his pants. "I'm her son. I'm Jack."

The idea of having to explain his existence exhausted him. When he walked into the living room, the woman was still clutching the candlestick—a lathe-turned beauty, to which Lisa had glued hundreds of tiny red beads. Jack had lent her the epoxy himself, a leftover tube from one of his build-it-yourself dinosaur sets.

"You can put that down," said Jack.

"Look," said the woman, "Beatrice isn't here. She won't be back for a while."

"Who?"

"You're looking for your mother?"

Jack felt a peculiar flutter in his gut.

"I'm meeting her in a—in a bit," stammered the woman. "I'll just—I'll let her know you were here."

"What did you call her?" asked Jack.

The woman took a step back. "Nothing. What?"

"Her name," Jack stated as calmly as possible, "is Bertie."

"Well, that's not how I know her," said the woman in yoga tights, who, even with the upraised candlestick, seemed to smile, a quick flash of arrogance.

"I can see your vulva," said Jack.

The woman covered her crotch with the candlestick. "My God, do you even know what you're saying?"

"It's inappropriate is all I'm saying," replied Jack, strolling over to the yellow couch. He sat at the far right, where the air of the swamp cooler always hit you square in the face. As kids, he and Lisa used to fight over this spot. "Fifteen minutes each," Bertie used to say, making them share the luxury equally. "Otherwise I'll shut the damn thing off." Frickin' Solomon, that was his mother all right. A part-time Christian with a gutter mouth.

Beatrice? For fucking real? How could Jack not have known this—or, more important, why had this information been kept from him? "I don't think you know what you're talking about," he said to the woman.

But she wasn't listening. She was on the telephone, giving an address Jack recognized. He made a blah-blah-blah gesture with his hand, as the woman prattled into the phone.

Why did no one wish to have a legitimate exchange with him? He was a good person, a personable person, a person with a heart the

size of a fucking bullfrog. Couldn't the woman in yoga tights understand that there was no need to involve the police?

"I live here," said Jack.

The woman said, "Thank you," and hung up the phone. "I've
called the—"

"I know," interrupted Jack. He crossed his legs, willing himself
to stay calm. Anyway, it would take them at least ten minutes to get
here. This wasn't a Zip Code anyone rushed to, especially the cops.

"Do you want to get arrested?" the woman asked. "I mean, do you
want to be like this?"

"Like what?" asked Jack.

"Do you realize how much pain you've caused Beatrice?"

"Who are you, exactly?" Jack had the thought to have Yoga Tights
arrested when the police arrived. "How do you even know my
mother?"

"We're *roommates*," the woman articulated with unnecessary aggression.

Jack had a vision of pillow fights, s'mores, backrubs.

"Disgusting," he said.

"What's disgusting?"

Jack didn't reply—glass houses and all. He might as well be talking about himself and Jamie. He stood, annoyed, and walked over
to the mirrored cabinet in the corner of the room. It seemed distinctly smaller than it had when he was little, like a toy version of
the real thing. He knelt before it, turned the silver latch, opened
the doors. He stared inside, uncomprehendingly *(What the fuck?)*,
pushed around envelopes and stamps, a pile of old phone bills. He
shoved his hands to the far back. Not even a bottle of Tio Pepe or
crème de menthe.

"We don't keep any in the house," the woman said.

Jack scowled. He knew Bertie better than that.

"In case you care to know, your mother is doing really well."

Wonderful! thought Jack. Applause!

He stood, dusted himself off regally, as if he might dismiss the in-
creeping panic. "I just need to get a few bottles of water."

In the kitchen, in the pantry, he pulled the cord, turned on the
light. Well stocked, as usual. For Judgment Day, Bertie had always

been prepared. With food, if not with mercy. "I can't be held responsible," Bertie liked to say. In a more generous mood, everything was God's plan, God's doing. Jack took six bottles of water and ten granola bars, stuffed them into his pack.

"Help yourself, why don't you?" the woman said.

Unbelievable. Un-fucking-believable. Jack turned to her. She was standing in the doorway, still holding the candlestick.

"Do you even know who that belongs to? Do you even know who made that?"

But the woman had no interest in discussing the relics of Jack's childhood. "Just take what you want and go," she said. "Beatrice would probably be pissed anyway, if I got you arrested. I don't know why she should be, though. You've been a very toxic influence on her." She shook her head, puffing air bullishly from her nose. "Everyone at Fellowship thinks so, too, but your mother is, like, deluded."

The woman moved the candlestick from one hand to the other. Jack looked at her hard, just to make sure she wasn't Lisa. No one really knew what Lisa looked like these days.

You could always tell by the eyes, though—and when Jack looked at those he knew that Yoga Tights was not his sister.

"You're not even a very good replacement," he said.

"Replacement for what?" she asked.

But Jack did not deign to answer. He zipped his pack and, without even bothering to take the loose change visible on the counter, scurried out the back door.

He cut through neighbors' yards to avoid running into the cops. He leaped over stones, over crevices, over brown lawns and tiny quicksilver lizards. His speed exhilarated him, and then made him feel distinctly ill. When he finally heard the sirens, he was three blocks away, in an alley frilly with trash. He lurched to a stop, sending up clouds of dust. A dry wind blew grit into his eye.

Fuck. He needed an improvement in his itinerary, like immediately. But he had no leverage. Not even two bucks for the bus. He should have taken the coins from Bertie's kitchen. Probably no more than a dollar, but a dollar was enough to get started. Four quarters in a newspaper lockbox and you could steal the lot, sell them from some busy intersection. Old-school, but it worked—even if, sometimes, it took five hours to make five bucks.

"What's that?" Jack said to his stomach, which was mumbling something vague but insistent. He fed it a granola bar, and immediately vomited. Drank some water. Vomited again.

Dirt, weeds, a huge prickly pear like a coral reef. Jack covered his burning head with his T-shirt, exposing his belly. Why hadn't the Founding Fathers planted more shade trees out here? Probably because the bastards had never made it this far west. The only people who'd ventured this far, back then, were derelicts and thieves. Uprooted types, not prone to plant things.

Jack was leaning philosophically against a fence for several minutes before he spotted the dog, sleeping on the other side. Not a pit, just some big floppy collie. Still, it reminded him of Lisa.

How could an animal sleep in this heat with all that fur? Jack knelt in the alley, winding his fingers through the chain-link. "*Psst.*" Rattled the fence. "Hey! Buster!"

The dog opened one eye, too stunned to get up. Shook a leg epileptically.

"You're just gonna lie there?" Piles of dried shit everywhere, like a miniature wigwam village. Again Jack rattled the fence.

"What are you doing? Why are you bothering him?" A little man with a lopsided beard, like a paintbrush that had dried crooked, appeared at a window.

"I'm not bothering him," said Jack. "I thought he was someone else."

"He's a dog," said the man. "He ain't got nothing to do with you."

Jack, riled, was ready to argue the point, but then let it go. He could see that the man was old, and so was the dog. Besides, his mouth was dry, and as he tried to get up his legs buckled.

The man snapped his fingers in Jack's direction. "No funny business!"

Jack nodded and backed away. "I'm going."

He walked about ten feet before he stopped, opened his backpack, and pulled out another granola bar—which he quickly unwrapped and tossed over the fence. "Get up for that, I bet."

The dog didn't hesitate. "I thought so," said Jack.

Instantly, though, the old man shot from the back door and pulled the food from the dog's mouth.

"It's not poison!" shouted Jack. "It's granola!"

A firecracker went off in the distance, and Jack turned. Next time, he thought, I'll do *that*—stick a firecracker in the damn granola.

For years, he'd hated every dog, and experienced a paralyzing weakness in their presence. Now, despite the occasional flash of cruel intention, Jack's anger had mostly turned into something else. A dog, any dog, was like the relentless sunshine: mind-alteringly sad. Jack sat on the curb, touched his hand to blazing macadam.

Sometimes it could be burned out of you—the pain.

But no, the past was here, before him now like a mirage, wavering with tiny figures, holograms he recognized.

Resistance is futile, the Borg say.

Because not only had he run into a dog; he'd run out of his stash as well—and running out of crystal was like running out of time, sinking back into the mud that was your life. No dusting of white snow to prettify the view. With a mad, flea-scratching intensity, Jack scraped out the stem of his pookie, but what fell from it was worthless: a few flakes of irredeemable tar. The holograms grew to full size, and came closer.

"*Grrr*," said Jack, hoping he didn't sound like an animal.

Jack had been with his sister that day—a summer morning, playing Frisbee in a field. The Frisbee had gone over a fence.

The dog was black, not huge, the size of a twenty-gallon ice chest.

After the attack, Jack wondered if they'd really killed it. The police had used the words *put to sleep*, but Jack had worried that the owners might have somehow woken the animal up, and were hiding it inside their house. Lisa's fears, no doubt, had been far worse—but Jack had known better than to ask her.

Anyway, Lisa couldn't really talk after it happened. She had a lot of problems with her jaw. With everything, really. Her right hand was so nerve-damaged that she had to use her left, which she never got very good at. She shook a lot, refused to eat, mostly drank smoothies. Her pinkie was missing.

Her face, though, was the worst. Even after two surgeries, it looked like something badly made, lumpy—as if a child had made it out of clay. It was less a face than the idea of one, preliminary, a sketch—but careless, with terrible proportions, and slightly skewed; primitive—a face that might be touching in art, but in life was hideous.

"Look at that!" Bertie had shouted at the lawyer, showing him pictures of what Lisa had looked like before. "*Beautiful*. And this is what they're saying she's worth?"

The settlement had not been much. "An outrage," Bertie said to anyone who would listen. She tried to get another lawyer to take on the case. Jack would sit with his mother in cluttered offices, staring at the floor, telling the suits what he'd seen. "Happens every seven seconds," one lawyer said with disturbing enthusiasm, as if discussing the odds of winning the lottery. "Plus, you know how people in Tucson love their Rotts and their pits." Unfortunately, he explained, a jackpot settlement was usually tied to an attack catching the right wave of publicity. "Your moment has probably passed," he said with a wince, a shrug.

"That baby," Bertie would complain, referring to what she considered Lisa's competition.

The same summer, a two-year-old had been mauled near Sabino Canyon. There'd been a fund-raising campaign. "Foothills," Bertie had scoffed, after seeing the child's parents on television, their big house on a ridge. "As if they need help! We should start our own campaign," she'd muttered, after a sip, to Jack.

"We could make posters," he'd suggested sheepishly.

"Posters, TV commercials, the whole shebang." His mother pulled more deeply from her Captain Morgan mug, the ice clinking like money inside a piggy bank.

"Wanna make them pop, though," she said of the posters. "Need to get us some big-ass pieces of paper."

It would have been easy. Jack was artistic (everyone said so), and Bertie had balls. But, in the end, they'd never done a thing; never called a TV station or decorated a coffee can with ribbons and a picture of Lisa's face. Never took the case back to court—even though it was clear, after the initial surgeries, that Lisa would require more. The procedures couldn't be rushed, though. The doctor had recommended that

Lisa wait before going back under the knife: "Too much trauma already. Let's see how the current work heals."

What little remained of the settlement money was kept in a separate account, like a vacation fund or a Christmas club, some perverse dowry. Money for the future, earmarked for surgery.

Jack had helped, at some point, hadn't he? Standing at the edge of the alley, he scratched his leg—a vague recollection that he'd given Lisa some of his own skin. It had been more compatible than Bertie's.

In the fall, Lisa had refused to go back to school for her junior year. She mostly stayed inside, in her bedroom. There was a lot of pain medication—which was apparently, Jack learned, something to be shared. "I'm in pain, too," Bertie had cried, defensively, when he caught her one night with the bottle. "Anyway," she chided, changing the subject, "your sister can't live in a fog for the rest of her life. She needs to get a job."

Jack didn't understand why a person in Lisa's position couldn't be allowed to stay inside, in a dark bedroom, for the rest of her life. Bertie had a thing, though, about self-improvement and positive thinking, which often made her children shrink from her as if she were a terrorist.

Amazingly, Lisa had found a job fairly quickly, full time at a telemarketing firm. "You see," Bertie had chirped. "Up and at 'em," practically shoving Lisa out the door, her hair strategically feathered over her cheeks. "Minimum wage," Lisa said, and Bertie replied that there was no shame in that. All day, Lisa had sat in a cubicle, talked on the phone in her new, funny voice. But maybe, thought Jack, the people his sister called just assumed she had a toothache, or an accent.

No one on the phone would have known that his sister was a high-school dropout in Tucson—or that she'd been mutilated. That was a word no one had used—not the doctors or Lisa's friends or even the truth-obsessed women from Bertie's so-called church. No one ever said *maimed, destroyed, ruined.*

Bitten, people preferred to say, modestly, as if Lisa's misfortune had been the work of an ant, or a fly.

* * *

Jack rubbed his eye, swatted his cheek. As he headed downtown in long, loping strides, his body was dangerously taut, a telephone wire stretched between time zones. He needed to bring his thinking back to 2000-whatever-the-fuck-it-was—*this* day, *this* street. "Excuse me," he said to a woman with a briefcase and praying-mantis sunglasses—but, before he could explain his purpose, she darted away and leaped into a black sedan. The woman obviously had issues; even from inside the vehicle, she was waving her hands at him in extreme sign language: *no tengo no tengo no tengo.*

After an hour and a half, he'd managed to assemble two dollars (a few quarters from a laundromat, a few obtained by outright begging). When he climbed on the bus and dropped the coins in the chute, they made a sound like a slot machine promising a payout.

"What are you waiting for?" asked the driver.

"Nothing," mumbled Jack, taking a seat at the back.

He'd been looking forward to the air-conditioning, but now it made him shake—the cold air, like pins on his face. Sometimes he'd met Lisa after her shift, to accompany her home. She hadn't liked to take the bus alone. She'd wanted Jack to ride with her in the mornings as well—but how could he? He was fifteen; he had school.

Anyway, the afternoons were enough. The walk to the back of the bus had always seemed to take a lifetime. People stared, kids laughed. Lisa never said anything, but sometimes she took Jack's hand, which embarrassed him: what if people thought she was his girlfriend? Sometimes he could hear her breathing; sometimes, a sound in her throat like twigs snapping.

That same year, Jack met Flaco. The first time they went fast together, in Flaco's enamel-black bedroom, it was like, *oh yes*—total understanding, total big picture, all the nagging little details washed away. Soon Jack stopped meeting Lisa after work. He let her take the bus alone, with nothing but her feathered hair to protect her; her head drooping like a dead flower; a white glove on her right hand like Michael Jackson, the pinkie stuffed with cotton.

It was okay, though. Because the funny thing was, he'd been able to love her more, and with less effort, from a distance. He felt that by going fast he was actually helping Lisa, he was helping all of them. He was building a white city out of crystal, inside his heart. When it was finished, there'd be room for everyone. For the first time in his life Jack had understood Bertie's nonsense about positive thinking, about taking responsibility for your own life. After Jack met Flaco, there were nights he didn't come home at all. Sometimes their flights lasted for days. Bertie might have complained, but she, too, was spending more and more time at her meetings. It was no surprise when Lisa said she was going away.

"Away? Where could you possibly go?" cried Bertie.

Lisa said she'd heard there was a good doctor in Phoenix; she'd start there.

"For how long?" Bertie had asked—and, when Lisa didn't answer—"And I suppose you plan on taking the money with you?"

"It *is* mine," said Lisa.

No one could argue with that.

Jack pulled the cord, made his way to the rear exit of the bus. The door opened with a life-support hiss.

Whiplash of light coming off a skyscraper. Jack held up his hand to block the sun's reflection, a roundish blur of ghostly ectoplasm that hovered somewhere around the twentieth floor—which the boy's street sense interpreted, correctly, as roughly five o'clock.

Please be over soon, he thought, knowing full well that the day would linger for hours yet. Even after sunset, the heat would be terrible—the sidewalks, the streets, the buildings, radiating back the fire they'd absorbed all day. There'd be no relief until well after midnight.

Jack walked south, toward the barrio, toward the sound of firecrackers, the whistle of bottle rockets. Later, at dark, the neon pompoms would come—the big holiday displays at the foothills resorts, and the city-sponsored show on Sentinel Peak, which half the time had to be stopped due to the scrub catching on fire. From the valley, you could watch the flames flowing down the mountain like lava. People looked forward to that as much as to the fireworks.

Jack walked with no particular purpose, and was surprised when he found himself standing before Flaco's house. There was the white storybook fence around the neatly swept yard; the saint with her garland of artificial flowers, standing on a lake of tinfoil. At the Virgin's feet, a weird mix of things: playing cards and plastic beads, and what looked like pieces of old bread. Jack had always loved this diorama, which lived inside a little cage like a chicken coop. To protect it from the rain, Flaco's mother had explained.

He wondered if she'd still recognize him, maybe give him some *carne seca* wrapped in a tortilla as thin as tissue paper. In so many ways, his life had started in this house. A thousand hopes and dreams. Jack wondered if they were still in there, inside Flaco's spray-painted bedroom. Wondered, too, if there might be any crystal left in one of the old hiding spots.

Five years was a long time, though. Someone would already have smoked it, or flushed it down the drain. And, besides, Jack didn't have the stamina to crawl through another window. He was done with windows and doors. He half considered climbing inside the chicken coop with the saint.

The sadness bloomed in his belly. It always started there—a radio-active flower, chaotic, spinning out in weird fractals until it found its way to his arms and legs, his quivering lips. Then the telltale buzz of electricity in his hair.

See, this was the reason it was better to go fast with another person—so that, when you crashed, you weren't alone. The high, too, was better when shared. Sometimes he and Flaco, as a team, could increase the effect of the drugs, pinballing around the bedroom, generating so much heat they could barely stand the feel of their clothing. Often they'd ripped off their shirts, lain next to each other on the bed, watched in amazement as their words turned into flames, rose into the air like rockets.

Flaco—and this was something Jack wished to mention in his documentary—Flaco had not died from crystal. It had been something else, something stupid, a car.

Walking away from the imprisoned saint, Jack passed old women putting lawn chairs along the street, claiming spots. *Brujas* in flowered smocks and slappy flip-flops, some with brooms, territorial. Later, they'd sit there with glasses of watermelon juice and watch the fireworks, the burning mountain.

Farther south now, past Birrieria Guadalajara, where he and Flaco used to eat everything, even tongue.

Lengua.

Words no longer seemed chimeric to Jack, no longer seemed approximations for something else. They were earthbound now, which was what happened when you were sober. Jack clenched his fists—untrimmed nails digging into his flesh. All he wanted was to find a safe place before the blooms made a mess of the sky.

He stopped at the railroad tracks. Stopped right between the iron rails, kicked aside some trash, and sat. In his dark jeans, his dirt-brown shirt, they might not even see him. "*Ow,*" he said, because of the stones as he lay down.

While the sun cooked him, he became aware of how dirty he was. He could smell himself, even a slight tang of shit. Disgusting. His breath stank—and his stomach was bubbling, an ungodly flatulence from a diet of protein bars and black smoke. It was understandable why others would despise him. Most people lived their entire lives straight, and had no ability whatsoever to see through surfaces—unlike Jack, who'd been schooled in crystal, and who understood how easy it was to forgive.

Who knew if Lisa forgave him? He hoped she didn't. He was the one who'd thrown the Frisbee over the fence, a total spaz, missing Lisa by a mile. She'd pulled a face and told him to go get it. "You're closer," he'd shouted back. "You get it."

Jack turned his head, to see if he could spot the train. Flicker of distant traffic: metal and glass. Lost saguaros, catatonic, above which birds drifted in slow circles, like pieces of ash. To the east, the mountains, shrouded in dust, were all but invisible. The train would come eventually, the crazy quilt of boxcars, the fractious whistle.

Oh, but it was so boring waiting for death! Jack had come to the tracks before. When the signal light began to flash, he jumped up. He wasn't an idiot.

Besides, he couldn't help himself; his sadness was like a river, carrying him home.

"You don't like your life, make up another one." Something Bertie used to say. Her children had, in the end, listened to her.

Jack kept running, and when he got to Jamie's he didn't knock; he walked right in, sat at the table.

It wasn't long before Jamie came into the kitchen in his phony orange kimono *("Mijo! Mijo!")*, flapping his arms, flushing, like something out of a Mexican soap opera.

And though Jack didn't laugh, he remembered the part of himself that had—and not so long ago. Still, he flinched when the man tried to touch his face.

In the silence that followed, Jamie began to smile.

"What?" said Jack—and Jamie said, "I'm just looking at you."

"Why?"

"Do I need a reason?"

Jack shrugged, evasive. "I'm sort of hungry."

"Well," Jamie said grandly, "you're dealing with an expert on that subject. The only question is: animal, vegetable, or *mineral*?" This last word sugarcoated, singsong.

Jack looked up, hopefully.

"Yes, *mijo*." Jamie patted the pocket of his kimono. "I do I do I do."

"I do," repeated Jack, feeling his heart leap straight into the man's fat little hand.

SHANE BAUER, JOSH FATTAL, SARAH SHOURD

■

780 Days of Solitude

FROM *Mother Jones*

SHANE

The nightmare began on July 31, 2009. I was living in Damascus, cover-ing the Middle East as a freelance journalist, with my girlfriend, Sarah Shourd, a teacher. Our friend Josh Fattal had come to see us, and to cel-ebrate, we took a short trip to Iraqi Kurdistan. The autonomous region—isolated from the violence that wracked the rest of Iraq—was a budding Western tourist destination. After two days of visiting castles and muse-ums, we headed to the Zagros Mountains, where locals directed us to a campground near a waterfall. After a breakfast of bread and cheese, we hiked up a trail we'd been told offered beautiful views. We walked for a few hours, up a winding valley between brown mountains mottled with patches of yellow grass that looked like lion's fur. We didn't know that we were headed toward the worst 26 months of our lives.

JOSH (July 31, 2009)

"You guys," Sarah says with hesitancy. "I think we should head back."

"Really?" Shane sounds surprised. "How could we not pop up to the ridge? We're so close."

Shane knows I want to reach the top. "Josh, what do you want to do?" he asks.

"I think we should just go to the ridge—it's only a couple minutes away. Let's take a quick peek, then come right back down." Just as we're setting out, Sarah stops in her tracks. "There's a soldier on the ridge. He's got a gun," she says. "He's waving us up the trail." I pause and look at my friends. Maybe it's an Iraqi army outpost. We stride silently uphill. I can feel my heart pounding against my ribs.

The soldier is young and nonchalant, and he beckons us to him with a wave. When we finally approach him, he asks, "Farsi?"

"*Faransi?*" Shane asks, then continues in Arabic. "I don't speak French. Do you speak Arabic?"

"Shane!" I whisper urgently. "He asked if we speak Farsi!" I notice the red, white, and green flag on the soldier's lapel. This isn't an Iraqi soldier. We're in Iran.

The soldier signals us to follow him to a small, unmarked building. Around us, mountains unfold in all directions. A portly man in a pink shirt who looks like he just woke up starts barking orders. He stays with us as his soldiers dig through our bags. His eyes are on Sarah—scanning up and down. I can feel her tensing up.

I keep asking, "Iran? Iraq?" trying to figure out where the border lies and pleading with them to let us go. Sarah finds a guy who speaks a little English and seems trustworthy. He points to the ground under his feet and says, "Iran." Then he points to the road we came on and says, "Iraq." We start making a fuss, insisting we should be allowed to leave because they called us over their border. He agrees and says in awkward English, "You are true." It's a remote outpost and our arrival is probably the most interesting thing that has happened for years.

The English speaker approaches us again after talking to the commander. "You. Go," he says. "You. Go. Iran."

SHANE (August 2, 2009)

Beneath the night sky, the city is smearing slowly past our windows. Who are these two men in the front seats? Where are they taking us? They aren't speaking. The pudgy man in the passenger seat is making the little movements that nervous people do: coughing fake coughs; adjusting his seating position compulsively. Everyone in the car is trying to prove to one another, and maybe to ourselves, that we aren't afraid.

But Sarah's hand is growing limp in mine. Something is very wrong.

"He's got a gun," Josh says, startled but calm. "He just put it on the dash."

"Where are we going?" Sarah asks in a disarming, honey-sweet voice. "Sssssss!" the pudgy man hisses, turning around and putting his finger to his lips. The headlights of the car trailing us light up his face, revealing his cold, bored eyes. He picks up the gun in his right hand and cocks it.

Sarah's eyes widen. She leans toward the man in front and, with a note of desperation, says, "Ahmadinejad good!" (thumbs up) "Obama bad!" (thumbs down). The pistol is resting in his lap. He turns to face us again and holds both his hands out with palms facing each other. "Iran," he says, nodding toward one hand. "America," he says, lifting the other. "Problem," he says, stretching out the distance between them.

Sarah turns to me. "Do you think he is going to hurt us?" she asks. I don't know whether to respond or just stare at her.

In my mind, I see us pulling over to the side of the road and leaving the car quietly. My tremulous legs will convey me mechanically over the rocky earth. I will be holding Sarah's hand and maybe Josh's too, but I will be mostly gone already, walking flesh with no spirit. We won't kiss passionately in our final moments before the trigger pull. We won't scream. We won't run. We won't utter fabulous words of defiance as we stare down the gun barrel. We will be like mice, paralyzed by fear, limp in the slack jaw of a cat.

Each of us will fall, one by one, hitting the gravelly earth with a thud.

Sarah pumps Josh's and my hands. Her eyes have sudden strength in them, forced yet somehow genuine. "We're going to be okay, you guys. They are just trying to scare us."

JOSH (August 4, 2009)

My sandals clap loudly on the floor as I try to catch my momentum and keep my balance. After every few steps, they spin me in circles. My mind tries desperately to remember the way back.

The door shuts behind me. The clanging metal reverberates until silence resumes. I stand at the door, distraught and disoriented. Whatever script, whatever drama I thought I was in, ends now. Whatever stage I thought I was on is now empty. I dodder to the corner of my cell and take a seat on the carpet. There is nothing in my 8-by-12-foot cell: no mattress, no chair—just a room, empty except for three wool blankets. My prison uniform—blue pants, blue collared shirt—blends with the blue marble wall behind me and the tight blue carpet below.

Shane and Sarah are probably sulking in the corners of their cells too. We agreed we'd hunger strike if we were split up. Now I don't feel defiant. I just feel lost.

Sarah's glasses are in my breast pocket. She gave them to me to hold when they made us wear blindfolds. She didn't have pockets in her prison uniform—they dressed her in heaps of dark clothes, including a brown hijab. I empty my other pockets: lip balm from the hike and a wafer wrapper—the remnant of my measly lunch.

I don't know what I'll do in here for the rest of the day. I sense the hovering blankness—a zone of mindlessness that looms over my psyche and lives in the silence of my cell.

SARAH (August 6, 2009)

"Sarah, eat this cookie."

"Not until I see Josh and Shane."

I'm sitting blindfolded in a classroom chair. A cookie is on the desk in front of me.

"Do you think we care if you eat, Sarah?"

They do care. I know that much. I've been on hunger strike since they split us up two days ago. At first it was difficult, but I'm learning how to conserve my energy. When I stand up, my heart beats furiously, so I lie on the floor most of the day. Terrible thoughts and images occupy my mind—my mom balled up on the floor screaming when she learns I've been captured, masked prison guards coming into my cell to rape me—but I've found ways to distract myself, like slowly going over multiplication tables in my head.

"Sarah, why did you come to the Middle East to live in Damascus?" the interrogator asks. "Don't you miss your family? Your country?"

"Yes, of course I do. But it's only for a couple of years. I can't believe you're asking me this—do you realize how scared and worried my family must be? Why can't I make a phone call and tell them I'm alive?"

There are four or five interrogators. The one who seems like the boss is pacing and talking angrily in Farsi. They tell me if I eat their cookie, I can see Shane and Josh.

"Let me see them first—then I'll eat."

"Sarah, you say you are a teacher. Have you ever been to the Pentagon?"

"No, I've never even been to Washington, DC."

"Please, Sarah, tell the truth. How can you be a teacher, an educated person, and never go to the Pentagon? Describe to us just the lobby."

"I've never been to the Pentagon. Teachers don't go to the Pentagon!" I almost have to stop myself from laughing, partly because I'm weak from not eating and partly because I can't really convince myself this nightmare is real.

JOSH (August 18, 2009)

In my mind I am already running. My feet patter quickly on the brick floor. All day, my energy is dammed up, but in the courtyard, energy courses through me. They take me for two half-hour sessions per day. I'm allotted a single lane next to other blindfolded prisoners. It's the only time I feel alive all day—when I'm out here and thinking about escaping.

Once, when I heard a helicopter whirring near the prison, I deluded myself into believing freedom was imminent. I decided US officials must be negotiating our release and that I'd be free within three days. Now I cling to the idea of being released on Day 30. In the corner of my cell, the corner most difficult to see from the entryway, there are a host of tally marks scratched into the wall. I check the mean, median, and mode of the data sample. The longest detentions last three or four months, but most markings are less than 30 days. I remember an Iranian American was recently detained and released from prison. How long was she held? Thirty days seems like a fair enough time for the political maneuvering to sort itself out.

JOSH (August 30, 2009)

Suddenly, the metal door rattles. A guard signals me to clean my room and gather my belongings. I am prepared for this. The floor is already immaculate—sweeping the floor with my hands is one of my favorite activities. I grab my book and three dried dates stuffed with pistachio nuts to share with Sarah and Shane. I wasn't crazy. Day 30 is for real.

When we're in the car, I can hardly control my joy. I turn to Shane and Sarah, and we start giggling—nervous laughter—at the comfort of our companionship. Now that we're together again, the weeks of solitude I've just endured seem like a distant memory. Was it really a month? Somehow this is funny to us.

Sarah tells me that she and Shane spoke to each other through a vent. They *what*? Sarah says, "I promise we didn't do it much." I can't believe they were near each other. They had each other! I had nothing.

These guys don't have a clue what I experienced. I would have done anything for a voice to talk to. I push the idea of them talking as far from my mind as possible, trying to convince myself of what I'd always assumed—we are in this together.

In the rearview mirror, I make eye contact with the stoic driver.

He slows to a stop, then lifts the emergency brake. His gaze, knowing and pitiless, conveys the truth. Shades and bars cover every window of the dirty, gray building before us. This is another prison.

JOSH (September 2, 2009)

In this prison, guards don't hide their faces like they did in the last one. Some even talk to me. One guard, who speaks a little English, taught me the Farsi word for the courtyard we go to, *hava khori*. He told me that it literally means "eating air."

I've even grown friendly with a guard I call "Friend." I treated him amiably and he has responded in kind. He speaks awkward English and tries out colloquial expressions on me. He makes small talk, which can be the most significant event of my day. Friend gave me a bed and mattress, pistachios, bottled water, and crackers. He even gave me a small personal fridge that he put in the hallway in front of my cell. With snacks in front of me, I allowed myself to feel how hungry I've been, and how my stomach shrank after 11 days of hunger striking and four weeks on a prison diet.

Friend shows up at my cell to escort me down the hallway to hava khori. "Do you know what a honey is?" He smiles goofily. "Do you have a honey?" "No," I say dismissively, "and I don't want a honey in here." I regret talking to him about English expressions. Why is he asking me about a honey? Why did he give me a bed last week? I push away the thought these questions raise.

SHANE (October 2009)

Solitary confinement is the slow erasure of who you thought you were. You think you are still you, but you have no real way of knowing. How can you know if you have no one to reflect you back to yourself? Would I know if I was going crazy? The longer I am alone, the more my mind slows. All I want to do is to forget about everything.

But I can't do it. I am unable to keep my mind from being sharply focused on one task: forcing myself not to look at the wall behind me. I know that eventually, a tiny sliver of sunlight will spill in through the grated window and place a quarter-size dot on the wall. It's ridiculous that I'm thinking about it this early. I've been awake only 10 minutes and I should know it will be hours before it appears.

They take everything from us—breezes, eye contact, human touch, the feeling of warm wet hands from washing a sink-load of dishes, the miracle of transforming thoughts into words on paper. They leave only the pause—those moments of waiting at bus stops, of cigarette breaks. They make time the object of our hatred.

I try not to look for the light.

Eventually, I pull myself up and out of bed. I take the few steps to one end of the cell, then back to the other. For a while, I had a few books to transport me out of this prison. The interrogators gave us Dostoyevsky's *The Idiot*, Virginia Woolf's *To the Lighthouse*, Edith Hamilton's *Mythology*, the Persian poet Ferdowsi's *Shahnameh*, and—without irony—Orwell's *Animal Farm*. But recently, they took them all away. Now I just have Whitman's *Leaves of Grass*. I recently memorized "To the Garden the World," so I recite it over and over again as

I pace, jutting my finger into the air at the line "Curious here behold my resurrection after slumber."

As I walk, my finger taps against my thigh in alternating short and long pulses, each accompanied by high-pitched vocal beeps. I recite the poem in Morse code, tapping out the lines, "By my side or back of me Eve following,/Or in front, and I following her just the same." I've been studying Morse code in the dictionary Sarah convinced the interrogators to give us by saying she wanted to learn it like Malcolm X did when he was in prison. We take turns with it for a week at a time, passing it to one another through our interrogators.

Somehow the study of Morse code seems useful to me. It makes me feel like my life isn't seeping down the drain for nothing. Maybe someday I'll be stranded somewhere with a flashlight and will be able to code my way to safety. Actually, I know that's bullshit. I study Morse code because I need challenges like this to survive.

I slide under my bed on my back and lift the end as though it were a bench press. I do sit-ups and pushups. I jog in place on a stack of blankets and do high head-kicks back and forth across the cell. I give myself a sponge bath in the sink and look at the wall again. The light is there now—a trickle of diagonal dots. The day has begun. I am hopeful that today my interrogator will come. Then, at least, I will have some human contact.

After lunch, the hours pass blankly until the light is on the long wall. The two large rectangles of 10 vertical bars of light have fully gone around the corner. The day is at its midpoint. My interrogator isn't coming. He never comes after lunch. All that's left of the day is stagnation. All I can do is wait for sleep. I've already juggled oranges and swept the floor clean with my hands. I do make one discovery: The color red is absent from my life, but if I close my eyes and put my face in the patch of sun, I can see it.

Then, still pacing, I start thinking of books. The titles comfort me: *The Brothers Karamazov, War and Peace, A People's History of the United States.* I'm afraid that when the time comes to tell somebody what books I want, I will forget one, so I recite them occasionally to remember. I know that if that opportunity arises, I will only have one chance. I've decided to keep a list of 10. Why 10? I don't know.

Eventually I realize how quickly I'm bouncing from one end of the cell to the next. I'm not walking so much as striding. And I'm speaking out loud. I stop and look around. How long have I been doing that, repeating these titles out loud and counting them on my fingers? Something about realizing that I've been hearing my own voice—merely hearing it, not commanding it—frightens me.

SHANE (November 2009)

At the end of each hallway, there's a small open-air cell. The guards sat me in one of those today. I've been in here, listening to Sarah's voice in a nearby room for a while now. "You have to let me call my mother!" she is shouting. "You can't do this!" Her cries sound desperate.

I am boiling inside. What are they saying to make her wail like that? The interrogators haven't come to me yet, but these sounds are making me nervous. We were caught a week ago using illegal pens and leaving notes at hava khori for one another to find. Ever since then, I've been waiting for them to come.

An interrogator comes in. He's the tall, oafish one I sometimes hear speaking to Sarah while she is being interrogated. He is always telling me not to worry about her, that she is doing wonderfully. "You are stupid, Shane," he says. "What did you think you were doing?" He comes in close behind me. "Stupid!" he says again, smacking me on the back of the head, not hard, just a humiliating slap that brings alive in me something reminiscent of all those school bullies who slapped, punched, kicked, and choked my younger, smaller, bespectacled self.

I jump out of my seat, pull my blindfold off, and spin around to face him. He is towering over me, at least a foot taller than I am.

"Don't you ever touch me like that again," I say, pointing my finger toward his face. I don't remember the last time I've been swept away with such heat.

His jaw lowers and his square, pale face goes cold. He looks frightened, not frightened that I will hurt him—he's huge—but frightened that he made some mistake. The slap felt routine, like something he does all the time. But we are high-value prisoners. He can't do this with us. He knows that, but until now, I don't think he knew that I knew that. I'm not quite sure why I do.

"Okay," he says, almost placatingly. "I won't do it again." I hold his gaze for a second longer than is comfortable, his eyes dripping remorse, mine full of fire.

Slowly and self-assuredly, I turn around, sit down, and begin to write: "I had a pen. I knew it was illegal, but I did it anyway. I needed to communicate with Sarah and Josh. It was a moment of weakness. It was a mistake and I will never do it again. If I do, I accept full punishment. I hope you find it in your heart to forgive us and to give us another chance."

I know that I have no choice. The interrogators can always punish me by punishing Sarah and Josh.

SHANE (December 8, 2009)

A guard is at my door. He is smiling slightly, which I've never seen him do. He takes me to the door of a cell with a fridge—an object I know to be the privilege of only a few prisoners—next to it. He opens the door and there is Josh, genuflecting with his head on the ground. He jolts up, looking stunned. "What's going on?" he says.

"It looks like I'm moving in," I reply. He leaps up, and we hug and laugh. The guard is now smiling widely. The cell door closes behind us.

This isn't the first time we've seen each other recently. For the past 10 days, they've been allowing the three of us to meet for half-hour sessions at hava khori. These meetings have been mostly frantic, each of us desperately trying to unload what we've been storing in our minds for months.

Now, in a cell together, Josh and I come back to life. After five months of isolation, the possibility of conversation on any topic for any length of time is overwhelming. We talk about *The Idiot* to an absurd extent, reading passages at random to discuss them as though they were Scripture. Josh gives me a lesson on the musical career of Bob Dylan and I school him on the Balkan Wars. Since we aren't allowed pens, I draw an invisible map with my finger on the wall.

Josh tries to remember the Hebrew alphabet. He teaches me the letters by writing them with sunflower seeds. The task becomes stressful because we have to destroy the letters every time we hear footsteps, lest we give the guards "evidence" that we are Israeli spies. We stay up late at night and discuss Josh's ideas about the city government in Cottage Grove, Oregon. We make lemonade with the lemons from our lunch. We shoot hoops with a wad of paper and an empty box. We draw a ring on the floor and see who can toss the greater number of candies inside it. We say "Good night" to each other before we go to sleep.

On our first day together, we come out to hava khori to find Sarah. "Guess what?" I say. "Josh and I are in the same cell now." I can barely contain my excitement.

She takes a deep breath. "It's okay," she says.

The next day, Josh stays behind so I can be alone with Sarah for the first time in months. When I pull my blindfold off, I see her at the opposite end of the courtyard, hunched over and staring at me with cold, angry eyes I barely recognize. I rush over to her and she steps back, like a cowering animal. For every advance I make, she makes a retreat, scowling. Then, her frigid eyes begin to tear. "It's not fair, Shane," she whimpers.

"I know, baby," I say, reaching my hand out. "It's not fair." I step toward her again.

As soon as I touch her, she starts screaming, kicking and punching the wall with each word. "It's! Not! Fair!"

I throw my arms around her as she tries desperately to pull away from me.

"It's okay, baby," I say. In my mind I'm saying these words softly, trying to soothe her pain, but in fact I'm shouting, competing with her screams. "It's okay! Sarah. Stop! It's okay."

"It's okay?" she says sharply, looking at me like I've just smacked her. "It's not okay, Shane. This is not okay!" She's right, of course. It's not okay that she is alone and I am not. But I don't know what else to say.

Eventually, her rage shifts into sorrow. She lets me hold her. But it doesn't feel like she has found comfort. It feels like something is fundamentally broken, in me, in her, between us. I feel like an accomplice in torture.

What if they'd asked me if I wanted to cell up with Josh? Would I have refused? If I could have, should I have? Every time I laugh or share a meal with Josh or stay awake longer than I would if I were alone, part of me feels like I'm turning my back on Sarah.

SARAH (December 12, 2009)

Fuck you, body, I think as I get out of bed. My head is a balloon filled with water, my shoulders are slack and lifeless, and my eyes feel like glass. I slowly pull on my pants, walk three steps to the sink, and drink two cups of water. My stomach makes an ugly sound, so I ring the bell for the second time even though I know it won't make the guards come any faster.

The bell is a round, black rubber button on the wall. When I push it, a green light, which the guards can see but often ignore, comes on outside my cell door. I need to use the bathroom, so I begin to pace the length of my 10-by-14-foot cell, punching the air like a boxer with my eyes fixed on my bare feet and the brown carpet. I let out a cry of frustration, pick up a plastic cup, and hurl it at the wall. I decide to pee in the sink.

Ever since I found out Shane and Josh were put together, I've been full of uncontrollable anger at everything and everyone. And hate—an almost violent hate.

If Shane and Josh can get through this, so can I. That's been my motto since we came here. Even during the months we didn't see each other, I knew they were enduring the same empty hours I was. Now that they are together in one cell, there's a rupture between us, a distance I don't know how to bridge.

When I'm with Shane and Josh in hava khori, I almost feel worse. Every touch reminds me of the absence of touch. Their situation seems heavenly to me—they're out of solitary! What could be better than sharing a leisurely game of chess, listening to endless stories about each other's lives, being able to connect without the fear of interference? They are halfway there, halfway to sanity and normalcy, halfway to freedom! I want to feel happy for them, but I don't know how much longer I can hold it together alone in this cell.

My time has become less and less structured as I get more depressed. I talk to myself, eat my food with my hands. Like an animal, I spend hours crouched by the slot at the bottom of my door listening for sounds. Sometimes I hear footsteps coming down the hall, race to the door, and realize they were imagined. Or flashing lights will dart across the periphery of my vision—but when I jerk around to see, they're gone.

These symptoms scare me. Sometimes when I try to read, I can't focus and end up reading the same line again and again, finally hurling my book in frustration. I've become extremely paranoid about my stuff, afraid the guards will take things when I'm gone. I hide the food and other junk I hoard all over my cell—under the carpet, in my mattress—and check it compulsively.

How will I know when I've left sane thought and behavior behind? When there's no turning back? I've always clung to the certainty that I can emerge from this place unbroken and unchanged, but I'm not sure I believe that any more. Why am I being singled out for this torture? How can they leave me in here to go crazy alone?

Suddenly I'm on my feet, running to the door. I start banging on it with my fists, kicking it again and again. The guard opens the door and I stare at her, breathless and angry, my hands balled into fists.

"I want hava khori," I demand, my voice trembling, my face locked.

"No, Sarah!" she yells. "No hava khori today!" I hear the door slam. I hear her footsteps running down the hall. I don't hear anything else. I want to die. I want to disappear. I want to kill.

I hear a scream. It's far away, maybe in the courtyard or the next row of cells. There's something familiar about it.

The door opens and a guard is in my cell. She looks at me with horror and through her eyes I see myself. The scream I heard wasn't coming from down the hall. It came from my own throat.

The guard grabs my shoulders, and begins to shake me. "Sarah, no! Sarah, no!" We fall to the floor, and I can feel her hands on my face. I open my eyes and follow her gaze to the wall. I see streaks of blood against the mottled white. I look down at my hands and begin to wail like a child. My knuckles are scraped from where I'd been beating them against the wall.

"I can't!" I yell at her. "I can't do this." Her arms encircle me now. "I can't!"

SARAH (December 27, 2009)

The guards in the hall are frantic as they lead us back to our cells from hava khori. I peek under my blindfold as we pass five or six young women lined up facing the wall. It's evident by their fitted jeans, long black jackets, and platform shoes that they've just been brought in from the streets. I sense their fear as I'm led past. One has a bandage wrapped around her head, caked with blood. Another is limping, her bright red hair streaming out of her torn headscarf. Based on the number of new women I've seen, I estimate there are now 10 or 12 packed into each cell.

I've had a hunch something like this might be coming. When I woke up this morning, the guard who brought me breakfast was uncharacteristically brisk. Then I heard helicopters circling outside my cell window. After my screaming episode two weeks ago, my interrogators attempted to pacify me by placing a small TV and DVD player in my cell. I've watched the one movie they gave me, the 2008 presidential assassination drama *Vantage Point*, about 18 times now, and I spend hours each day reading the English ticker on the Farsi news channel. This week, thinly veiled threats against "hooliganism" on the news caught my attention. Then boxes of new prison uniforms and plastic slippers arrived at the end of the corridor. I assumed the "Green Revolution" protests we watched on TV in Damascus last spring were over, but the government-controlled media has been gearing up for something for weeks.

I decide to ring for the guard and ask for my nightly shower. "Nah," she says, exasperated, *"kaar daaram."* I'm busy. I begin to pantomime, performing like a trained monkey, smelling my armpits and crinkling up my nose.

"Okay, enough, Sarah, quickly!" I grab my towel, hastily tie my blindfold around my head, and charge down the hall toward the showers.

I crank the hot-water knob as high as it will go, steaming up the room like a sauna. Is it really a revolution this time? If this government's overthrown, what will happen to us? Things could get really ugly before the opposition assumes power. We could get hurt, separated, or killed in the interim.

I suddenly hear the door open in the small room next to the showers. I quietly unlatch the barred window, peering into the small courtyard. A young woman stares back at me.

Think fast, I tell myself. It's been several months since one of the guards has made such a slip, leaving me alone in the bathroom with another prisoner nearby. I grab the bars between us, bringing my face as close to hers as I can. "I Sarah. American. Long time here, no freedom," I whisper in my ridiculous, infantile Farsi. "You please phone mother Sarah. Sarah no spy, Sarah love Iran people, Sarah teacher, Damascus. Please you freedom phone mother Sarah, okay?" The woman looks straight at me. "I know you, Sarah," she says in awkward but good English. "I am sorry, but I am not free, so I cannot help you."

At that moment the door opens and a guard starts yelling at both of us. She hands the prisoner a stack of navy blue clothes and ushers her down the hallway.

SHANE (Early January 2010)

Little cakes and candies wrapped in cellophane dash across the cell floor. The disruption freezes me momentarily as I kneel over tiny flash cards, each displaying a name, arrayed in a large network on the carpet. I was in the middle of something important: constructing an elaborate Greek family tree of gods and mortals. I'd been frustrated because I couldn't remember which marriages connected the House of Atreus to the House of Thebes. How many days must I study this before it finally sticks? It takes me a moment to realize that the sweets were tossed in through the window in the door. Josh and I lunge to the floor and rip open some cakes. We each put a morsel into our mouths, chewing slowly with our eyes closed. It's spongy, like a Twinkie. The concentrated blast of sugar is like an injection of well-being.

After we finish, we set to work splitting open some dates, removing the pits, and pressing some dark chocolate and a glob of butter into each of them. We put six of these in a small plastic bag that I put in my pocket. Later, a guard comes to take us to hava khori. As I pass the neighboring cell, I jam the plastic bag through the little bars. Behind the door, I hear people scramble.

I know the cakes came from someone in that cell—I am guessing the guy I often hear whispering to another person across the hall in Arabic, a language rarely heard in this prison and one that, unlike Farsi, I understand. Judging by their accents, I assume that our neighbor is a Saudi and the man across the hall is from Iraq or Kuwait. I've gathered that the man across the hall has a television, which is why he is always the bearer of tidings. Our neighbor has been asking for updates on the "Brotherhood," which seems to roughly mean Al Qaeda, some other militant Sunni group, or all of them generally.

Sometimes, they've talked about us.

"Hey, the other day when I went to the bathroom I looked in the cell of those Americans. It's like a five-star hotel in there. They have beds and a TV. And every day they go outside twice. Yeah, Iran is good to the Americans." So badly I've wanted to interject, to tell them we didn't, in fact, have a television and that we weren't allowed to even make phone calls. But I've resisted.

I've refused to talk, despite our neighbor's pounding on our wall and the coughs out into the hallway to get our attention.

I've refused because Sarah, Josh, and I made an agreement not to talk to anyone. The longer Sarah is alone, the more afraid—and paranoid—she has become that one of us will get caught doing something and that we will be separated again. For her sake, we don't break the rules.

But now he is throwing cakes into our cell.

As the days pass, it becomes harder and harder to resist the urge to communicate. I am convinced it is safe—these two men talk to each other every day, loudly—and I am frustrated with Sarah's lack of faith in my judgment. Eventually, Josh and I set a date: In two weeks, we will tell Sarah we want to actually talk to him.

Then one day, at hava khori, Sarah says, "Guys, I really want to talk to my neighbor. I will be really careful. Do you think it would be okay?"

"Sure," I say. I am genuinely happy, because I want Sarah to connect with more people. She has been deteriorating. Her excitement at seeing us every day is desperate. She almost always leaves hava khori deflated and disappointed. People need people, and Sarah needs people more than most. It's as if they found a special little torture just for her, and put it on a screen for us to watch every day.

"I'd really like to talk to our neighbor too," I say. "He seems to know a lot about what's going on."

"Okay, just be careful," she says.

Our neighbor says his name is Hamid, and when we start talking to him, our hall feels suddenly alive. He tells us that we are in Section 209, one of the political wards of Tehran's giant Evin Prison. He teaches us the Farsi word for hostage, *gurugan*, which we use whenever we are frustrated with the guards, because they hate the idea.

He tries to reassure me: "America can do anything it wants to. You will be out soon. Trust me." I disagree. "I think the US is just going to leave us here. We aren't worth much to our government. If we really were spies, we'd be out by now. Iran is going to keep making demands for things like prisoner swaps, and the US will refuse. Iran won't be able to back down. So how will we get out?"

The more I get to know Hamid, the more I see how similar his situation is to ours, except that no one, not even his family, knows what is happening to him. He says he was arrested for a visa technicality, that he has never been allowed to call anybody, and that he has never seen a lawyer or his embassy. He just went to court and they gave him a one-year sentence for visa forgery. "But don't worry," he tells me. "Illegal entry is only a six-month sentence." We are coming up on five.

SARAH (Early January 2010)

I wake to insistent knocking on my wall. The new prisoner hasn't stopped trying to get my attention since she came here after the protests. If I knock back, it will only lead to more communication, like whispering into the hallway or passing notes. There's nothing I can do to help her, I tell myself sternly, trying to focus my attention back on my book.

"Sarah." I suddenly hear a soft whisper. The voice is close, almost as if it were in my room. "Sarah." My head darts to the right and left, looking for the source of the sound. Am I imagining it? "Sarah." The voice is louder now. "Please." It seems to be coming from the corner near the door, where my sink is. Above the sink is a vent. I leap off my bare mattress and climb onto the sink. I press my mouth to the vent.

"Who are you?" I ask the voice. "How do you know my name?"

"My name is Zahra, almost the same as yours, Sarah. I know you."

"You know me?" "Yes, I saw your mother on TV. I am so sorry for you, Sarah. I am a mother too." "Did you talk to my mother?" I almost yell, then remember to hush my voice. "Did you talk to her?" As soon as the question escapes my mouth, I realize how irrational it is.

"No, Sarah. But I saw many pictures of you on BBC. You are a small, beautiful girl. I know it must be easy for you to be standing on the sink. For me, it is difficult. They beat me. They kicked me and tortured me. My hips hurt and it is difficult for me to stand." Her English is almost perfect, strongly accented with a sensuous, scratchy quality.

I feel tears welling up in my eyes. It's a miracle, I think. She knows me! We can talk to each other! "Is—" I hesitate, but I have to ask. "Is my mother okay?" "I don't know, dear Sarah. I am Dutch," she says, "and Iranian. I live in the Netherlands, but my daughter is here, in Iran. They will not let me talk to my embassy. I don't know if my embassy understands that I am here. When you see your embassy, please tell them about me, Zahra Bahrami."

"They never let me see anyone," I tell her. "I don't know what's happening. I've had no court, no trial. They won't let me see my lawyer." "Yes, I know. They are liars, Sarah. Don't believe anything they say to you. I am your friend now, I love you." I try to imagine her, hurt and alone, being taken out every day for beatings and interrogation and then put back in a cage. "Why did they arrest you?" I ask.

"I was at the protest," she says, "Ashura."

Suddenly, the door bursts open. Leila's small, voluptuous silhouette is outlined in the doorway.

Not Leila, I think, of all people. I've managed to stay on her good side, and she's helped me a lot—even complaining to the warden about how long they've kept me in solitary. I can't afford to lose her.

But now her kind, motherly face slams shut like a steel door. She says she will tell my interrogators what I've done. Zahra is immediately transferred.

Now, when Leila comes to my cell, there are no more smiles, no conversations in Arabic. She hands me my food with a cold, unfocused stare, then wordlessly leads me out to the courtyard for a few minutes of sun. I'm no longer her *ukhtee al-aziza,* her sweet sister. I'm a plant that she gets paid to keep alive.

JOSH (Early January 2010)

At hava khori I have to hide from Sarah the depth of my relationship with Shane. Sarah has said that she felt left out around Shane and me on the hike, and now the prison has institutionalized that arrangement.

Shane and I try to avoid talking about funny moments in our cell or even the fact that the interrogators let us have a plastic chair. Sarah asked us not to say "we," but we don't always succeed, and she invariably shudders when we slip. I try to remind her that one day it will all be set straight: "When we're released, you and Shane will be together all the time. I'll be on my own."

Sarah and I work to build our friendship so our triad's dynamic doesn't all hinge on Shane. She tells me about her days as a punk and about her relationship with her mother. She suggests friends of hers I should date in San Francisco. I tell her about Jenny, the friend I've wanted to marry since we dated in middle school, how I received long letters from her in September, and how I finally feel ready for her.

We schedule two weekly hava khori sessions in which Sarah and Shane can be alone. On Saturday mornings and Wednesday nights, I go to "small hava khori," a room smaller than my cell but with a glass roof that allows me to see the sky.

SHANE (January 10, 2010)

The censors neglected to remove a staple from our letters. I pull it out with my long fingernails and bend the end to make a little hook.

I stick the hook delicately under the hem of my pink towel and pull the thread out, one stitch at a time. I do the same with my underwear, pulling out two long, white threads.

I tie the ends of these little threads to the zipper handle on my mattress. Like my sisters and I did as kids, I take three threads and weave them together, tying little knots over and over again. The knots form into a tiny little ring.

When we were all in solitary, I read books like *Pride and Prejudice* and *Tess of the D'Urbervilles* and paced my cell. I would only read a few pages at a time before I would put the book down, pace, and think. What have I been doing all these years? I'd ask myself. Why haven't I proposed to Sarah yet? Are we going to just roll along together year by year, without ever deciding that it will be forever? I turned over these questions for months. I've never really believed in marriage, so part of me wondered whether I was being seduced into it by my isolation and those 19th-century novels.

But I love her so much. I do want to be with her forever. Though I see her every day now, she is still ripped away over and over again. I want to be Sarah's sanctuary and I want her to be mine.

I tie off the thread spirals and leave enough loose string at the ends to make sure I can tie them onto our fingers. It's date night, which means that Josh is going to stay in the cell while Sarah and I go out alone. I have the two little rings in my hand, white with a strip of red in the middle, like a stone.

Josh has no idea what I'm about to do. I don't tell him because I'm afraid I might chicken out. I'm so nervous. What if she says no?

I get to hava khori before Sarah. It is dark and the late-winter air is a little cold. I lay a blanket down for us to sit on, under the camera so the guards won't be able to watch.

When she comes out, I ask her if she wants to walk. We do a few rounds, my heart pounding as I try to make small talk. Then I stop and sit us down on the blanket.

I take her hands in mine. The single light, high up on the opposite wall, drowns out any view of the stars, but it casts a soft yellow glow on her face. Her hair is long now, drawn back in a ponytail, but I can't see much of it under her purple hijab. Her lips are slightly redder than usual, probably from the strawberry jelly she uses sometimes for lipstick. She is beautiful.

I can see in her eyes that she doesn't know what I'm going to say. I'm shivering even though it isn't cold.

"Baby, I didn't want to do this here. I wanted it to be somewhere beautiful, but—" She looks confused and a little worried. "Will you marry me?" Her body jolts with surprise. She squeezes my fingers. For a few moments, she says nothing. I hold my breath. Then she says yes.

I tie the rings onto each of our fingers and we hold each other, looking into each other's eyes, smiling.

SARAH (February 2010)

About a week ago, the guard opened my door to hand me my lunch. Suddenly, another guard called her from down the hall and she left in a hurry. Standing with my food in my hand, I noticed a narrow, open crack in the door's seam, which usually let in no light. She'd left it open. What difference does it make, I thought to myself—frozen with my eyes fixed on the crack—if my stupid door is open? In the hallway outside my cell, there is a video camera mounted on the wall. This hallway leads to another hallway with another camera. With no help from the outside, there's no possibility of escape.

For months I had dreams of that damn door being left open— of magically walking out to freedom. Now that it actually was, all I wanted to do was close it. So I did.

JOSH (March 2010)

What I look forward to most is hava khori. It's the time of day when I stop reading, writing, exercising, and just connect with my two friends. Increasingly, though, it doesn't work out like that.

The arguments can be about anything. Shane wants to share meals at hava khori; Sarah doesn't want food to distract us during these precious times together. Sarah and I want us three to read the same books at the same time; Shane doesn't. Sarah wants us to appeal for clemency and apologize, but Shane and I don't want anything that hints at admitting guilt.

I wrack my brain for an escape from our routine. I propose that we celebrate as many holidays as we can think of—as creatively as we possibly can, disregarding the actual calendar if we feel like it.

The night before Palm Sunday, each of us creates a personal system for palm reading. A few days later we decide it's Ash Wednesday.

We smear our faces with the chalky prayer stone, laughing at how ridiculous we look.

On Friday, I arrange a makeshift Seder plate: a hard-boiled egg, salt water, a fish bone as a lamb shank, lettuce as a bitter herb, and dried, flat Persian bread for matzo. Halfway through the Passover story, Sarah gets the giggles and can't stop. She curls into Shane's arms, laughing and embarrassed by her girlishness.

Shane looks at me, clearly uncomfortable. I call off the meal, a little ticked. I put effort into making the Seder special, and I refreshed my memory by reading the story of Moses in the Koran. Passover is my favorite Jewish holiday.

I peer down at my pathetic Seder plate, then over at Shane and Sarah balled together, and then I look over the walls to the cloudy spring sky. I quickly let it go. It was a nice week, but these distractions couldn't last forever. Our holiday season is over.

SARAH (April 2010)

I'm in the middle of my exercise routine, doing jumping jacks and pushups, when I see a flurry of motion outside the slot on my door. I look down to find a tight ball of tissue paper on my floor. If the guards catch whoever threw this, my door will burst open any second. I will eat the note before they can take it.

Carefully smoothing out the crumpled note, I read: "Dearest Sarah, I am Zahra. Do you remember me? I have been very worried about you, my dear Sarah. They took me to a different section for talking with you, but now they have brought me back. Are you okay? Do you need help? I will talk to you tonight when the guards are sleeping."

I can't believe it's her! It was almost four months ago that they moved Zahra. I'd often wondered what happened to her, but I never expected to see her again.

Later that night, there are loud knocks on my wall. I hear my name being whispered into the hallway. I crawl toward my cell door.

"Hello," I whisper timidly through the slot.

"Sarah," the voice replies, "I am Zahra. Do you remember me? I've missed you. Are you okay? Are you still alone? I've been very worried about you." That night we devise a method of communicating through notes written on scraps of cardboard. She will write with a pen she stole from her interrogators and I will use a small piece of metal I've fashioned from a tube of Vaseline that leaves a mark like a pencil.

Zahra and I decide to hide our notes in the trash can in the bathroom. She balls hers up in toilet paper and I stuff mine inside soiled-looking maxi-pads—places the guards will never look. When one of us has a new note waiting, we will let the other one know by three hard knocks on our common wall.

I sometimes wait for days or weeks for the right opportunity to pass a note or exchange a few words with Zahra. I wait till the right guard is working—the one who never bothers to check on me through my peephole—so I won't get caught writing. I memorize the guards' footsteps and the patterns they walk in through the halls. I save a portion of beef stew in which I carefully soak a maxi-pad overnight, then let it dry for a day or two until it authentically looks like menstrual blood. If anything feels off, even the smallest detail, I abort the project.

Zahra is bold with the guards, sometimes making jokes, sometimes yelling at them. "I will not cry for these bastards," she writes me. "I will not show them my tears."

"We have to stop," I write to her one morning. "I'm afraid we'll get caught and they'll move you. Zahra, when we are both free, I'll come to see you in the Netherlands. We'll spend days together dancing and talking. We will be friends forever." A few days later Zahra passes by my cell and leaves another note balled up on my carpet.

"They are moving me again—don't cry, Sarah! I don't know what will happen to us, but remember you are never alone here. Sarah, please remember that Iranians are not bad people. We love the American people. I love you. No matter where they take me now, I will try to find you. Remember to listen for me—I will call out your name at night."

Over the next several months I sometimes catch a glimpse of Zahra's pink jumpsuit hanging on the prison clothesline. When the guards aren't looking, I run my hands across the pretty color and sneak a few nuts or a piece of candy into her back pocket.

SHANE (May 20, 2010)

The guard we've nicknamed Dumb Guy is at our door. He hands us a bag of brand new jeans, shirts, socks, and sneakers with shoelaces. "Put these on, quickly," he says, and leaves. We've been planning for this moment. Our moms have told us in letters they were trying to come and visit us.

After Dumb Guy is gone, I go to the bathroom. A tiny note, covered in microscopic writing, is wrapped tightly in plastic and stuck inside the outer lip of the sink. It's small enough to fit discreetly between my middle and ring finger.

Josh and I have practiced this many times. I tape the note to my penis.

They took Sarah's pen first, so we knew to hide one of ours before they raided our cell. I scribed this letter with our secret pen over several days while Josh stood watch for guards. It describes in detail what happened when we were captured and lays out a schedule of all of the events of our detainment, including prison transfers, hunger strikes, the arrival of books. It describes our daily routine and lists our email passwords in the hope that someone will change them. It has a list of songs we sing that we want our friends and family to listen to.

We are transported in a van with fogged windows to a hotel in another part of the city. Large, unsmiling men with radios and bellhop uniforms take us to the 15th floor. I ask to use the restroom, where I untape the note and put it in the coin pocket of my jeans.

They line us up in front of a set of double doors, where we stand on a red carpet, the kind movie stars walk down. Lights and cameras are blazing. The next thing I know, my mom is in my arms. I feel a warmth so pure that it awakens an old, lost part of me. I become loose in a way I haven't been since we were hiking up that mountain 10 months ago. I pull the note out of my pocket and squeeze it into my mom's hand. As I hug her, I tell her to hide it. She tucks it into her bra. Then, she whispers into my ear, "I love you, Shane. I can't wait to have you home." In this moment, I feel halfway there.

The men in suits sit us all down on a couch in front of a wall of cameras. Livia Leu Agosti, the Swiss ambassador, sits with us. I don't understand how this is happening. After all those months of not letting us have pens in order to prevent any chance of communication to the outside world, why are they putting us in front of cameras, giving us a chance to say anything we want?

"What happened at the border?" a reporter asks.

"We never walked into Iran," I say, then stop myself. I know our interrogators wouldn't want us to answer that question. I feel an overwhelming need to self-censor. "We can't really talk about that," I say.

Suddenly, I realize why they brought us here—they aren't afraid of us saying anything they don't want us to. They control us. If I say anything even slightly offensive, any plans they might have to release us could be canceled. They exercise the same power over our mothers.

Something is different about my mom. She has always been a tough, no-nonsense kind of woman. Now she won't let go of me.

"I hope they let you come home with us," she says. Her words make my heart drop into my stomach. "I don't think that's going to happen, Mom," I say gently, squeezing her hand. The three of us believe we'll get out eventually, but we know the Iranians arranged this visit in order to hold us longer. By allowing us to see each other, they can claim they are making "humanitarian gestures," subdue international pressure, and put the focus back on the United States to reciprocate.

The suits tell our moms they can remove their hijabs. They leave the room. At last, we are alone.

Leu Agosti jumps up and walks around the room, lifting up garbage cans and carpets to check for recording bugs. "This hotel is very famous," she whispers. "This is where they bring prisoners to do videotaped confessions." We ask her about the on-again, off-again talks over Iran's nuclear program. She says she doesn't believe that our detainment is directly tied to the nuclear issue, but "it doesn't help."

Mom talks about my friends as if they were hers. She and Sarah's mom have been living together, working on our campaign full time. Our friend Shon Meckfessel, who was with us in Kurdistan, is moving in with them. Dad is raising money through hog roasts in rural Minnesota and by raffling off Bobcat skid loaders.

Sarah and I signal each other with our eyes and come together. We kneel on the floor in front of our moms and hold their hands. "Shane and I are getting married," Sarah says.

"Congratulations," they both say, somewhat nervously. I try to read their thoughts. Are they worried that we're being rash, planning out our futures in such an extreme situation? Are they, both divorced, trying to hold back their own fears of marriage? Sarah shows them her ring of thread, and they soften, cooing about how romantic we are. Sarah's mom asks, "Can we tell the media?"

SARAH

I can't get over how strong my mom looks. All these months I've been imagining her defeated and broken, but I was wrong. I don't have to protect her from what's happening to me. Even if I want to, I can't.

I ask her to follow me into the bathroom. We walk past the secret police hand in hand and lock the door behind us. "Mom," I whisper, "about four months ago I found a lump in my left breast. It's big and sore, and wasn't there before. They took me to the prison doctor but didn't allow me to ask her any questions. A few weeks later, they took me to a real hospital for a mammogram, but I haven't seen the results. They say I'm fine, but I'm not sure I believe them." I lift up my shirt and guide my mom's hand to the spot that's been tormenting me. Her skilled fingers gently prod the area—after a few seconds she looks up at me and shakes her head.

"It's not cancer, sweetie. It's just a totally normal lump. You don't need to worry anymore." My mom has been a nurse for more than thirty years—I know she wouldn't lie to me about this. We hear a knock at the door and Dumb Guy tells us to come out.

"You're fine," my mom says. "Know that—but don't stop demanding medical care. This is really important, okay?"

SHANE

The suits bring us menus and encourage us to order. I ask for shrimp and a chicken sandwich and fries and Coke and coffee. I eat it all, as well as some of the fruit heaped up on the table in front of us. Sarah sings songs she has written in prison. It is starting to feel surreal, like someone telling us to have fun at gunpoint.

Two hours after we eat, the Iranians tell us it's time to go. We hug and kiss our moms and say every last thought we can think of as they usher us slowly down the hall. We wait in front of an elevator. When it opens, a man invites our moms to enter. They do, and we stare at each other, them on one side of the threshold and us on the other. Just as my heart starts to break, something inside me turns off.

Four months later, following international publicity about her health problems, Sarah is released on medical grounds. Over the next year, she meets with everyone from President Obama and Mahmoud Ahmadinejad to Oprah Winfrey and Sean Penn, working nonstop with our friends and families on a campaign to get us released.

Josh and I are tried by the Revolutionary Court, on charges of master-minding an American-Israeli conspiracy against Iran, and sentenced to eight years. Eventually, the sultan of Oman pays a million-dollar "bail" and the two of us come home. (The sultan goes on to use the back channel opened up during the negotiations for our release to rekindle US-Iran nuclear talks.) Josh connects with his middle-school sweetheart, Jenny, and two years later their son, Isaiah, is born.

We also hear news about Sarah's cell neighbor, Zahra with the pink jumpsuit. One morning, nine months after Sarah last saw her, she is taken out of her cell to Evin Prison's death chamber. She is executed by hanging.

CHRISTOPHER MYERS

■

Letter to My Grandnephew

FROM *PEN America*

Dear PEN,

The following is not a typical memoir. I chose to submit it in the memoir category because it is a "snapshot" of a (fairly recent) moment in my life and vividly (I feel) expresses my emotional state at that moment. Furthermore, the images and details in the piece are drawn largely from my life experiences. Anyone reading the simple sentence, "The Indians are in third place" (to give just one example) ought to be able to see at least the general outline of the forty-year narrative underlying it, and it is hoped that such latent narrative richness characterizes the entire piece, making it a true memoir. As a bonus, it is rhythmic and uplifting. I hope you enjoy this nonstandard offering.

Christopher Myers
Lovelock Correctional Center

Letter to My Grandnephew , 7-28-12

Dear Jack,

My spoon broke. My roommate moved out. The Olympics are starting. The dictator of North Korea got married. Albania has never won an Olympic medal. I have made a pair of plastic balls out of compressed plastic wrap. I only have three ballpoint pens left. I ate a big hot dog today with mustard and onions on it. (There was an extra bun and I ate it with just sauerkraut.) I don't like the color blue. I wrote a poem about a little girl who drowned in a river. I like

"The Rifleman". There is a turkey sandwich
in a paper sack at the foot of my bed.
I just saw the flag of Bosnia and
Herzegovina for the first time in my
life. I have a little yellow plastic bead
shaped like an elephant. It is standing
on a small, red, hexagonal box that sits
on top of my TV set. The box is painted
with glittery paint and has a picture
of the Buddha on it. Inside the box is
the 1,000th paper crane I folded wishing
you would come visit me. My TV set has
a 13" screen and a transparent case so
you can see all the wires and components
and electronic stuff inside. (It has a

real cathode ray tube—I bet none of your
TV sets do.) I would wear a kilt if I
had one. I have an Arabic language CD
but no CD player. When I was six years
old I wore thick eyeglasses. I wish my
sister Alyssa didn't have cancer. Today
math I had
nd steady.
oga class. The
you on is 8" x
pposed to be
uter program
r equations.
uter I'm writing
almost six

years old. All the Czech Republic athletes are wearing blue boots. My brother Bob used to live in the Czech Republic. I get very nervous sometimes. I don't believe that our eternal destiny is determined by what we do in this lifetime. The greatest clarinet player of all time was Henry Cuesta. I have written 721 pages of letters to you. It is possible to chew a piece of celery forever, because its cellulose does not break down. A British guy won the Tour de France this year. My beard is long and the hair on my head is thin. I look in the mirror more than I used to. My favorite TV show is "Cake

Boss", I own two rubber bands — no, wait, it's three... I just remembered I have a rubber band around a bundle of 26 artificial-sweetener packets. I visited Idaho once and saw the state capitol building. My watch battery went dead so now I sometimes carry a digital clock in my pocket. The Indians are in third place. I heard that lightning starts on the earth and strikes upward toward the sky. I like the trumpet solo in "Penny Lane". Dogs are cool, I have decided. Unless my sister accidentally wrote the same name twice, I recently had two grandnephews born who are both named Carson. The world is astonishingly beautiful. Happiness is easy. I love you.

Chris

A N D E R S   C A R L S O N - W E E

Dynamite

FROM *Ninth Letter*

My brother hits me hard with a stick
so I whip a choke-chain

across his face. We're playing
a game called *Dynamite*

where everything you throw
is a stick of dynamite,

unless it's pine. Pine sticks
are rifles and pinecones are grenades,

but everything else is dynamite.
I run down the driveway

and back behind the garage
where we keep the leopard frogs

in buckets of water
with logs and rock islands.

When he comes around the corner
the blood is pouring

out of his nose and down his neck
and he has a hammer in his hand.

I pick up his favorite frog
and say If you come any closer

I'll squeeze. He tells me
I won't. He starts coming closer.

I say a hammer isn't dynamite.
He reminds me that everything is dynamite.

■

The Contestant

FROM *The California Sunday Magazine*

THE PERUVIAN VERSION of the international television game show franchise the *Moment of Truth* arrived in Lima in mid-2012. By that time, the program had been produced in dozens of countries around the world, including the United States, where it aired on Fox in 2008 and 2009. In Peru, the show was called *El Valor de la Verdad* ("the value of the truth"), and the format was essentially the same as it had been everywhere else: A contestant is brought into the station and asked a set of questions, some banal, some uncomfortable, some bordering on cruel, all while hooked to a polygraph.

The answers are cataloged. Then, a few days later, the contestant is brought back to go through the questions once more, this time before a studio audience. The answers given are compared to the results of the polygraph, and for each truthful response, the contestant wins money. If she lies—or rather, if the polygraph says she lies—she loses it all. Naturally, the more money at stake, the more compromising the questions become. The contestant has the option of calling it off after each answer.

In Peru, the show's host was Beto Ortiz, who in a recent national poll was named the country's most powerful TV journalist. A balding, heavyset man in his mid-forties, Beto has long been one of the more successful and controversial figures in Peru. He is sharp, inquisitive, funny, and has gained millions of fans; the television critic Fernando Vivas, who writes for *El Comercio*, Peru's most influential newspaper, described Beto as "a monster on the scene, with all the ambivalence implied by the word '*monster*.'"

When Beto first made the transition from print to television, he was known for his deeply reported stories about the seedier aspects of urban life: street kids, punks, prostitutes. He was unlike anyone else on the air. Today, in Lima, you need only say "Beto," and everyone knows whom you're talking about. When asked what it was like being famous, Beto responded: "That's like asking me what it's like being fat. I don't remember what it was like being skinny."

The show's first contestant was a young woman named Ruth Thalía Sayas Sánchez. She was nineteen years old, with shoulder-length brown hair and an easy smile. She and her siblings were born in the province of Huancavelica, hundreds of miles from Lima, but had been raised on the outskirts of the capital in a working-class area called Huachipa. Not long ago, this area was a provincial escape from Lima's humid, miserable winters, but by the time the Sayas Sánchez family moved in, the neighborhood was in the midst of an unseemly transition, away from its agricultural past and toward its frenetic, urban future. And so both ways of life coexisted, sometimes uneasily: Young men tended to mototaxis; slightly older men grazed horses. Stray dogs lapped water from dirty puddles in the middle of rutted, unpaved roads, and large plots of farmland sat amid half-built houses, rebar poking out of the concrete, piles of bricks lying in the street.

This was where Ruth Thalía grew up, though she would admit to Beto that she longed for something better. For his part, Beto was, at least initially, unimpressed with Ruth Thalía: "Average," he said, when asked to describe his first contestant. "Pretty, but nothing special." When the cameras began to roll, however, something changed. Ruth Thalía brightened, carrying herself with the confidence of a young striver, comfortable under the lights, even playful. "She liked being on television," her sister, Eva, would say later.

According to the rules of the program, every contestant could bring three guests. Ruth Thalía was accompanied by her parents, Leoncio and Vilma. Leoncio seemed worried from the outset. "I'm afraid of what I might learn about my daughter," he told Beto when he was introduced on camera. Vilma was more optimistic. She was a small woman, with a wide smile and glowing light-brown skin. Ruth Thalía's parents had an Andean pop band, *Vilma Sánchez y los Chu-*

pachichis del Perú, that often performed in the dustier sections of the capital. Vilma sang, and Leoncio played the harp. As far as Vilma knew—as far as her daughter had told her—Beto would be asking about her arrival in Lima; about how the family had survived those first years in the capital, selling watermelon and pineapple in the market; about those days when the girls still spoke only Quechua, one of Peru's indigenous languages, and were bullied at school for it. These were satisfying memories for Vilma. They'd worked hard, through difficult circumstances, and though they would never have a lot of money, their two daughters were studying at a local university. It's the typical, heroic story of Lima's hundreds of thousands of migrants, no less admirable for being common. "I was happy to go," Vilma said later. "I was going to say, 'I'm from Huancavelica and proud of it, Mr. Beto!'"

Ruth Thalía's third guest was a handsome, timid young man named Bryan Romero Leiva. He wore his brown hair short and combed forward slightly. He was twenty years old, drove a mototaxi, and had been raised on a steeply sloping dirt road near Ruth Thalía's home. He had soccer posters adorning the walls of his old room just off the dirt-floor kitchen, and he kept a cat and a rabbit as pets, both black, as was his preference. He wasn't a dour or unpleasant boy, though; in fact, Bryan's mother, Mery, described her son as helpful and kind. And he hadn't had it easy, that was for sure. He'd stuttered, Mery said, ever since an old boyfriend of hers had pushed him down the stairs when the child was only eight. For years, Bryan had accompanied her to the market at dawn, helping her sell breakfast plates to the workers. At the time of the taping, he was renting a room in the neighborhood, just a few minutes' walk from his mother's house.

"I don't know why," said Vilma, "but I hated that kid."

On the show, in front of the cameras, Bryan was tense, his right leg shaking anxiously.

"You seem nervous," Beto said. "What are you so nervous about?"

"That she may have cheated on me."

Everyone laughed, including Ruth Thalía.

Beto paused. "Let's not forget this is just a game," he said.

The show's opening questions were light: Have you ever skipped school without your mother's knowledge? If you found 1,000 soles, would you return them? Ruth Thalía's parents joked along with Beto, as their daughter copped to these minor moral failings. There was more, of course. David Novoa, who was a producer with the show at the time, later admitted he felt bad. He'd done the initial interview with Ruth Thalía, had helped Beto formulate the questions that would be part of the show. He'd visited the Sayas Sánchez family in Huachipa and knew their story well. The afternoon of the taping, he was in the control booth, whispering into Beto's earpiece. "I knew it was going to be a surprise, and a shameful moment for them."

Which made Ruth Thalía a perfect contestant for *El Valor de la Verdad*. It all happened in a matter of minutes, a kind of onslaught. Ruth Thalía revealed that she'd had a nose job, that she didn't like her body, that she wished she were white, that she was only with her boyfriend until someone better came along, that she was ashamed of her parents' manners, that she didn't work at a call center, that she danced at a nightclub. The result was undeniably riveting: this young, reckless woman sharing secrets with an entire country.

Reality television was relatively new on Peruvian airwaves. Peru's economic growth in recent years had led to growing advertisement dollars for local television stations and growing budgets for bigger and more ambitious productions. For the region, however, Peru was still catching up. Formats like *Big Brother*, which had exploded across Latin America, skipped Peru for years. Importing an international format like *El Valor de la Verdad* would have been unthinkable until quite recently, and audiences were understandably drawn to shows like these. While Ruth Thalía answered Beto's questions, her parents and boyfriend sat onstage. Over the course of the hour, they crumbled. Vilma all but begged her daughter to stop. Bryan was too stunned to offer much resistance, never stringing together more than a couple of sentences. At one point, he admitted he loved Ruth Thalía. "I don't want to hear more," he said.

She went on anyway. Beto asked Ruth Thalía if she thought Bryan was handsome.

"Uh . . . yes," she said, hedging a bit.

"And is he smart?"

She laughed. "More or less."

"Does he have a good heart?"

For this response, at least, she didn't vacillate: "Yes," Ruth Thalía said, and the studio audience applauded.

Then came question number eighteen: Have you ever accepted money for sex?

Vilma bent over, as if in physical pain.

Ruth Thalía answered yes, and the show's announcer, a disembodied, almost robotically precise woman's voice, called out:

"The answer is . . . true."

There was a long silence.

"Just twice," Ruth Thalía explained. "We needed money. We were in a bad situation. It hasn't happened since, and it won't happen again."

For this truthful admission, Ruth Thalía had won 15,000 soles, or about $5,300—almost ten months' wages for someone living in Lima. Beto asked if she wanted to go on, in search of 50,000 soles. Before responding, Ruth Thalía said she was sorry for all this. "My mother, my father, my brother and sister are the most beautiful thing in the world to me. I love them with all my heart. Bryan, forgive me for making you go through this."

Then she announced she was done. The audience cheered her decision.

"The truth is always illuminating," Beto said to the cameras. "It will not do harm, even though it hurts."

Ruth Thalía hugged Bryan. His face registered nothing. As the credits rolled, she got down on her knees before her ashen-faced mother and begged for forgiveness.

The show was taped in June and aired a month later, on Saturday, July 12, 2012. That month of waiting wasn't an easy one. Something had been shattered in the Sayas Sánchez family. Vilma was moody and confused; Leoncio was distant. They couldn't understand why their daughter had done the show. When Vilma asked, Ruth Thalía was almost flippant.

"For the money," she said.

She had fantasized about being famous, to be sure, and had even auditioned for soap operas and other game shows—but her more immediate goal was practical. She wanted to open a salon. She'd already saved the equivalent of $7,000, and the winnings from the show brought her closer to that dream. If she had to make a spectacle of herself, perhaps this was the price to be paid.

Once the show aired, that position became harder to justify. *El Valor de la Verdad* was an instant success, knocking one of Peru's television icons, Gisela Valcárcel, from her number one spot. In fact, for the next eighteen weeks that it aired, *El Valor de la Verdad* would win the ratings battle against Gisela fifteen times. Ruth Thalía's secrets were suddenly part of the national conversation. "It was a celebration," said producer David Novoa. "We beat Gisela. That's all that mattered. The ratings! They were drinking champagne up on the second floor"—the executive offices at the station, Frecuencia Latina. Ruth Thalía was the face of Beto's new hit show. She was photographed with a Frecuencia Latina executive, grinning and holding one of those oversize checks, and splashed on the cover of newspapers across the capital.

Ruth Thalía's notoriety, though, had come at a great cost. "This neighborhood we live in is a hellhole of gossip," Leoncio said. It seemed everyone had seen Ruth Thalía on the show, and everyone had an opinion. Relatives the family hadn't heard from in years were calling to say how ashamed they were. Ruth Thalía withdrew. "She didn't even want to leave the house," Eva said. Ruth Thalía confessed to her mother that she'd thought of suicide.

For Bryan, one could argue, it was even worse. He'd been exposed as a cuckold in front of millions, something unforgivable in Peru's macho culture. One day, at the bridge in Huachipa, Bryan was taunted by a busload of high school students. He had to go hide in a nearby store. In the weeks after the airing, he showed up at the station a few times, demanding some kind of recompense for his public humiliation. He was accompanied by his uncle, Redy Leiva, who was studying law and did most of the talking.

One afternoon, just a few weeks after the show had aired, a television crew from Frecuencia Latina caught up with Bryan at the front door of his house. The host asked him how he felt.

"Ashamed. All the things I learned on that show," Bryan said, eyes avoiding the camera. "How would you feel?"

"But they say that if you love someone, you can forgive them."

"Depends what they did. The things she said that day, I can't forgive."

In other interviews, Bryan claimed that it had all been a setup. He and Ruth Thalía had broken up months before the taping. She'd approached him and asked him for a favor. Pretend to be my boyfriend on television, she'd said, and if I win, I'll share the money with you. He'd agreed, with no idea what he was getting into. It had been an ambush. Weeks had passed, and he still hadn't seen a cent. Then he went further: The producers of the show had known all along that he and Ruth Thalía weren't together. Frecuencia Latina was complicit in the charade.

"After the show," Eva said, "he started asking for money. First 500, then 1,000, then 2,000." One day, someone broke into the Sayas Sánchez house and stole Ruth Thalía's laptop. None of Eva's things was taken. The family assumed that Bryan had stolen it, but he denied it, and in the end, there was no proof. Leoncio filed a police report, and that was that.

On September 11, 2012, eight weeks after *El Valor de la Verdad* debuted, Leoncio and Vilma went to bed watching a World Cup qualifying match between Peru and Argentina. When they woke up, Leoncio heard his wife say, "Thalía hasn't come home." Ruth Thalía had never done this before. Eva was out of town, but eventually, they were able to contact her. She called some of her sister's friends and managed to reach a young man who'd seen Ruth Thalía the night before as she left the university. He said she'd gotten a call from Bryan. Vilma went straight to Bryan's house for answers. She feared the worst. "I was crying, screaming," she said. "Everyone in the street, the neighbors, they must have seen me. I was kneeling, as if he were a god. Bryan, give me back Thalía."

But Bryan was unmoved. He said he hadn't spoken to her in a while, and then he turned and went inside.

When faced with a situation like this one, people like the Sayas Sánchez family don't have a lot of options. This is a fact of life in Peru, though not just there, of course. If you're poor, if you come from a place like Huachipa, the authorities aren't always on your side. The police can be slow to react, even negligent, and corruption weighs most heavily on those least able to withstand it. Leoncio filed a missing persons report on September 12, 2012, without much hope. Then he went to the one place where he felt he had a chance to be heard: to Frecuencia Latina, the station that had aired *El Valor de la Verdad*.

"Here in the city," Leoncio said later, "the only way to get help is through the media. Where else can you go?"

The studios of Frecuencia Latina sit behind a high green wall in a residential neighborhood of the city called Jesús María, and look more like a military bunker than a television station. Still, on any given day, at any given hour, there are mobs of young fans out front, hoping to catch a peek of their idols or get picked to be in the audience at their favorite show. There's another crowd, too, often older than the fans, people like Leoncio, who've come to the television station for help. Supplicants. They press their documents against the mirrored glass security window; they stammer their sad stories and ask to speak to a producer. They've suffered one of the many indignities that life in a city like Lima can deal to a person: They need work; they've been swindled; they have a sick child and no hope of access to health care. From a turret above the scene, a guard stands watch.

Leoncio was fortunate: He was able to speak to a producer from Beto's morning news show, *Abre los Ojos*, who promised to get them on the air the next day, to publicize their plight.

When Leoncio got home, he found Vilma in anguish. He did what he could to calm her. They talked for a while, speculating where their daughter might be, trying not to fall into despair. Maybe she'd gone on a trip. Maybe someone had drugged her or was holding her for ransom. That night, Leoncio and Vilma didn't sleep. Tomorrow, they hoped, after their daughter's disappearance was made known, the search for her would begin in earnest.

The next morning at 5:00 a.m., the phone rang. It was the producer from *Abre los Ojos*. She was apologetic: Their appearance had been canceled. A problem with scheduling, she said, and promised to call again soon.

Three days passed, and no one from Frecuencia Latina had called. There was still no sign of Ruth Thalía, and the police hadn't done much investigating. Vilma and Leoncio went out every morning, asking for help at all the television stations in Lima, with no results.

During those first anxious days, while Ruth Thalía's parents visited the local television stations, they never mentioned *El Valor de la Verdad* or Beto Ortiz. They were omitting the most crucial and valuable detail: that their daughter was famous. Or infamous. Instead, they told a simpler version of events. Our daughter hasn't come home. We're poor people, and we need help.

It's a story, incidentally, that is heard every day at the door of every television station in Peru.

On the third day, at Channel 9, also called ATV, Vilma finally shared the key piece of information that would once more land her daughter on the front pages of newspapers all over the country. "I explained it to the man," Vilma said, referring to the security guard at ATV. "I said, my daughter, she was the girl from *El Valor de la Verdad*. Right away he went to get the cameraman."

That night, three days after Ruth Thalía's disappearance, the case was mentioned for the first time on national television. Vilma happened to be watching ATV while she waited to speak to a detective at police headquarters in downtown Lima. "I was sitting there, and on the television, I hear Ruth Thalía's name, and I thought: Sweet Lord, for sure I'll find my daughter now!"

There was only one problem: ATV didn't introduce Ruth Thalía as "the girl from *El Valor de la Verdad*." Instead, the host called her "the prostitute from *El Valor de la Verdad*."

"They killed me in my heart," Vilma said.

Now the story had changed. This was no longer about the disappearance of a young woman from a faraway neighborhood of the sprawling capital. Everyone wanted exclusive access to Ruth Thalía's family, and Vilma, Leoncio, and Eva found themselves under siege. Every station in Lima sent producers and cameramen to the family home in Huachipa. They took long panning shots of the unpaved street, the train tracks, the mototaxis. They talked to neighbors and passersby and hounded Vilma and Leoncio wherever they went.

When stories like these happen in Lima, the competition between the various channels can be brutal. Every television news program—and there are dozens—peddles a steady diet of crime reporting. The morning news shows recount the overnight death toll from shootings, robberies gone awry, kidnappings, domestic disputes that escalate into violence. It's not uncommon for the producers of a news show to buy their way into a wake, offering grieving families DVD players and stereos for exclusive shots of the tearful mother or the mourning husband. "There's a tradition in Peruvian journalism, not a good one, in my opinion," explained Maribel Toledo, a journalist with more than 15 years of experience working in television. "In order to secure exclusives, the reporters, the stations, the producers grab people and almost kidnap them."

Every news program in Lima aired a story on Ruth Thalía, but ATV had the family. By the sixth day, Leoncio recalled, "ATV was here all the time. They even slept here. They wouldn't leave us alone."

Leoncio and Vilma got up each morning to ask for help. This task—knocking on doors, hoping someone might listen—constituted the entirety of their lives in those days. They traveled in a car provided by ATV, filmed by ATV cameramen. They went to the Ministry of Women's Affairs, to police headquarters, to the hospitals, to the morgue. They knocked on the door of the presidential palace in central Lima and managed to get an audience with an adviser to the first lady. A phone call from the palace got some movement out of the police. Things were happening, and to be fair, for people like Leoncio and Vilma, much of this would've been impossible without the help of a station like ATV. Leoncio was uneasy with the situation, but he knew there was no other way.

Leoncio didn't eat; Vilma didn't sleep. They received all kinds of terrifying phone calls, including extortion attempts traced to police officers in towns outside Lima, claiming they had a lead but needed money to investigate. One day, Leoncio recounted, "a mototaxi driver came and said, 'You know what? I found your daughter.'" According to this stranger, Ruth Thalía was being held in a hotel not far from their home. He would take Leoncio there, for the right price. They negotiated and agreed on 2,000 soles, half upfront. Leoncio felt he had no choice, but he was afraid. He climbed onto the man's mototaxi, and they headed toward an area called Carapongo. When they arrived at the hotel, the man told him to wait, and Leoncio was left alone. "I called Channel 9. I just let it ring a couple of times. In case I disappeared, too, my last call would be from there."

A few minutes later, the mototaxi driver brought down a young woman, but it wasn't Ruth Thalía, just another girl, a runaway, who looked like her. Leoncio was crushed. "Go home," he told the girl, and she started crying. "Those were desperate days," he later recalled. "I felt like I was floating. There were moments where I couldn't tell if I was asleep or awake."

By then it had been a week since Ruth Thalía had disappeared. The police and, crucially, the media knew that Bryan had been the last one to speak to her. On the morning of September 22, he was interviewed by Alejandra Puente, a reporter from ATV. When asked if he'd seen Ruth Thalía on the night in question, Bryan said he couldn't remember. He'd been drunk.

The reporter pushed him: "If you were me, would you believe yourself?"

"Like I said, I don't remember that day."

"But your conscience is clean?"

"Yes," Bryan said.

That same afternoon, eleven days after Ruth Thalía's disappearance, Leoncio got a call from someone at Channel 9. The police, he was told, had found the body of a young woman, buried in a well and covered by rocks and concrete, on a piece of land on the outskirts of Lima. The land belonged to Redy Leiva, Bryan's uncle, and they suspected it was Ruth Thalía.

Leoncio and Eva went to the scene and found themselves confronted with cameras and microphones and photographers from every media outlet in Lima. "The newspapers were desperate, the radio was desperate, and I was desperate," Leoncio said. "It was all desperation." For more than an hour, the police wouldn't let Leoncio and Eva on the property, so they waited, surrounded by reporters. When it was confirmed that the woman at the bottom of the well was Ruth Thalía, the cameras filmed Leoncio and Eva sobbing, bent over, embracing.

Eventually Bryan was brought to the scene, and Leoncio pressed the police to let him see the young man. He was told he had to control himself, and Leoncio assured the officer he would, but he grabbed a rock and put it in his pocket. "And then Bryan started talking about my daughter . . . I just reacted." Leoncio took out the rock and surged toward Bryan, swinging at his head. The police managed to hold Leoncio back.

Across town, in Huachipa, the reporter Maribel Toledo arrived at Leoncio and Vilma's house. She had been at home when she got a call from her producer at *Día D*, a news magazine on ATV, where she worked at the time. "He says to me, they found Ruth Thalía," Toledo recalled. "Go to the family's house as quick as you can."

Toledo and her cameraman were the first journalists to arrive. Vilma and some neighbors were holding candles and signs. Toledo went up to Vilma. "I think I gave her my condolences," Toledo said later, "and I asked her something, assuming she knew her daughter was dead. And I realized she didn't understand what I was saying. It wasn't that she didn't understand me; *she didn't know.*

"The only thing I could bring myself to say was, 'Ma'am, they've found a girl.'" Vilma went inside the house, up to the second floor, and locked herself in her room. For the next few minutes, Toledo watched as people, friends of the family, she supposed, came and went from the second floor. She was so disconcerted that she called her producer again, just to confirm that it was true, that the police had found Ruth Thalía. Her producer assured her it was. Bryan had confessed.

"I decided to do the most uncomfortable and perhaps the most morbid thing possible in that situation," Toledo recalled. She summoned her cameraman and headed up the stairs. "And just as I went up and was about to knock on the door, I hear this cry, something like, 'No, it can't be her.'" Toledo's cameraman urged her to knock anyway, but she refused. "Another reporter might have insisted on an interview with the mother right then and there, but I felt I couldn't do anything more."

In the segment that aired on ATV, you can hear a dog barking and Vilma's anguished screams, muffled from behind the door. Toledo stands there, with a microphone in her hands, seemingly unsure of what to do next.

Not long afterward, Toledo quit working in television news.

That night, Peruvian television viewers saw the alleged murderer, Bryan Romero Leiva, being led away in handcuffs, surrounded by police in riot gear. The death of Ruth Thalía was the lead story on the evening news on every channel in Peru—except Frecuencia Latina. It was a Saturday, and Frecuencia Latina stayed with its regularly scheduled programming: *El Valor de la Verdad.*

In his videotaped confession, Bryan wore the same clothes he had worn in his interview with Alejandra Puente from ATV: a black-and-turquoise hooded jacket and acid-washed jeans. He spoke firmly and told investigators a simple story. He called Ruth Thalía as she was leaving the university, and they made plans to meet. "I waited for her by the bridge," he told police. "She got into my mototaxi. I said, let's go have some wine, and she said, OK." They rode to the house where he rented a room. Once there, he and Ruth Thalía drank a $3 bottle of red wine in the street and eventually went upstairs. They had sex and, afterward, started to fight. "She tells me, I don't know what I'm doing talking to a poor mototaxi driver," Bryan said. "And that's when I grabbed her by the throat." Bryan admitted to police that he choked her for thirty seconds or more. "I thought she had passed out," he told police. "I listened to her heart. I didn't hear anything. I grabbed her and shook her hard. But nothing. I got scared."

The following day, Bryan took police to the scene of the crime, where the murder had occurred. He toured them around the small, unfurnished room and simulated carrying a woman's body down the stairs.

The difference between a crime of passion and premeditated homicide is the difference between spending a decade in prison or one's entire life. This question, then, became central to the case: Bryan had confessed to killing Ruth Thalía, but had he planned it? No, his lawyer, Felipe Ramos, would argue. Bryan had snapped under the pressure of his national humiliation. The crime could be traced directly to the show. "The format couldn't have existed without Bryan," Ramos said. "That's the truth. The program had impact so long as you had a cuckold sitting up there, call him Bryan, Juan, Pedro. They needed a victim for Ruth Thalía's lies."

In a matter of hours, the story was all over the front pages. Every last detail of the murder was reported again and again on television. Beto's rivals saw an opportunity to link Peru's most powerful journalist to a scandal, and many called for Frecuencia Latina to cancel his show. The station refused. Fernando Vivas, the influential critic, described Ruth Thalía's death as "an extraordinary case of televicide" and called on the trade group of television advertisers to withdraw its support for the program.

That evening, Sunday, the day after Ruth Thalía's body had been found, Beto called a group of friends to his apartment to discuss his options. The guests were mostly journalists and television veterans of Beto's generation, trusted confidants. One proposal was that Beto and the production team go to the Sayas Sánchez house and give their condolences. All dressed in black, very formal, very serious. A few of Beto's closest friends supported the idea, but Beto wasn't convinced. According to producer David Novoa, who was present at the meeting, Beto feared for his safety. "He thought they might attack him," Novoa said.

Beto made no comment until Monday, on his morning news program, *Abre los Ojos*. He sat alone at a desk, wearing a black suit, a black dress shirt, a black tie, and black-framed glasses; Beto extended his condolences to Ruth Thalía's family. Then he shot back at his critics: "Unfortunately, this case, which is all over the news, which happened to a person who was on television, has been used by some people for sinister purposes." *El Valor de la Verdad* played no role whatsoever in the death of Ruth Thalía, he argued. "The murderer of Ruth Thalía Sayas Sánchez is Bryan Romero Leiva."

Which is true, of course. But when asked if he thought Ruth Thalía would be alive if she hadn't appeared on *El Valor de la Verdad*, Novoa didn't hesitate. "Of course," he said. Then he paused for a moment. "Well, I don't know if she would be alive. Maybe she'd have died some other way."

In court, Bryan's lawyer was determined to tie Beto Ortiz and *El Valor de la Verdad* to the crime. A few days before the trial began, Ramos read a handwritten letter to the press, in which Bryan asked Ruth Thalía's parents to forgive him. "I want to confront Mr. Beto Ortiz and take off his mask," Bryan said in the letter, "so that the people can understand his manipulative and frivolous attitude in the face of the harm he caused in our lives."

Ramos petitioned to call Beto to testify, and the judge agreed, and so, on January 21, 2014, Peru's most famous television journalist appeared in a courtroom inside the country's largest penitentiary, on the outskirts of Lima. He wore a dark-gray suit, a blue dress shirt, and no tie. He spent most of his testimony standing, while Bryan and his uncle sat on the other side of a glass barrier.

Bryan accused Beto of peddling fake reality to his audience and attempting to buy his silence about the show's manipulation with a job offer, then later going back on his word. He described the job, as Beto had allegedly explained it to him. "All you'll have to do is get me water," Bryan told the court.

Beto raised his eyebrows. "Get me water?" he asked incredulously.

"Tell the truth," Bryan said. "Tell the truth."

Beto denied it all.

When it was over, Beto was all smiles and asked the judge for permission to add one more thing. The judge agreed. Beto pointed out that Ramos had been the lawyer for another famous murderer. The animosity between them predated Ruth Thalía's death. "I was very harsh with him," Beto explained, "and now he's trying to get back at me."

On February 27, 2014, the court declared Bryan Romero Leiva guilty of the murder of Ruth Thalía. The vast majority of Bryan's confession was found to be false. The police had tracked down a witness, an adolescent boy from the neighborhood, who said that the night Ruth Thalía disappeared, Bryan had paid him fifty soles to let him know when Ruth Thalía got off the bus. The boy claimed to have seen Bryan and another man force her into his mototaxi. The court determined that Bryan's accomplice was his uncle, Redy Leiva, the owner of the property where her body was found. Both were sentenced to life imprisonment. The motive for the crime was robbery. They had attempted to get Ruth Thalía's bank security code. They wanted her winnings from *El Valor de la Verdad.*

Vilma, Leoncio, and Eva were in court on the day of the sentencing. Afterward, they gave statements to the media, saying that justice had been served. Vilma, her voice cracking, told the press: "When I die, that's when I will stop crying. That's when I will stop suffering." She visits her daughter's tomb once a week to wash the gravestone and pray.

A few months after Ruth Thalía's murder, Eva was invited to audition for a talent show called *Rojo*, broadcast on Frecuencia Latina. She accepted, and dedicated her performance to her sister, dancing to a mix of traditional music from Huancavelica and pop. The judges said Eva's rhythm was "imprecise," and she didn't make it past the first round.

The second season of *El Valor de la Verdad* was produced with only celebrity contestants: politicians, showbiz folks, the kind of people who are used to dealing with the media. It was a hit. One highly placed source at Frecuencia Latina stated that this decision, to use only celebrities, was in direct response to the murder of Ruth Thalía, but Beto Ortiz denied it. "The show is entertainment, and I don't lose sight of that. We need contestants whose stories are interesting enough that people will watch."

REBECCA CURTIS

■

The Christmas Miracle

FROM *The New Yorker*

CATS WERE DYING. This happens, of course. But in this case they were dying in a gory way, one after another, and my nieces, who were six and seven years old, were witnessing the deaths, and it was Christmas, the most magical, horrible, spiritual, dark, and stressful time of the year, so we—my older sister and her husband, my younger twin brothers, my sister's in-laws, our mother and our uncle, and the other relatives who were gathered at my sister's house in Revelstoke for the holiday—were trying to prevent more cat deaths. My sister had had five cats. She'd adopted them from the pound, because they were going to be killed. She wanted every living being to be happy. I am telling this story to you, K, even though you are a Russian Communist and a Jewish person who doesn't believe Jesus was the son of God, and even though Christmas is an obnoxious holiday when millions of people decapitate pine trees and watch them slowly die in their living rooms, because miracles can happen on any day, and as long as man has existed he's celebrated this weirdest time of year, the shortest stretch of sunlight, the winter solstice, as a time of fear, change, courage, and passion. I'm going to tell you the story of a miracle that happened at Christmas.

I was not at a great point in my life leading up to the miracle. I was teaching creative-writing classes, but I hadn't managed to think clearly enough to write and publish anything in years. I had Lyme disease and some co-infections that I was treating with intravenous antibiotics: babesiosis, a malaria-like virus that drains red blood cells and causes fatigue; and bartonellosis, a bacterial infection common among homeless men, which causes vascular inflammation in the brain and bouts of madness, fantastical visions, and frank or rude speech, usually set off by eating carbohydrates. I'd completed my degree in nutrition, and had luck helping clients overcome ailments, especially infertile women who wanted to conceive, so I knew which foods I *should* eat and which I *shouldn't*. But if cake was nearby I wasn't always able to prevent myself from having one bite; then the sugar fed the Bartonella bacteria, which *commanded* me to eat more, and I would, and then I'd go insane.

With this in mind, I'd asked my sister to cancel the traditions of: 1) baking, frosting, and decorating forty dozen sugar cookies; 2) constructing a ginger-bread mansion; 3) baking eight pecan pies; 4) stuffing everyone's stocking full of milk chocolate. My sister had replied that these traditions were integral to the joy of Christmas. I knew that her response was reasonable. But I was literally unable to control myself around sugar, and I worried about containing my fits of madness. I was also concerned about our family's ability to prevent the remaining cats from dying, though my sister assured me she'd implemented a system to achieve this; I was worried, too, that no one would like the cheap, ugly Christmas presents I'd got them; I'd also become aware of my strong urge to inform my sister's sister-in-law Kunda, a shy, forty-four-year-old neurosurgeon and Canadian Medical Officer of Health, that I knew she'd been trying to get pregnant, and that if she'd accept my help I could make it happen, despite my sister's warning that no one was supposed to know Kunda was "trying" and that I must not accost her; finally, I was concerned, as always during family visits, about the safety and comfort of my nieces around our uncle, who was a pedophile, especially since the previous Christmas, when my sister and I weren't vigilant enough, I'd caught him rubbing the butt of the elder girl, then six years old, in a dark, empty room. That, too, my sister assured me, was under control: the girls would never be left alone with him, and at night they'd sleep on cots in her room. Everyone in our family meant well and wanted to be a family.

I know too, K, that you cringe whenever I mention the pedophile thing, and feel that it should not be placed in any story, because it overwhelms it and is too terrible for words. But I'd like to point out that my nieces are two beautiful, talented, and privileged girls, who see their grand-uncle only a few days a year; and that our uncle is not a bad man, just a sick one. So please quell any squeamishness or horror and bear in mind that it could be worse.

I'd also like to say—regarding the Christmas miracle—that it was my elder niece who instigated the Kamikaze Cat Training, not me. I have two nieces but only one goddaughter. And though I've abandoned Catholicism, the cult that I was born into, and am one of about eight godmothers, I take my duty seriously. Perhaps I can be forgiven at least one mistake I made that holiday.

Clara died first. She was eaten by a coyote. She was a nice cat. I don't expect you to care about the cats. Clara was a long-haired Maine coon mix who loved to be petted. She went outside to use the bathroom, or frolic, or whatever cats do, around sunset, and never came back.

The problem was an influx of hungry coyotes into the development where my sister lived. As the town crawled up the mountain, coyotes, bears, and lynxes were displaced from their habitats and wandered down the mountain, where they discovered the delicious new food, cat. In September, when my sister's family barbecued on their back deck, they saw coyotes trot through the pines at their yard's edge.

Clara was eaten in October. Afterward, my nieces cried, blahblahblah. My sister, too; Clara had been her first cat. And through the years, whenever my sister felt sad about anything—fight, failed test, car accident, etc.—Clara sensed it, came to her, and sat in her lap.

My sister instituted a lockdown. The cats got one outing, at dusk, to use the bathroom in the yard. They were let out for five minutes, watched, and lured back in with cooked shrimp.

The other cats were Chocolate, a diabetic brown male with postnasal drip who made stinky farts and loved all people, but especially loved to sit on the chest of my brother-in-law (who once spent five thousand dollars on an operation to save Chocolate's pancreas and life); Patches, a brindle who loved playing in the bathroom sink; Simmy, a bony Siamese loner who fought other cats and never purred; and Crow, a black cat. Crow was fit, above average size, and a mouser. She left dead mice in my sister's bed, which displeased my sister, because Crow first bit out the eyes. Crow did not curl up in anyone's lap. But she slept on my elder niece's bed most nights.

Wildfires burned throughout the Monashee Mountains that fall; though it was now December, there'd been no snow. Rather than disappearing, bears, lynxes, and coyotes foraged in the developments, thinking it still time to fatten up. Patches was eaten next. One evening, she sneaked past the yard's edge when no one was looking, probably to investigate a mouse smell, and never came back.

My sister made a new rule: no cats outside.

But two weeks later Simmy, the Siamese who fought other cats, sped past my brother-in-law one night as he opened the door to the deck. When he lunged for her, she slipped into the forest. My sister's family walked the woods until midnight, calling her name.

When I arrived in Revelstoke for the holiday, everyone was still shell-shocked about the cat deaths. My elder niece, Adira, a pale, black-haired tomboy, would occasionally mutter, "We shouldn't have let her out"—about Clara or Patches, I guess—and my sister would say that if she hadn't been able to go out at *all* she wouldn't have been happy; and my niece would say, "But she'd be *alive*"; and so forth.

My sister's house was large—its kitchen opened to a dining area and a "circle room" with a fifty-foot solar-panelled glass dome—but contained few rooms. So I was given my elder niece's second-floor bedroom, my brothers shared my younger niece's room, and our mother and our uncle took the sleeper couch in the library, on whose carpet Crow often peed.

Because we were aware of the traumatic cat deaths, we all behaved well, even me, and when our uncle knelt down and spread his arms wide and said to my nieces, "Come give Uncle D a kiss!" and I had to watch my nieces tense up, walk stiffly toward him, and let him grab their faces and kiss their lips, I didn't say anything. I just smiled widely and continued to behave, that afternoon, by not eating any gumdrops while my family spent several hours baking and constructing the gingerbread mansion, and we all felt, I think, good after the mansion was completed. It was late afternoon on December 23rd, and I probably never would have instituted the Kamikaze Training if it hadn't been for what happened *after* the gingerbread mansion was finished, which was that we all went for a walk in the woods.

The fires hadn't reached Revelstoke. The ground in the forest was a soft red-and-bronze carpet of pine needles, and the fields around the forest were gold brush. Revelstoke is set beside a river formed by glaciers circled by six-thousand-foot-high craggy mountains, and the sky above was velveteen blue. We were all breathing hard, laughing, running along the forest path when my younger niece giggled, pointed to an opening in the pines, and said, "What's that thing?" and ran off the path, and my mother said, "Lily, be careful, don't touch it," but she was touching it, and it turned out to be Simmy. The cat's mouth was open, her gums shrunk, her teeth exposed, her tan torso gutted. My brother-in-law wrapped the cat remainder in dead leaves and carried it home, and then he and my uncle worked for an hour to dig a hole in the frozen back yard.

We all felt, I think, eager to bring calm back to Christmas, so after dinner my brother-in-law went to bathe, as did my mother; my sister took refuge in doing dishes; my brothers and my younger niece played Super Mario Kart together on one living-room couch; and, on the other, my elder niece, Adira, read a book, one of her easy-readers, "Ramona Quimby, Age 8." My uncle entered the room, still dirty from digging the cat-hole, and said kindly, "Adira, would you like a foot rub?" and the girl tensed and a small "Nnnneh" sound came out of her mouth, and my uncle sat down next to her and began rubbing her feet.

I felt the Bartonella bacteria in my head move. They had been fed when I ate my dinner of chicken and broccoli. I'd been careful not to eat a speck of sugar, but even the carbohydrates in broccoli could feed them. I felt them grow strong and say to me, "There's a gingerbread house on the counter. Its frosting is sugar and cream, it's soft and warm, you can eat some!"

Meanwhile, Adira sat stiffly, staring at her book but not reading; my uncle had pulled her legs onto his lap and was kneading her calves. I sat in a leather chair nearby, not reading, either, because I heard the Bartonella bacteria yelling, "Sugar! Sugar!" I don't know how many minutes passed before my sister asked our uncle, from the kitchen, whether Adira had said that she wanted a foot rub. Our uncle answered, in a soothing, asset-management-specialist's voice, Yes, she had; my sister responded in a clipped voice that *she* thought she'd heard my niece say, "Nnnneh." Our uncle continued to rub my niece's feet, and then my sister said angrily to my niece that she needed help in the kitchen, and Adira put her book down and walked into the kitchen without looking right or left and said quietly, "What do you want me to do?"

My sister said, "Dry these dishes."

Our uncle went downstairs to shower, and I helped do dishes, too, because sugar was in the kitchen—and not just the gingerbread house. In the cupboards, I knew, there were Mint Milano cookies. Full dark pulsed outside the sliding glass doors to the deck, and a coyote yip-yip-yip-yipped in the woods. When my sister looked over her shoulder through the dark glass, I just dipped my finger into the gingerbread mansion's white trim. From the living room, my brothers saw me do it, and one told me loudly not to eat the mansion with my fingers, because that was gross and others would get my germs, but Bartonella said, "Ignore him. Do again." And so I finger-dipped again, and the other twin yelled that I was disgusting and was destroying the mansion, and that hurt my feelings and made me angry, so that before my sister went to bed I cornered her in the empty kitchen and told her that I did not think my nieces felt comfortable when our uncle kissed their lips, and that we should stop it. My sister, in a stretched voice, reminded me that grand-uncles kissing grand-nieces was normal, and that she'd spoken to a professional family counsellor about correct procedures in these cases, and the real me said, "Okay," but Bartonella me, who was larger than me and lived outside me, said, "Not okay."

My sister added that she was the mother.

The real me said, "I know."

But Bartonella me said, "You are the mother. Big deal. I am the *god*mother!"

The counsellor had warned her, my sister said, that telling her daughters our concerns would damage their psychological development, and that the issue must never be addressed.

My sister said, "*Promise* you won't say anything about Uncle D to the girls," and the real me said, "Okay," and she said, "*Also*, don't bring up the fact that Kunda's trying to conceive when Kunda comes over—it's *secret*," and I said, "I won't," but Bartonella said, "Eat sugar."

The only notable thing about Kunda, besides that she was a hot, nice, Hindi immigrant who had put herself through college by wait-ressing, is that she worshipped her husband, a pimply blond govern-ment secretary in her department. She met him when she was thirty-seven, and after they started dating she told me, "I love him." I said, "Really? He's so ugly, pink-faced, and blond," and she said, "He's a good one, a keeper." She always worked the same schedule as he, so that no other female official could "get him." For the past five years, apparently, she'd been failing to have his baby, owing to "mystery in-fertility," and was racked by shame.

At 3 A.M. I woke and ate half the gingerbread mansion. I'm not proud of that, but I do blame it for the rest of the story.

At 7 A.M., I awakened dizzy, wanting more sugar, already tasting it in my mouth. When I entered the barely lit circle room and found Adira alone, playing Super Mario Kart on a couch, it was Bartonella who said, "Kamikaze Training."

On the loft stairs, the large black cat, Crow, curled and watched. Beside my niece, the fat brown cat, Chocolate, licked its rear.

My niece paused her game and said, "What?" and Bartonella ex-plained that I'd pay her to say a few phrases. The *real* me remembered my sister's warning, but Bartonella said, "The therapist's wrong."

Bartonella felt that our difference of opinion stemmed from the previous holiday, at our uncle's Texas ranch, when my sister hadn't seen what I had. Christmas night, she'd played backgammon with most of our family in the living room; I'd wandered the house look-ing for a quiet place to read, and gone into the dark den, where we'd all watched a movie earlier. She hadn't seen my elder niece asleep on her belly on the couch—or feigning sleep—and our uncle seated behind her, massaging her ass. She hadn't had to think, Christ, why me? or notice that my niece's tiny hands were clenched. I'd told my niece I had a present for her upstairs, and she'd vaulted up and run with me to my bedroom, where I gave her an old rubber eraser; I'd got her out of there, but like a thousand-per-cent wuss I said noth-ing to my uncle. Later I told my sister what had happened, said we should do something, and she said we'd be more vigilant. But she hadn't seen what I had.

So, about fifteen feet from the couch, I squatted down in the posture that our uncle always adopted when he spread his arms and said, "Come give Uncle D a kiss," and I informed my niece that I was going to tell her to give me a kiss, and that she should respond by saying she didn't feel like giving me one, and that if she followed my instructions I'd pay her a dollar.

My niece started playing her game again.

I said, "I'll pay you a dollar!"

She smiled a little. She said, "Aunt D, do you know what my allowance is?"

I said, "Five dollars?"

She shook her head.

Her hand waved upward.

I said, "Is your allowance *ten* dollars?"

Guiltily, she nodded.

On the screen, she leaped over a mushroom.

She whispered, "I don't want to say it."

I knelt in his posture, I opened my arms the way he did, and I growled in his voice, being careful not to be so loud I'd wake everybody, "Come give me a kiss!"

Her eyes were wide.

I said, "Now you say, 'I don't feel kissy.' I'll pay you ten dollars."

On the stairs, Crow got up. Her black pupils went large.

On the couch, my niece shook her head.

Bartonella exhorted my niece to say it. If she can't say it she's a sucker, Bartonella said. If she can't say it she's doomed.

My niece said she didn't want to say it.

I kept exhorting. I offered her the choice of two phrases—"I don't feel kissy right now" or "No thanks, I must go clean my room"— and was telling her again that I'd pay her ten dollars, when my niece started breathing as if she couldn't get enough air. Her posture wasn't good; she'd hunched.

She whispered, "It's too scary."

My real self said, Stop, you're being a jerk, you made her cry, jerk; but Bartonella said, Someone's gotta train her.

Bartonella said, "Adira, if you say it, I'll buy you a ruby necklace."
She looked at me.

I added, "And matching earrings."

I knew from experience that one could buy a "real" ruby necklace and earrings on eBay for ten dollars.

My niece looked down. Wiped her cheek. Said, "Okay."

Crow licked her right paw. She stared at me.

I squatted down and said in my uncle's voice, "*Come* give me a *kiss!*"

She breathed shallowly, and whispered in a high, artificial voice, "I don't feel—"; Chocolate farted, a smell of cheese/egg filled the room, and at that second my uncle walked in and yelled, "Hellooo! What's everybody doing?"

He paused, sniffed.

Crow's tail whipped.

I said, "Nothing"; Adira said, "Nothing."

My sister entered behind my uncle and announced that she'd found a mouse by her bed. She held it up by the tail. Its paws dangled. Where its eyes had been were deep holes. She stared at Crow and said, "Crow, I *don't* want you to do this again." Crow's head lifted. She closed and reopened her eyes, then stood, stretched, and padded up the loft stairs. My sister watched her go. Then she saw my niece's face. She looked at me. Her brow furrowed. She asked my niece why she was crying. Was it something Aunt D had said? Bartonella said, "Ohnoooyourefucked!!!!!!!!!!!!!!!!!" and my niece said calmly, "I was remembering Simmy." Then my *sister* started crying, and I did, too—for fun and because I wanted sugar so bad—and my niece re-started her video game and my uncle baked us all cinnamon buns for breakfast.

That afternoon, in preparation for guests, we made forty dozen sugar cookies in the shape of jingle bells, angels, and snowmen. My sister watched me eat three, and said carefully, "Drip your I.V. yet?" and I said, "Yeah," although I had not, and decorating cookies was so much fun that everyone got along well up until the tragedy.

It's hard to describe one family frosting cookies, or maybe not worth the effort, but: picture bowls with colored frosting on a kitchen island. Picture my younger niece, a round-faced, brown-eyed six-year-old in a loose red dress sitting on a stool at the island; across from her was my mother, a plump sixty-something Swede with blond hair and a puffy, sad face, bent over giving directions like "Use pink for the bell, Lily," and "Why don't you put three Red Hots on the holly?" I was also frosting, beside my younger niece, only I was creating, using colored jimmies, bespoke snowmen who resembled family members; I'd secretly frosted an extra bump onto one and given it curly black licorice hair to make it represent a pregnant Kunda. Outside the kitchen's sliding glass doors, the sun shone upon golden-brown grass; it was fifty degrees; everyone was happy. My sister laid wheat noodles in vats for lasagna; her husband dumped sixteen cans of corn syrup into four mixing bowls to make eight pecan pies; my elder niece sat across from me, cutting cookies into squares and icing them yellow to resemble SpongeBob; our uncle, a handsome, red-haired retired asset-management specialist in his mid-sixties who loved to ride horses, build furniture, and collect antique books, sat on my younger niece's other side and frosted cookies as best he could, without particular imagination, slabbing pink on a heart and yellow on a bell, and holding it up for everyone and saying, "Hey, guys. I did a bell. See?" From time to time he dropped his butter knife, and when he did he'd say, "Whoops, I dropped my butter knife," and get down and crawl around underneath my younger niece's stool; at which my niece, whose bare legs dangled from her dress, giggled nervously. Then our uncle would pop over to the sink, near where my sister was working, and say, "Excuse me, my knife's dirty. I'm going to wash it." He dropped his knife five times, I guess.

I know, K, that you'll protest that that's not realistic: how can a man drop a butter knife five times? I'm sorry to say that it's easy—the fingers spread, the knife drops. And you bet that part of me observed the proceedings and thought, This is crazy, I'm going to kill something, I'm gonna tear down *walls* or some shit! But the rational me thought, So he crawls under her stool, maybe sees panties, so what? Respect your sister's wishes. Everybody wants a peaceful Christmas.

Also, I was distracted by the fact that my sister was preparing wheat-based lasagna for dinner: my sister and my elder niece had both had Lyme disease, and were warned by doctors never to eat dairy (mucus-forming), soy (goitrogenic), or wheat, which spiked blood sugar, caused inflammation, and depressed the immune system. I *knew* that I was not supposed to criticize my sister's food choices, because she'd told me not to, but the third time our uncle dropped his butter knife I felt my frustration surge, and said, "Nina, why can't we make chicken stir-fry? You're not supposed to eat wheat!" and my sister replied that guests were arriving, and everyone liked lasagna, and I said, "They might like *gluten-free* lasagna," and she said that *no one* liked gluten-free lasagna, and added that normally she did not eat lasagna, but today was Christmas Eve, she was making it, and I needed to lay off her food choices, and outside a V of fat geese floated through the slate sky, and I thought wistfully how, if I could muscle-test Kunda to identify the supplements that would best replenish her iodine and support her adrenals, I could get her pregnant, and our uncle's butter knife clattered and he said, "Whoops! I'm clumsy!" and crawled under my younger niece's chair and the kid's legs kicked, and I *knew* I shouldn't say anything, I knew I shouldn't cause trouble, but I felt dizzy. I saw Crow, who was crouched on the loft stairs, shimmer and float above and beside herself, as if she were three cats, and I yelled, "But I see that you have wheat *bread* on your counter!" and my sister said coldly, "That's for the girls," and I said, "But *they* shouldn't eat wheat either—it's a Frankenfood!" and I was describing wheat's thyroid-hampering properties when my sister turned to our mother, who was petting Chocolate, and said, "Mother, I *said* don't pet Chocolate, *stop!*"

Our mother was allergic to most animals. But my sister's reprimand probably hurt her feelings, so she ushered my nieces into the circle room and told them a Jesus story. One about his entering a town and healing a blind man by spitting on his eyes. As our mother spoke, my sister banged pots and pans. Our mother always loved Christ, but she probably loved him more after her husband died and she was left broke, not fully bipolar but not right in the head, with four kids age six and under. She prayed to Jesus for help, and later that week our father's older brother, a confirmed bachelor and an asset-management specialist, offered to let her bring us all to his ranch and live with him, and to send her kids to college. To thank him, our mother cleaned and cooked for our uncle and the arrangement worked out, mostly. To thank God, she attended church twice weekly and spoke with Jesus for an hour every day.

From the kitchen, my sister ordered our mother to stop proselytizing; our mother kept speaking. Her voice was sweet in a way it rarely was. Our mother loved Jesus. I didn't condemn her. Personally, I agreed that many Jewish guys were extra-talented, kind, and good with touch, and I'd had "relationships" with emotionally distant, mostly unavailable Jewish guys myself, so I sympathized; my older sister did not.

When my sister repeated her request, our mother yelled, "*Then* Jesus asked, 'What do you see?' and the blind man said, 'I see *people!* They look like *trees*, walking around!'" and, temper shot, my sister ordered my nieces to play in their rooms.

Everyone slumped in the living room. Our uncle asked who wanted to go for a walk; no one did. Our mother sneezed. Our uncle said, "I guess I'll go by myself, then!" and left. We all read—my siblings books, my mother a magazine called *Real Simple*. The bells' carol played and the tree's lights twinkled. I was reading a biography of my favorite writer, who at forty-five begged Stalin to be allowed to finish his work before he was shot by a firing squad, when we heard a *thump thump thump* in the hall.

"What's that?" one of my brothers said.

"I don't know," my sister said.

We heard shrieks and giggles.

"Jump!" a voice cried.

We entered the hall and saw that my nieces had used their old tights to affix a coyote to the bannister. It was a donkey piñata, really; but they'd glued red-brown felt to it and taped coyote ears to its head. They'd cut holes where the donkey eyes had been, and in the holes they'd taped Doritos. My elder niece dangled a cat toy on a wire and made its attractive end bounce near the Doritos. Chocolate panted and lunged at the toy madly, fatly, his belly heaving. But each time he failed to reach it and fell with a thump. Crow watched from the top of the stairs.

Adira peered at her.

"Crow!" she urged. "Get it! Come!"

My sister asked what they were doing.

Adira muttered.

My sister said, "'Kamikaze Cat Training'???"

"We're teaching them to fight coyotes."

Her blue-black hair flared, tangled, around her shoulders.

"We'd train Crow," Adira said, "but she won't come near Chocolate. He bullies her and she's scared."

"First of all," my sister said, "that's not a coyote. It's a donkey. Chocolate does not see a coyote. He sees Doritos." Cats were not smart, she said. Cats were dumb. Crow was not being trained. She was watching the girls act stupid. No cat could kill a coyote. Furthermore, no cat was in danger, because no cat was ever going outside.

My sister said that she needed help in the kitchen, and told my nieces to clean up their mess.

I'm sure other families have fallen into bad holiday moods over similarly trivial incidents.

But I felt a sadness. I couldn't knock it; I don't know why. At any rate, I had to contemplate the prospect of my family eating wheat lasagna, which had goitrogenic effects; though, regarding that, they didn't believe me. My family found my health ideas absurd. My brothers, both dentists, had told me that my nutritionist work should be illegal, because only doctors are qualified to dispense supplements; my sister said that I'd never make rent as a nutritionist, and that I should give up. I was forbidden to offer Kunda the most common-sense advice. I considered, still with wonder, my clients who'd got pregnant: a dozen women in their mid-forties who had each had three failed I.V.F. treatments before they did protocols with me. Many had had repeat miscarriages, several had ovarian cysts, and all had tried unsuccessfully for years; but once we had replenished their minerals, supported their thyroid and adrenals, used herbs to balance their hormones, and changed their diets, they'd all conceived. They'd all had healthy, non-retarded babies. They'd sent me referrals, but not enough. My sister was right: I couldn't pay my bills. I'd spent a few hundred bucks on Google AdWords, but I made bad ads and they didn't work. My Web site was ugly. I'd had some unsatisfied clients, old ladies who'd gained weight instead of losing it, and they'd Yelped me, calling me a quack. I thought about how, if I helped Kunda, I'd have a district medical officer's Yelp endorsement, and how many clients that'd get me. I didn't give a fig about Kunda's sensitivity; I was dizzy, from actual dizziness or from grandiosity; I thought, So what if my degree's an Internet diploma?

I was slicing onions when I noticed, beyond the kitchen's glass doors, my mother standing in the back yard, staring contemplatively into the distant pines, under that pale vast Shuswap sky.

My sister said, "What's she doing?"

We wandered toward the glass—my sister and I, her husband, my nieces behind him—and saw that my mother was watching Chocolate, who was hunched privately at yard's edge, depositing number twos into the grass; as we observed, a handsome coyote the size of a large dog, but more yellow-gray and with a long narrow snout, strolled into the yard, bent down to Chocolate as if to whisper in his ear, and bit his throat. It pulled, ripping flesh, and the cat convulsed. The coyote plucked up Chocolate's body and trotted into the trees.

All I remember of the ensuing chaos is my sister's husband shouting in a high, almost teen-age voice, "You weren't supposed to let the cat out! Why'd you let the cat out? You weren't supposed to do that!"

Apparently, our mother had thought the cats were still allowed outside to use the bathroom at dusk. She was watching Chocolate, she explained. "I was *right there*," she said.

We had thirty minutes until our guests arrived.

I dripped medicine in my room. I'd put it off because there's a thing called a Herxheimer reaction: when you kill thousands of bacteria the remaining billions heighten their activity. I often hallucinated after dripping. I disliked feeling cold fluid slide through my veins. Also, inserting tubes into my arm-port was embarrassing and I tried to do it privately, so as not to repulse my family. Now I had to make a sixty-minute I.V. drip in thirty, so the pressure was high. I was lying on my bed, feeling logy, when the door swung open. A second later, Crow jumped onto the bed. A minute later, a hand tapped the door; Adira asked to enter.

I said it was her room.

She was wearing her gray track pants and a SpongeBob T-shirt. She hopped onto the bed and lay to my left. She asked what I was doing; I said I was dripping; she nodded. She'd been "tick sick," so she knew what it was. She reached across me to pet Crow; Crow let her. She read her book, then said, "I don't want Crow to die," into the pillow. I told her not to be stupid; she said, "Someone will let her outside, I know it," and I said, "You're being stupid" and she said, "*You're* stupid," and I said, "You're stupid like SpongeBob" and she said, "SpongeBob's awesome, I love SpongeBob!" and I swore that no one would let Crow out. Then I looked to my right and saw an old woman, as dark as night, bent and withered but still strong and smiling grimly. She had sharp teeth and yellow eyes, and was crouching. I jumped. My niece asked why I'd jumped. I explained that I'd dripped too fast. My niece said reasonably, "Why don't you slow it down?" and I said because we had guests coming. I wiped my eyes, gook came out; I looked at my fingers, they'd puffed like sausages. My niece asked what I'd got her for Christmas, and I said something cheap and small, which was true.

She smiled and said, "I bet I like it."

I said, "Listen, tardface, no one's letting Crow outside."

We slept.

The thing with nieces, K, is that they just happen. You may be a broke, semi-jobless loser who's never loved, hates kids, and is repelled by marriage, and suddenly your successful sibling may have these things: babies that look like you and know your name. And there's nothing you can do. I remember this one time, the year I took a job in Vancouver (the worst place on earth) to be near my sister, and she drove down to visit with her husband and my nieces, Lily still a baby, Adira then two, this wild fast skinny thing with an elf face and ebony hair, and we hiked through Lighthouse Park, along a trail that wound two miles through thousand-year-old cedars and descended steeply to an inlet called Starboat Cove, and my niece ran its length but on the way back got tired, and I asked if she wanted a piggy-back ride. I probably said, "Smellface, want a ride?" and she said, "Yes!" and my older sister got an odd look and asked my niece, "Do you want *me* to give you a piggy-back ride?"; there was a pause, these white clouds moved in the perfect sky above the cove, the ocean smacked saltily, fishily on the rocks below our feet, and my niece composed her face as if contemplating how to put things; I knew my sister would always be her one love—we all knew that—but she said, in her breathy two-year-old voice, "Sometimes when your heart is big, all you really want is Aunt D," and I was, like, "Great, I'm fucked, I'm going to like this kid, this niece thing, forever."

We'd slept through dinner. I was glad, because I'd decided to starve myself in order to starve the Bartonella. My sister offered me food and I declined, though ravenous. I saw by the remnants on the counter that my family had consumed ten pans of buttered squash, twelve loaves of bread, and eight vats of lasagna. I was surprised but didn't dwell on it. Holidays make people hungry. My relatives are fit and they exercise and have good metabolisms. However, the sight of ricotta droppings made me nauseous, and when I pulled the trash compactor out from the counter I saw thousands of silverfish sliding atop squash peels. My stomach rolled; they sparkled and slithered. I closed the drawer. My sister asked what was wrong; I said nothing, opened the trash, saw only squash rinds. I helped carry eight pecan pies into the circle room, where relatives were settling into couches, and a strange thing happened, or I guess not so strange, when you consider that I'd dripped my I.V. too fast; instead of my beloved family and pleasant in-laws gathered around the tree, sitting on the circle room's several couches, I saw animals. My sister's father-in-law, a witty, retired postal worker who was now making well-deserved cash selling disaster insurance, was a wily wild boar, wearing plaid pants, a blue polo, and a bow tie, with a bald boar's head and bristles coming out of his large tan ears. He was telling my brother-in-law—a timid giraffe in a blue T-shirt, with two hooves poking out of each jean leg—about some fire/tornado/hurricane packages he'd sold in new developments, and his snout nodded as his maw said, "Went like hotcakes."

My sister's mother-in-law, in real life a beautiful textile designer, was a kangaroo, her soft brown legs splayed on the couch, knitting next to my younger niece, who looked up at her adoringly; my sister, I'm sorry to say—don't think badly of me, blame the Bartonella—was a Chihuahua who went yipping around the room bringing everyone a slice of pie by carrying each plate in her mouth, and whenever her mouth was free she'd yip, "How are you? We have mulled wine!" Everyone was talking happily. The kangaroo told my sister in a warbly voice, while stroking her pelt with one paw, that she and her husband had coyotes in their back yard, too, and had kept their cats inside for years now; she looked over to the boar, who was adjusting his bow tie, and said, "Greg's thinking of shooting some! Good money for the pelts!" and my sister panted and yipped, "Let's not talk about that right now! I don't want to upset the girls! It's Christmas!" and the kangaroo said, "Of course!" and my mother, a flushed potbellied pig who wore a pink velour dress and was seated next to a hairy gentleman with dark fur and a fedora, snorted, "Marianne, how are your fair-trade scarves doing? Are your scarves in a department store?" and all these people—or animals, I have no idea—were eating pecan pie. I knew I was hallucinating, but the part I felt sure was real was that they were consuming eight pies, and the Chihuahua yipped, "Cassandra! Do you want a piece, maybe a small one?"

I shook my head. I knew she didn't want me to eat it, even when she offered me the plate in her mouth, because her tail flattened and her mouth growled, so I declined and the Chihuahua said, "Adira? Pie?" and my niece, beside me on the couch, accepted. As she ate, a hairy orangutan with a big pink nose and beady eyes, who in real life was her uncle, the secretary, gnashed his teeth from across the room and said, "Adira, you've gotten taller! If you eat another bite of pie, you'll be taller than your mother!" and the Chihuahua jumped up and down angrily and said, "Nononono, not yet!" and a beautiful gray-skinned elephant wearing a purple sari, seated on the couch beside the orangutan, touched his shoulder with her trunk, and her gray lips said, "She's got another year before she'll catch her mother," and, beside me, my niece grinned.

I don't know, K, why my inflamed brain turned my district medical officer sister-in-law, a tall Hindi woman with wide cheeks and curly black hair, into an elephant—I think it was the association of elephants and Hinduism, plus I'm racist. At any rate, all was well. I'd accepted that I was hallucinating and decided to retire, pleading illness, when the Chihuahua declared it time for the *most important* Christmas Eve tradition: everyone must open one gift from under the tree; both my nieces exclaimed "Yay!" and in the ensuing pause the hairy gentleman across the room, who wore a fedora and a gray suit and had gray fur on his chin, appraised my elder niece and said, "Adira, you look very attractive this evening."

No one spoke. The kangaroo frowned and her needles paused; the potbellied pig turned pinker. I felt my niece push backward, into the couch. I thought, Ah well, it's *done*. I don't know why I thought that, except that suddenly I tasted corn syrup, lard, and stale pecans in my mouth; I don't know who put them there. The Chihuahua yipped, "Uncle D! You should compliment Lily! *Lily* has a new dress on and a bow in her hair! *Adira's* wearing *old* track pants and a *dirty* T-shirt! Lily is the one who looks pretty!" The distinguished gentleman turned to my younger niece, who was now admiring her own dress, and said, "Lily, you also look very pretty."

Everyone observed my nieces.

As the pie sugar hit my blood I felt a surge of—adrenaline? neuron death? It was true about the track pants—for the last year, my elder niece had worn nothing but nylon track pants, because anything else bothered her skin. The word "skin" flashed through my mind as I considered this, and I felt wired, alert, crazed, and I saw the elephant across the room. Her gray skin was wrinkled, and as she peered at the grandfather clock in the hall I remembered that wrinkles indicate iodine deficiency, and that the elephant was trying to get pregnant, and I yelled, "Kunda, do you think lately you have wrinkles?"

The kangaroo frowned and said, "Everyone has wrinkles!"

The Chihuahua jumped up and down and said, "Yes, that was rude! Everyone has wrinkles!"

I was implementing a business strategy from a book called "How to Master the Art of Selling," whereby you ask your potential clients questions they're bound to say "yes" to. You start with something easy, like "It's a nice day out, isn't it?" and keep going. Once they get in the pattern of saying "Yes," they can't stop—that's the idea. I knew certain things about Kunda, because she was a woman suffering from infertility, plus she was an elephant, so I said, "Kunda, I suspect your body temperature's low. Do you often feel cold?"

The elephant stared at me. Her trunk curled down. She said, "I do feel cold often. Why?"

I looked at her gray, bald head and sad brown eyes. I said, "Kunda, your eyebrows are thinning at the outer edges, aren't they? In fact,

I don't think you have eyebrows at all! Are you losing hair in the shower drain?"

The elephant's hooves went to her forehead. Her mouth dropped open.

The orangutan next to her frowned.

Everyone stared at me.

I thought, Yes!

I said, "Kunda, do you crave sugar in the afternoon? Salt? Caffeine?"

The elephant peered at me. Slowly she said, "Yes. Why?"

"Ignore her!" the Chihuahua yipped. "She's tick sick! She has Lyme disease!"

Beside me, my older niece said, "Aunt D, what are you doing?"

The kangaroo said that she didn't think this was a nice conversation.

I peered at the elephant, on the couch. "Kunda," I said. "You look big to me. Do you have belly fat? Are you having trouble losing weight?"

In reality, K, Kunda was slender. But I knew that women in their forties are paranoid about everything, and for no reason that I understand I was intent on showing Kunda that she was suffering from iodine deficiency.

I said, "You're cold and fat around your middle, right?"

The elephant nodded.

The orangutan yelled, "I won't stand for this! You're saying things that are totally inappropriate!" It came at me from across the room; I was afraid, in fact terrified, and my niece whispered, "Aunt D, stop," and I yelled, "Too bad, Kunda. Those are all symptoms of a deficiency in iodine, the mineral most essential for fertility. That's why you can't conceive!"

The orangutan stopped inches from me. "That's enough!" he said.

The elephant turned mauve. She rose clumsily and headed toward the kitchen.

I struggled to frame my closer as a "Yes" question. I yelled, "Kunda, if a cheap nutritionist in-law who charges cheap rates could help you fix these problems cheaply, you'd want help, wouldn't you?"

Suddenly it was done. Instead of an elephant I saw a lithe, forty-something Indian woman striding toward my sister's back door. She opened the door, closed it carefully behind her, and walked into the dark yard. My sister, not a Chihuahua but a tallish blond investment banker with great skin and runner's legs, twisted my right wrist. She said, "Everything you said is unacceptable."

Some of our relatives—our gray-suited uncle, his mouth curled as if a friend had told him a joke; our mother, in her pink velour dress; my sister's husband's parents, the ex-postal worker with his bald head and bristly black brows and his slope-faced, brown-eyed wife—stared at me, appalled, from a couch; on a love seat, one of my brothers leaned toward the other and whispered, "We might commit her; Nina will pay."

Beyond the glass dome of the circle room was clear black sky; under the Christmas tree sat mounds of gifts decked in sparkling gold-and-red paper and tied with organza ribbons.

I said, "I apologize."

I kept saying it.

My sister sighed and said that someone should go to Kunda; her husband said that he would, but my sister said, "No, let me." She walked through the kitchen, slid the heavy glass door open, and strode out. Behind her, the black cat sauntered across the kitchen tiles and out the door and into the grass. It padded left, past the swing set, and headed into the trees.

That's how we reentered the forest, now frigid and pitch black. Though it was late, all of us lurched through the woods, calling the cat's name. My sister didn't own enough flashlights for everyone, so we searched in clusters and pairs. The trees were dark, still shapes; I heard twigs crack and people in distant places call the cat's name. It was terrible and no one spoke much, but at one point my sister ended up next to me, and said, "I don't want to discuss this evening right now, because I'm too upset, but . . ." She'd worked hard to make the holiday nice for everyone, she said, and to enable everyone to get along. She'd worked hard to make *me* happy, too, and it seemed that all I wanted to do was criticize her and make people upset; I wasn't myself, and she was curious—what had she done to me, to deserve this? And I was, like, Christ. I felt terrible. I knew she'd spent days shopping for gifts, party favors, groceries, stocking stuffers; she'd bought us all snow boards and ski passes—time she barely had, since she worked eighty hours a week at her banking job. She tried so hard and no one thanked her. "I'm so sorry," I said. "I didn't mean to, I'm sick—" and she said, "Don't use that excuse." She'd had Lyme disease, too, she said. Maybe she hadn't had Bartonella, but she'd had spirochetes in her nervous system, they'd affected her neurologically, and she hadn't acted like I was now; her throat caught. The real me felt ashamed and said, "You're right, I'm so sorry," but Bartonella heard her say, "Bartonella," and awakened. Bartonella me yelled, "You want to know why? Because I'm *pissed* at you, bitch!" and she gasped and asked how *dare* I call her that? And added that, truthfully, she was angry at me, too; I heard branches rustle and, distantly, someone call, "Who's there?" but, out of my head, I said, "Bring it on, bitch! Here's my chin!" I saw my sister frown and rear back. Then an immense fist like a sledgehammer punched my jaw.

I fell on my butt on the trail. An orange pain was my jaw and also the world. I had three faces and saw three sisters. It wasn't she who'd hit me—it was the orangutan. Rather, the secretary, Kunda's husband; I heard him say, "I've never punched anyone before, I was just so mad about what she said to Kunda," and my sister muttered, "Done is done," and the willowy black shadow of one of my brothers said, "She sort of . . ." and the other's said, "Deserved it," and the secretary touched my face and said, "No worries, it's not dislocated"; the others showed up, my nieces asked what happened, my sister's mouth opened and closed, as did the secretary's, and I said, "I fell and hit my jaw on a stone." My sister announced that we weren't finding Crow tonight and should go home. My nieces protested that we couldn't leave Crow, so my sister told them that she was probably hiding in a safe place in the forest, just waiting for daylight to come home.

Adira begged us to leave the sliding door open for the cat. My sister didn't want to wake up to raccoons in the kitchen, but my niece insisted. So my sister—who couldn't deny her daughters anything—said okay.

The weird thing about blood-sugar issues is that they don't go away just because you've had a bad Christmas. I woke up at 3 A.M. The house was quiet. I guessed everyone was asleep. I figured I could sneak into the kitchen and eat half a pecan pie and no one would know. I entered the kitchen and found half a pecan pie, covered in foil, on the counter. I unwrapped it. I already tasted it in my mouth, even before eating it; that's the horrible thing. Stale pecans, wheat crust, lard, and corn syrup—I was desperate for it. Outside, it was coal-black. Cold wind blew through the open door. I stuck my finger in the pie and scooped out a big blob. The pecan-syrup blob was moving toward my mouth when I heard a high-pitched cry, outside in the yard. I felt afraid. I put the blob back in the pie tin, and stepped away; a black ball shot into the kitchen, moving toward me fast, uttering a high sound, once-cat, but it moved on its belly, pulled itself forward by using its front paws, which scraped madly, nails clicking, across the floor; it had no legs, only a head and a torso, it seemed to roll past me, it paused between the circle room and the kitchen and looked at me. It was Crow, but her back legs seemed to have disappeared—she was half a cat and her face looked gigantic, puffed to twice its size. I've never been so terrified of anything in my life, and nothing else has ever made me so sad as hearing that pitiful cry and seeing the cat with no hindquarters.

My sister appeared in the hall. "God," she said. "We have to get it out of here. I don't want the girls to see it, it will upset them—"

My elder niece appeared. She said simply, "The coyote ate her legs," and walked toward her cat, and my sister yelled, "Don't touch her! She's hurt, she may bite you," but the kid knelt by the cat and pressed her hand along its back; it didn't move, and my sister rushed forward to pull my niece away, but as soon as she neared the animal it opened its mouth, its enormous swollen face twitched, and it released two gelatinous orbs.

Once they came out, the cat's face became normal-sized. The whitish blobs slid across the floor—golf-ball size, like undercooked eggs with red tendrils. In one I could see the golden disk and the dark pupil.

My sister said, "What are those? Ugh!"

My niece said, "She got them."

Revelstoke is an unusual town. The veterinary clinic's reception contains Oriental rugs and damask couches, and the clinic stays open all night, even on Christmas. We took the cat in and they operated immediately, saving one hind leg, which had been folded behind her; the technicians weren't certain, but they said that the thighs appeared serrated by coyote's teeth, and all seven of them—there were seven technicians—said they'd never seen a cat get away from a coyote, and that it was a miracle that she was alive. We left the clinic at 6 A.M., the pet's remaining leg in a cast, and I'm sure you saw this coming, K, but the sky had grayed over, and, as we left the clinic and saw the firs on the distant mountains, down came white flakes, huge, far apart, as large as in picture books, the first of the year, and they fell onto our tongues, as if the earth were saying, "Jesus is Lord," or else, "Here is some snow," or just, "Global warming hasn't killed me yet, I'm alive."

A somewhat odd thing happened that morning. My sister, who stuck up for me when she was a kid, but whom no one stuck up for—ever, in any way—thanked our mother and uncle for coming, and told our uncle that he had to go.

Some say that those born between December 22nd and January 19th carry existential sadness within them. They say that Capricorns are at the end of their line; everything they want to do, they have to do within this life. Perhaps that's why they're stubborn plodders who'll trek step by tiny step to reach their goals. I'm a hundred per cent sure that, as a Russian Communist, K, you'll say that that's bunk, and that I should never mention astrology in a story again. For what it's worth, I write to you as one child of winter to another.

SHEILA HETI, HEIDI JULAVITS, LEANNE SHAPTON

■

Wear Areas

FROM *Women in Clothes*

THREE YEARS AGO, *Heidi Julavits, Sheila Heti, and Leanne Shapton sent out a series of questions about fashion to hundreds of women. From these surveys they compiled* Women in Clothes, *a panoramic look at female style and its relationship to identity and story. As Julavits says in the introduction to the book, "I don't check out men on the street. I check out women. I am always checking out women because I love stories, and women in clothes tell stories." The book discusses wetsuits, knee socks, pantsuits, pearls, floral-prints, and everything in between. And it also examines women's diverse and complex relationships with their bodies. For example, in the following images, which were dispersed throughout the book, several women annotate a blank body outline drawn by Shapton.*

PROJECT

WEAR AREAS | GINTARE PARULYTE

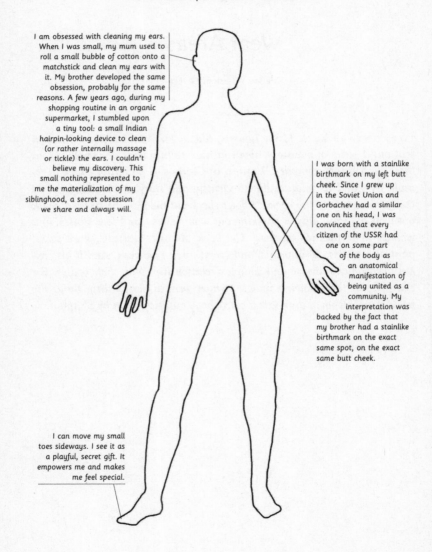

I am obsessed with cleaning my ears. When I was small, my mum used to roll a small bubble of cotton onto a matchstick and clean my ears with it. My brother developed the same obsession, probably for the same reasons. A few years ago, during my shopping routine in an organic supermarket, I stumbled upon a tiny tool: a small Indian hairpin-looking device to clean (or rather internally massage or tickle) the ears. I couldn't believe my discovery. This small nothing represented to me the materialization of my siblinghood, a secret obsession we share and always will.

I was born with a stainlike birthmark on my left butt cheek. Since I grew up in the Soviet Union and Gorbachev had a similar one on his head, I was convinced that every citizen of the USSR had one on some part of the body as an anatomical manifestation of being united as a community. My interpretation was backed by the fact that my brother had a stainlike birthmark on the exact same spot, on the exact same butt cheek.

I can move my small toes sideways. I see it as a playful, secret gift. It empowers me and makes me feel special.

PROJECT

WEAR AREAS | RIVKA GALCHEN

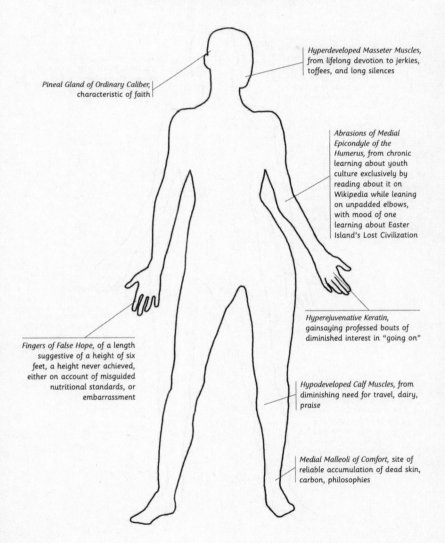

Hyperdeveloped Masseter Muscles, from lifelong devotion to jerkies, toffees, and long silences

Pineal Gland of Ordinary Caliber, characteristic of faith

Abrasions of Medial Epicondyle of the Humerus, from chronic learning about youth culture exclusively by reading about it on Wikipedia while leaning on unpadded elbows, with mood of one learning about Easter Island's Lost Civilization

Hyperejuvenative Keratin, gainsaying professed bouts of diminished interest in "going on"

Fingers of False Hope, of a length suggestive of a height of six feet, a height never achieved, either on account of misguided nutritional standards, or embarrassment

Hypodeveloped Calf Muscles, from diminishing need for travel, dairy, praise

Medial Malleoli of Comfort, site of reliable accumulation of dead skin, carbon, philosophies

PROJECT

WEAR AREAS | ANA BUNČIĆ

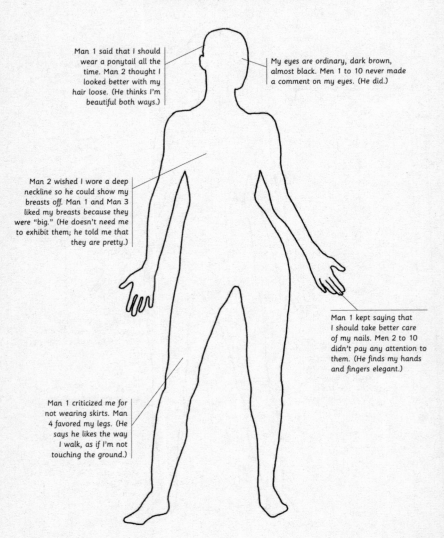

Man 1 said that I should wear a ponytail all the time. Man 2 thought I looked better with my hair loose. (He thinks I'm beautiful both ways.)

My eyes are ordinary, dark brown, almost black. Men 1 to 10 never made a comment on my eyes. (He did.)

Man 2 wished I wore a deep neckline so he could show my breasts off. Man 1 and Man 3 liked my breasts because they were "big." (He doesn't need me to exhibit them; he told me that they are pretty.)

Man 1 kept saying that I should take better care of my nails. Men 2 to 10 didn't pay any attention to them. (He finds my hands and fingers elegant.)

Man 1 criticized me for not wearing skirts. Man 4 favored my legs. (He says he likes the way I walk, as if I'm not touching the ground.)

WEAR AREAS | JINNIE LEE

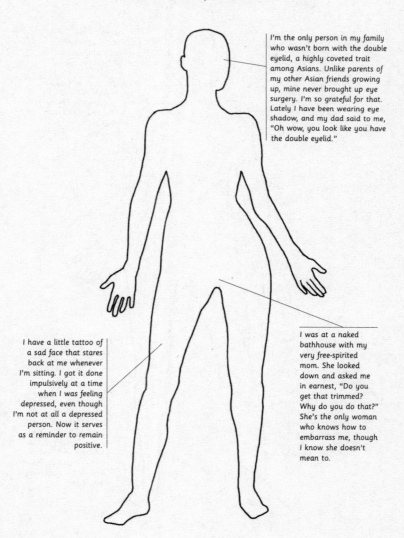

I'm the only person in my family who wasn't born with the double eyelid, a highly coveted trait among Asians. Unlike parents of my other Asian friends growing up, mine never brought up eye surgery. I'm so grateful for that. Lately I have been wearing eye shadow, and my dad said to me, "Oh wow, you look like you have the double eyelid."

I have a little tattoo of a sad face that stares back at me whenever I'm sitting. I got it done impulsively at a time when I was feeling depressed, even though I'm not at all a depressed person. Now it serves as a reminder to remain positive.

I was at a naked bathhouse with my very free-spirited mom. She looked down and asked me in earnest, "Do you get that trimmed? Why do you do that?" She's the only woman who knows how to embarrass me, though I know she doesn't mean to.

PROJECT

WEAR AREAS | ADITI SADEQA RAO

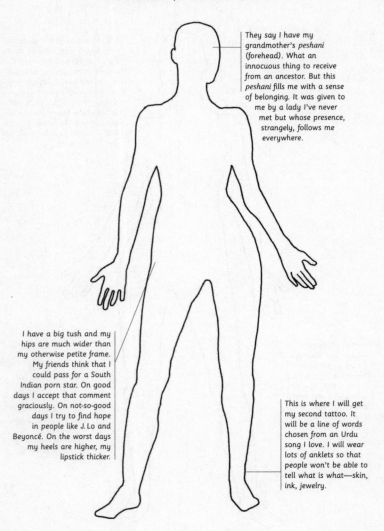

They say I have my grandmother's *peshani* (forehead). What an innocuous thing to receive from an ancestor. But this *peshani* fills me with a sense of belonging. It was given to me by a lady I've never met but whose presence, strangely, follows me everywhere.

I have a big tush and my hips are much wider than my otherwise petite frame. My friends think that I could pass for a South Indian porn star. On good days I accept that comment graciously. On not-so-good days I try to find hope in people like J. Lo and Beyoncé. On the worst days my heels are higher, my lipstick thicker.

This is where I will get my second tattoo. It will be a line of words chosen from an Urdu song I love. I will wear lots of anklets so that people won't be able to tell what is what—skin, ink, jewelry.

PROJECT

WEAR AREAS | JILL MARGO

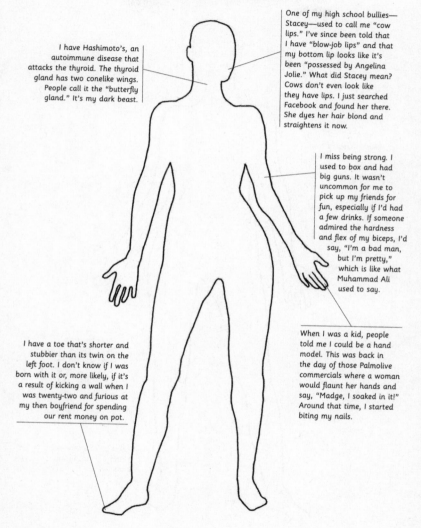

I have Hashimoto's, an autoimmune disease that attacks the thyroid. The thyroid gland has two conelike wings. People call it the "butterfly gland." It's my dark beast.

One of my high school bullies—Stacey—used to call me "cow lips." I've since been told that I have "blow-job lips" and that my bottom lip looks like it's been "possessed by Angelina Jolie." What did Stacey mean? Cows don't even look like they have lips. I just searched Facebook and found her there. She dyes her hair blond and straightens it now.

I miss being strong. I used to box and had big guns. It wasn't uncommon for me to pick up my friends for fun, especially if I'd had a few drinks. If someone admired the hardness and flex of my biceps, I'd say, "I'm a bad man, but I'm pretty," which is like what Muhammad Ali used to say.

I have a toe that's shorter and stubbier than its twin on the left foot. I don't know if I was born with it or, more likely, if it's a result of kicking a wall when I was twenty-two and furious at my then boyfriend for spending our rent money on pot.

When I was a kid, people told me I could be a hand model. This was back in the day of those Palmolive commercials where a woman would flaunt her hands and say, "Madge, I soaked in it!" Around that time, I started biting my nails.

PROJECT

WEAR AREAS | ANNA BACKMAN ROGERS

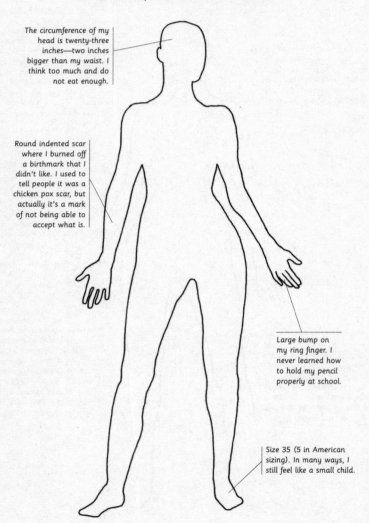

The circumference of my head is twenty-three inches—two inches bigger than my waist. I think too much and do not eat enough.

Round indented scar where I burned off a birthmark that I didn't like. I used to tell people it was a chicken pox scar, but actually it's a mark of not being able to accept what is.

Large bump on my ring finger. I never learned how to hold my pencil properly at school.

Size 35 (5 in American sizing). In many ways, I still feel like a small child.

WEAR AREAS | MARGO JEFFERSON

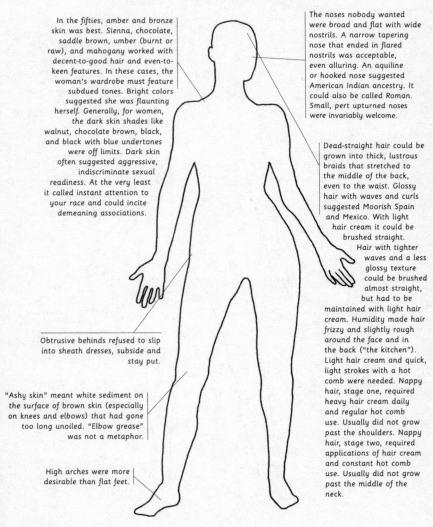

In the fifties, amber and bronze skin was best. Sienna, chocolate, saddle brown, umber (burnt or raw), and mahogany worked with decent-to-good hair and even-to-keen features. In these cases, the woman's wardrobe must feature subdued tones. Bright colors suggested she was flaunting herself. Generally, for women, the dark skin shades like walnut, chocolate brown, black, and black with blue undertones were off limits. Dark skin often suggested aggressive, indiscriminate sexual readiness. At the very least it called instant attention to your race and could incite demeaning associations.

The noses nobody wanted were broad and flat with wide nostrils. A narrow tapering nose that ended in flared nostrils was acceptable, even alluring. An aquiline or hooked nose suggested American Indian ancestry. It could also be called Roman. Small, pert upturned noses were invariably welcome.

Dead-straight hair could be grown into thick, lustrous braids that stretched to the middle of the back, even to the waist. Glossy hair with waves and curls suggested Moorish Spain and Mexico. With light hair cream it could be brushed straight.

Hair with tighter waves and a less glossy texture could be brushed almost straight, but had to be maintained with light hair cream. Humidity made hair frizzy and slightly rough around the face and in the back ("the kitchen"). Light hair cream and quick, light strokes with a hot comb were needed. Nappy hair, stage one, required heavy hair cream daily and regular hot comb use. Usually did not grow past the shoulders. Nappy hair, stage two, required applications of hair cream and constant hot comb use. Usually did not grow past the middle of the neck.

Obtrusive behinds refused to slip into sheath dresses, subside and stay put.

"Ashy skin" meant white sediment on the surface of brown skin (especially on knees and elbows) that had gone too long unoiled. "Elbow grease" was not a metaphor.

High arches were more desirable than flat feet.

PROJECT

WEAR AREAS | ANNIKA WAHLSTRÖM

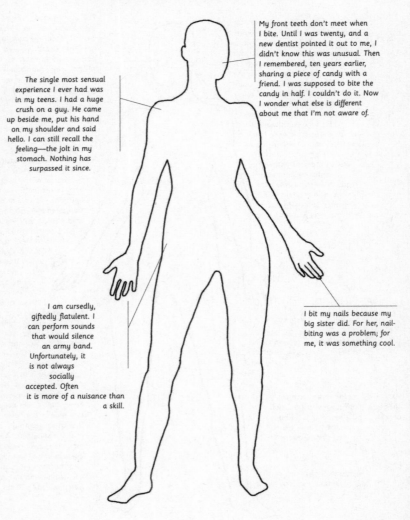

My front teeth don't meet when I bite. Until I was twenty, and a new dentist pointed it out to me, I didn't know this was unusual. Then I remembered, ten years earlier, sharing a piece of candy with a friend. I was supposed to bite the candy in half. I couldn't do it. Now I wonder what else is different about me that I'm not aware of.

The single most sensual experience I ever had was in my teens. I had a huge crush on a guy. He came up beside me, put his hand on my shoulder and said hello. I can still recall the feeling—the jolt in my stomach. Nothing has surpassed it since.

I am cursedly, giftedly flatulent. I can perform sounds that would silence an army band. Unfortunately, it is not always socially accepted. Often it is more of a nuisance than a skill.

I bit my nails because my big sister did. For her, nail-biting was a problem; for me, it was something cool.

WEAR AREAS | LITHE SEBESTA

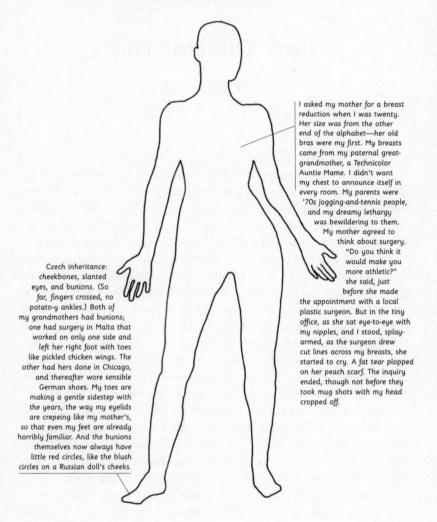

I asked my mother for a breast reduction when I was twenty. Her size was from the other end of the alphabet—her old bras were my first. My breasts came from my paternal great-grandmother, a Technicolor Auntie Mame. I didn't want my chest to announce itself in every room. My parents were '70s jogging-and-tennis people, and my dreamy lethargy was bewildering to them. My mother agreed to think about surgery. "Do you think it would make you more athletic?" she said, just before she made the appointment with a local plastic surgeon. But in the tiny office, as she sat eye-to-eye with my nipples, and I stood, splay-armed, as the surgeon drew cut lines across my breasts, she started to cry. A fat tear plopped on her peach scarf. The inquiry ended, though not before they took mug shots with my head cropped off.

Czech inheritance: cheekbones, slanted eyes, and bunions. (So far, fingers crossed, no potato-y ankles.) Both of my grandmothers had bunions; one had surgery in Malta that worked on only one side and left her right foot with toes like pickled chicken wings. The other had hers done in Chicago, and thereafter wore sensible German shoes. My toes are making a gentle sidestep with the years, the way my eyelids are creping like my mother's, so that even my feet are already horribly familiar. And the bunions themselves now always have little red circles, like the blush circles on a Russian doll's cheeks.

AMMI KELLER

■

Isaac Cameron Hill

FROM *American Short Fiction*

HIS CHILDHOOD WAS IDYLLIC but strange. Isaac spent a lot of time alone, wondering how every grass and leaf and creek reflecting dense branches could be a different color of green, was excused from Sunday school after taking up a precise count of people killed by God in the Bible. Isaac began reading adult books from the library in the fourth grade. He was not physically bullied because he was female.

In high school he connected with other kids who were a bit different: the local doctor's girl, ethnically Chinese; the Indian twins whose parents owned the paint store, the very smart girl whose face had a layer of fat over one cheek covered in fine downy hair. That was about it for Calhoun County, West Virginia. He excelled in school, chose a small college where the focus was on classics. He could have gone anywhere: he'd received a near-perfect score on his ACT test, was brilliant and female from one of the poorest counties in the United States. But he chose what he chose and graduated early, then left for Mexico with his best friend. I might have met him there—my parents were missionaries, mostly in the rural areas, though we spent my high school years in D.F.—but I didn't. Isaac went on to Guatemala by bus, then Honduras, which was dangerous in those days. The girl he'd gone with came back to the States to study social work. Isaac got work in the kitchen of a cruise ship and rode it to Greece. One night, he was assaulted in the fifth-level basement below decks and broke the man's wrist. So he off-boarded without his final paycheck in Catalonia, where I might also have met him—I was doing study abroad in Barcelona because it was far from my family—but again, we did not meet.

Isaac worked in restaurants, became as proficient in Spanish as he was in Greek and French, had his first affair with a woman. It was a good time to be in Barcelona. I was back in college at Brigham Young. Isaac wanted to be a writer, had the sense he was a writer, but when he sat down to write stories he simply could not make his characters do anything. He lost his job and stole like the natives and Australians and Germans he squatted with. When he got down to his last three hundred dollars, he booked a ticket home.

He was twenty-four now, the year when most young people think themselves adult. But he did not yet know where he was supposed to be. He followed a friend he'd met abroad, an American boy, skinny and fey, to San Francisco and lived in the boy's kitchen, where he discovered sex. He slept with men and women and people who didn't consider themselves either and was surprised to learn afterwards he could maintain eye contact during job interviews. Isaac moved into a lesbian commune, which became a queer commune when three of his housemates began taking hormones that deepened their voices and broadened their features. It was here he learned to frame walls and do plumbing, but when a building-code inspector passed over their renovations only to refer to Isaac as his housemate's "girlfriend," Isaac found himself hollowed out by a sense of dissonance so strong it bordered on grief. Isaac was not a woman. All his life, he had struggled to make a place for girls—in machine shops and calculus classrooms, S&M bars and kitchens—but it had yet to cause him to arrive in himself as a girl. And now the other people who'd made the compromises he had made were leaving.

One night Isaac climbed the gate of an abandoned Victorian, then shimmied up a drainage pipe to the roof overlooking Capp Street, where he plunged a syringe filled with testosterone into his thigh. He was not looking forward to telling his mother and sister but otherwise felt no shame. There was only a quarter moon, and Isaac scraped the inside of his calf climbing down, where an infection grew for which he needed to go to the ER and give a fake name.

He continued taking hormones and working in kitchens, leaving each when the pronoun some of his coworkers used conflicted with the pronoun others used. One day a conflict over the rack of ribs Isaac was handling, in which two waiters tripped over their cross use of *he* and *she*, then turned to him with predatory eyes, changed something. Isaac bought a pick-up truck and drove out to the national forest outside Arcata, got on food stamps and slept in a tent some nights, under the camper top others, for six months. He found the nearest library and kept the books dry in the front seat, cooked beans and grains on a camp stove, knew something about gathering wild greens, decided hunting wasn't worth the effort after a cost-benefit analysis. His mother and sister sent letters General Delivery to the town's post office, ten miles from the mouth of the logging road that led to his camp.

Isaac rarely saw another human during those months, and he did not miss them. But he was missed by friends in the city, was well loved for his unconventionality, his spirit, by people who knew better than to try to bring him back. I'd moved to San Francisco by then on a writer's fellowship applied for on a whim, and though I was not remarkable in any way, I went to performances sometimes, at the Bearded Lady and elsewhere, crossed paths with his friends, remember his name being mentioned with affection. We still hadn't met. Isaac's genetics had set him up to be hairy, and by the time the year was over he had a wooly beard, looked for all the world like a West Virginia mountain man become a California weird one, no trace of girl visible to the outside world. Being a man is a rougher life, but it's far easier to be left alone and this suited him. Having been raised a girl caused Isaac to act in ways that seemed, for a man, gracious. On visits to the city, in his truck stinking of motor oil and whiskey and mud through so many layers of army canvas, he was more beloved than ever. But he had no money and so could do little. His diet was not good, his world was too small, his face more weathered than it should have been. He was twenty-eight when he went back to trying to write. He had a long-term lover now, a man like himself, and they invented characters jointly, then each tried to write separately.

He'd smoked half a pack of cigarettes and sweat through his clothes when I met him outside an Oakland bar that could have been anywhere. He was heading back north the next day to sleep on a friend's land and build with her. Isaac was agitated because he could not make the old man he and his boyfriend had created perform any action whatsoever. Later, he succeeded in writing a short piece featuring a purple sky with stars like arrows, in which the man finally changed a tire.

I was instantly taken with him. I did not know he had not been born a man and I did not date men, so I thought it was simple affection. I told him I was a writer, and though this means nothing to most people until you prove you are not a bad one, he bought me a whiskey. He was wearing cowboy boots and a Western shirt like many of the more hip bar goers, but there was nothing artificial about him. Maybe I noticed the rings of dirt around his wrists or the smell of him, I don't remember. But I had the sense he could have appeared at any moment in history with the same facial expression, a credit I would not have given myself. We exchanged email addresses but never wrote. And I forgot about him the way you forget about a dream until you have it again and wake up stunned, only then sure it meant something the first time and something more for coming back.

When I saw Isaac again it was a year later in San Francisco. I had a teaching appointment at the prestigious university where I'd done my fellowship, but I hadn't written in six months. At twenty-seven, on the verge of becoming a writer, I was watching this dream slip away, a plate spinning out of control on the long finger of an acrobat. In the mornings I would drink coffee and sit at the desk, then look down to the dark hairs on my stomach, alternately feeling exhausted by my own revulsion and ready to make friends with it. I was pretty sure all human beings steeled themselves against the ungovernableness of their own flesh, but also: it was too easy to make my characters do things. It became clear to me as I imagined them yelling what I could not myself say, or convulsing without losing fluid during chemotherapy, or working joylessly to make a small part of their environment better: I feared and resented them all.

The last BART train had gone; I offered to take Isaac back to my shared apartment. Though we'd been talking intensely, our breath hot enough to condense in the warm fog, we became oddly delicate as we crossed the threshold of my sealed and empty living room. I threw open the windows. I thought about Isaac saying, earlier, that a work of literature "changed the way I have sex." I wanted the night to keep going. But I still set him up on the couch.

I don't exactly know why. Maybe I wasn't absolutely sure then he liked boys who'd been born boys, which is what, at the time, you would have told me I was. Some part of me knew that if this changed I could say goodbye to things at the prestigious university, but so long as I hadn't told a single soul I was going to transition, the consequences weren't real. I opened my mouth, but just then Isaac yawned like a teddy bear. I saw how badly I wanted to keep his attention, and I saw that this was not the way. I said, Goodnight Moon. In the morning, my housemate's box of orange juice was half-empty and on the wrong shelf, and Isaac was gone. I put my bottom lip against the torn eaves of the carton. I did not see him again for two years.

During those years, yes, I was let go from the university. Not for being transsexual, there are laws against that (or there are now), but for being "unstable," at least according to the paperwork I received from Human Resources. I began blockers, then hormones and felt my body change, so suddenly I needed to spend a lot of time regarding myself and thinking. I wanted to write about this, thought I could keep a valuable record, but the work of trying to explain felt heavy, even to myself. And my feeling of wonder felt private and in need of protection. I had been short for a man but was tall for a woman and avoided anything more than one-inch heels. The voice training and electrolysis I put on my credit cards after my savings ran out. I spent a lot on salon haircuts but did the color myself, used Ivory soap in the bath and still cooked like I always had, hardboiled eggs with torn up fresh dill on crackers. I figured I'd earned the right to be as I pleased. Still, I thought of Isaac frequently and imagined his reaction to me as I was now, worried he would let through some sliver of revulsion or regret. When we crossed paths again I was thirty and he was thirty-three. I had gone from precocious to lived-in, but I was told regularly I was beautiful, not just by those who knew me but by strangers on the street, only a third of whom must have known I was transsexual. I was slimmer than ever, due to the way I ate and because it made passing easier. And so that year had a waifish look: round almond eyes and talcum soft skin, jewelry that balanced my wider and leaner parts, hands I kept folded so the rose-colored nails hung over the knuckles, making them look smaller.

He was living here again, he said. He was a partner in a health food restaurant that gave all its profits to groups that fought hunger. I had missed the moment when he saw me again, but when he'd spun me from behind it was clear he recognized me, that I was the same person to him. Moments like these had become rare. He gave me a business card and I went a week later, alone. He was busy in the kitchen, plating ingredients I did not recognize with complete devotion to each dish. I didn't think he knew I was there, but when I got up to leave he intercepted me, bringing a vodka drink with fresh pomegranate and floating seeds and floating mint and coriander. And so I waited while the rest of the patrons and the waiters and the assistant chefs all left.

I drank my drink, debating whether I should confess my feelings for him while I pointed and flexed my foot so the wedge sandal released and re-gripped my heel. I thought: this is all of it. This is my life. When he returned he was warm and joyful. He asked me about my writing; I shook my head. He'd begun composing poetry, which was why he was so happy. That's perfect, I told him, thinking he was so well-read and had had such a difficult life. He walked me home and I almost said something, but I could not be the pathetic transsexual, even if he was one too. The guys have different problems, but for most, including Isaac, passing wasn't among them. I gave him my email address again, and this time he did contact me, three weeks later when he was accepted into a graduate poetry program. I mourned.

I developed more confidence in my thirties and began wearing heels. I felt the dawning of a different kind of self-acceptance and began toying with a novel, a very private novel, about my experience as the late and only child of missionaries. I was surprised to find the project had its own momentum. It was a relief not to be watched. Nobody remembered the prestigious appointment from my youth. I'd become simply a never was, a mistake. I began meditating and heard the birds exquisitely in the mornings. Then I moved temporarily to a small town north of the city. It was lonely, but I accepted this; I couldn't figure out who was supposed to love me.

When I returned, I wrote to tell Isaac I'd finished a draft of my novel. I had been working, except when I was in Guerneville, in a bookshop, which took a lot of my time but not much of my energy. The pay scale had changed, and I soon had a week's paid vacation. I suggested a visit, never thinking he'd agree or could commit to a plan. He wrote me with an enthusiastic yes, and though we drove to the Ice Age National Trail, and I learned to camp, nothing romantic happened. I was so struck by him I felt woozy. I'd turned that side of myself off so totally that it now gave me a constant hum, like a machine whose power has been left on, to be around him, day in and day out, for a week. We grew closer, but our discussions were always theoretical—Kathy Acker, the Rapture, why beavers are important ecologically. I never doubted that he loved me as a human being. But as a woman? As a lover? I'd been through too much already; I could not ask.

We spent two days of the trip at his house in Madison, and on the last night one of the women he lived with took me to bed, surprising no one more than me, though it must have been my hum she noticed. She was very butch and had no idea about me, though I assumed she knew or that he would have told her. There was a moment of awful, throat-tearing silence, and then we had the most authentically delightful sex. I'd been with people in the five years since transitioning but mostly one night stands, encounters that left me with some kernel of sadness. This person simply did not care that I had a penis. She was a terrifying, deeply silly lover, whose growling turned me on and made me giggle, and after I left she got my postal address and wrote me love letters.

I considered moving to Wisconsin and knew I had to do it. Life was now unbearable, and it seemed as though every experience I'd had—including my writing, my corporeality, the birds in the morning—was a waste or an error or a regrettable preface to this present, which must have been waiting for me all along. Love shattered the filthy glass I hadn't realized had been standing between myself and the world. Sexual, romantic love could bestow personhood, I now understood, and suddenly I belonged not only to her but to everyone: to those around me on the street and in grocery stores, just the whole human race.

It was spring in San Francisco when I applied for a teaching position at the college in her town, but without a published book I did not receive a response. So I sent my draft to agents. I inquired about bookshops in my letters to her and abruptly the tone of her replies changed. They became less frequent and, after I spent two terrible months waiting for one, I knew it would not come. Or if it did, it would not be enough to give me back the lust and security I'd known. My pride was like a sword buried to the hilt in my body, making me want to faint when I looked in the mirror. I wished I was a kid again, a teenager or a person in their twenties, so that I could travel to her, beg her to love me again, if she ever had. But I was thirty-four and sick with pride and with the understanding that I could not change the situation. I even understood that the world had not wronged me. But I did not know what to do.

I considered telling Isaac, but all he knew was the shadow of my legs on her wall as I walked to her bedroom; he'd never asked what happened after. And I did not want to seem desperate or hysterical or uncool. Also, I was very good at suffering very quietly. So I retreated to my San Francisco studio, and said I could not get off work when he suggested I visit that summer, and slowly I felt my soul wash the grit out of my body. Isaac graduated from the program and could not get a job.

I'd turned thirty-six. He was thirty-eight. I told him America did not want us, that we should go to Barcelona or to Mexico City, which I still had faint, fond memories of, notwithstanding my current estrangement from my parents. Isaac lived on my couch and though my feelings for him had not changed, he soon became the person I was closest to. I saw I would soon be forty. I did not tell him I loved him. It's different for men. He and his old lover reunited, and together saw me as an important friend and resource because if they lived together they would fight.

An agent found me. I'd misspelled my email address on my postal queries. She wanted to sell my very private novel and in the end she did, not for an enormous amount of money, but the way I lived, it was a year's expenses. That spring Isaac received a fellowship to England, the first of many we assumed, and when he took it I went to Spain. But being outside the Bay Area was a shock for me. I felt invisible as a transsexual woman, then suddenly afraid. I understood in a new way my world had gotten smaller. When I returned four months later, they gave me my job back at the bookstore and I should have been grateful; the economy was not good. But I was angry. I rebelled and had sex with a number of people I met online, some of whom were very nice and some of whom dehumanized me, but I'd become obsessed with certain kinds of sex, and I did not have enough intelligent people to talk to. The world is always smaller than it ought to be.

When Isaac came back from England he looked for jobs for a year. Though he could have stayed on my couch forever, he went to Oakland to live with his lover. My publicist hadn't known I was transsexual (why would she?). There was a brief storm, me fielding calls in the empty apartment because, as luck would have it, transexuality was in vogue that year, on talk shows. The book came out but, transsexual or not, few people noticed. Some of my old colleagues got in touch and a few of the more esoteric places had good reviews, but it came nowhere near earning back its advance. I continued working at the bookshop. The butch in Wisconsin contacted me; she wanted to be friends. I had so many lovers now, I thought it wouldn't hurt, but it did.

Isaac went back to the woods and began building a shack on a friend's land. He believed in his work, but his values were very different from the values around him; he typed poems onto postcards and sent them away in the mail. I began another novel, discouraged, a transsexual coming-of-age story. I owed my publisher a second book; this was the publicist's idea. I remember feeling like I was lying though I knew I was writing things that were indeed true, for myself and other people. It was a very confusing process, from drafting through publication, and against all odds it became a mainstream success. I was offered a faculty position at a less prestigious and less stodgy university in the city than the one where I had begun. They were progressive for the time, and the health insurance paid for the surgery I'd despaired of ever getting. So quite rapidly I was where I wanted to be at forty-two—but I was forty-two. I was called striking. But my skin was becoming that of a middle-aged person, I had a waddle under my chin, and though I still I kept myself scrupulously thin, my face was gaunt because of it. I was a popular enough teacher but aloof; I had passed the point when I could have learned to trust other people on contact. But I had coffee with a few of my colleagues from fifteen years before, and, now that I was one of the more successful of our group and the lines had been well-drawn, they were comfortable with me. What I was surprised to find: I was comfortable with them, too.

Isaac suffered. He began to mention recurrent muscle tears and debts, to express bewilderment that the same financial and professional struggles were still waiting for him each morning. Men became more attractive in their forties, and the physical labor he did living out on the land made me feel so much older beside him when I went out to visit, though I was more than two years younger. My footing was off on the mud slope that led to his cabin. He apologized but I knew it was my fault, not the slope. In an awkward moment one night toward the end of that trip I thought he might kiss me, but I was wrong and we got over it. His mother died and he used the money to buy the land; he was there permanently now. He wrote poems six months out of every year, but journals rarely wanted to publish them. They published the most obvious poems instead. This enraged me and I tried to pull a string or two for him, but the tide of my influence had receded. I'd been overrated, some said, hired only for the novelty of having a trans professor.

But I had tenure. I was shocked to find my days portioned out, to be going to sleep at night without fear. I began work on a third novel, unterrified. I'd ripened as a writer enough to cover my own shortcomings, and I no longer worried about a certain style of humiliation from reviews. I knew the window I'd been given to write something undeniably great had closed, but I still loved my characters, my garden, my stature, my students, my friends, and my city. I reunited with my family, a welcome surprise, and though they were frail it wasn't poor health that brought them back to me. And I headed towards middle-middle age with less strife then ever before, even dated for a few months or a year here and there, though something about me always made me remove myself. They weren't smart enough or

I could not be loved, or both. But these relationships helped with the loneliness. Surviving what you were never meant to survive creates a hard rock of happiness under the bones of the chest. My happiness wasn't fanciful or expansive, but I had survived, and I was happy.

I went to see Isaac for his fifty-sixth birthday and was shocked to find a grizzled, grey-haired mountain man staring back at me. I'd gone grey of course, and dyed it, but the pure white of his temples silenced me. His arms were red and pocked, part muscle and part soft. He'd never gotten surgery on his chest and because he'd thickened, his small breasts bunched at his lower ribs. It had been more than five years, and though I knew enough to buy hiking boots, he had to help me over the rise. I felt an unbearable ache for what had and had not happened. My success; his terminal beauty. He cooked me a meal that night that could not have been purchased in the city for any amount of money. Roast squash and a roast chicken just killed, herbs and garlic under the skin; potatoes dark and purple as a screaming baby; beer he'd brewed in a cool square hole in the earth beneath the table. Tears came to my eyes as I chewed. My throat seized around the food.

After dinner I read a sheaf of his poetry while he picked at a guitar, a new hobby. He played terribly but his poems were so good I stopped hearing him. When I was done I felt sure I was not happy, that a joke had been played on me. I'd enjoyed writing my last two novels, and I knew they did not matter. My hands around his poems were shaking so I rested them on my knees. I asked him if he'd sent them anywhere. He nodded. I put the papers down on a couch stinking of dog and snow, stood to look through the pane we'd set in the mudbale wall when for two days a long time ago I had helped him work on this house. It was far too late for me to ask him to make love to me. We were such different people. He put his arms around my shoulders from behind. I in hiking boots, he in work boots—we were the same height. I knew because his breath moistened the hair directly behind my mouth.

A feeling of pure joy flooded me, but I felt my body stiffen. He let go. He put me to bed in the hut he'd built for guests, and when I awoke to the sound of the birds it was with an intensity of sorrow I didn't know one could feel and not shatter. I was only fifty-three. I opened my journal and made a list of everything I wanted to do before I died, putting lines through what was no longer possible.

I was never asked to be a visiting professor, though others with my rank left every year or two for this purpose. Still, I had my place in the Bay. I was thought of as outspoken, a situation I found darkly comic. I dated a man for four years and at last he wore me down and we moved in together. He made more money than I did, and I gained all sorts of new problems—to vacation or redo the kitchen? The Galapagos or San Miguel de Allende? There is much less violence against older people, and I was rarely scared when we traveled. We took cabs everywhere and people were paid to respect us. He'd been wealthy and male all his life, my lover, whereas I covered my discomfort at being waited on, and after a period I ceased to feel it. I added to and crossed things off my list, especially when both Publisher's Triangle and the Lambda Association awarded me lifetime achievement designations within the span of three years. This was after my sixth book, a memoir, I liked to joke, about the first five. I offered to pay for Isaac to attend the second awards ceremony, in September, but I think he was involved in harvesting marijuana. He could not come.

When he came the next year, for my sixtieth birthday, I noticed he had no table manners. He just began eating when the food was handed to him, though my lover was still in the kitchen. He liked my lover, he liked everyone, but they had little to talk about. When the three of us stayed up late with a bottle of wine, I was impatient, as uncomfortable as when the butch from years ago had abandoned me, as when I was in my twenties and applying for the fellowship, begging an institution to save me from the prospect of life as a Mormon husband and father. I asked my lover to go to sleep, and after making a face, he did.

Isaac and I then talked about: bitterness. What leaves you satisfied, I asked him, and what isn't yet done?

"I am angry because if they want to kill us they can. Still."

I frowned because I hadn't been thinking about that. Everyone where he lived carried a gun. If I'd convinced him to touch me so many years back, I might be there too.

"You know," I said, the shape of him in my home so perfect in its incongruity it would become the image I returned to most after he was gone, a quiet death. Every wrinkle in his plaid snap-up shirt, the hint of jagged yellow tooth, the eyes defenseless and at once every color of green, "I always wanted you to be my lover."

"I knew." His cheeks reddened under long grey lashes. "But it's better this way."

"Better," I said, nodding into my wine. I had no idea whether or not I believed it. The hands of the clock above the fireplace drew themselves over its oiled oak face.

CLAUDIA RANKINE

■

"You are in the dark, in the car ..."

FROM *Citizen*

/

You are in the dark, in the car, watching the black-tarred street being swallowed by speed; he tells you his dean is making him hire a person of color when there are so many great writers out there.

You think maybe this is an experiment and you are being tested or retroactively insulted or you have done something that communicates this is an okay conversation to be having.

Why do you feel okay saying this to me? You wish the light would turn red or a police siren would go off so you could slam on the brakes, slam into the car ahead of you, be propelled forward so quickly both your faces would suddenly be exposed to the wind.

As usual you drive straight through the moment with the expected backing off of what was previously said. It is not only that confrontation is headache producing; it is also that you have a destination that doesn't include acting like this moment isn't inhabitable, hasn't happened before, and the before isn't part of the now as the night darkens and the time shortens between where we are and where we are going.

/

When you arrive in your driveway and turn off the car, you remain behind the wheel another ten minutes. You fear the night is being locked in and coded on a cellular level and want time to function as a power wash. Sitting there staring at the closed garage door you are reminded that a friend once told you there exists a medical term—John Henryism—for people exposed to stresses stemming from racism. They achieve themselves to death trying to dodge the build up of erasure. Sherman James, the researcher who came up with the term, claimed the physiological costs were high. You hope by sitting in silence you are bucking the trend.

/

When the stranger asks, Why do you care? you just stand there staring at him. He has just referred to the boisterous teenagers in Starbucks as niggers. Hey, I am standing right here, you responded, not necessarily expecting him to turn to you.

He is holding the lidded paper cup in one hand and a small paper bag in the other. They are just being kids. Come on, no need to get all KKK on them, you say.

Now there you go, he responds.

The people around you have turned away from their screens. The teenagers are on pause. There I go? you ask, feeling irritation begin to rain down. Yes, and something about hearing yourself repeating this stranger's accusation in a voice usually reserved for your partner makes you smile.

/

A man knocked over her son in the subway. You feel your own body wince. He's okay, but the son of a bitch kept walking. She says she grabbed the stranger's arm and told him to apologize: I told him to look at the boy and apologize. And yes, you want it to stop, you want the black child pushed to the ground to be seen, to be helped to his feet and be brushed off, not brushed off by the person that did not see him, has never seen him, has perhaps never seen anyone who is not a reflection of himself.

The beautiful thing is that a group of men began to stand behind me like a fleet of bodyguards, she says, like newly found uncles and brothers.

/

The new therapist specializes in trauma counseling. You have only ever spoken on the phone. Her house has a side gate that leads to a back entrance she uses for patients. You walk down a path bordered on both sides with deer grass and rosemary to the gate, which turns out to be locked.

At the front door the bell is a small round disc that you press firmly. When the door finally opens, the woman standing there yells, at the top of her lungs, Get away from my house. What are you doing in my yard?

It's as if a wounded Doberman pinscher or a German shepherd has gained the power of speech. And though you back up a few steps, you manage to tell her you have an appointment. You have an appointment? she spits back. Then she pauses. Everything pauses. Oh, she says, followed by, oh, yes, that's right. I am sorry.

I am so sorry, so, so sorry.

/

PAUL TOUGH

∎

A Speck in the Sea

FROM *The New York Times Magazine*

LOOKING BACK, John Aldridge knew it was a stupid move. When you're alone on the deck of a lobster boat in the middle of the night, forty miles off the tip of Long Island, you don't take chances. But he had work to do: He needed to start pumping water into the Anna Mary's holding tanks to chill, so that when he and his partner, Anthony Sosinski, reached their first string of traps a few miles farther south, the water would be cold enough to keep the lobsters alive for the return trip. In order to get to the tanks, he had to open a metal hatch on the deck. And the hatch was covered by two thirty-five-gallon Coleman coolers, giant plastic insulated ice chests that he and Sosinski filled before leaving the dock in Montauk harbor seven hours earlier. The coolers, full, weighed about 200 pounds, and the only way for Aldridge to move them alone was to snag a box hook onto the plastic handle of the bottom one, brace his legs, lean back and pull with all his might.

And then the handle snapped.

Suddenly Aldridge was flying backward, tumbling across the deck toward the back of the boat, which was wide open, just a flat, slick ramp leading straight into the black ocean a few inches below. Aldridge grabbed for the side of the boat as it went past, his fingertips missing it by inches. The water hit him like a slap. He went under, took in a mouthful of Atlantic Ocean and then surfaced, sputtering. He yelled as loud as he could, hoping to wake Sosinski, who was asleep on a bunk below the front deck. But the diesel engine was too loud, and the Anna Mary, on autopilot, moving due south at six and a half knots, was already out of reach, its navigation lights receding into the night. Aldridge shouted once more, panic rising in his throat, and then silence descended. He was alone in the darkness. A single thought gripped his mind: This is how I'm going to die.

Aldridge was forty-five, a fisherman for almost two decades. Most commercial fishermen in Montauk were born to the work, the sons and sometimes the grandsons of Montauk fishermen. But Aldridge was different—he chose fishing in his mid-twenties, moving east on Long Island from the suburban sprawl where he grew up to be closer to something that felt real to him. He found work on a dragger and then on a lobster boat, and then, in 2006, he bought the Anna Mary with Sosinski, his best friend since grade school. Now they had a thriving business, 800 traps sitting on the bottom of the Atlantic, and two times a week they'd take the boat out overnight, spend an eighteen-hour day hauling in their catch and return the next morning to Montauk loaded down with lobster and crab.

Sosinski had a reputation on the docks as a fun-loving loudmouth, a bit of a clown—he actually rode a unicycle—but Aldridge was the opposite: quiet, intense, determined. Work on the Anna Mary was physically demanding, and Aldridge, who was lean but strong, drew a sense of accomplishment, even pride, in how much he was able to endure each trip—how long he could keep working without sleep, how many heavy traps he pulled out of the water, how quickly and precisely he and Sosinski were able to unload them, restock them with bait and toss them back in. Now, alone in the water, he tried to use that strength to push down the fear that was threatening to overtake him. *No negative thoughts*, he told himself. *Stay positive. Stay strong.*

The first thing you're supposed to do, if you're a fisherman and you fall in the ocean, is to kick off your boots. They're dead weight that will pull you down. But as Aldridge treaded water, he realized that his boots were not pulling him down; in fact, they were lifting him up, weirdly elevating his feet and tipping him backward. Aldridge's boots were an oddity among the members of Montauk's commercial fishing fleet: thick green rubber monstrosities that were guaranteed to keep your feet warm down to minus fifty-eight degrees Fahrenheit, a temperature Montauk had not experienced since the ice age. Sosinski made fun of the boots, but Aldridge liked them:

they were comfortable and sturdy and easy to slip on and off. And now, as he bobbed in the Atlantic, he had an idea of how they might save his life.

Treading water awkwardly, Aldridge reached down and pulled off his left boot. Straining, he turned it upside down, raised it up until it cleared the waves, then plunged it back into the water, trapping a boot-size bubble of air inside. He tucked the inverted boot under his left armpit. Then he did the same thing with the right boot. It worked; they were like twin pontoons, and treading water with his feet alone was now enough to keep him stable and afloat.

The boots gave Aldridge a chance to think. He wasn't going to sink—not right away, anyway. But he was still in a very bad situation. He tried to take stock: It was about 3:30 a.m. on July 24, a clear, starry night lit by a full moon. The wind was calm, but there was a five-foot swell, a remnant of a storm that blew through a couple of days earlier. The North Atlantic water was chilly—seventy-two degrees—but bearable, for now. Dawn was still two hours away. Aldridge set a goal, the first of many he would assign himself that day: Just stay afloat till sunrise.

Once the sun came up, Aldridge knew, someone was bound to start searching for him, and he could begin to look for something bigger and more stable to hold on to. For now, though, there was nothing to do but scan the horizon for daylight and watch the water for predators. For the first hour, the sea life mostly left him alone. But then, in the moonlight, he saw two shark fins circling him, less than ten feet away—blue sharks, they looked like, 350 pounds or so. Aldridge pulled his buck knife out of his pocket, snapped it open and gripped it tightly, ready to slash or stab if the sharks tried to attack. Eventually, though, they swam away, and Aldridge was alone again, rising and falling with the ocean's swell. He kept trying to drive away those negative thoughts, but he couldn't help it: Who would get his apartment if he didn't make it back? Who would take care of his dog? He thought about fisherman friends who died, funerals he'd been to at St. Therese, the Catholic church in Montauk. He thought about who would come to his own funeral if he didn't make it.

But mostly he thought about his family back in Oakdale, the Long Island town where he grew up: his parents, who had been married for almost fifty years and still lived in the house where Aldridge was born; his brother; his sister; his little nephew, Jake. It was a close-knit, middle-class, Italian-and-Irish family. His father was retired from the Oldsmobile dealership in Queens where he commuted to work for decades. Aldridge pictured them all, asleep in their beds, and thought about the phone calls they would soon be getting.

His family didn't bring it up much anymore, but Aldridge knew that none of them liked the fact that he had taken up such a danger-ous profession. In his twenties, when he was starting out as a fish-erman, his parents were constantly trying to talk him out of it. They gave up, eventually, but even now, every time he said goodbye to his mother, she looked at him as if it were the last time she was going to see him.

Alone in the darkness, he remembered a conversation he had a few months earlier with his sister, over beers in her backyard. They were talking about a friend of Aldridge's named Wallace Gray, a fish-erman who drowned off Cape Cod when his scallop boat sank in bad weather. It wasn't a very cheerful conversation, and they both knew that they weren't talking only about Gray. Out of nowhere, Aldridge felt compelled to make his sister a promise: *If I ever get into trouble out there*, he told her, *just know that I'm going to do everything I can to get back home.*

It was a little after 6 a.m. when Anthony Sosinski woke up onboard the Anna Mary. The mate he and Aldridge hired to work this particu-lar trip, an old friend named Mike Migliaccio, got up first, and when he saw that Aldridge was missing, he yelled for Sosinski. They were both sleep-dazed, confused by the daylight. What time was it? Where were they? Sosinski tried to puzzle it out: Just before he went to sleep at 9 p.m., he told Aldridge to wake him at 11:30 p.m. Now it was past dawn. Even if Aldridge had decided to let him sleep (as he some-times did), surely he would have woken Sosinski by the time they got to their first trawl. But they were more than fifteen miles past their traps—almost sixty miles offshore. What could have happened?

The Anna Mary is a forty-five-foot boat, and most of its surface is taken up by a flat, open deck, so there aren't that many places to search for a missing person. Still, Sosinski and Migliaccio looked everywhere. One hatch cover on the deck was off, and Sosinski thought maybe Aldridge had fallen into the open lobster tank, hit his head and drowned. He lay facedown on the deck and stuck his head through the hatch, ignoring the powerful smell. No sign of Aldridge.

Sosinski ran to the VHF radio, which was bolted to the ceiling in the small wheelhouse toward the front of the boat, and grabbed the microphone. He switched to channel sixteen, the distress channel, and at 6:22 a.m., he called for help, his voice shaking: "Coast Guard, this is the Anna Mary. We've got a man overboard."

The Coast Guard's headquarters for Long Island and coastal Connecticut is in New Haven. Sean Davis is a petty officer there, and it was his job that morning to stand watch at the station's communications unit. Davis was part of a five-person watch that had just come on duty. Davis radioed back, asking Sosinski for details, and Sosinski started feeding them to him: when he last saw Aldridge, the course the boat was on, where they were now. No, Aldridge wasn't wearing a life preserver. No, he wasn't wearing a G.P.S. distress beacon. No, he didn't leave a note. Yes, he could swim.

Davis asked Sosinski to stand by, and he turned to the rest of the team in the command center, a dimly lit room on the second floor of the base. The front wall was covered with maps and charts and video screens, which could show everything from a live radar image of Long Island Sound to the local news. Sitting nearest to Davis was Pete Winters, a Coast Guard veteran who was now working as a civilian search-and-rescue controller. That morning, he was the Operations Unit watch stander, which would normally mean that he'd be the person running the search-and-rescue computers. On this morning, though, there was a second person in the Operations Unit: Jason Rodocker, a petty officer who that week was "breaking in," or being trained. Rodocker was new to Long Island Sound—he had just transferred two days earlier from the Coast Guard station in Baltimore. But as it happened, he was an expert in the Coast Guard's search-and-rescue computer program, known as Sarops.

The first calculation the search team ran that morning was a survival simulation, taking into account Aldridge's height (5-9) and weight (150 pounds), plus the weather and water temperature. It told them that the longest Aldridge could likely stay afloat before hypothermia took over and his muscles gave out was nineteen hours. But that, they knew, was a best case. The reality was that very few people survived more than three or four hours in the North Atlantic, especially without a flotation device.

By 6:28, the command center had notified the search mission commander in New Haven, Jonathan Theel, and the search coordinator at the district headquarters in Boston, who would have to approve the use of any aircraft in the search. At 6:30, Davis issued a universal distress call on channel sixteen: "Pan pan. Pan pan. Pan pan," he intoned, the international maritime code for an urgent broadcast. "This is United States Coast Guard Sector Long Island Sound. The Coast Guard has received a report of a man overboard off the fishing vessel Anna Mary, south of Montauk, between five and sixty miles offshore. All mariners are requested to keep a sharp lookout."

Davis kept working the radio. He contacted the Coast Guard station in Montauk with instructions to launch whatever boats were available. Boston approved the use of two helicopters and a search plane, and Davis radioed Air Station Cape Cod and told them to get airborne as soon as possible. The closest Coast Guard cutter, an eighty-seven-footer called the Sailfish, was in New York Harbor, and Davis directed its crew to start heading east.

Rodocker, meanwhile, was manning the computer. The Coast Guard has used computer simulations in search and rescue since the mid-1970s, but Sarops has been in use since only 2007. At its heart is a Monte Carlo-style simulator that can generate, in just a few minutes, as many as 10,000 points to represent how far and in what direction a "search object" might have drifted. Operators input a variety of data, from the last known location of a lost mariner to the ocean currents and wind direction. Sarops then creates a map of a search area—in this case, of the ocean south of Montauk—with colored squares representing each potential location for the search object. Red and orange squares represent the most likely locations; gray squares represent the least likely.

The challenge in Aldridge's case was that the search team had no clear idea when—and therefore where—he fell overboard. It might have been five minutes after Sosinski went to sleep, or it might have been five minutes before he woke up. That created a potential search area the size of Rhode Island, a sweep of ocean thirty miles wide, starting at the Montauk lighthouse and extending sixty miles south. This was a big problem: In contrast to the sophisticated algorithms of Sarops, the Coast Guard's basic searching technique is a low-tech one—human beings staring at the ocean, looking for a person's head bobbing in the waves. An 1,800-square-mile search area would be almost impossible to cover.

The team in New Haven based its initial calculations on Sosinski's report that Aldridge was supposed to wake him up at 11:30 p.m. That suggested to them that Aldridge fell overboard between 9:30 p.m. and 11:30 p.m., which would put him somewhere between five and twenty miles south of the Long Island coast. Rodocker input those assumptions, and Sarops came back with an "Alpha Drift"—its first scatter plot of search particles—that curved in a thick parabola from Montauk Point southward, bulging out toward the east, with the highest-probability locations, the reddest squares on the map, clustered about fifteen miles offshore.

The next step for Sarops was to develop search patterns for each boat and aircraft, dividing up the search area into squares and rectangles and assigning each vessel a zone to search and a pattern to use. A little before 8 a.m., New Haven started issuing patterns to the first three assets on the scene: the plane, a helicopter and a forty-seven-foot patrol boat from Montauk. Sarops can assign all kinds of patterns, depending on the conditions—a track line, a creeping line, an expanding square—but in this case, each search crew was assigned what's called a parallel search: a rectangular S-shaped pattern, with long search tracks proceeding roughly north and south and a small jog to the west between each track.

The helicopter was a Sikorsky Jayhawk piloted by two young lieutenants from Air Station Cape Cod named Mike Deal and Ray Jamros. Flying a Jayhawk in the Coast Guard, like many jobs these days, involves looking at a lot of screens: seven in total, spread out in front of Deal and Jamros in the cockpit, showing live maps, radar images and search patterns. When the parallel pattern came in from New Haven, the coordinates fed directly into the helicopter's navigation system, meaning that the pilots were able to simply turn on the autopilot and let the helicopter fly the search pattern on its own. That allowed Deal and Jamros to turn their attention away from the screens and toward the water below them. They were joined in their search by two crew members who sat in the back of the helicopter: a rescue swimmer named Bob Hovey and a flight mechanic named Ethan Hill. Deal and Jamros scanned the ocean through their cockpit windows; Hill sat perched in the wide-open door on the right side of the helicopter, where he had the clearest view of the water below. Hovey spent most of his time staring at yet another screen, this one displaying the output of an infrared radar camera mounted on the bottom of the helicopter.

The Coast Guard search was off to an excellent start. It was a clear day with good visibility, and they had plenty of assets in place. The only problem, of course, was that everyone involved was searching in entirely the wrong place. Aldridge did not fall in the water at 10:30 p.m.; he fell in at 3:30 a.m. Almost thirty miles south of where the Jayhawk crew was carefully searching for him, Aldridge was clinging to his boots in the cold water.

Back in New Haven, Pete Winters was having second thoughts about the Alpha Drift. He borrowed the microphone from Sean Davis and radioed the Anna Mary directly. "Talk to me, Captain," he said to Sosinski. "Fisherman to fisherman. Help me reduce this search area. We need to narrow it down so we can find John."

Throughout his long career with the Coast Guard, Winters worked on the side as a commercial fisherman on the North Fork of Long Island, like his grandfather and his uncle before him. This gave him an advantage when a search-and-rescue operation involved commercial fishermen, especially Long Island fishermen: He spoke their language.

Sosinski had also been having second thoughts about the search area. After his initial conversation with Davis, he inspected the boat more carefully, and he found a few important clues. One hatch cover was upside down on the deck, which every mariner knows is bad luck—an upside-down hatch cover means your boat is going to wind up upside down, too. Aldridge must have left it propped up against the side of the boat when he opened the hatch—and he wouldn't have left it there for long. The pumps were on, sluicing cool ocean water through the lobster tanks, which meant that Aldridge had been pre-paring them for the day's catch. And in the warm summer months, Aldridge and Sosinski would usually wait to start filling the tanks until their boat reached the forty-fathom curve, the line on maritime charts that marks where the ocean's depth hits forty fathoms, or 240 feet, which is the point at which the water temperature tends to drop. The forty-fathom curve is only about fifteen miles north of the Anna Mary's first trawl. Then Sosinski found the broken handle on the ice chest, and he realized exactly how Aldridge had fallen over-board. It was still difficult for Sosinski to reconcile this new informa-tion with the fact that Aldridge hadn't woken him up at 11:30 p.m., as scheduled, but he knew that Aldridge liked to push himself, and it didn't seem entirely uncharacteristic that his friend might have just decided to stay up all night, alone, before working an eighteen-hour day pulling in traps.

Together Sosinski and Winters came up with a new theory: Al-dridge had gone overboard somewhere between the forty-fathom curve, about twenty-five miles offshore, and the Anna Mary's first trawl, about forty miles offshore. At 8:30 a.m., Winters passed this new information to Rodocker, who punched it into Sarops. When the new map emerged, most of the dark-red search particles had mi-grated south of the forty-fathom curve, and Sarops quickly developed a second, more southerly, set of search patterns.

Theel, the search-mission commander in New Haven, then turned his attention to a more difficult duty: informing Aldridge's parents. He called John Aldridge Sr., who called his wife to the phone, and they sat together, listening to Theel deliver the news of their son's disappearance. Mrs. Aldridge was hopeful, but Mr. Aldridge felt cer-tain his son was already dead. If he hadn't been killed by the propel-lers when he fell overboard, he had surely drowned by now. Pretty soon, he thought, Theel would be calling back to say that the helicop-ters had found John's lifeless body floating in the waves, or that the Coast Guard had decided to suspend the search.

The news about Aldridge was also spreading through Montauk's fishing community. Much of the town's commercial fleet was out on the water that morning. Some fishermen heard Sosinski's anguished first call for help. Others heard Sean Davis's pan-pan broadcast. And then word traveled from boat to boat, back to the dock and then all over Montauk. The mood in town was grim. Everyone knew the odds: a man overboard, that far off the coast, would very likely never be found alive.

Most of the fishermen who heard the news had the same immediate response, wherever they were: They wanted to help with the search. Richard Etzel, the captain of a Montauk charter boat, had taken a group of customers out at dawn that morning to fish for striped bass. When he heard the news over the radio, he took his customers back in, fueled up and headed south. At the Montauk Marine Basin, a mechanic borrowed a customer's center-console boat—without actually mentioning it to the customer—and took off toward the fishing grounds. Jimmy Buffett, the singer, who has a summer house in Montauk, had that morning hired Paul Stern, one of the best big-tuna fishermen on the East Coast, to take him out in Buffett's boat, the Last Mango. When Stern heard about Aldridge, he asked Buffett if they could join the search. Buffett agreed, and the Last Mango headed south as well.

In total, twenty-one commercial boats volunteered to look for Aldridge. And as they set out, one by one, they flipped their radios over to channel sixteen and alerted the Coast Guard that they were joining the search. Usually, when good Samaritans volunteer to take part in a search-and-rescue mission, the Coast Guard politely declines. It's too complicated; the civilians don't know the search patterns; and their searches aren't always reliable. In this case, though, the search area was so vast that the Coast Guard needed all the help it could get. And these were highly motivated volunteers who knew the area well. Theel didn't want to turn down that kind of help. Still, Sean Davis couldn't possibly coordinate twenty-one new search patterns on top of all the Coast Guard craft he was already directing. So Winters hit on an idea: They would put Anthony Sosinski in charge of the volunteer fishing fleet.

Sosinski said yes to the assignment, of course—he would have done anything to find Aldridge—but organizing twenty-one fishing boats into a search party would be a daunting task for anyone, and Sosinski was distraught and disoriented, standing alone in the cramped wheelhouse of the Anna Mary in his bare feet and shorts. In contrast to the high-tech work stations in New Haven, Sosinski's only work surface was a chest-high countertop by the boat's front window that was always piled high with unopened mail, newspaper clippings, notebooks, tide charts and rolls of paper towel and electrical tape. Sosinski dug through the mess until he found a pen, then got on the radio and asked the volunteer searchers to give him their latitude and longitude.

To outsiders, Sosinski looked more like a surfer than a fisherman: long, sun-bleached blond hair that he was constantly pushing back from his eyes, untamed facial hair and a face tanned and creased by years in the sun. On his days off, he would usually smoke some marijuana to calm himself; when he was in charge of the boat's satellite radio, he inevitably chose the '70s station. He was short and muscular, always humming with energy, talkative, jittery—all of which made for a sharp contrast with most Montauk fishermen, who tended to be laconic and reserved. But Sosinski had been on the dock since he was a teenager, and he had earned a certain kind of respect—or at least affection—among the Montauk fishing fleet.

When Sosinski was growing up in Oakdale, his father worked as a tractor-trailer driver during the week, delivering lumber up and down Long Island. But most Friday nights, his father would drive to Montauk for the weekend, where he'd work a second job as a deckhand for the Viking fleet, Montauk's biggest charter company, helping out on half-day party-boat charters. When Sosinski turned twelve, he started tagging along on his father's weekend trips, and in high school, Sosinski spent each summer living on a houseboat moored at the Montauk dock, working full time for Viking. As soon as he finished high school, Sosinski moved to Montauk and started commercial fishing. He married at twenty, and by the time he was twenty-four, he had two daughters and a job on a long-line tilefish boat, going out for ten days at a time.

Then Sosinski returned from a fishing trip to find that his wife had left town with their children. No note, no forwarding address. For 14 months he searched for his family, until he finally found them in Laguna, Calif. After a long legal battle, Sosinski won custody of both of his daughters and brought them back to Montauk, where he raised them as a single father, doing everything from attending

P.T.A. meetings to cooking dinner to making sure they both got into college. While the girls were young, he worked close to shore on a small lobster boat so that he could be home every night.

Aldridge and Sosinski first fished together as boys, riding their bikes to a spot they found under Sunrise Highway and pedaling home with their bicycle baskets filled with trout. Once Aldridge joined Sosinski in Montauk, they fished for years on separate boats, but when a beat-up lobster boat called the Anna Mary came up for sale, they decided to pool their money and buy it together. It took more than a year of repair work in the boatyard to make the Anna Mary seaworthy, and the men were in their late thirties by the time they finally got it out on the water. But it felt to both of them like the opportunity they had been waiting for—no boss, working together, setting their own hours, charting their own course.

Throughout the 1990s and early 2000s, Montauk's commercial fisheries had been contracting, a casualty, depending on whom you asked, of rampant overfishing or excessive government regulation. Every year, there were fewer commercial boats going out. But Sosinski and Aldridge made it work. They found a buyer for their lobsters in Sayville who would ship them on the ferries to Fire Island. They sold their crabs to Chinese markets in Queens. They weren't getting rich—maintaining lobster traps and a boat is an expensive undertaking—but they were doing all right. And they were still fishing side by side, more than 30 years after they first dropped their hooks in the water.

Now, quite literally, Sosinski had lost his best friend. All day, as he stared out at the vast rolling ocean, he felt helpless and guilty. If only he'd woken up a few hours earlier, he told himself, Aldridge would have taken his shift in the bunk, and right now they'd be pulling in lobster traps together. He tried to focus all his energy on directing the commercial boats in north-south tracking lines, trying to keep all their locations straight. But none of it felt like enough. Aldridge had left his driver's license in the wheelhouse, propped up next to the radio, and every once in a while, during the search, Sosinski would pick it up and hold it in his hand. He'd stare at it and say out loud: *Where are you, John?*

* * *

The sun rose on John Aldridge at about 5:30 on the morning of July 24. He was cold, thirsty and tired—he'd been awake for twenty-four hours—but he was still alive and afloat. Now that it was light, he gave himself a new assignment: find a buoy. To most people, the Atlantic Ocean forty miles south of Montauk is just a big, undifferentiated expanse of waves, but Aldridge knew roughly where he fell overboard—a few miles south of the forty-fathom curve. And he knew that several lobster fishermen had trawls nearby—he knew them by name, in fact. Each lobster trawl is a string of thirty to fifty traps, spaced 150 feet apart at the bottom of the ocean, and at the end of each string, a rope extends up from the last trap to the surface, where it is tied to a big round vinyl buoy. If Aldridge could make his way to a buoy, he figured, he would be more visible to the searchers, and it would be easier to stay afloat.

But where to find one? For the first couple of hours of daylight, Aldridge just drifted and looked. Every ten seconds or so, a swell would carry him up a few feet, and when he got to the top of the wave, he'd scan the horizon for a buoy. Finally, at the peak of one wave, he spotted a buoy a couple of hundred yards away and began swimming toward it. He took a sock off one foot and stretched it over his right hand, to give himself more pull. But it was slow going with the boots under his arms, and the current was against him. Each time he looked up, the buoy was a little farther away.

Aldridge realized he was exhausting himself, and he decided to cut his losses. He was able to see that the buoy he had been swimming toward had a flag on top of it, which lobster fishermen attach to the west end of their strings. Lobster traps are always laid out along an east-west line, so Aldridge figured that a mile or so to the east of the unreachable buoy, he would find the other end of that string of traps, and with it, another buoy. He started swimming east—*with* the current this time instead of against it—stopping briefly at the top of each swell to see if he could catch sight of the eastern buoy. It was painful work. His legs were cramping. He couldn't feel his fingers. The sun, rising higher in front of him, was blinding. But finally, after more than an hour, he spotted a buoy, and using the current, he was able to angle himself directly into it. He grabbed the rope and held on.

After a minute or two of relief, Aldridge discovered that the buoy wasn't quite the deliverance he was hoping for. Lobster buoys can be big—two feet or more in diameter—so it was impossible to get his arms around it or ride on top of it in any way. His only option was to grab on to the black vinyl eye at the bottom of the buoy that the rope was threaded through. The problem was, since the buoy was tethered to the traps at the bottom of the ocean, it didn't rise, entirely, with the waves. Each time a swell rose, much of the buoy would submerge. Which meant that Aldridge would be dunked underwater as well.

By noon, Aldridge had been in the water for almost nine hours. He was starting to shiver uncontrollably. Sea shrimp and sea lice were fastening themselves to his T-shirt and shorts, claiming him as part of the sea. Storm petrels swarmed around occasionally, squawking and diving.

Aldridge could see the plane and the helicopters running their patterns, but everyone searching for him seemed to be at least a mile to the east. Clinging to the buoy, he realized that the Coast Guard thought he was still drifting. Even if they'd figured out more or less where he fell in, their search patterns hadn't taken into account the possibility that he snagged a buoy. Aldridge knew if he wanted to have a chance of being found, he had to get himself farther east. He took out his buck knife and started chopping away at the rope that held the buoy in place. When he got it free, he tied it around his wrist and began swimming east again, holding the buoy in front of him.

As he went, he felt the energy drain from his body. His kicks and strokes were weakening. The sun rose higher, and the skin on his face and neck began to blister and burn. Then, at the top of one swell, impossibly, he spotted the Anna Mary, less than a quarter-mile in front of him. Mike Migliaccio was standing on the roof, and Aldridge hollered with all the strength he could muster. He tried to throw the buoy up in the air to attract attention, but the boat was too far away. For the second time that day, Aldridge watched as the Anna Mary receded into the distance without him, and he began to contemplate the reality he'd kept at bay in his mind for all these hours, that no matter what he did, he might not be rescued after all.

He willed himself to keep kicking until eventually—he doesn't know how much time went by—he reached another buoy. He recognized that it belonged to his friend Pete Spong, a Rhode Island fisherman who owned a lobster boat called the Brooke C. He untied the rope from his wrist and tied it to the anchor rope underneath the new buoy. Now he had two buoys connected by a few feet of rope. He swung his leg over the rope and straddled it, facing east. The thick rope rubbed back and forth on his crotch and his legs as the waves rose and fell, chafing them raw, but at least he wasn't being pulled underwater anymore. He repositioned the boots under his arms, and he waited, knowing that this was as far as he could go, that he couldn't survive another swim. If he was still in the water at sundown, he decided, he would tie himself to the Brooke C's buoy. That way, at least someone would find his body, and his parents would have something to bury.

Up in the Jayhawk helicopter, Deal and Jamros and Hovey and Hill had been staring at the water since about 7 a.m., and by early afternoon, they were growing discouraged. They had a few false alarms during the day—sea turtles and mylar balloons—and with each possible sighting, they followed the same protocol: the person who saw the object would call out: "Mark. Mark. Mark." One pilot would hit a button in the cockpit that would mark the location, and they would swing the helicopter back around to check it out. Each time, nothing.

The truth of working as a search-and-rescue helicopter pilot for the Coast Guard is that you don't get to do a lot of actual rescuing. Deal had been in the Coast Guard for eight years, flying a Jayhawk for three, and he had never once pulled anyone alive from the water. They had all trained for it countless times, plucked dummies out of the ocean, run through checklists and drills until they had them memorized. But the reality was that almost every time a person went overboard in the North Atlantic, he drowned.

At 2:19 p.m., the helicopter crew finished another parallel search pattern—their third of the day—and radioed to Sean Davis to request a new one. They were about an hour from bingo fuel, the moment at which they would have only enough gas to make it home. And once they stopped to refuel, they knew, they would be in fatigue status, and Coast Guard regulations would then stipulate that they couldn't take off again until the next day—at which point Aldridge would be well past his nineteen-hour survivability window.

Davis radioed back from New Haven with some unwelcome news: Sarops had crashed. The search had been going on so long and involved so many assets that the system became overloaded; the screens in the command center simply froze. After much shouting and cursing and pounding on keyboards, Rodocker had to restart the system, and now he was typing in all the relevant information again. For the time being, Sarops couldn't produce search patterns. Davis instructed the Jayhawk crew to return to its base in Cape Cod—even if Rodocker was able to get Sarops running soon, bingo fuel was fast approaching, and there wouldn't be time for them to do a full search pattern anyway.

They radioed back and argued with Davis. They were out there anyway, and they still had a *little* fuel—why not give them something to do? The search unit in New Haven finally agreed, and in the command center, Rodocker, Winters and the command duty officer, a civilian named Mark Averill, huddled around Rodocker's computer and looked at the latest Sarops map. Pointing with his finger on the screen, Averill proposed a simple track-line search: the Jayhawk would head south-southeast for about ten miles, straight through the main search area, then turn sharply to the north for another ten miles, then veer north-northwest, which would take the crew straight back to Air Station Cape Cod. It wasn't a conventional pattern, and it wasn't Sarops-generated, but it would have to do. Davis radioed the coordinates to Deal and Jamros, who fed them manually into their autopilot, and at 2:46 p.m., the helicopter started moving again.

Twelve minutes later, Ray Jamros called out "Mark! Mark! Mark!"—only now he was much louder and more insistent than he had been all day. Deal hit the mark button in the cockpit and turned the helicopter around. And there was John Aldridge, sitting on the rope between his two buoys, clutching his boots and waving frantically. Bob Hovey, the rescue swimmer, clipped his harness onto the helicopter's hoist cable, and Hill lowered him into the water. As Hovey swam to Aldridge, Hill lowered a rescue basket, and Hovey helped Aldridge climb in. Just as Hill was about to raise him up, Aldridge realized that his boots were floating away, and he yelled to Hovey to grab them and put them in the basket with him.

After Aldridge was safely in the helicopter huddled under blankets, Deal flipped the radio to channel twenty-one and called Sosinski, who was somewhere below them, staring out at the water, still looking for Aldridge. "Anna Mary," Deal said, "we have your man. He's alive."

There's a bar in Montauk, a few steps from the Anna Mary's slip, called the Dock, a dark, wood-paneled place with stuffed animal heads on the wall and signs that say things like "No Shrimpers, No Scallopers," and "We've upped our standards. Up yours." It is one of the dwindling number of places in town that feels as if it belongs to the people who live and work there year-round. If you step inside the Dock any given afternoon, you'll very likely find fishermen drinking and talking about ballgames and elections, D.U.I.'s and divorces. You're very likely, too, to hear them talking, sometimes overtly, sometimes not, about the loss of a way of life—the government regulations that make it harder to make a living as a commercial fisherman, the vanishingly small margins for doing the dangerous work they do, the way this place where they've made their home is less recognizable to them with each passing year.

In the weeks after Aldridge's rescue, I talked to several local fishermen on the docks about the search, and not only did they all admit that they cried when they heard the news that Aldridge was safe, but most of them teared up again, despite themselves, as they were telling me the story. It was hard to say what, exactly, was bringing them to tears. But what seems to go mostly unspoken in their lives is the inescapable risk of their jobs, and the improbable fact that Aldridge hadn't drowned in the Atlantic somehow underscored that risk for them even more. He'd kept himself alive in a way that few people could, had managed to think and work his way through a situation that, for most of us, would have been immediately and completely overwhelming. And he'd willed himself to live. To be a fisherman and to really know the danger of the sea, and to think of Aldridge in the middle of the ocean for all those hours refusing to go under—maybe that was too much to contain.

The person who seems least shaken by the experience is John Aldridge. He spent the night after his rescue in a hospital in Cape Cod, being treated for hypothermia, dehydration and exposure, but he has no post-traumatic stress, he told me: no nightmares, no flashbacks, no fear when he goes out on the water to work. The Coast Guard pilots and the men in the search unit in New Haven express a certain understandable pride when they talk about their work that day, and when Aldridge talks about it, he sounds the same way. "I always felt like I was conditioning myself for that situation," he told me one day in September while we were sitting in the Dock. "So once you're in it, it's like: All right, I can do that. I did it. I had that sense of accomplishment. I mean, thank God I was saved, yes. Thank God they saved me. There's no better entity than the U.S. Coast Guard to come save your ass when you're on the water. But I felt I did my part."

For the people around him, though, things haven't been quite so easy. Aldridge's father told me that he still often wakes up around 3 a.m. and can't get back to sleep. "It's something that you can't kick," he said. "It's never out of my mind. Never." A few weeks after his son's rescue, John Sr. got a tattoo on his arm: a pair of big green fishing boots, and between them, the G.P.S. coordinates where his son was found.

Anthony Sosinski still seems shaken as well. For all his happy-go-lucky charm, his love of life, something changed for him on July 24. The last time he and I talked about it, we were sitting in the wheelhouse of the Anna Mary, which was tied up at the Town Dock. "More than anything, I think about it when I'm out there working," he explained. "It was the whole feeling of helplessness. Something was torn out of me, and that part doesn't just show back up."

For Montauk as a community, the ocean remains a blessing and a curse. It is the lifeblood of the town, the essence of its economic livelihood, the reason the tourists keep coming back. But it is also a constant threat. In September, a twenty-four-year-old Montauk commercial fisherman named Donald Alversa was killed on a fishing trip on a dragger off the coast of North Carolina. Alversa grew up in Montauk—he went to school with Sosinski's older daughter—and Sosinski and Aldridge attended his wake.

The funeral home was crowded, and the mood was somber. When it was over, the Dock filled up, and the mourners drank late into the night. The next evening, after Alversa's funeral, Sosinski and Aldridge met at the Anna Mary. They loaded on bait and ice, steered her past the lighthouse and went back to work.

TOM MCALLISTER

■

Things You're Not Proud Of

FROM *Unstuck*

"ARE THERE PEOPLE living inside our pipes?" my wife asks.

"Of course there are not people living inside our pipes," I say, but: of course there are people living inside our pipes. Where does she expect them to stay? A hotel?

The thing she has never understood, will clearly never understand, is this: real estate. Capital. Supply, demand. It's the reality of the world. Homes are not affordable. Banks are broken. So you move inside somebody's pipes if you have to move inside somebody's pipes. It's happening everywhere.

They're not proud of it. But life is full of things you're not proud of.

She tells me to Drano the pipes, so I ask her if she's okay with the moral implications of massacring the people inside the pipes just because she doesn't like undrained water rising above her ankles when she showers.

"I thought you said nobody lived in there," she says.

"They don't," I say.

While she's out buying the Drano, I'm lying facedown in the tub, warning the people in the pipes. She doesn't know them like I do, doesn't respect them, but I understand where she's coming from. The tub drains too slowly. They pose legitimate health and safety hazards—it has to be against the health code to have people living in there, with their back hair and fluids and communicable diseases. The chaos of their conversations rattles within the pipes, and when they shout at one another about money, the walls hum and clang. They claim they can't see our bodies when we're showering, but I suspect they can see our bodies when we're showering.

So I get it. I do.

Still and also, I am not enthused about killing them just because their existence is a little inconvenient to my own.

They think I'm bluffing. They say: You don't have the guts. They say: Could you stop peeing in the shower?

I say, "If you're going to stay here, we need to establish some ground rules."

I am still in the tub when she returns from the hardware store, am still working out a verbal contract with the people in the pipes. Negotiations have been arduous; they won't even make simple concessions, i.e., they won't tell me how many people are in there, let alone agree to stop inviting friends over for parties.

"Listen," I said. "She's home, and I'm the only one who can stop her from killing you."

This isn't right, the patriarch says. He says: Threats of violence. What happened to good-faith negotiations? What happened to constitutional rights?

Deeper in the pipes there is a flush of applause. He says: I'm sending an email to my congressman.

I didn't even know they had Internet access in there.

My wife is downstairs mixing something in a bucket. Two parts water, three parts mystery powder, one part frustration. The mixture seems to be thickening, because she needs two hands to twist an old paint stirrer through it, and she's hunkering to generate torque with her midsection and to power through with the legs. Her back is turned to me, and I think about making some kind of joke about witches and cauldrons, but I can't quite come up with the right phrasing and anyway, she does not like jokes at her expense, not even flirty ones.

We are both in our kitchen, which is fully upgraded and has new granite counters and custom cabinets and a heated tile floor and recessed lighting and everything else you're supposed to have, according to the people on TV. When you don't have children to pay for, you can afford the so-called finer things in life. The plan was to have three children. It would go like this: girl, boy, boy, and their names would all begin with the letter B, because my wife read on the internet that B is a letter of strength, is a structurally sound letter that would equip them for handling the daily grind, but the plan was flawed because you cannot make your bodies do what you want them to do on cue, you cannot predict that you will have faulty equipment incapable of impregnating your wife. We financed the kitchen upgrades with money that had been earmarked for Barbara's college fund, the same way Buster's summer camp money had paid for our bathroom remodel and Blake's sports equipment and travel budget had been diverted to pay for last year's seven-day, six-night, three-fight Caribbean cruise.

She is wearing a tank top and her shoulders are more muscular than I remember. She seems to be calling on a younger version of herself to aid in the stirring, and I am moved, mindlessly, to sneak up behind her and grab onto her hips, kiss her behind her ear, tease her bra strap out of place with my teeth.

She shrugs me away. "I'm stirring, can't you see I'm stirring?"

I can see it. I just thought she looked good, felt myself flashing back to weekends fifteen years ago, afternoons when she casually walked around the house nude and we cooked meals as a team and made plans with friends just so that later we could break them and spend the time together. Now we order Chinese. Now I have guys' nights and she has girls' weekends. Now she wears socks to bed so I can't see her toes. Now I spend nights sitting in the bathtub and talking to the people who live in my pipes.

She hands me the bucket and says, "Keep stirring."

The man at the hardware store—his name was Timothy, she tells me, even though I don't care what his name is, or that the letter T is a bridge-building letter which means he's skilled at connecting with people—was very helpful. He was waiting at the front door and when he asked if he could help her with anything, she told him she needed all the help she could get. My wife says he took her hands in his and looked her in the eyes in a really serious way, like a hypnotist or a furniture salesman, and he told her he had exactly what she needed. He led her to the storage room in the back to show her something special.

"I don't like where this is going," I say, which is meant to be kind of a lascivious joke.

"Okay, anyway," she says, "He takes me back there and he pulls down a box from the top shelf that says Do Not Open." It's an elixir, Timothy told her, banned in the US because of some bureaucratic nonsense, accidentally shipped to this hardware store instead of some toy factory in China.

What does the elixir do? It does everything. It solves problems. It's like having a mom you can call on any time of day. "Why do you think Chinese people are so happy?" she says Timothy said. "Why do you think they've advanced so far beyond us?"

What Timothy told her was we could use it on the drain, but we wouldn't be exploiting its full potential. We're supposed to apply it to any problem area. Two coats if necessary. I ask her if she's sure this is a good idea, isn't it maybe possible that this is a dangerous thing to do, and what if we get a second opinion from another person at a different hardware store? Or a doctor even.

"One of us needs to be willing to solve problems," she says. "One of us needs to be a doer."

It's true, she's the doer and I'm the reactor. Like when that swampy smell creeped up from the basement and I told her it's just what happens to older houses—they start to smell—but she called in the building inspector and they found all that mold in the walls. Or like the time the sinkhole formed in our backyard and she wanted me to fill it but I didn't fill it because it seemed like backbreaking work and anyway the new dirt was just going to sink too. So why delay the inevitable? But she called in a guy—she always wants to call a guy, and I have to admit the guy usually knows how to fix things. It seems to me that as long as things get fixed, it doesn't much matter who gets the credit for the fixing, but my wife does not agree. When she wants something badly enough, she is a missile bearing down on an insurgent, she is momentum personified. "What if one of us needs to be a not-doer," I say. "What if the thing to do sometimes is to not do anything?"

"You've tried not doing anything for five years," she says. "There's nothing noble about moping around the house and wondering what happened to us. Sometimes you just need to hammer a nail a little harder. You need to tighten the screw." She dips a finger in the bucket then swipes it across my gumline, says it ought to fix my crooked incisor, and maybe it will make my jokes funnier.

Texture of a pulverized crayon, taste of an overripe orange.

My jokes are equally as funny as they were fifteen years ago, when she thought they were plenty funny. I want that on the record.

I dab some of the paste on her chin where she seems to have given up the fight against her persistent sprouting hairs. I rub some into her ears so maybe she'll become a more generous listener. She shoves her index finger up my nose to stop my snoring.

"What happened with the Drano?" I ask, her finger still in my nose. My mouth feels alien and my voice is distant, like I'm hearing an actor on a TV in another room.

"I forgot about the Drano," she says. She forgot about the Drano.

There is a sound like cheering in the ceiling above us.

Two days later, the elixir is half gone, and we are both covered head to toe in a turgid paste. She is nude and I am nude, both of us spectral in the glowing whiteness of the elixir, my joints feeling like a twenty-year-old's joints—not my twenty-year-old self, but some other, better twenty-year-old, a high-jumper who can squat two-fifty and who never wakes up in the middle of the night with cramps in his legs. It's easier to feel optimistic when your body feels so charged with possibilities; when you hit a certain age, you have to focus on just staying awake all day, and you don't have time to work on marriage anymore, you want the marriage to work on itself. When we met, it was because the algorithms on a website determined that we were a good match; she wanted a man who didn't drink and who ran 5Ks on weekends and who had a well-kempt beard and perfect vision and a decent job with potential for promotion and the know-how to make minor home repairs, and I wanted a woman who wanted a man like me, and the website delivered me to her. Computers are amazing, but they cannot predict everything. There was no way it could predict that I would have faulty equipment or that I would hate spending time with her family or that if I spent a couple of hours in the mornings browsing porn sites she would want to call it an addiction. The computer never could have known that even though we had fun on dates and we had the same taste in music and held roughly similar religious views, that we were not cut out for living together, couldn't predict how quickly we would discover all the ways to irritate each other day to day and wear each other down to raw nerve endings that could be inflamed by even the slightest misstep. Couples counseling didn't work for me. Eventually it turned into solo counseling for her every Monday and Wednesday evening.

My wife's eyes are psychedelically charged, changing color from blue to green to a deep orange like a tabby. Her laugh is sharper and more crystalline. Her voice sounds luxurious but accessible, like a wind chime made of rare sea glass. She grabs a handful of the elixir and rubs it all over my groin and my faulty equipment, and immediately I can feel myself producing vibrant, potent semen, envision millions of B-named children swelling inside of me, begging to be released. We call out of work and pull the curtains and do things to each other's bodies that we have never done, and she says she already feels like she is pregnant, already feels like a mother. Triplets inside of her, growing.

The next day we are already running low on the compound, but we still have enough to keep us going. We hold hands because we want to, not because we need to put on a show for everyone at the company picnic. Her heart thumps against her ribs and we hear it like a bass drum. I tell her we ought to trade hearts, put mine in her and hers in me, see what happens. She says okay, but later, and then she says as long as we feel like we're twenty, we should do what twenty-year-olds do. She says, "we were both so much better before," and I look at her and I realize how sad she is to be getting old. I see how hard it is on her to be this deep into a life she doesn't want.

So I agree with her: let's be twenty. Acting like a twenty-year-old means being reckless, it means feeling no pain ever, it means being oblivious to both past and future.

We put on clothes and we go for a run, beyond our suburban development and alongside traffic and through woods as far and as fast as we can go until we are lost but we are not afraid. She climbs a tree and says she's a squirrel and wants me to chase her so I chase her from tree to tree.

We don't get home until early morning, because we spend hours wandering the woods and then we hitch with a man who looks like his side job is modeling for Wanted posters. We sneak in through the bedroom window—I give her a boost, then she lowers the fire ladder for me to climb up. It's as if we are young and our old, beaten selves are our parents waiting for us in the living room. She shushes me and I shush her and in the dark of our bedroom we both see everything so clearly it's blinding.

On the fifth day, there is no more elixir and the paste is flaking off of our bodies. My eyes feel heavy like ball bearings, and my throat sometimes closes involuntarily, forces me to consciously attend to my own breathing. My wife checks her pulse every ten minutes, says she feels like a bird, hollow-boned and graceful. She rubs her belly now and then, the absent-minded way an expectant mother is supposed to do. She presses my hand against her so that together we can feel the kicking of the triplets she is incubating. This wasn't the plan exactly, but it's better than having no plan at all, she says. The people inside the pipes seem to be having a party, the pipes groaning and whistling urgently, the house clattering like an overworked radiator.

On the sixth day, she rolls out of bed, spends a long time in the bathroom. I watch her still shadow beneath the door. She turns on the exhaust so I can't hear her crying—an old trick.

My body is turning forty-three again. I feel growing pains like I've never felt before.

The door swings open and she emerges slowly. Her eyes are swollen and her mouth looks like a collapsed bridge.

"I got my period," she says. Even in the pipes there is silence.

My tongue tingles, my hearing is alarmingly acute, but otherwise, I am back to normal, which is to say I am worse off than I was a week ago because I've tasted the good life and lost it. We both go back to work on Monday. And we revert to watching television quietly next to each other on the couch. We order Chinese for dinner and eat leftovers for four days. At night, I lie in the tub and talk to the people in the pipes. They seem happy, relatively. They seem settled. They're developing a small business in there, removing unwanted body hairs from other people's home pipes, and they don't think there is any reason to ever return to the surface. They say it was bad at first, but the fresh start has rejuvenated them.

I ask if maybe I can come down and visit sometimes.

This isn't a tourist resort, the patriarch says. This is our home.

My wife wants to know who I'm talking to at night. She says she can hear me, says I should level with her and tell her if I'm having an affair.

I tell her I must be talking in my sleep.

"But you're not in bed," she says.

"I'm thinking of moving into the pipes," I say.

She goes to the hardware store that weekend, saying as she leaves, "I am going to fix this thing." Because divorce is not in her plan. Having a husband in the pipes is not in the plan. The elixir will get us back on track. She will buy enough to last as long as we need to feel something other than what we feel.

When she comes home, she tells me Timothy is gone, nobody knows what happened to him. Nobody has ever heard of the mystery elixir.

She removes a bottle of extra strength Drano from her bag. The label says *eliminates even the toughest clogs*, and there is a picture of an anthropomorphized clog—a mucousy, sinister knot of sludge and grime—screaming in terror as the patented formula advances on it.

She says, "If you can't take care of the problem, then I will."

I chase her up the stairs, but what am I going to do, tackle her? I am not going to tackle my wife. I don't want to hurt her. I don't hate her. I just also don't love her.

She pours the entire bottle into the tub's drain, even though the label says a half-bottle will do the job. The liquid is silver like mercury, glugs out of the bottle with drunken hiccups. The label says to allow thirty minutes for the liquid to penetrate the obstruction, and I envision it creeping like lava through the homes of my friends in the pipes, drowning them, igniting their lungs and chewing through their intestines. My wife and I sit beside each other on the tub's edge for a half hour listening to a shrieking like failing brakes. She won't let me leave, says I need to hear this, and I tell her she is a monster, ask how could you do this to anyone, let alone the harmless people in the pipes? I turn on the faucet, but that seems to expedite the process, the echoing, gurgling screams more frantic than ever. My wife sits behind me sweating, crying onto my shoulder, decade-old tears welling up from her, and I think, I should be in there too. Even as they're dying, I want to crawl down inside with them, to feel the burn on my skin, to feel myself purged, to be propelled through fevered heat and anguish and terror into whatever lies on the other side.

PAUL SALOPEK

■

Out of Eden Walk

FROM *National Geographic*

IN 2013 PULITZER PRIZE-WINNING *journalist Paul Salopek began walking through the Great Rift Valley of Ethiopa. For the next seven years he planned to retrace the footsteps of human migration, out of Africa and across the world. He is currently in his third year of walking, somewhere near Tbilisi, Georgia at the time of this writing. Along the way Salopek has been posting dispatches about the things he sees and the people he meets. His writing effortlessly blends historical information with contemporary observations, painting a rich, layered portrait of each location he visits. We have gathered some of our favorite posts here, beginning in Jordan, in the first few days of 2014.*

Tomatoes
January 9, 2014
Near Al Quweirah, Jordan, 29° 42' 56" N 35° 17' 14" E

We walk out of the desert and come to where the earth rises and falls beneath our footsteps in long, regular wales, like corduroy—fields of plowed sand. The hills of Wadi Rum fade in iron-colored light. Dusk is falling. It grows colder by the minute. A path leads through the thickening dark to tents that glow yellowly from within, like belled medusas adrift in a sunless sea. We tether our two cargo mules to large stones. We approach the first tent.

"*Sala'am aleukum,*" calls Hamoudi Enwaje' al Bedul, my guide.

The tent, which had been noisy with voices, falls silent. A man throws back the flap, and after an exchange in Arabic that lasts no longer than thirty seconds, he waves us in. Fifteen people sit inside atop foam mattresses. A sad-faced woman layered in sweaters—blue tribal tattoos dot each of her wrinkled cheeks, dot her chin—loads more sticks into a small woodstove. She beckons us to sit near the heat, in a circle of staring, wild-haired children. She pours us glasses of syrupy tea. She serves us a platter of fresh tomatoes, pickled green tomatoes, fried broccoli.

"There is no meat," the man apologizes. "Here, we only dream of chicken." Everyone in the tent laughs.

They are tomato pickers. They are Bedouins from Syria.

Officially, there are 550,000 Syrian war refugees in Jordan. But most people know better. The true number might be twice that. Tens of thousands of refugees languish inside two gigantic UN camps. Others drift into urban slums where they beg at potholed intersections. And many more, like the 104 people encamped outside Al Quweirah, rent out their muscles at desert farms. Many Jordanians complain bitterly about these guests. Unemployment is ruinously high in Jordan, where the local poor can't find work. The small country has been staggered over the years by throngs of Iraqi refugees, by long-homeless Palestinians, by émigrés fleeing troubled Egypt. Syrians are just the latest neighbors to arrive in exodus. They are a breaking wave of war-displaced people that ripples back millennia, to the conquests of Babylon, to the wanderers led by Moses through the wilderness.

Our host, a small, friendly, energetic man, tells this story:

Bashar al-Assad, the chinless ophthalmologist who presides over the abattoir called Syria, sent tanks against his own people the summer of 2011, following the popular uprisings of the Arab Spring. Shells ripped into bakeries, plowed into parks, drilled into apartment blocks. Soldiers shot every sheep and cow in sight. Wheat crops were torched. "We burned our family papers, our shoes, to survive the winter," the man says. "There was no bread. We tried grass to try to stop our hunger." Then one night he and his family—he sweeps an arm around the tent—grabbed their chance. They slipped through the siege lines and crossed into Jordan. The snow on the mountain passes reached their knees. They carried the smallest children.

"War, war, war. Syria goodbye." He slaps his palms together, cleaning off imagined dust. "It's finished!"

All of the tomato pickers came from the same Syrian province, from villages near the ancient city of Hamāh. Poor, star-crossed Hamāh! In 1982, the country's then-dictator—Al-Bashar's father—leveled the city during a previous uprising. (The CIA is believed to have supported the toppling of Syria's first elected president in 1949, initiating an unforeseen chain of coups that led to the Al-Bashar regime.) Hamāh fell to Tamerlane in 1400. It fell to Crusaders in 1108 and before that to Muslim armies in the seventh century. Almost 3,000 years ago, an Assyrian conqueror named Sargon II captured Hamāh and flayed alive its king.

About 120,000 people have died in the current civil war. I ask the man if he has lost any family members. He nods. A brother. A son. Shot by government troops in Hamāh. The woman gets up and leaves the tent. She doesn't come back. We all sit quietly for a moment under her beautiful handiwork: fine embroideries called *sarma*, which she has pinned to the inside walls of the canvas. She lugged these gold and white remnants of home with her across the Jordanian frontier.

In the icy morning Hamoudi and I heft our saddlebags onto the mules. The animals have gorged overnight on too-ripe tomatoes. The fields around the camp are garish with them. Hamoudi, a tribal man, a Bedouin, gives the woman, who has reappeared to brew tea, the jacket off his back. He gives her our cheese.

"It's cheese," he assures her when she stares at the foil-wrapped wedges in her calloused palms. She raises the cheese to her forehead. "Praise God," she says.

We walk on.

"*Solvatur ambulando,*" Diogenes proclaimed: "It is resolved by walking." But do you actually believe that grief can be walked away? It is like these goddamned tomatoes. Given the hands that picked them for $11 a day, you would think they would be inedible—too bitter to swallow. Toxic with pain. But they aren't. They are good tomatoes. They taste just fine.

(Note: Names of refugees have been intentionally withheld for their safety.)

The Eddy
March 27, 2014
Ghor Al Safi, Jordan 31°02'22" N 35°29'16" E

A sodden dusk.

We walk into the small market town soaked, muddied, dizzied by an astonishment: the first rains in a year of trekking. Rain varnishes the town's cratered pavements. Electric shop signs glint and glitter in the rain. Car taillights spill their cherry hues into puddles. In the drizzle, the street lamps burn like fireballs. A carnival of reflected light. Yet the rain deters no one! The streets are filled with splashing people. We tug our two weary pack mules through damp crowds at intersections. We are seeking lodging—a roof, a room, anything. But what are these townsmen doing outside? Are they celebrating the precipitation? It seems plausible, in such a parched Middle Eastern town. I glimpse their faces. I am startled. They are African.

"Never use the word abed here!" Hamoudi Enwaje' al Bedul, my Bedouin guide, whispers into my ear. He wags a finger in warning. "Big problem!"

As if I would. *Abed*: slave, an Arabic insult for Africans. A painful slur. Hamoudi is tense. He is out of his element—a tribal man, this citizen of the desert—in such an alien place. But I am warmed, comforted, charmed even: I lived in Africa for more than a decade. It is my favorite continent. And here, somehow, I have stumbled across a remnant population of Africans living in the Jordan Valley. I am transported instantly back to the walk's starting line. As it turns out, though, we may both be mistaken, Hamoudi and I.

"I don't know where we come from," says Muhammad Zahran, the director of the local museum, who permits us to sleep in the guard's kiosk. "I'm not sure we came from Africa. We could have been Ottoman soldiers. Many people here are from Amman. Or Bedouin tribes or Egyptians. Or Palestinians or Syrians. We are mixed."

Zahran refers to his ethnic group, the Ghawarna—dark-skinned Jordanians who farm the great alluvial fans south of the Dead Sea. I stare at him, puzzled. He looks like my friends from Ethiopia or Somalia. Moreover, cursory research reveals that scholars agree: The Ghawarna, who number in the tens of thousands, are genetically African. They came to Middle East unwillingly, as slaves, either to work in twelfth-century sugarcane fields (a colossal sugar mill has been unearthed near Ghor al Safi) or as house slaves in the nineteenth-century. But the townspeople I question, like Zahran, bat away the idea. They frown. They shrug. They disagree.

"Maybe it's the sun here," the manager of women's sewing coop, Nawfa al Nawasra, suggests. "Maybe it just burns us darker." Al Nawasra informs me that her ancestors come from Iraq.

What is going on?

"The Ghawarna have been the subject of color prejudices for a very long time in Jordan," says Edward Curtis, a professor of religious studies at Indiana University, in Indianapolis. "The local solution, in this context, is to adopt a totally Arab identity."

Curtis recently conducted an ethnographic study in Ghor al Safi and concluded that no identifiably African folk traditions exist. No oral histories peg Africa as the ancestral home. Such is the power of discrimination, underdevelopment, and shame in one of Jordan's poorest regions. Relatively little intermarriage goes on between the Ghawarna and other Jordanian ethnic groups.

"I came looking for a narrative of black Muslim pride," Curtis says. "But that turned out to be my own American idea. These folks don't even see themselves as African. They are Arabs who happen to be black."

The basis of identity, of race, is not in any sense granitic.

It is highly fluid. It is like a river—a tidal stream, in fact: Its flow is not linear, but one that winds and bends, drifting first in one direction, then in another. Not only could our direct ancestors have been different colors through time: Given the right combination of migratory patterns and solar exposure, they could have been different colors several times over. This isn't a philosophical viewpoint. It is genetics. Scientists think that skin pigmentation can change appreciably in as little as 100 generations.

The next morning Hamoudi and I plod north up the Jordan Valley. We drive the two mules before us.

We are both mistaken about the river's eddy called Ghor al Safi. Walking fast, Hamoudi puts uneasy distance between himself and a town of apparent outlanders—Africans—who are as culturally "Arab" as he. And I am far more African, in my memory, than the wary black residents of Ghor al Safi whose kinship I clumsily seek out. The Ghawarna teach us this. We are, for better or worse, whoever we say we are.

Bang
July 7, 2014
Nabi Salih, West Bank, 32°01'0" N 35°7'29" E

We turn the corner of the road when the first round whips in. It kicks up dust one yard in front of Bassam Almohor. He stops walking.

"We're being shot at," my guide says. His voice is aggrieved. "That was a bullet."

It was, to be precise, a rubber bullet. Or, more exactly still: a rubber-coated bullet, a slug of steel dipped in hard plastic. The term "rubber bullet" connotes non-lethality, harmlessness, a comical form of deterrence—a bouncing ball, a children's toy, a pea-shooter. Yet anyone who has been struck by these projectiles knows differently. Rubber-coated, metal-cored bullets can flatten people with the force of a swung baseball bat. They can kill at close range. The source of this particular rubber bullet: the Israel Defense Force, the IDF.

This comes as a shock. Why? Because it is Wednesday.

We have strolled, Bassam and I, out of a small Palestinian village called Nabi Salih.

Nabi Salih: a clutch of stucco houses clinging to a sun-hammered hill in the West Bank. Clashes between local Palestinians and the Israeli army are common here. In fact, they are predictable. Every Friday, like clockwork, a ritual begins. After midday prayers, scores of civilians—men and women, old and young—march, chanting, out of the village mosque, usually toward a nearby spring. This spring, a watering hole for cattle, has been encroached on illegally by a nearby Israeli settlement. (Such settlements are themselves deemed illegal by most governments of the world, because they occupy the territory of a proposed homeland for Palestinians.) The Israeli army is waiting. Platoons of soldiers block the crowd's progress. A provocation occurs. A slur. A shove. And the dance of violence starts. From the Palestinian side: a hail of rocks flung by boys and young men armed with slingshots. From the Israelis: rubber bullets, teargas canisters, stun grenades and, sometimes, a high-pressure stream of "skunk water," a stinking chemical brew sprayed from a police truck.

I imagine seeing this battle from the air, a strange diorama, with men, women, and children running about on roads and in open fields, amid white blooms of teargas, to the sound of gunfire: These figures sometimes topple over wounded or, on rarer occassions, fall dead. (Since 2009, two villagers have been killed in the protests.) The green-clad soldiers maneuver in lines, in clusters. Occasionally, one of them may drop out, too, injured. Such weekly violence is a minor set piece in an older, much larger, more layered standoff in the West Bank. In toxic summary:

The commandeering of the village spring, an ancient trickle called Ein al-Qaws, is to many Palestinians just another outrage in a military occupation that began forty-seven years ago, following the Six Day War between Israel and its Arab neighbors. The people of Nabi Salih want their waterhole back, but they also wish to be free of checkpoints, of walls, of segregation, of humiliation. The Israelis, meanwhile, demand to be safe from Palestinian terrorism. (A radicalized young woman from Nabi Salih, for example, assisted in a 2001 suicide bombing in Jerusalem that killed fifteen people.) Palestinians curse the armed Israeli settlers proliferating in their midst—in a future Palestine. Ultra-religious and nationalist settlers claim the West Bank for themselves, either by right of conquest, or as Samaria and Judea, part of the 3,000-year-old homeland for Jews. Such rival narratives of primacy and grievance have been refined, purified, distilled, faceted, polished, and codified through years of conflict. They are petrified.

Which is why Bassam and I are caught off guard. The shooting at Nabi Salih happens on Fridays. (It is Wednesday!) Something has upset the schedule.

We blunder, chatting, around a bend and into the free-fire zone. We don't hear the pop-pop-pop of the rifles until it is too late. Israeli soldiers, mistaking us for village protesters, begin firing our way. We retreat. We scramble behind a road embankment. We see boys slinging stones. We circle around the battle in a low crouch.

"I feel bad," Bassam says, as teargas drifts across the grassy pastures. "Just walking away like this."

But I do not feel bad. I have walked away from dozens of conflicts before. Few were mine. Most were obscure bush wars in Africa, the type of bloodlettings that nobody anywhere else much cared about. Once, in Congo, where between one and five million people have perished, I could not pitch a story about a battle that killed one thousand civilians because nine people—Palestinians and Israelis—had died in the West Bank. (The dead Congolese got their due only later, in a special project.) The world's gaze burns on Israel, on the West Bank, on Gaza. Yet this is no solution. There must be some virtuous fulcrum point—an ideal balancing line between outside concern and utter neglect—at which mass violence can more easily, naturally subside: exhaust itself. Few outsiders witness Somalia's agonies. In Nabi Salih, perhaps too many do. (Palestinians videotape their clashes. So do Israeli settlers.) These disparate wars grind on.

In either case, little of war's madness can ever be accurately communicated.

"A person who lived through a great war is different from someone who never lived through any war," wrote the Polish foreign correspondent Ryszard Kapuscinski. "They are two different species of human beings. They will never find a common language, because you cannot really describe the war, you cannot share it, you cannot tell someone: Here, take a little bit of my war. Everyone has to live out his own war to the end."

Bassam and I walk on.

The valleys of the West Bank are golden in the low afternoon sun. We stop and brew a pot of tea in a grove of silver-leaved olive trees. Palestine, the West Bank, Samaria, Judea—the tiny enclave that Palestinians and Israeli settlers die for—is one of the most beautiful inhabited landscapes in the world: Its broad valleys, serried hills, orange groves, and bone-smooth deserts are a Middle Eastern California. The only difference, I tell Bassam, are the faint gunshots that can often be heard, mostly from IDF firing ranges, echoing in the distance.

"Distant gunfire?" Bassam says looking up from his cup. He smiles sadly, nodding. "I never noticed that."

Aftertaste
July 26, 2014
Nablus, West Bank 32°13'15" N 35°15'15" E

We are cooking: cutting up zucchinis, rolling dough, stirring pots of boiling yoghurt. We are with the women of Bait al Karama. They are teaching us about the flavors of remembrance—about its frailty, its persistence, its loss.

What is Bait al Karama?

It is a cooperative, the "House of Dignity": dozens of women gather each month in a stone house in Nablus, a trading center founded by the Roman emperor Vespasian around the time of Christ, an ancient town bloodied by the Second Intifada, and famed outside of Arab-Israeli conflict for its olive-oil soap, its baked sweets, its still-vibrant medieval souk. The women teach cooking classes. They are writing a local cookbook. They are reviving their traditional Nablusi recipes, with all the original ingredients. This afternoon, three members, Ohood Bedawi, Beesan Ramadan, and Fatima Kadoumy, are busy making shish barak, a meat dumpling stew.

"It comes originally from Lebanon, some say Syria," explains Kadoumy, the coop founder, solemn and soft-spoken in her black hijab.

"When we talk about Palestinian cooking, we talk about the influences from the outside," she says. "Our history is mixed into our food. It is the food of a crossroads. It contains migrations. It is about colonialism, conquest. Our sumac [a tart, lemony spice] is a Roman ingredient. Our sweets, called *canafe*, are Turkish, from the Ottomans. Our bulgur grain is Mediterranean, much older here than rice. Only the *akub*, a thorny wild artichoke, is native to our hills. Today, we are losing the habit of cooking these things. Now we eat the Kentucky Fried Chicken."

So we pitch in, my guide Bassam Almohor and I. We do our part. We have stopped walking. We lay aside the GPS. We pick up a spoon. We pick up a paring knife. We report for duty on the front lines of cultural preservation. It is no easy task. It comes at a price: Our appetites must be sacrificed. We stuff ourselves with delicious Arabic foods.

Everyone likes to eat. In peace or war, the ultimate refuge—the sanctuary of all that is humane—lies distilled within the warmth of the kitchen. Watching the women of Nablus move briskly, efficiently, purposefully about their tasks, chatting, often joking (about men, politics, life), I am reminded of all the meals that admitted me briefly into the conflicted lives of Israelis and Palestinians.

In the tiny village of Deir es-Sudan, the West Bank: Bassam and I slogged in, exhausted, at sunset, not knowing a soul. We camped on the concrete floor of a half-built clinic. The shopkeepers next door brought us a large platter of treats—eggs, olives, French fries, yoghurt, fresh bread. They waved away our weak, startled thanks. "The innermost chamber of my home"—one benefactor said—"is yours."

A side trip to Tel Aviv: My Israeli walking partner, Yuval Ben-Ami, threw together, in a bowl, whatever resided at that time in his refrigerator. What was it? Even he didn't know—a concoction of cooked beans, of greens, of rice, of mystery sauces. It was like his living space, a bohemian apartment, packed with books, musical instruments, clothes, art. A typical Yuval sentence begins, "The poet Rachel Bluwstein wrote about the Galilee as if it were another planet." His leftover stew was a reflection of his restless nomad mind.

On a kibbutz north of Haifa: Dark Georgian wine drunk from a ram's horn, courtesy of cousins David and Moshe Beery. They emigrated from Tbilisi as children. They have grown up in uncertainty. They have known war and death. Now, they are building hotels. "To live in this place, you got to pay the rent, so to speak, my friend," says David, ruefully. "But hey—isn't this meal beautiful?"

A house in Ramallah, in the West bank: Bassam's wife, Haya, served a simple, perfect meal of pickles, hummus, sausage, and vermillion tomatoes. The house vibrated with the energy of two small children. The couple lives under Israeli occupation. The daily restrictions on travel, the military raids, the roadblocks, the loss of scarce jobs to political maneuvers by the Palestinian Authority and Israel—all these humiliations are forgotten over the clean taste of olive oil. Bassam looks giddily at his son, Adam, eating. A tightness around his mouth relaxes. A certain loneliness that accompanies him everywhere, even while walking together, dissolves.

I watch Bassam now. The capable women of Nablus order him about their kitchen. He and I will part ways, soon.

We will trek north, Bassam and I, atop straw-colored ridgelines and through lemon orchards: a foot-worn landscape once traveled by Abraham, patriarch of the Middle East's three great religions. (A development organization, Abraham Path, has surveyed such interfaith routes for foreign hikers to walk, thus aiding local communities with tourist dollars.) We will climb the dry wadis. We will part herds of goats. He will talk of the love poetry of Darwish. He will discuss, as everyone does, the mythical peace. ("It's called a 'process' for a reason, Paul," Bassam mutters. "That's because powerful interests on all sides don't want peace. They're making too much money off the process.") He will look with infinite weariness on anyone—Israeli or Palestinian—in uniform. We will part ways in Jenin, at night, outside a bakery. I will walk on.

I watch Bassam. At this instant, in the old stone house in Nablus, he stands with a spoon raised to his lips, eyes closed.

The Hinge
September 10, 2014
Kirit, Turkey 31° 04'49" N 34° 53'45" E

"How did you find our mule?" I ask Deniz Kilic.

"Taxi driver."

"You asked a taxi driver where to buy a cargo mule?"

"I have never bought a mule before. I know nothing about mules. Where do you buy a mule? Who knows? So I asked my taxi driver driving me in from the airport. I said to him, 'Don't laugh. This is serious. Where do I buy a mule?'"

Kilic is my walking partner in Asia Minor.

We meet in Mersin, a large industrial port in southeastern Turkey. I have just disembarked from a ferry from Cyprus. And Kilic has agreed, based on two emails and one long-distance phone call, to join my traverse of Anatolia—600 to 700 miles on foot across the sprawling Asiatic heartland of Turkey.

"Crazy people"—he says—"attract other crazy people."

Kilic is a professional tour guide, a compulsive world traveler.

(Joined by his wife, Elif, he has driven motorbikes through twenty-nine countries.) He is from Bodrum, a resort town in Turkey's cosmopolitan European fringe. But he is proud of the rustic glories of Anatolia, the little visited eastern peninsula that comprises more than 90 percent of his country. The Trojans, immortalized by Homer in the *Iliad*, were Anatolians, Kilic informs me. The historic Santa Claus was an Anatolian, too. (The fourth-century patron saint of children and pawnbrokers stood five feet tall and had a broken nose.) The world's Indo-European languages may be rooted in Anatolia. Anatolian nomads might well have invented agriculture. Their history is complex, bottomless, Kilic says: We will stub our toes daily on artifacts. Moreover, Anatolians are the true Turks—a tough steppe people of varied origins. Kilic is their advocate. He is a man of granite opinions. Of limitless ingenuity. He suffers fools badly: He calls them "geniuses."

"Walking in August will be miserable! What genius planned this?"

"I did."

"Nice."

We tug the mule over farm roads. (According to her $350 bill of sale, she is prehistoric: twenty-two years old. More about this creature later.) We trudge into amber sunrises toward the dusty Iranian Plateau. We stir the quivering heat waves of molten afternoons. We climb the pleated foothills of the Taurus Mountains. We slog through fields of dried sunflowers. Past hand-pumped wells. Down to the sweltering Cilician Plain, perhaps the oldest continuously farmed landscape in the world. We sleep on village roofs.

Millions of families still dream outdoors in southeastern Turkey.

Summer days are a furnace. The earth sizzles underfoot. The humidity of the nearby Mediterranean is smothering: It clogs the lungs; it drenches the skin with sweat. Yet at dusk, on the flat roofs of farmers' homes, loom hidden refuges: a wisp of breeze, a dip in temperature, a refreshing oasis. Anatolians are like birds. They return to roost atop their houses after laboring in their fields. They recline on baize mattresses twenty or thirty feet above ground. (Houses in rural Turkey are typically two or three stories tall.) They sip tea and stare out across their old, old world through a clutter of water tanks, television antennas and airy clotheslines. On rooftops, they picnic on yoghurt, meatballs, and watermelon. They converse and make love under starlight. Neighbors one house away perform these exact same rituals. This practice, a remnant of open-air life, of camping while settled, has survived in Anatolia since our Stone Age youth. It is an echo of hunting and gathering—from the Pleistocene trails that I follow out of Africa.

"The villages are dying out," a farmer named Sami Gortuk says. "The government gives us subsidized fuel. It gives us cheap seeds. It gives us loans for tractors. But our children are moving to jobs in Mersin, to Adana."

The young abandon the sky in Anatolia. Only the poor sleep al fresco in the city.

Wearing baggy peasant pants and clogs, Gortuk and his wife, Hayirli, bring our mule a bucket of ground oats. They lead us to their roof. They set out bowls of *fasulye*, a bean and tomato stew. They unspool power cords to recharge our electronic devices. We are total strangers. This generosity, this impulsive kindness, is repeated everywhere along our route. Rural Anatolians are the most hospitable people on Earth.

This is a cheering surprise, given the blood-steeped soil.

The plains of eastern Turkey are not simply a strategic corridor between Asia and Europe. They are a hinge of history. Civilizations have swiveled violently back and forth atop this plateau for more than 6,000 years. Armed migrations, invasions, conquests, incursions, retreats—books on Anatolia contain numbing variations on this: "and a new wave of Indo-European raiders swept over the land."

Because that land is so fertile. Because it ramps westward to four seas: the Black, the Aegean, the Marmara, the Mediterranean. Because much of Anatolia is flat and impossible to defend.

"[T]he fields of one community came into contact with those of another," writes Robert D. Kaplan in *The Revenge of Geography: What the Map Tells Us About Coming Conflicts and the Battle Against Fate*. "[C]hronic war emerged, as there was no central authority to settle boundary disputes, or to apportion water in times of shortage."

The Akkadians and Assyrians claimed the prize of Anatolia. So did the Hittites, aboriginal Anatolians whose 3,500-year-old legal code, etched on clay tablets, includes the bylaw: "If anyone bites off the nose of a free person, he shall pay forty shekels of silver." Then the Phrygians invaded, and then the Scythians, Greeks, Neo-Assyrians,

Persians, Armenians, Macedonians, Seleucids, Parthians, and Sassanid Persians. The Romans marched in over stone roads to the Euphrates. Christianity turned them into Byzantines. Then came Arab armies bearing the green banner of Islam. The conquering Seljuks (and their Sultanate of Rum) were overrun in turn by bandy-legged cavalrymen galloping in from the east—the Mongols. Later, the Ottomans cobbled together nearly 600 years of continuous rule. Their aging, multiethnic Sultanate—the "sick man of Europe"—cracked apart in the wake of WWI. The Europeans gobbled up the pieces of Anatolia, but the Turks fought back. Modern Turkey was born here in brutal spasms of ethnic cleansing (Christian Armenians, Greeks, Assyrians were massacred and driven out; Muslim Bosnians, Albanians, and Bulgarians fleeing similar fates beyond Ottoman borders streamed in). Only ninety years ago, a radical Turkish general with a fondness for tuxedos—Mustafa Kemal Ataturk—yanked the fledging country into modernity. He banned sharia, abolished the Caliphate, gave women the vote, and forced Turkish men, on pain of prison, to exchange their fezzes for Western fedoras. (The Hat Law of 1925.)

The *Out of Eden Walk*, too, will swing on Anatolia's ancient hinge. For the next two years, maybe three, I will trek eastward to China.

We navigate using village minarets, Deniz Kilic and I.

Blinded by the midday sun, we echolocate our way ahead using the heat-distorted calls to prayer that moan in the steamy distances.

We stagger past 1,900-year-old Corinthian plinths being used as backyard coffee tables. By new OPET gas stations with "Chat Cola" in their fogged-glass coolers. Past worn limestone mosques that had been churches for half a millennium, and before that, synagogues. Over beaches strewn with a mile of broken Iron Age potsherds. Under the fleeting shadows of KC-135 jets launched from the U.S. airbase at Incirlik. (They were arrowing towards Iraq.) And among hundreds of old Anatolian men sitting on wooden stools in village squares, slapping down numbered tiles in eternal games of okey.

"Why are you doing this?" one of them asked. He rotated his palms skyward in query.

"Why do you sit here day after day playing okey?" I said.

"I don't know."

"I don't know, either," I said. And he nodded.

Loose Thread on the Silk Road

October 31, 2014
Sanliurfa, Turkey, 37°08'54"N 38°47'24"E

We parked the mule on the Euphrates and took a hire car to Edessa: a famous pilgrimage town in Mesopotamia. Founded by Assyrians. Traded at the point of a sword between the Greeks, Nabateans, Romans, Sassanids, Byzantines, Arabs, Armenians, Seljuks, Crusaders, and Seljuks again. About 4,000 years ago its cruel king, Nimrod, ordered Abraham burned alive for rejecting the Assyrian pantheon. Abraham's God saved the prophet by turning the flames into water and the coals into fish. According to Muslim tradition, God then punished Nimrod by sending a mosquito up his nose to bite his brain. The deranged king ordered his men to knock his head with felt-wrapped mallets, then with wooden clubs. Nimrod died that way. A pool in the modern city, now called Sanliurfa, commemorates Abraham's miracle. The pool is filled with sacred carp. People feed the fish with a lira's worth of pellets. The fish are immortal and quite fat. Eat one and you go blind.

Next to Abraham's pool is an old bazaar from the days of the Silk Road. The tailors there are Kurds. They sit in a shady courtyard where menders have patched holes for a thousand years. They sip tea. They ruin their eyesight spearing licked thread through needles.

The fates of mighty empires once rose and fell according to the flow of commodities across the worn plank shop counters of Sanliurfa. Maybe they still do. Today, the tailors hunch over antique American-made sewing machines that were sold a century ago by Sears, Roebuck & Company. The tailors pump the machines by foot. Sturdy artifacts from another time. From an age before the rise of disposable Chinese polyester. From a world where America exported more than its titanic debt.

"We're the last generation," tailor Muhammed Sadik Demir says with no self-pity. He shrugs. "People don't repair clothes anymore. They throw them away."

Actually, it is Deniz Kilic who says this.

Kilic, my Turkish guide, my interpreter, is going home.

He has suffered like no other walking partner on the long *Out of Eden Walk* trail out of Ethiopia. Shin splints. Sore feet. Blisters on top of blisters. He has endured, too, the torment of my lectures on walking landscapes—avoiding beelines, contouring hills. Yet Kilic never stopped. In the mornings, he pounded on his boots. He tottered on. He loved the slow journey. It allowed him to deploy his streetwise charm. Teasing, joking, he disarmed all we meet. He called the humblest farmer *hoca*—master, teacher. From Mersin to Sanliurfa, across more than 200 miles of mountains, roads, beaches, and fields, he was my wise-guy window to Anatolia. He forced me to watch my first 3-D movie—*Dawn of the Planet of the Apes*—claiming it was research. His parents had named him after the 1960s revolutionary Deniz Gezmis, Turkey's version of Che, and he was bracingly cynical about all politicians. He completed his thoughts with snatches of pop songs.

Crossing a creek with the mule: "*We all live in a yellow submarine . . .*"

Frowning up at storm clouds: "*Here comes the rain again, falling on my head like a memory . . .*"

I will see you again, I tell him.

Like all of the walk's guides, Kilic is invited to Beagle Channel between Argentina and Chile, to the finish line of the journey. This is the dream: Every walk partner who has helped shape the walk's route will regroup in 2020. I see Mohamad Banounah; a son of Mecca, walking in Tierra del Fuego bundled against the Antarctic wind. I see Noa Burshtein, a young woman recently discharged from the Israeli army, walking the cobbled shores there. And Elema Hessan, the Afar fossil hunter from the bone-colored plains of the African Rift. And the Bedouin guide Hamoudi Alweijah al Bedul from Petra. And Bassam Almohor from Ramallah. There will be Russian guides. Chinese and Colombian guides. Twenty-one thousand miles worth of fellow voyagers. We will stride together, en masse, along the final mile of the human journey, to last beach of human imagining. Kilic will sing, "*Baby, it's cold outside . . .*" This journey belongs to them. Warp and weft, they have sewed its story into existence.

> *Your absence has gone through me*
> *Like thread through a needle*
> *Everything I do is stitched with its color.*

—W. S. Merwin

Mule-ology
December 11, 2014
Near Siverek, Turkey 37° 46' 32" N 39° 16' 22" E

First things first: A mule is not a donkey.

A *donkey* is a member of the equine family burdened by low self-esteem: a small, modest, long-eared creature from which mules are bred when mated with a horse. In other words, a donkey is the crude base metal from which a superior alloy—the mule—is forged. To call a mule a donkey, then, is at best a beginner's mistake that will earn the squinting contempt of veteran muleskinners. At worst, they are fighting words.

There are jack mules (male) and jenny or molly mules (female). There are blue mules, cotton mules, sugar mules, and mining mules. There is a mammoth mule that weighs a thousand pounds. George Washington was a mule breeder. But all mules are immune to politics. There is no idealistic mule.

Being hybrids, mules are biologically sterile, which helps explain their dispositions: angry at the world.

The Mexicans have a saying: *Una mula piensa por lo menos siete veces al día como matar el amo.* "A mule thinks at least seven times a day how to kill is master." This is doubtless an exaggeration. Nobody, however, disagrees with the drift of this aphorism.

Mules do not tolerate names.

This fact might surprise the lay public. True, one can call a mule anything one wishes. Our white jenny, for example, has been baptized differently by each of my walking partners across Turkey. Deniz Kilic called her Barbara for reasons only he can explain. Mustafa Filiz dubbed her Sunshine. Murat Yazar calls her Sweetie. John Stanmeyer, my photographer colleague, refers to her as Snowflake. My preference is Kirkatir, a Turkish name meaning "grey mule." It is the original moniker bestowed by her previous owner, an Alevi woodcutter from the forested hills above Mersin. The truth is that, like all mules, she answers to no label meted out by mere humans. Kirkatir does not come when called, or when whistled to. She comes when she feels like it. This is not very often.

Kirkatir is twenty-two years old.

How old is this in mule years? About five millennia. Walking along a trail with Kirkatir is like trekking with the oldest living being on the planet Earth: It is like taking a Sunday stroll while tethered to a redwood, or a bristlecone pine tree. When I first took her for a test walk, back in July, I noticed that her hide was wrinkled around the edges of the packsaddle. "How old is she?" I asked the owner. The owner, Ahmed, looked heavenward. He held up his palms. He shrugged his shoulders. Ahmed was a passable thespian. Her documents, procured after the sale, spelled out the truth.

"She's not *that* old," sniffed Deniz Kilic, who had agreed to her purchase before I arrived in Turkey, and who now felt responsible. Deniz spent the first afternoon of the walk in Turkey peering grimly down into his smart phone. He was looking hard for a Web site that would attest that mules could live for fifty years, or perhaps even a century.

Mules eat everything.

On a cross-country foot journey, this tolerant belly is a useful quality. Horses are much too finicky. That said, the mulish appetite does have its disadvantages. In Jordan, where I traveled with cargo mules, one of the animals, Selwa, ate my Bedouin guide Hamoudi Enwaje' al Bedul's walking stick. Walking sticks are very hard to come by in empty deserts. Hamoudi cursed Selwa. Days later, after much intense searching, he at last found another stick. Selwa ate that one, too.

Mules are smarter than horses.

This is a well-known fact about the mule race. Mules, for instance, take no unnecessary chances. Look into a mule's dark, benthic eyeballs: You will detect quadratic equations cascading down like plankton behind their depthless retinas. Mules are forever calculating their odds. Kirkatir is a careful mule. She observes all posted traffic laws. She stops at all speed bumps installed on roads to slow automobiles. She does this for a very long time.

One afternoon, Deniz and I walked into a veterinarian's office outside of the Turkish city of Gaziantep. We needed an expert opinion.

"We have a problem with our mule," we informed the animal doctor, a thin, appraising young man who stood behind the counter in a white medical smock. "Our mule does this strange thing *all night long.* Whenever we tie her to a tree at a camp, she paces back and forth—yes, back and forth—constantly. She does this odd dance."

And then, Deniz and I reenacted, to the best of our ability, the rumba of Kirkatir: Standing elbow to elbow, we took three steps forward, tossed our heads dramatically—in a wide, clockwise circle— and then took three steps back. Perhaps, we asked the vet, our mule suffered an obscure mule neuroses? Was she a mule insomniac? Was our mule insane?

We repeated these steps three or four times. For clarity's sake. For an accurate diagnosis.

The vet's eyes zigzagged between us and a crowd of people growing at the open clinic door. No, the vet said at last. Our mule, he assured us, was perfectly normal.

JOAN WICKERSHAM

■

An Inventory

FROM *One Story*

BOY I WAS SMALL AND SOFT. He seemed breakable. Serious, soft
brown eyes. He built careful buildings in the block corner—this was
in kindergarten—a tower on one side and a tower on the other side,
an arch in the middle. He didn't say much. Over spring vacation, he
went to visit his grandparents in Texas. You had heard that there were
rattlesnakes in Texas, and you worried all week. You kept thinking of
him walking around in Texas, his small, unguarded ankles.

Boy 2 rescued you on the playground. There was a kid who always showed up dressed like a cowboy, who one day climbed the ladder just behind you, put his lasso around your neck, and pushed you
down the slide. Boy 2 ran over to see if you were hurt—you weren't,
just shocked by the sudden viciousness of it—and to shout at the
other boy, "Leave her alone!" He stood over you while you loosened
the rope and helped you pull the noose off over your head. After that
day neither of them paid much attention to you, though you taunted
the kid in the cowboy suit and looked behind you whenever you
climbed the ladder to the slide.

Boys 3-5 were the boys of elementary school, interchangeable:
bright, sturdy, clean looking. You and a lot of other girls liked them;
they liked you and a lot of other girls. You ate lunch together in the
cafeteria and played at one another's houses. You knew their mothers
and what their bedspreads looked like and what books they read. You
talked with them about the things that happened to other people—
the operation one kid had to have to, well, no one knew exactly what,
but to widen the, you know, *hole*; the girl suddenly sent to live with an

aunt after her father stabbed her mother—but nothing like that ever happened to any of you.*

Boy 6 was the one you loved, the one who kept asking you to be his partner for science and social-studies projects. He was your introduction to the conundrum that would occupy you for the next decade: the boy who liked you but didn't *like* you. (Which brings up the concurrent but barely noticed Boy 6b, who liked and *liked* you, and whom you liked but didn't *like*.) These italics made sense to every girl you knew, and were for a long time the currency of every female friendship, nearly every female conversation. Its coins were gossip, speculation, exhilarating confidences, assurances that somehow provoked more anxiety than they allayed, and devastating revelation, as in the time someone told you that Boy 6 not only *liked* another girl, but also had taken her to a party and felt her up (and you said, "But there's nothing there to feel").

Boy 7 was the first boy who kissed you, and the last for several years. Which surprised you: you had assumed that this door, once open, would stay ajar. Boy 7 himself turned out to be bafflingly forgettable even though, for the three months or so when he was kissing you and the six months before that when you had wanted him to, thoughts of him had consumed you. Eighth grade ended and Boy 7 disappeared, along with Boy 7b, who had annoyed you all year by pulling your chair out from under you in morning assembly just as you were sitting down, but then sent you letters from summer camp on bright green stationery (you still didn't like him, but you found the stationery—his mother must have bought it for him—endearingly at odds with his bratty attempts to be cool), which he signed "Love."

Then came a frantic clot of boys with whom nothing happened, who each seemed to make brief sense of why nothing had happened with the one before. You were dazzled by a gentle voice and a kind smile; no, a cold stare and an air of having been mysteriously hurt; no, expertise, a violinist; no, pragmatism, altruism, a sweet head bent over a microscope; no, nervous brilliance and a kind of crooked off-

---

* Years later, after you'd all scattered to various high schools, you heard that Boy 5's mother had died of a brain tumor, and you instantly remembered the smell of her perfume, and the time she asked you if you'd go out to her car to get her cigarettes. "Would you be an angel?" she'd said.

centeredness, Mercutio, not Romeo, in the drama club production where you were playing the nurse. The boys talked to you or didn't, were aware of you or weren't. For one of them—Boy 10—you baked a birthday cake, and so did the other girl who had her eye on him; there was a terrible moment on a staircase, when you were running down from the second floor with your cake and she came charging up from the lobby with hers, both of you racing to be the first to reach and surprise Boy 10, who stood bewildered on the landing. With Boy 13 (a poet's chiseled nostrils), things actually progressed to the point where you were sitting on his lap one afternoon in the library, tucked behind the stacks in his carrel which you had been haunting for several weeks. Then—he must have looked down at your bunchy peasant blouse—he said, "My God, you have copious boobs," and you didn't know what was more chilling, his use of the word "boobs" or his misuse of the word "copious," and you slid off his knee and never spoke to him again.*

There was a devoted couple at your high school—she was a sophomore and he a senior, she was Juliet and Rosalind and Lydia Languish and he was the director. They were always together; they talked solemnly of a certain book, important to them both, a novel called *Islandia*, which you got from the library and were bored by—it seemed at once arid and overwrought. You returned it. In some confused irritated way you felt your failure to have penetrated it also barred you from love: there was something to get and you just didn't get it. The couple in your school, with their relentless soulful glued-togetherness, appalled you, but you knew you would never rest until you had what they had.

You wondered if they were sleeping together, supposed they might be, though you couldn't really imagine it, for them or for anyone,

---

* You were in college when, on a late-night train ride to Boston, you told another woman this story, and she said that a boy had once told her she had pneumatic boobs. You both laughed, and wondered if it was a trend among teenaged boys, to create new derogatory phrases by linking preposterous adjectives to the word "boobs." Well, at that age they're afraid of women's bodies, she said. You didn't know her well; she'd been in one of your classes the year before. She was on her way to visit her boyfriend for the weekend, as were you (Boy 19), and at first you spoke about them proudly, bragging a little; but as the dark train slid and rattled through the hours, she eventually told you she didn't really love her boyfriend and you said you weren't sure you even liked yours.

the mechanics of it, the geometry and the angles, the feelings. The nameless shattering thing you did alone in your room most afternoons had nothing to do with what you thought of as sex. Sex, as you understood it, was about being naked with another person and engaging in insertions that made sense in diagrams, but seemed too awkward and terrifying to actually do, or want to do, or let someone do to you, in real life.

One afternoon a boy—older, someone who sang in the school choir with you—asked if you wanted to go for a walk. Boy X.* You said sure. You were not feeling any particular interest or dread, just: Why not? Later you'd wonder how you could have been so stupid. Did you think he wanted to talk about Benjamin Britten, or Mozart's *Regina Coeli*? Well, yes, you sort of did. You'd thought he had wanted to talk about *something*, anyway, even if it was only going to be the stilted exchange of facts and preferences that constituted getting to know another person. That's what you said, after you'd walked into the woods with him and the two of you were sitting side by side with your backs against a fallen tree and he made his laconic suggestion. "But we don't even know each other!"

He looked at you. "What better way is there to get to know somebody?" His eyes were half-closed, he was drawling. You stood up and ran. Your disgust verged on terror and was almost indescribable—at least, you had trouble describing it to Boy 12, whose kindness had elated you and made you wistful at the beginning of freshman year, and who had since evolved into a friend. "But what's the big deal?" he said now. "Nothing happened."

You couldn't explain. The fakeness of it, the vacancy.

"Isn't it supposed to mean something?" you asked, and Boy 12

---

* Followed, in later years, by Boy—no, Man—Xb, a stranger who fell asleep, or pretended to, next to you on a train, and whose head slipped onto your shoulder and then down to your breast where his face then began to burrow and you tried gently to push him off but his sleep-heavy, or pseudo-sleep-heavy head, didn't move and so you let him stay there because maybe he really was sleeping and you didn't know what else to do. And Man Xc, another stranger who pressed his hard self against your ass on a packed New York City bus, and there was no room to move and you were afraid that if you said "Stop that" he would announce to the crowded bus that you were crazy, and finally another woman passenger noticed what was going on and stopped it by saying loudly, "Honey, why you let him do that to you?"

laughed and reminded you again that nothing had happened and you were okay, and you left him, uneasily. Maybe he was right and it really hadn't been so bad? So why were you feeling nearly destroyed?

Part of it, you thought, was that nothing about you had mattered to Boy X except your gender. You could have been any girl. But no— bad as that was, there was something else, something you couldn't have admitted to Boy 12 and couldn't even clearly articulate to yourself. In fact there was something special about you that had drawn Boy X to invite you into the woods: you were not pretty. Boy X had been gauging the odds when he looked at you with those half-closed eyes. He'd been aiming low, and he'd felt he had nothing to lose if he missed. Your lack of beauty not only made him think he might succeed, it somehow gave him the right to try.*

You knew that there were things a boy would have to see past in order to fall in love with you—your weight, your skin, a general too-muchness (too many words, too many fierce opinions, too big, too loud, too voluble) that you could not seem to damp down. You thought—or tried to think—of these things as a thicket, the brambles a prince would one day hack through to get to you. You had wise consoling words for friends of yours who also worried about being too much, too intense: "That is the very thing that someone will one day love about you." But what the hell did you know? You would have liked to be a tragic pale girl on the moors, or some other kind of mysterious sufferer, a poet, a muse, a wayfarer; but you knew—your mother told you—that you mostly came across as sullen. You were waiting for the boy who would—would what? Not just kiss or flatter you, but recognize you, and whom you would recognize.

By now you had begun to gaze at Boy 18, who was in your English class in the spring of junior year. You liked his quiet, sprightly, manly dignity. He had a way in class of reading poetry aloud that conferred on each poem the tone it required. "Margaret, are you grieving / Over Goldengrove unleaving"—you don't remember anymore who wrote the poem, but you can still summon up the mournful bell-toll

---

* While you might have been right about this particular Boy X and his contempt for you, you'd been wrong about beauty guarding against the X Boys and X Men of the world. Every woman you would ever get to know—no matter how beautiful—had stories like this one. Or worse. You'd been lucky.

of his voice reading it. He had delicate yellow hair, pale blue eyes; every day he wore a tweed sport coat and a white shirt, while the other boys were all dressing like lumberjacks and stevedores. He had an air of sadness, you thought, but it was somehow a pragmatic sadness, as if he were saying, "Yes, life is pointless, but then why not just get on with it?"

You talked with him about books. Virginia Woolf, Nathanael West, Maupassant, Faulkner, Kafka—you could be glib about all of them, even the ones you hadn't read. You giddily paraphrased Katherine Mansfield to him on the novels of E.M. Forster—something about how he warms the tea pot beautifully, only there ain't going to be no tea, and he said gravely, passionately that no, there really *was* tea, and that you should re-read *Howards End*. You did read it then (for the first time), and told him he was right, there was tea; and he paraphrased Katherine Mansfield to you on the difficulty of discerning whether Helen Schlegel had been impregnated by Leonard Bast or by Leonard Bast's forgotten umbrella. You discovered that you both liked, and were good at, writing limericks, and you started slipping them through the vents in each other's lockers. This was all it took, that spring, to flood you with happiness: the moment when you would open your locker and see, lying on top of your book bag or half in and half out of your cruddy gym shoes, a slip of white paper, with five lines of his small sloping letters, written in black fountain pen. Conversely, opening your locker and not finding a limerick was beyond disappointing—it felt crushing, as if you'd been abandoned, though you knew that the rarity of his offerings, and the suspense, was part of what kept you interested, and you worked to match your pace to his, to restrain yourself from littering him with too much rhyming confetti.

During your senior year, you and he were co-editors of the literary magazine. The art director was your best friend: the girl who knew all your secrets. She could understand why you liked him—she liked him, too—but *liking* him? What did you *like* about him? You would try to enumerate, and she would look politely dubious, which made him seem more entirely yours, or at least more entirely intended for you. You kept waiting for him to see this. In the darkening fall afternoons, while other people played football or programmed in the computer lab or made out in the theater lighting booth, you and your best friend and Boy 18 sat at a table at the back of the library, sorting through poems and stories and drawings. She was small, vivacious, elegant. She was also, you knew, unhappy. She liked bad boys, brutal boys, motorcycle boys. She worried every month that she might be pregnant—who knew if foam worked the way it was supposed to, and he refused to wear a rubber. She worried that she was dumb, while you worried you were ugly; you reassured each other, no no she was smart, and you were very attractive. All of this was hidden during the afternoons when you sat around that table with Boy 18, choosing and pruning and discussing and arranging. The three of you laughed and laughed.

A touring theater company was coming to your town with a production of *Our Town*. You invited Boy 18 to go with you. He blushed and cleared his throat and told you that he had, uh, actually already invited your best friend to go with him. (You fastened on that word "actually"—the pomposity of it, the self-regarding, inhibited precision. You stood there looking at him, mentally imitating him: "Uh, actually," "*ac*-tually,"—it was the first remotely critical thought you'd ever had about him—and imagined the fun of mocking him aloud, later; but of course the two people with whom you would have mocked this sort of thing had suddenly become unavailable.) But, he added, you'd be welcome to join them.

Incredibly, you did. It was partly that you couldn't figure out how to say you were doing something else that night when having issued the invitation made it clear that you weren't, and partly that you simply couldn't let them go without you; jealousy, and curiosity to see them together in this new way, and hope that maybe he would change his mind or that maybe you were misinterpreting the situation, beat out pride. You waited alone outside the town hall and watched as they came walking toward you together; and then you went in and watched the play and thought of how convenient things were in art, where there seemed to be only two young people in town and so they fell in love (the fact that it ended in death and grief seemed to you, that night, beside the point). The three of you kept working together on the magazine. He kept taking her to things—a movie, a coffee shop. She kept saying yes and going, even while she kept sleeping

with the motorcycle boy. She didn't seem to notice that your friendship had cooled, that you'd stopped confiding in her.* Meanwhile Boy
19, who was Boy 18's antipode, was beginning to shine in the distance.

He was handsome, Boy 19, in a way you thought yourself indif-
ferent to (though you knew this indifference was at least in part pre-
emptive, a resolution to spurn something you weren't going to be
allowed to have). He was also generally thought of as a jerk. Wait—
that's not quite true. It was more that he was not generally thought
of at all. He had come into your school partway through the year
and had somehow failed to register on the social Richter scale—he
wasn't a brain or an athlete, he didn't play an instrument, he didn't
do anything, except stand around looking vaguely sardonic. You
asked a couple of your friends who had classes with him what he was
like, and they shrugged. Did they think he was good-looking? They
guessed so, they'd never really noticed. It was almost as if he were
invisible to everyone but you, like the murderer in a horror movie
who can only be seen by his eventual victim. You watched him circling around at lunchtime, sometimes sitting next to one girl for a
few days, not getting anywhere, and then a week or two later moving
on to another. You had your own busy lunch life going on, but you
could have charted his like a sociologist; you were always aware, in
some half-conscious way, of where he was in that vast school cafeteria, his pattern of movement, his trajectory.

Finally, a few weeks before graduation, he worked his way around
to the table where you sat with some of your friends. The girl he

---

* She wrote to you in college, to ask what had gone wrong in the friendship. You wrote
back, curtly, and told her. She wrote back pages of apology. She honestly had not realized, she said. She had never thought of it as stealing—nothing had ever really happened between them, he'd never even tried to kiss her. *It was really just that I admired
you so much*, she wrote, *and you admired him, so I tried to admire him too. You were both
so smart*, she wrote, *I wanted you both to approve of me.* You crumpled up this letter and
didn't write back; but she kept trying. She wanted to see you, she wrote, when she
came East for Christmas vacation. Finally you said yes, worn down by her persistence
and her distress, which seemed real; and you went out to lunch with her and kept in
touch after that. And though it took years for you to really trust her again, and you and
she have lived in different states for years now, she is still one of the people you are
closest to.

was targeting didn't want him. You weren't sure you did either—up close like this, real, he scared you, not anything he said or did, but a trapped uneasy sense that the tractable, almost fictional, object of surveillance had suddenly become aware of you, as if you'd looked into your telescope one day and found an eye looking back at you. Now what? Now banter, for a couple of weeks. None of it memorable—you couldn't even remember it later the same day, unlike your conversations with Boy 18 which you could have written out afterward and attributed to Noel Coward.

"Ah," said Boy 19. "Well, then."

"Well, then," you agreed.

All of it just lay there, a leaden placeholder where you felt wit should have been. Or if not wit, then some shared way of seeing, thinking, feeling. Wasn't that, or the hope of it, the mirage of it, the thing that had always driven your longing? But here you were, walking into the woods one afternoon with Boy 19, lying on the ground in a grassy clearing propped on your elbows, chattering away. Then, abruptly, he told you to turn over, and you turned over.

A triumphant sense of relief, even that first afternoon when all you did was kiss each other. Oh, so this was it. This, not that dutiful checklist pecking you had done with the long-ago Boy 7. This was what people meant—what they did, what they liked. When his tongue came into your mouth, you were startled and exhilarated, you almost wanted to say, Oh you read that book too? You felt that way again a week or two later, when he was kissing you up against the wall inside your parents' garage—it was a hot day, he was wearing gym shorts and a light loose Indian cotton shirt and when he pulled away, his shirt was tented out in front of him, and you thought Oh so it really is, he really does—you'd been reading about and trying to imagine all of this for so long that you were surprised to discover it was true. He saw where you were looking and grinned and told you to give him a minute, it'd go down; and he was so relaxed with it, with you, not wheedling or pressuring you, that you put your hand there and his eyes slipped closed. It fascinated you, a real cock in your hand, the live strong veiny heat of it, and what you could do to him when you touched it. I want to go down on you, he said a few days after that, and you weren't sure what he meant but then that was another happy surprise—the thing you'd done for years alone in your room suddenly confirmed and magnified, connected up with this, in the way you'd suspected it might be without ever quite knowing—along with the brazen luxury of his hands on your breasts and the salty, grass-tasting slide of him in your mouth.

At the same time, you were troubled by love.* Where was it? How could you be loving all of this without loving him? His chuckly euphemisms—he called his wallet "the old exchequer." Once, after you and he had a fight about something—you were always having fights, and you, not he, picked them—he put a note in your locker. When you first saw it lying there, you felt a wild stab of hope that it might be another of Boy 18's limericks, which had stopped coming months before; but you saw that it was Boy 19's scrawly writing, also in fountain pen (fountain pen was big among the boys of your year): "I am yours / You are not mine / You are what you are." That he would quote Crosby Stills and Nash was bad enough. That he would change the lyrics was even worse. Why not just pick an apt quotation in the first place? Why *alter* something to make it apt?

"It's just sex," you said to your friends, when they asked why you were with Boy 19. You liked the tough, worldly sound of it. Finally you had caught up with everyone else—not just caught up, but leapt

---

* Troubled too, not then but years afterward, by remorse. He told you on that first walk that his mother, with whom he'd been living in New York City, had died a few months before, after a long illness, and so he'd had to come live with his father of whom he said, chuckling in the fakely sardonic way that you found so annoying, let's just say that he's oil and I'm water. He told you also—not on that first day but later—that his mother had had a drinking problem and some breakdowns, for which he blamed his father. And another time he said that his mother had done something to him once, when he was twelve, after his bath; but, he said, I don't think she really knew what she was doing. When he told you this it made you remember something strange he had said that first day, right after he first kissed you: he had buried his face in your neck and said, Oh my God you smell so good, I thought all girls smelled like mothers. You were too young to realize how young he was, and how wrong all this was, and how recently his mother had died. Would you have loved him, or at least have been less irritable, if you'd known? No, but you wish you had known—you wish someone had known. His loneliness, back then, must have felt infinite, hopeless. From searching online you've learned he is a judge now, living in Minneapolis, married, with a son and a daughter. Somewhere in your house you have a white silk scarf he gave you, that belonged to his mother.

over the conventional linking of sex and love, and flown, like Evel Knievel clearing an impossibly long string of barrels, to land triumphantly farther down the road, where sex had a sophisticated, detached, unencumbered life of its own.

But

a) what you meant when you said this was "Hey, listen, he's good for something." You were ashamed of Boy 19. You were also ashamed of yourself, for disowning him.

b) you were not really a "just sex" person. You thought about him, planned for him, missed him; were happy when he wrote to you that summer from Edinburgh, where he had gone to spend a month with an uncle; kept seeing him all through your freshman year and part of your sophomore year in college, even though he went to school in Boston and you were in New York; said you loved him when he said he loved you—and you did love him in a way, while continuing to find him irritating.

c) you weren't actually fucking him.

This last, c), is worth closer inspection. You were scared. Not that it might hurt, not that you might not like it, not of pregnancy, not of him leaving you. You were scared of doing something that, once done, would never again be something you'd never done. You had always planned to wait until it felt right, and this was not what you'd thought "right" would feel like. If you could somehow have combined Boy 18's soul, the excitement and rightness of those conversations, the *sacredness* of your feeling for him, together with Boy 19's frank desire, his physical ease and confidence (and maybe, too, his smell, and the way he tasted)—if you could have combined all that in one person, you would have slept with that person.

Were your expectations unrealistic, were you being too picky? You felt you'd been waiting, waiting, and hadn't even really come close to what you were waiting for—you could be waiting forever. But if you gave in just to get it over with (and because you kind of knew it would be terrific), were you betraying yourself, taking lightly something that, for you, needed to retain its meaning? You went back and forth about this for months, while continuing to go back and forth on the train between New York and Boston. Boy 19 was actually lovely about your indecision—he could have been frustrated and fed up with you, but he was patient. He let you know what he wanted, but didn't pressure you and liked the many things that did go on between you in those narrow little dorm beds on the weekends. In fact, you spent most of your time together in bed, and when you weren't in bed you ate. You couldn't remember ever having been as happy as you were in his dorm room on Sunday mornings, wearing only his shirt, sitting with him in the bright sunlight in front of the open window while he played Bach cantatas for you on his stereo and handed you pieces of Entenmann's coffee cake.

You ate with him in delicatessens and chowder houses and Chinese places and Italian restaurants where everything was covered in breading, cheese, and red sauce; and in a different kind of Italian restaurant, pale and severe, where you had *tortellini in brodo* and veal with truffles. You got dressed up and went with him on Saturday afternoons to glittering or dowdy hotels (he was rich), where starchy string quartets and velvet-gowned harpists sat being efficiently romantic amid potted palms while you and he drank tea and ate scones with clotted cream and talked about where you wanted to go for dinner. There was a deli you both liked on 43rd Street, and you would walk there together on Friday nights, late, from Penn Station where you'd just met his train. You ate borscht with sour cream, and potato pancakes with sour cream and applesauce, and onion bagels with cream cheese and smoked salmon or whitefish, all in the same meal—a clatter of white plates crowded onto the tabletop, along with tall glasses of fresh orange juice, furry with pulp. You loved these Friday nights, the startling lanky wolfish beauty of him rising from the train platform to the place where you always waited at the top of the stairs, the first kisses, the walk through the dark cold windy streets to the deli, that clean feeling of the weekend in front of you, with nothing yet to mar it, no blot on the paper (though he would always say, "I refuse to call it Avenue of the Americas. To me it will always be Sixth Avenue," and you would think, Who asked you?—it wasn't the remark itself, it was the fact that he said it every time, in the same words), you hadn't fought yet, the meal was still ahead of you to be eaten with a greed that was new each time, always innocent, as if you had never known the feeling that invariably came afterward: too much, too full, too heavy, regret, atonement, resolution to do it differently, carefully, next week.

You could eat in front of him without shame, without hesitation, without dissembling. Once he took you to a department store and told you to close your eyes, and he held your hand and led you gently, eagerly across the floor until—"Open your eyes!", and you were standing inside a gilded alcove devoted to a kind of Belgian chocolate you had heard of but never tasted. There was a little radar blip of shame then, as you imagined for a moment what it had looked like: a solicitous boy leading a fat girl across the selling floor—past the gloves, the perfume, the jewelry—to paradise; but you put it aside and gave yourself over to the pleasure of choosing exquisite little squares and mounds and fluted ovals for the saleslady to seize with deft fingers and arrange for you in a deep and costly golden box.

He said you were beautiful, and maybe he meant it: once he gave you a pair of silver earrings and looked at you in them so unremittingly that he bloodied his nose walking into a lamppost on the Boston Common. But even the credibility of a bloody nose couldn't take away the deep sting of the occasional but terrible signals you'd gotten from other boys over the years: the one in high school who, you had heard, when asked to name the girl he would least want to sleep with, named you; and Boy 20, whom you'd met during freshman orientation at your college and hung around with for several weeks by what seemed like mutual agreement, until you had blurted out one evening that you *liked* him and he had told you apologetically that he only went out with pretty girls.

Yes, even while you and Boy 19 were commuting back and forth, you were still sort of looking around. Boy 21 was an elegant pre-med student from India who spoke with a British accent and struck you as kind and heroic (he was playing Henry Higgins in *Pygmalion*—you were Mrs. Pierce, the housekeeper—and when the director, who was always fighting with his girlfriend, slapped her across the face one evening during a rehearsal, Boy 21 intervened, in a robust, morally incisive way that reminded you of Boy 2 rescuing you on the playground all those years ago). (Oddly, Boy 2 had recently and briefly reappeared: he was a student at your college. You noticed his name one day when you were thumbing through the freshman directory, and went over to his dorm to knock on his door. He remembered the playground, but had no memory of the boy in the cowboy suit or of you. He was polite, but neither of you could think of anything else to say, and so your fantasy that—that—oh, never mind.) Boy 21 seemed to like you, but he also liked your roommate, one of those ethereal girl-on-the-moors types that you would have liked to be. For Valentine's Day he gave her a dozen roses and you a gigantic heart-shaped box of chocolates; and not long after that he started going out with someone else.

Boy 18 wrote to you—you had not heard from him since graduation—to ask if you would like to come down to his college for a crew regatta. He was not a rower, as far as you knew; nor were you; and neither of you had ever expressed any interest in watching crew races. What could this invitation mean, if not that he had finally recognized that you and he were right for each other? Even as you formulated this theory, you knew that it was wrong—knew, in the language that you and Boy 18 had once seemed to share, that there wasn't going to be no tea.* You took the train down Friday night and he met you on a dark little platform, his face bleached and ghastly under the overhead light. He hugged you and told you that he'd arranged for you to stay with a girl whose roommate had gone home with mono, and he got you to her room very quickly. You lay awake that night in a top bunk under a moonlit ceiling, listening to the deep-sleep breathing of a girl you didn't know, feeling that you needed to be very still, vigilant, though you didn't know what you were on the lookout for, or hiding from. The next day he showed you over the campus, introduced you to some of his friends, stood with you in the hot sun on the riverbank watching the crew shells slide by. It was impeccable, he was perfectly nice, but you still had that pinched feeling—not sadness, not dread, but a kind of cautious baffled alertness. Why did you invite me? you might have asked, not reproachfully, but out of curiosity—except that, surprisingly, you weren't really curious. You'd wanted him for so long, it was as if your wanting had worn a deep groove in the land-

---

* He came to the twenty-fifth reunion of your high school class with a younger man who sat silently on a bench outside the library smoking. Boy 18 sat next to him, smoking too, and you sat next to Boy 18. He was a writer, a reporter for one of the big weekly law journals. He looked almost the same – his white hair was no more pale than his yellow hair had been – but instead of his old tweedy costume he was wearing jeans and a T-shirt.

scape; and now the groove was still there, but it was empty, the river-bed was dry. That night you sat up late with him talking; it was pleasant but formal, effortful. You both fell asleep on his bed, you with your head on the pillow and he with his head resting against the footboard. When you woke up Sunday morning, you lay very quietly, still clenched and vigilant, so you wouldn't wake him; and you found you were thinking of Boy 19 and the sun coming into his dorm room and the soft hair on his legs and his excitement when he played you Bach and the coffee cake with its wet tunnels of cinnamon.

There was no blood, but it hurt the first time even though Boy 19 was gentle, and it was awkward for a few times after that. Then it got good. It changed the way you felt about Boy 19: now when you told him you loved him, you thought you meant it (before, it had just been an exciting thing to say to someone and to hear). It seemed to change the way he felt too—he was sleeker, more confident, a little more careless with you. You got more careful, anxious. Sometimes when you called him at night the phone rang and rang.

That summer you went to France to be a waitress at a music festival, and he went to the uncle in Edinburgh again. You were living with a French family, finding your French was not as good as you'd thought it was, nor apparently was your voice; cowed by the jostling ambition at the festival; lonely, hungry, missing your parents, missing Boy 19. He wrote to you, but less often as the summer went along. He also called you occasionally, using what turned out to be, to your chagrin and the baffled outrage of your French hosts, a stolen credit card number. You were discovering love as inertia, and discovering that inertia could be something passionate and fierce, a stubborn persistence in adhering to a vantage point. At home, in your parents' bedroom, there was a painting of a bowl of fruit; one day as a child you had looked at it and seen a face—two eyes, a nose, a mouth—and since then you had never been able to see the fruit bowl, only the face. Now, it seemed, no matter what he did or how he treated you, you could only see Boy 19 as the boy you loved.

You were supposed to meet him in Paris for a few days at the end of the summer. He'd stopped calling you once the credit card fraud had been discovered, and you kept waiting for him to write and let you know when and where in Paris he wanted to meet, but no letter came. Did he still love you? Of course, he said when you were both back in America. Things had gotten complicated and busy, and he'd lost the address. Of course he'd wanted to see you. It had all just gotten away from him. Relax, why didn't you?

To be talked to that way. To have caused someone to talk to you that way. It was a chicken-or-egg question: which came first, your anxiety or his evasive brusqueness?

Just tell me, you kept saying, and he said: There's nothing to tell. He had bought a car and liked to drive it, very fast, up and down the East Coast. On this particular weekend, he had picked you up in New York and was driving you down to the house where his dead grandparents had summered in Maryland. Please, you said again, late that night at a rest stop in New Jersey, I know something's wrong, just tell me. And he told you: He'd fallen in love with someone else. Your mouth was full of mashed potatoes, which you struggled to swallow. You cried, you asked questions, and he answered with a monosyllabic reticence that seemed partly an attempt (futile) at chivalry and partly self-importance. She taught the calisthenics class he had started taking last spring. No, nothing had happened back then—he'd noticed she was attractive, that's all. She was forty-one. She rode a motorcycle. Divorced, with a nineteen-year-old son. Yes, he knew he and the son were the same age, and yes, he agreed it was a little weird. No, nothing had happened even now, but he could tell that it was going to. Then you were out in the parking lot and he had his arms around you—ssssh, ssssh, stop, it's going to be all right—but you couldn't stop, and you didn't want him comforting you for this thing that he was the cause of; but without him there was no comfort; you clung to him and soaked him and scared the hell out of him, and scared the hell out of yourself, out there under this big dull sky in the sulphur-smelling middle of nowhere.

In the grandparents' empty, cold house, you insisted on a guest room, not the big bedroom where he wanted you to stay with him; but then you fucked him on the narrow guest room bed, as if that could hold him or remind him of what he would be missing. It was a plea, and a deeper excursion into self-abasement; but you did it again in the morning. In between you stayed awake for most of the night, alone in the mothball-smelling guest room with its ancient silvery-gray carpet stained white in places by the old messes of long-dead pets, reading a warped, swollen paperback you found in a shelf, an account of soccer players surviving after a plane crash in the Andes by eating the flesh of their dead teammates. In the morning you had a headache and your eyeballs hurt from crying. You told him not to call you again. Even if nothing happened with the calisthenics teacher, you were through.

You proved to yourself that you meant it by seducing Boy 22, an act that was barely premeditated; he was known as someone who had a lot of casual sex, and you went to his room one afternoon with an apple, took a bite, and then held it out so that he could take a bite. Afterward, you and the sheets were littered with black hairs. When you were dressed again and ready to leave, he said, "Well, it's been real," and you thought, yeah, exactly. Casual sex was too casual for you. It had been purely factual, like your old notions of insertions and angles, no longer alarming the way it would have been once, but also uninteresting. The job had gotten done, but you could do that job by yourself at your convenience without involving another person.

This was where things stood when Boy 19 called you again. You'd been alone for several months by then. For the first time ever, you had no one in your sights. Your romantic education, at once so eventful and so tame, seemed exhaustive, complete. You couldn't imagine, nor did you want, further permutations.*

So you were surprised, but not otherwise moved—not angry, not thrilled (well, maybe a little gratified)—to hear from Boy 19 late in the fall of your sophomore year. He said he missed you. You asked about the calisthenics teacher, and he said yes, he'd been seeing her, but, he repeated, he missed you. Then he made a comparison between her and you that was crude and unsporting and morally bankrupt—you felt compelled to defend her, pointing out that she had given birth—but that also, shamefully, turned you on; and when he said again, lowering his voice almost to a whisper, that he missed

---

* You were feeling the way you would later in your life every January, with the blaze and clutter and over-richness of Christmas over, the children back in school, the ornaments back in the basement, the tree lying on the curb, nothing on the calendar: a little bleak, but also peaceful, clean, looking out at a landscape of packed ice and bare black trees.

you and wanted to see you again, you didn't say yes, but you didn't quite say no. There were more phone calls in the weeks after that, and eventually he came down to New York, and you went up to Boston once more.

In some ways those were the best weekends you ever had with him: pleasant, free, a little melancholy, not looking forward or backward. You both knew you wouldn't stay together.* You spent the time in bed. Sometimes he would stroke your hair while you lay with your cheek against the hollow just below his rib cage. But sometimes he would say something that would make you wonder why you were doing this—why you had done any of it, all that yearning and energy and self-reproach spent on people who seemed central and then didn't really figure at all, and why you were seeing him, even temporarily—like the time he said he would have to ask his analyst (he had started seeing one after you and he had broken up the first time) to explain why he was now able to let himself come in your mouth when, no matter how much he might have wanted to, he never could before. You were still lying next to him when he said it; you had never felt lonelier, but you could not figure out how to answer him: how to begin to say what you meant, or where it might end.

---

* You didn't know that you were about to meet your husband, who never felt like Boy 23; he felt like your husband almost at once. He had had his own odyssey, before he got to you. He wasn't there, and then he was, sitting on the floor next to a couch you sat on at a party you hadn't really wanted to go to.

EMILY CARROLL

■

Our Neighbor's House

FROM *Through the Woods*

Seven days ago our father left us
while he went hunting.

He left my older sister in charge
of me and
my younger sister.

Mary

Beth

Hannah

"I'll be gone for three days,"
he said.

"But if I'm not back
by sunset on the
third day,

pack some food,
dress up warm,
and travel to
our neighbor's house."

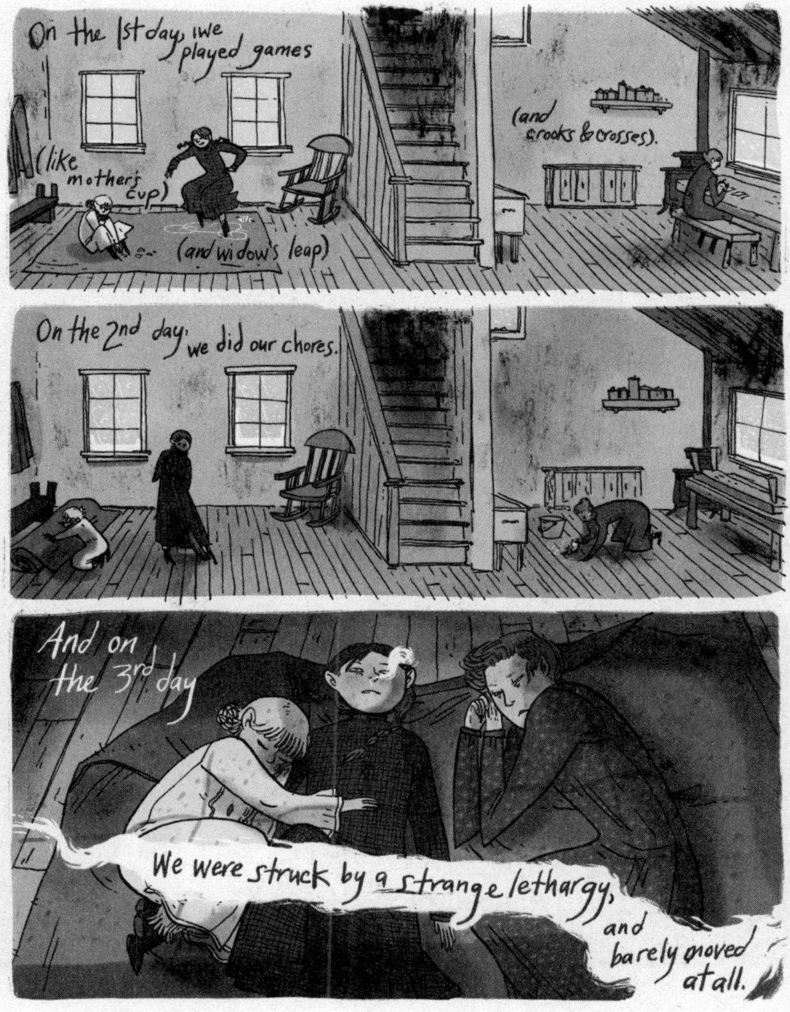
On the 1st day, we played games
(like mother's cup)
(and widow's leap)
(and crooks & crosses).
On the 2nd day, we did our chores.
And on the 3rd day
We were struck by a strange lethargy,
and barely moved at all.

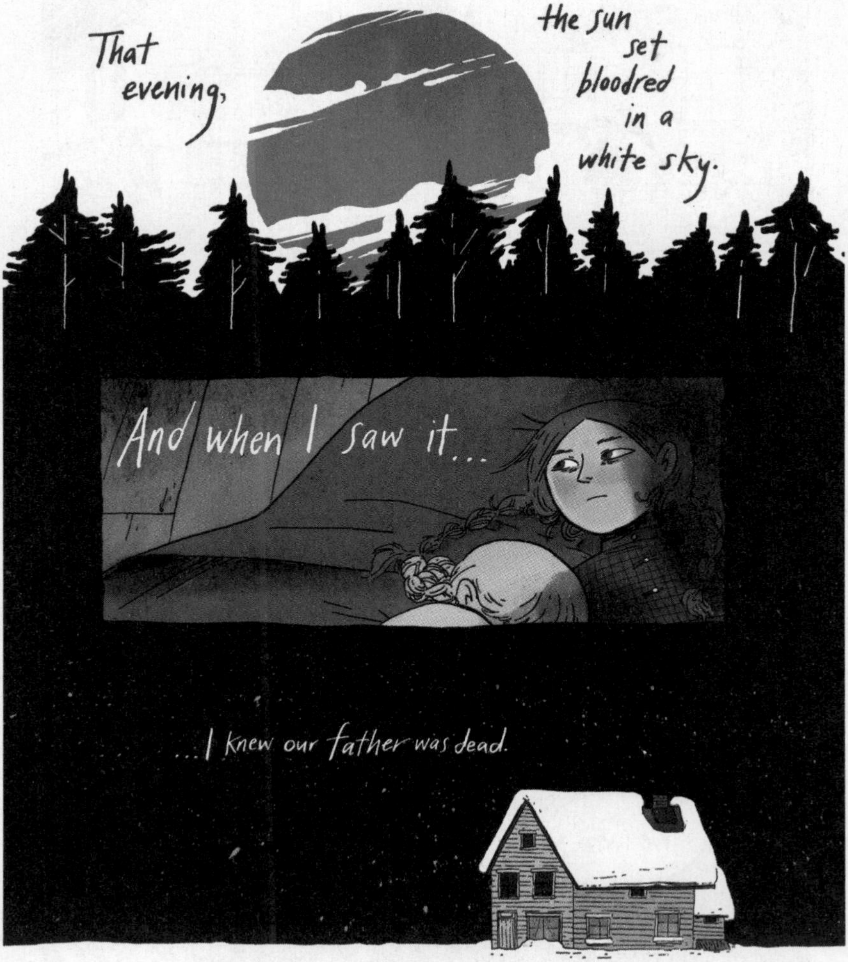
That evening,
the sun set bloodred in a white sky.
And when I saw it...
...I knew our father was dead.

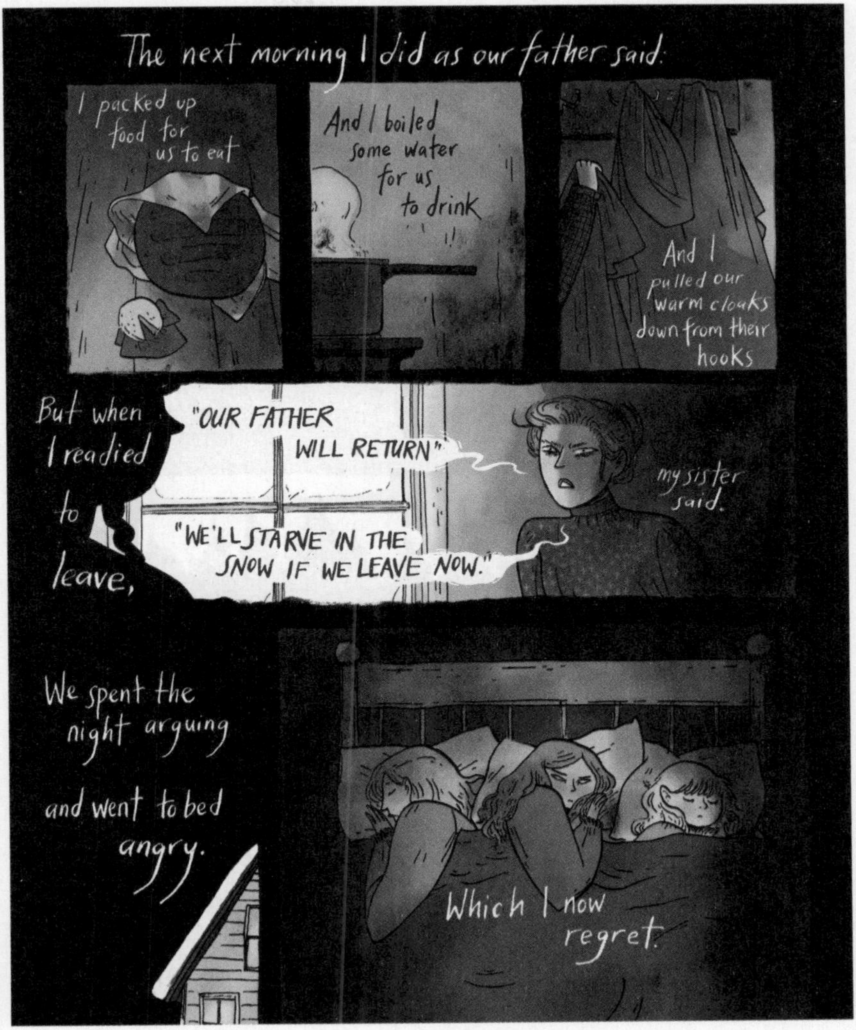
The next morning I did as our father said.
I packed up food for us to eat
And I boiled some water for us to drink
And I pulled our warm cloaks down from their hooks
But when I readied to leave,
"OUR FATHER WILL RETURN"
"WE'LL STARVE IN THE SNOW IF WE LEAVE NOW."
my sister said.
We spent the night arguing
and went to bed angry.
Which I now regret.

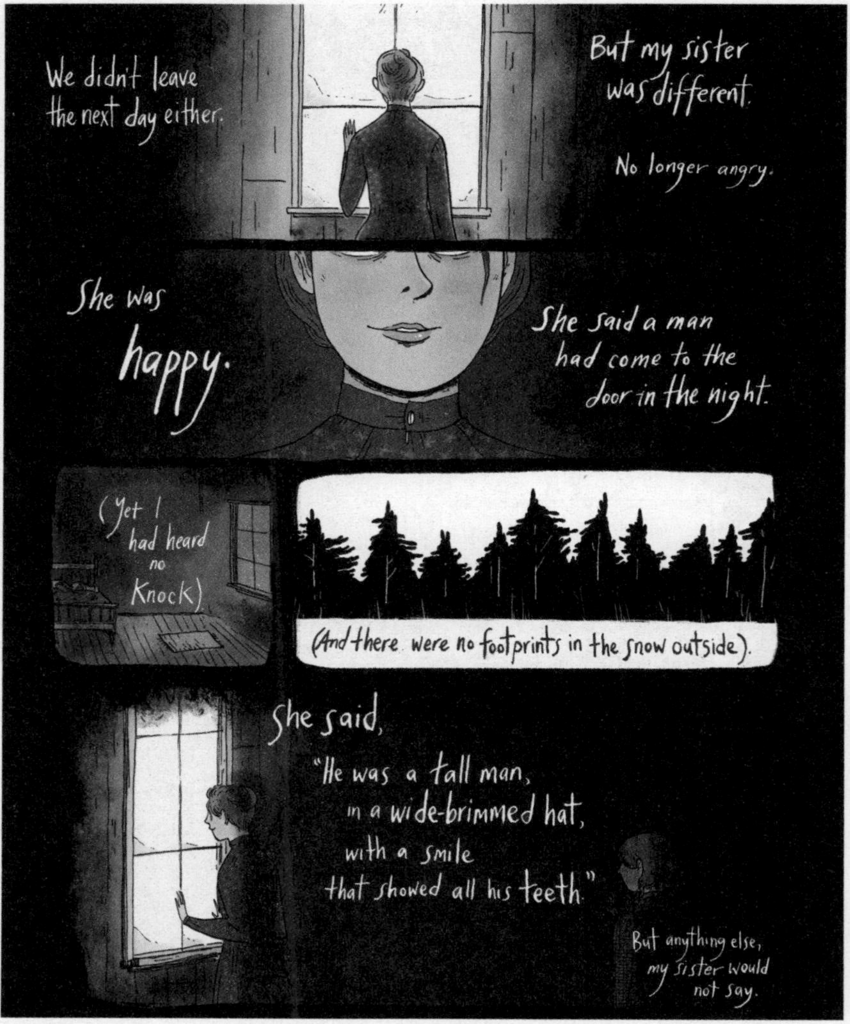
We didn't leave the next day either.
But my sister was different.
No longer angry.
She was happy.
She said a man had come to the door in the night.
(Yet I had heard no Knock)
(And there were no footprints in the snow outside).
She said,
"He was a tall man, in a wide-brimmed hat, with a smile that showed all his teeth."
But anything else, my sister would not say.

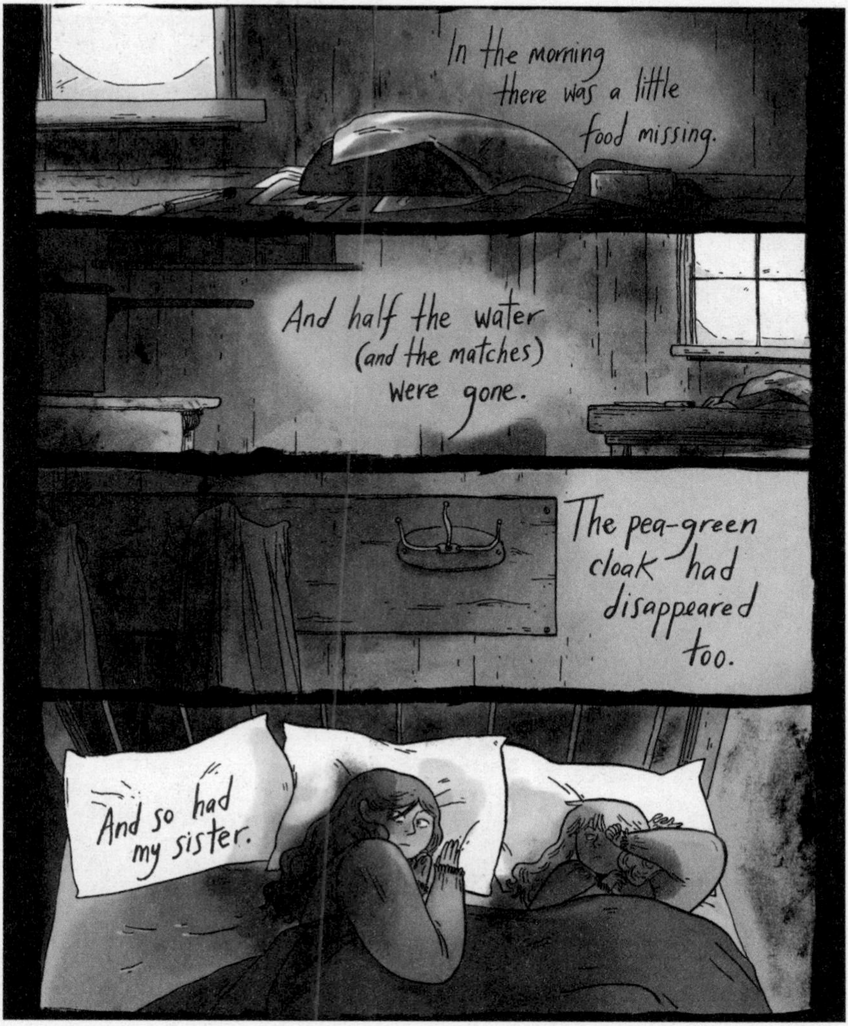
In the morning there was a little food missing.
And half the water (and the matches) were gone.
The pea-green cloak had disappeared too.
And so had my sister.

My little sister cried all morning.

There was no place in the house to escape the wailing.

By the afternoon her eyes were slick and puffy.

Outside, the snow had reached the windows, burying any footsteps or paths.

And inside, there was a stillness, like the air itself had frozen.

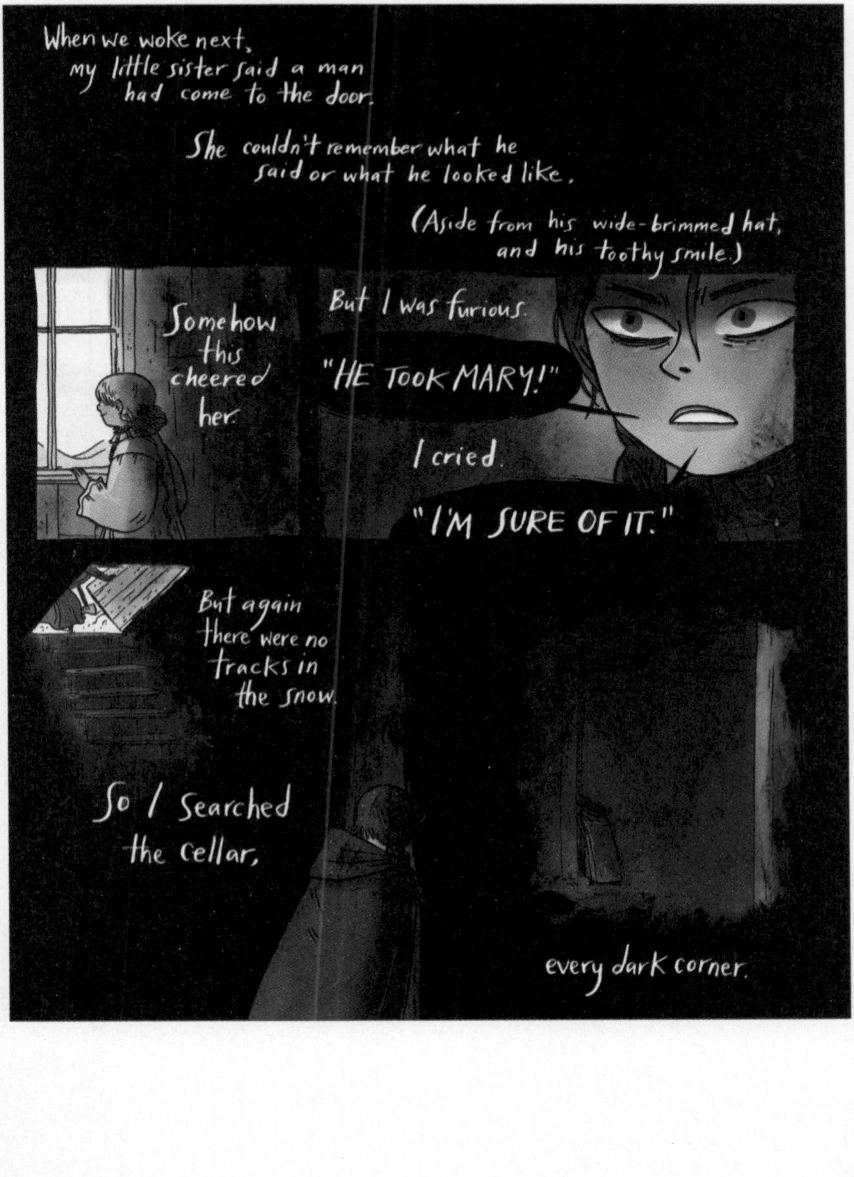
When we woke next,
my little sister said a man
had come to the door.
She couldn't remember what he
said or what he looked like.
(Aside from his wide-brimmed hat,
and his toothy smile.)
Somehow
this
cheered
her.
But I was furious.
"HE TOOK MARY!"
I cried.
"I'M SURE OF IT."
But again
there were no
tracks in
the snow.
So I searched
the cellar,
every dark corner.

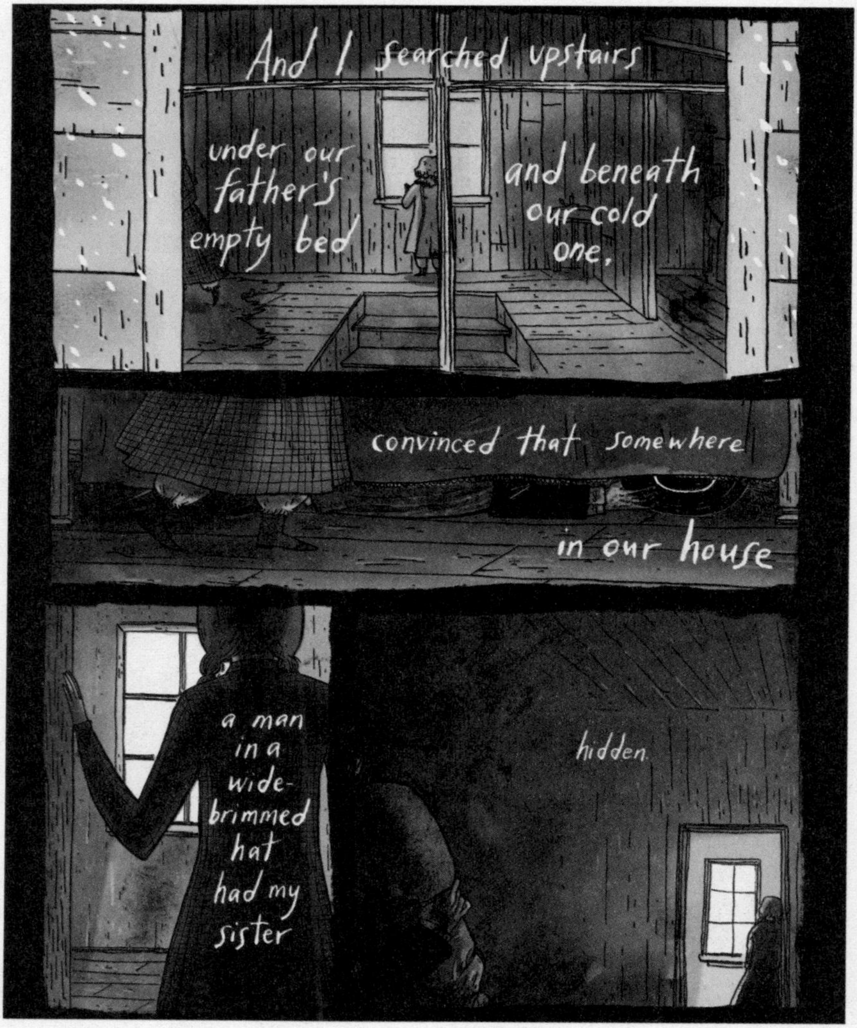
And I searched upstairs
under our father's empty bed
and beneath our cold one,
convinced that somewhere
in our house
a man in a wide-brimmed hat had my sister
hidden.

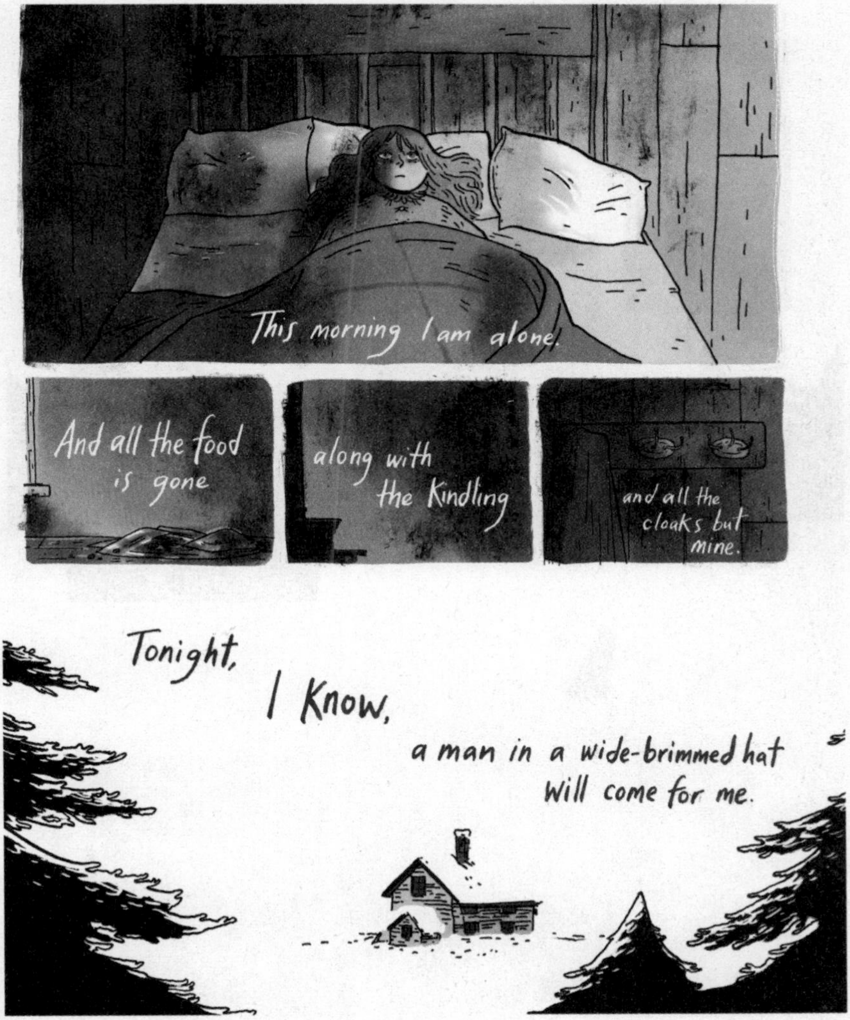
This morning I am alone.
And all the food is gone
along with the Kindling
and all the cloaks but mine.
Tonight,
I Know,
a man in a wide-brimmed hat will come for me.

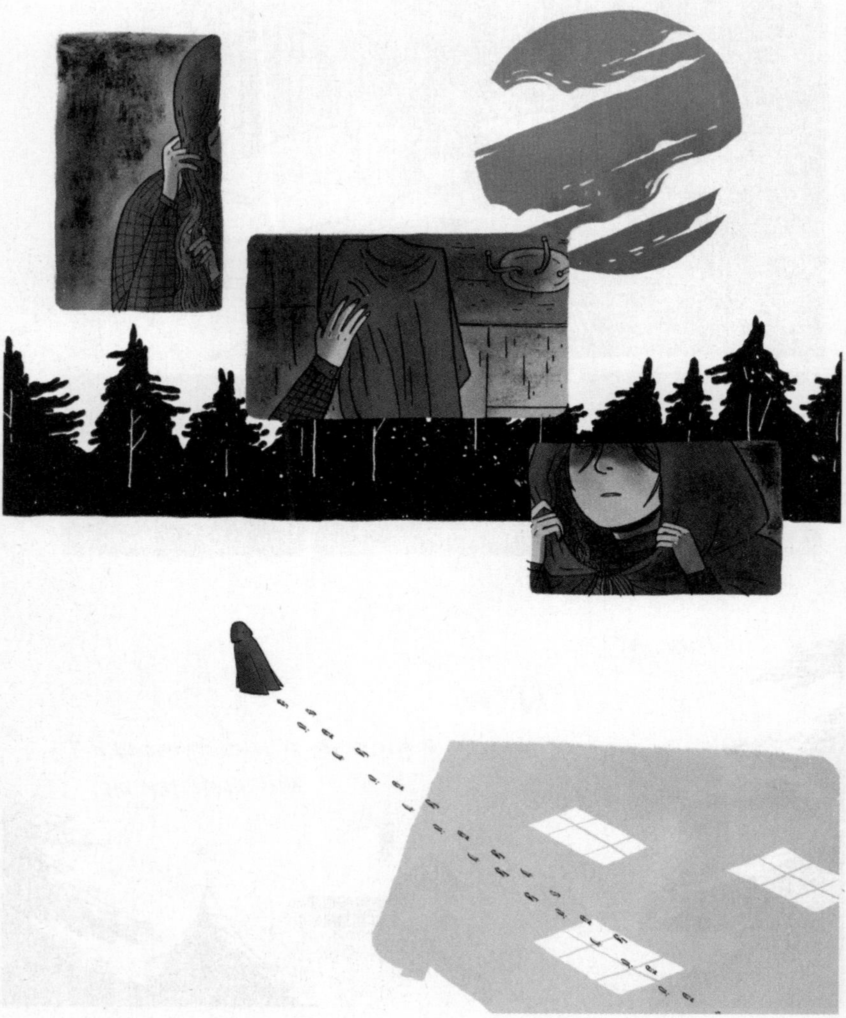

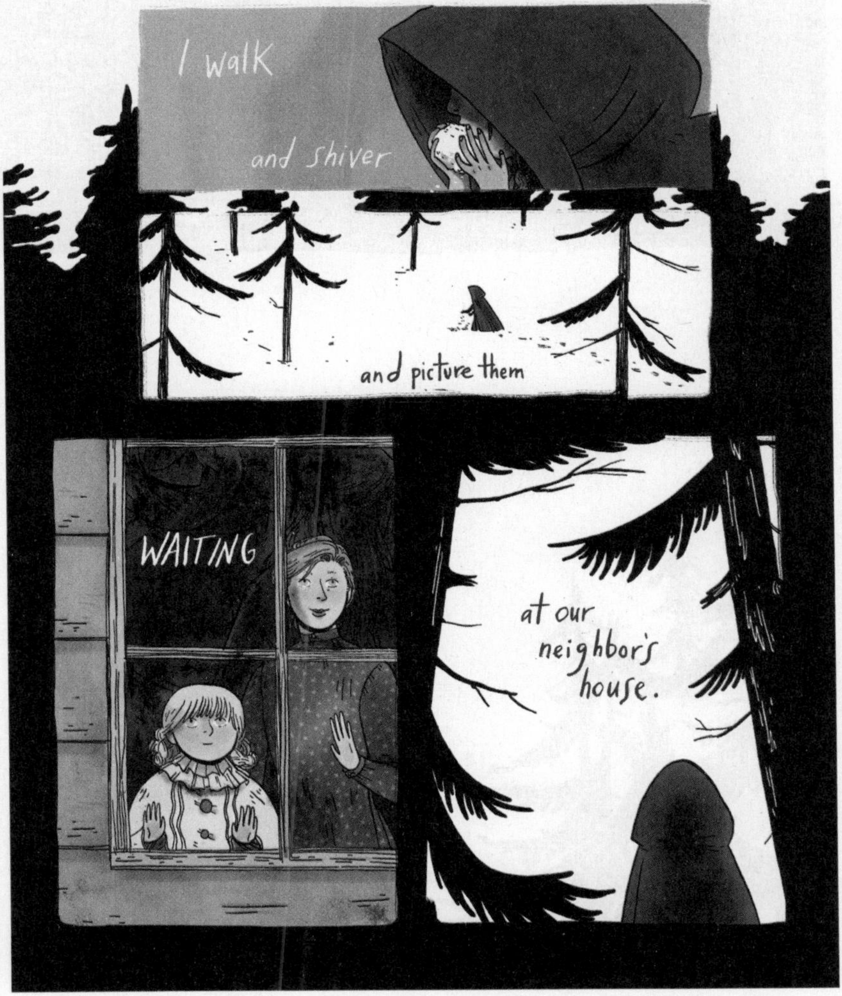
I walk
and shiver
and picture them
WAITING
at our neighbor's house.

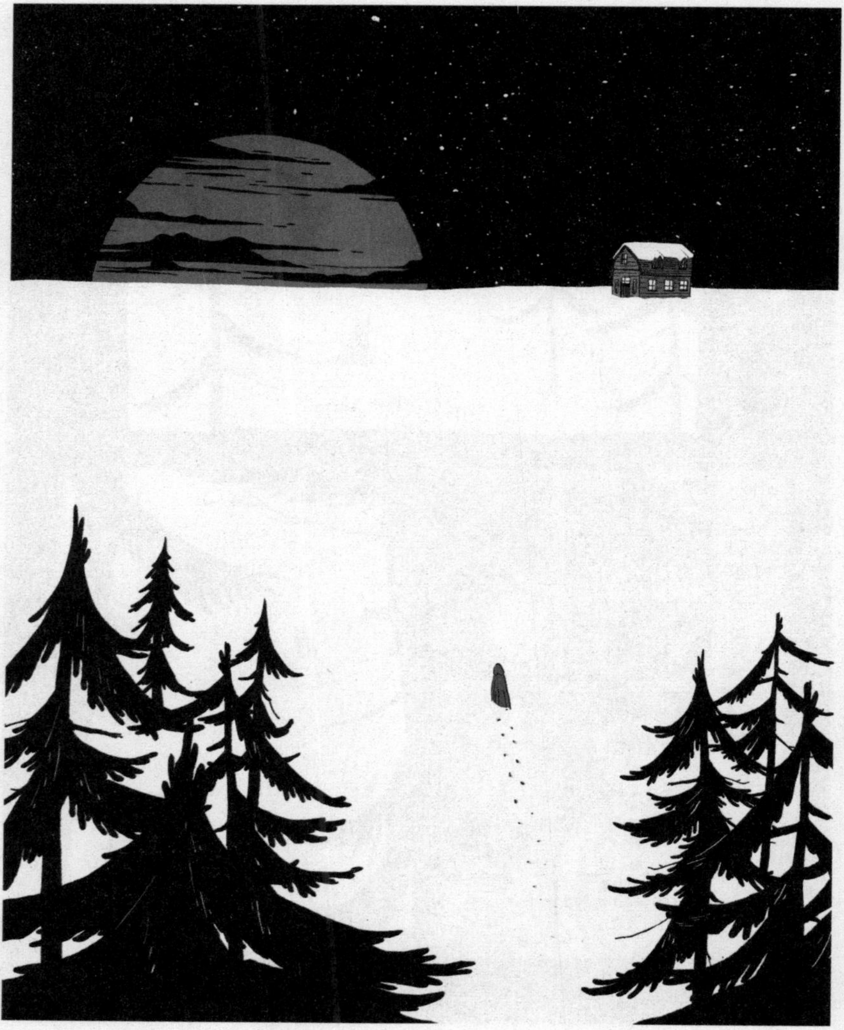

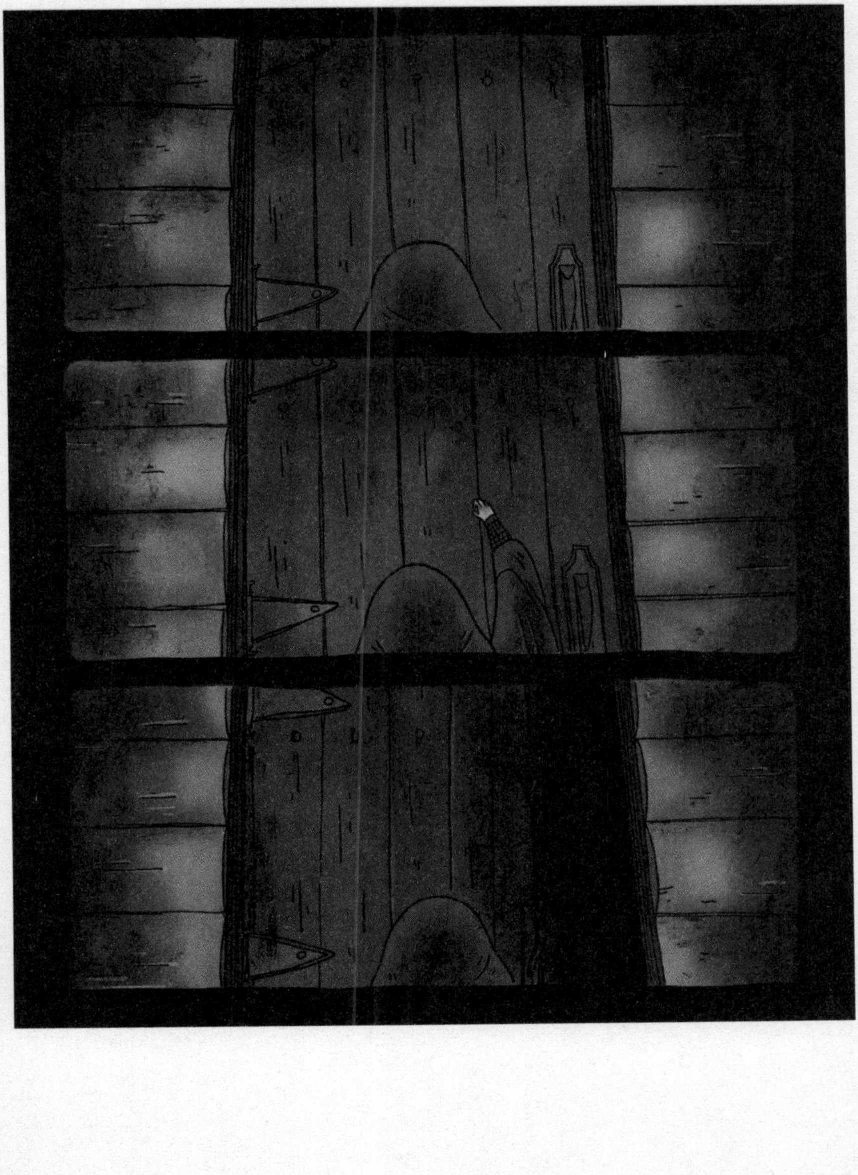

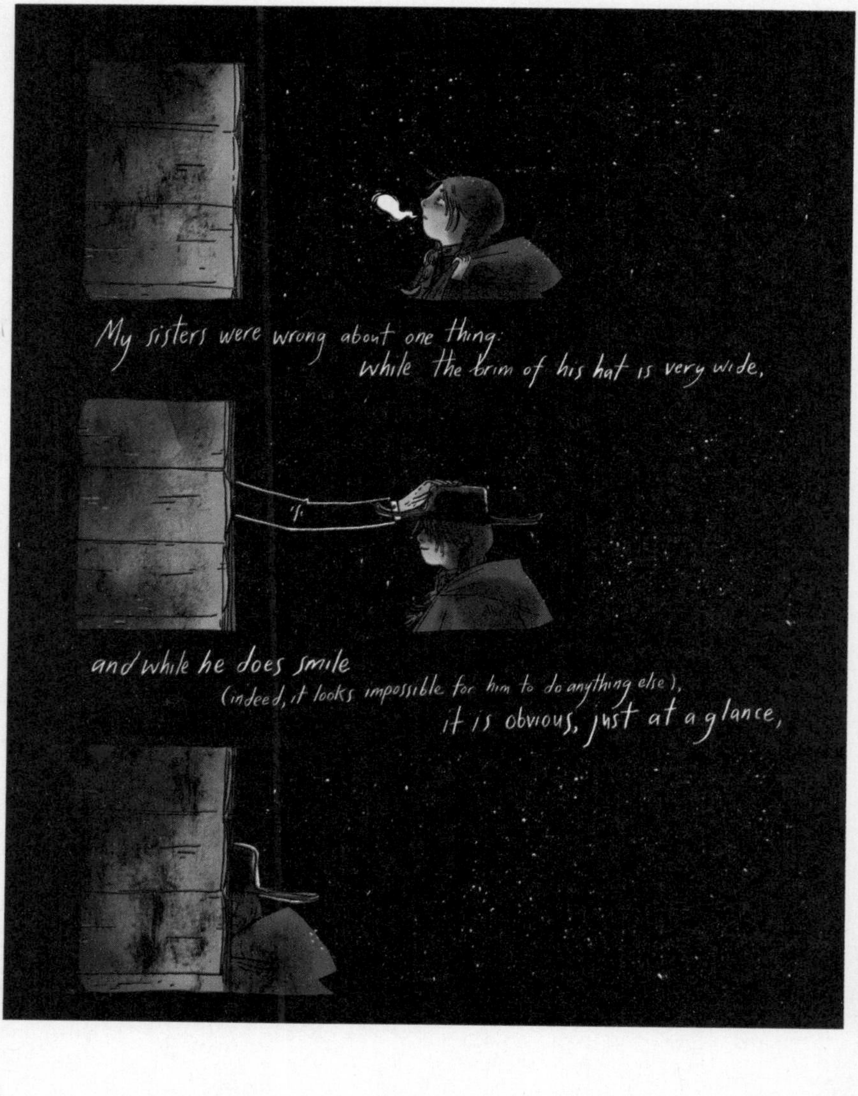
My sisters were wrong about one thing.
while the brim of his hat is very wide,
and while he does smile
(indeed, it looks impossible for him to do anything else),
it is obvious, just at a glance,

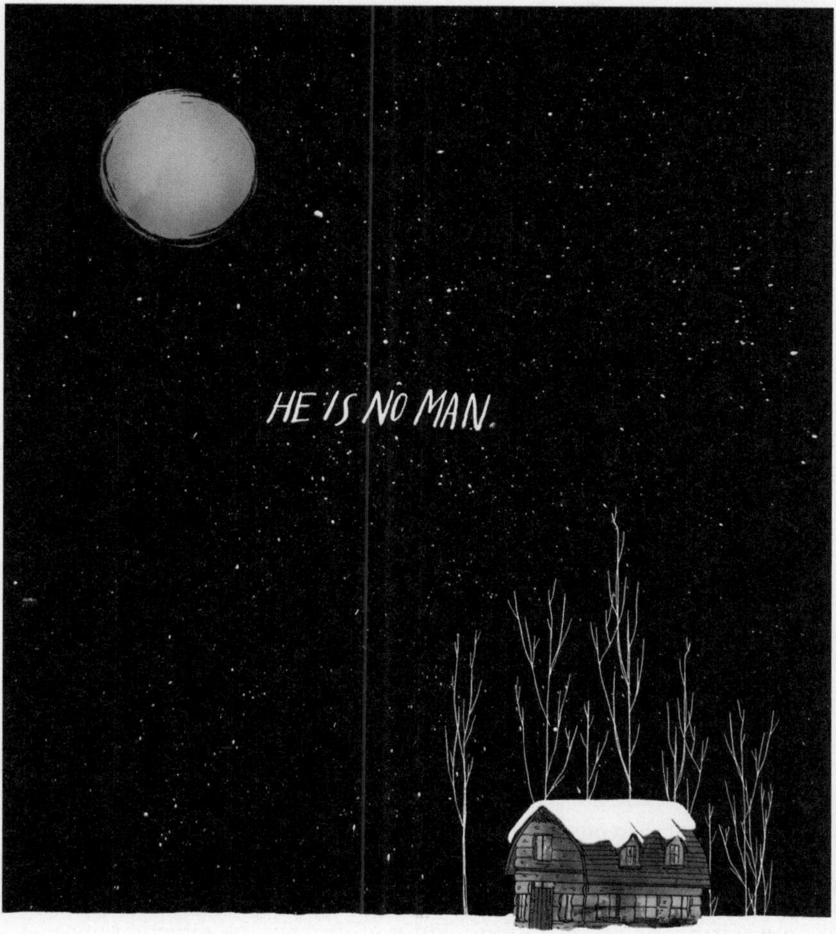
HE IS NO MAN.

INÉS FERNÁNDEZ MORENO

TRANSLATED BY RICHARD V. MCGEHEE

■

Miracle in Parque Chas

FROM *The Southern Review*

THAT NIGHT THE STREETS in the little barrio of Parque Chas reminded me more than ever of La Chacarita cemetery. Those modest little houses of Berlín and Varsovia Streets, their narrow windows and gray walls, no doubt corresponded to the marble and stone vaults of the neighboring cemetery. Houses a little smaller, of course, a little more silent, but essentially the same.

Vault or small house, each had the same proud enclosure of private property, the same persistent desire for a front yard, the pot of flowers, the same respectful barrier at the entrance. Even the garden dwarfs and the dogs on the terraces maintained their relationship with certain figures of virgins or of guardian angels in the friezes of the mausoleums.

I admit I was depressed.

A few days earlier I had found myself out of work, and the Brazilians were beating us, 1–0, in the final round of the Copa América. That's what the voice of the commentator was telling me, drilling my brain through the earpieces of my Walkman. Maybe that's why that cloud of funereal thoughts were arranging themselves to wear down my spirits, in the background, but uniformly in the direction of sadness and defeat.

I arrived at Triunvirato Avenue, looking for an open stand to buy cigarettes, and I stopped in front of the display window of a store that sold household articles.

A group of six or seven men was following the action of the game that appeared on the illuminated screens of several television sets. It always made me a little uneasy to see these solitary men; it's easy to imagine them hungry, cold, suffering with a desire that attains only the crumbs of comfort. In spite of everything, within the deserted and dimly lit avenue, the group seemed an island of hope for humanity.

I stood behind all of them, and, like them, I became mesmerized by the mute images on the screens. I had the doubtful advantage of sound, with the voice of the commentator detailing the movement of the players. That's to say, the errors of our team and the devastating advance of the Brazilians.

Suddenly the lights blinked, the screens faded to a final, luminous glow, and afterward they went completely black, leaving us disconsolate and gasping like puppies that had been pulled off a teat. I don't know why, maybe because I was the one who had arrived last, all their faces turned toward me. I shrugged my shoulders, a little disconcerted.

"A fuse must have blown," I proposed.

They kept looking at me. What did they want from me? I knew little or nothing about electricity.

"Come on, man," an old guy wearing a gray beret finally revealed the situation. "Since you're still connected, tell us how the game is going."

As children we've all had the fantasy of being soccer commentators, we've all tried, at some time, to attain the impressive velocity necessary to follow the path of a ball and the players running after it. I don't deny it. But to have myself launched like that to narrate, suddenly and without any preparation, that's another story.

Some of them advanced a step toward me; I didn't know, at that point, whether with a menacing attitude or probably they were just trying to position themselves better. I looked at them. I saw in the front of the group a youngster with rings under his eyes, wrapped up in a green scarf, a heavyset, tough-looking man in a leather jacket, a light-complexioned man with a worn face and a folded newspaper under his arm. . .

They were dejected men, punished sufficiently by the politicians, by the lack of work and of hope, by the clumsiness of our national team, and now, on top of everything else, by this unexpected power outage that left them again outside the game.

It was a duty of solidarity to grab that ball.

I began timidly to repeat the words of the commentator.

"How well the Brazilian did it . . ." I said, "what precision . . . the indirect kick is for Carvalho . . . there comes so-and-so . . . and so-and-so . . . and so-and-so . . . the striker heads with the left side of his head . . . it's a curving, centering shot . . . seeking the head of number nine . . . the ball's in the area . . . there's danger of a goal . . . "

I had barely begun the account when I realized that my words, sluggish at the start, were heating up, as if they became determined and even reckless—one time a friend who studied acting had commented to me that a voice used publicly becomes animated as from an outside force; it falls in love with its own lullaby and ends up creating its own game.

I was almost the first to be surprised when, instead of calling out the powerful goal by Gonçalvez that put Brazil ahead, 2–0, I made the ball curve a few centimeters in the air and strike the crossbar.

"The ball hits the crossbar . . ." I said, "incredible, gentlemen," I added, "incredible . . . Argentina is saved miraculously from a new goal by the player from Rio de Janeiro."

My crowd sighed in relief and I kept on going. "There comes Lefty . . . he passes to Angelini . . . Angelini to Pedrete . . . Pedrete to Pascualito . . . Pascualito . . . Pascualitoooo."

Argentina's offense would have continued its advance cleanly if it were not for Quindim, the Brazilian marker, a huge mulatto who slides over the field like an eel. "Quindim crosses to his right, engages Pascualito, takes the ball away and launches it far into the Argentine area . . ."

It wasn't so easy to change the direction in which my words were rolling. So I said, "Quindim on the right, tries to intercept . . . Pascualito feints right and left . . . the mulatto falls and rolls on the grass . . . and now nobody stops Pascualito, who arrives now to the goal area, shoots, and gooooooal! gooooooal! gooooooooooooooooooooooooooooal!!!! By Argentinaaaa!!!!" I cry, "that puts the score one to one with the Brazilians, greeeaaat Pascualito!!!" I note, "with a goal won sincerely through the emotion of obtaining the tie."

My crowd jumps for joy. The shouting grows until it shakes the unperturbed quiet of Triunvirato Avenue.

The retired man pulls off his beret and swings it in an enormous arc, as if he wanted to salute the entire universe with it.

The haggard kid in the scarf jumps onto the back of the big guy, who grabs his legs and whirls him around several times, piggyback. Farther back, a group of three or four hug each other and jump rhythmically. I, myself, run toward the corner with my arms over my head. A motorcyclist, infected by our enthusiasm, stops at the traffic light and blows his horn.

The festivities quiet down as soon as I resume my commentary, but they persist in the shining eyes and expectant attitude of the group.

With vertiginous anxiety, I understand that it all remains now in my hands, in my voice. That I can cause them to fall again into despair or make them live moments of glory.

In the middle of the second half, with the impulse of the cold and our enthusiasm, we move along Triunvirato toward La Haya. I'm out in front, followed by the crowd of fans, recording with increasing professionalism the incredible turnaround of the Argentinean team.

It's enough for me to correct the announcer slightly. When he speaks of the confident advance "of the Brazilians," I say, "of the Argentineans." When he says, "Bertorto went to sleep on that pass," I say, "Das Portas went to sleep." When he says, "Uhhh how the Argentinean goalie let that shot go through!" I say, "Uhhh how the Brazilian goalie let that ball through!"

A couple kissing slowly on La Haya joins the crowd of fans. On Berna Street an old man in a wheelchair comes to his door and applauds us. A man who's walking two sausage dogs on the sidewalk of Berlín Street begins to follow us. A woman with uncombed hair and in house slippers runs along Varsovia and reaches us. Also two boys who are smoking a joint on Amsterdam. Like the piper of Hamelin, the harmonious and consistent exhibition of the Argentinean team proves to be an irresistible music.

We arrive at the Plaza Éxodo Jujeño. Although summer is now in the past, there's a reminiscence of jasmine in the air. Then I stop listening to the commentator, the one who had spoken only to me, with the arrogant and strident voice of someone who believes himself owner of the truth. I don't need him. He irritates me with his common voice and his false goals. The members of my congregation listen only to my voice, they see by means of my words, they rise up and enjoy and fear, but only to return to jubilation because, like never before, the action adjusts itself to an intelligent and rigorous strategy: the forwards attack, the defenders defend, the goalkeeper saves goals.

The Brazilian errors, on the other hand, multiply.

They misdirect passes, they're taken in by our fakes, they set up their back line badly, they miss two penalty kicks that should have been sure things. . .

The Argentinean team perfects its technique; it becomes imaginative, they make plays—a shot between the legs of an opponent, a shot with the toe, a goal from midfield—that will be remembered for years. The goals, in this fiesta of greatness, are almost unimportant and are made with startling regularity. We win 5–1.

Neither the fog that descends on the Parque nor the weak glow from the streetlights is able to darken the joy. On the contrary, they bestow the dimension of a mysterious epic on the hugs, the unfurled jackets and scarves, the waving hands, on those who fall to their knees, cross themselves, kiss each other, and sing and dance.

Parque Chas is a liberated land, and its liberation was produced by the vibration of my words, by the images my words have convoked in front of all those eyes.

The cold presses on us and the group of fans finally, slowly disperses. I walk aimlessly. I go along like I'm in the clouds, worn out, but serene and proud.

A little light, like a buoy, guides me to the kiosk at the corner of Gándara and Tréveris, that is open now.

"Earlier you weren't open," I comment to the proprietor.

"Things change," he tells me philosophically.

"Did you perhaps see how the game ended?" He says this with a smile bright enough to light up the entire barrio.

"We all saw it," I say, trying to remember his face among the men in my group of fans.

Afterward I nod a good-bye to him and continue my walk.

I launch a puff of smoke toward the sky; it extends itself in a tenuous cloud of steam.

On the roof of a little house, a dark figure whirls crazily. It's a weather vane. A dog on a flat roof. An angel that celebrates the miracle of Parque Chas.

CORINNE GORIA

∎

An Oral History of Neftali Cuello

FROM *Invisible Hands: Voices from the Global Economy*

VOICE OF WITNESS *is a nonprofit organization that publishes oral histories of human rights crises. The following is an excerpt drawn from their book* Invisible Hands, *which featured narratives of workers struggling to survive in the global economy. The book was edited by Corinne Goria and this specific interview was conducted by writer and journalist Gabriel Thompson.*

AGE: 17
OCCUPATION: High school student, tobacco field worker
BIRTHPLACE: Los Angeles, CA
INTERVIEWED IN: Pink Hill, North Carolina

In North Carolina, when school gets out each summer, a stream of young people—nearly all Latino—head into the fields to help bring in the state's most profitable crop: tobacco. Neftali was twelve years old when she first accompanied her family into the fields. At the time, she and her older sisters wanted to help their single mother pay the household's bills. Now seventeen and a senior in high school, Neftali has spent five summers in the fields, working sixty-hour weeks and contending with extreme heat and humidity, along with nicotine and pesticide exposure.

We first meet Neftali at a gathering of young farmworkers advocating for better wages and working conditions, held in a doublewide trailer not far from her home in Pink Hill. At the gathering, Neftali speaks eloquently of the pressures that forced her parents and many of her peers to leave home and search for work in the United States, many of them uproot-

ing themselves and their families year to year to pursue available work to avoid the attention of immigration authorities.

Over the course of several subsequent phone conversations (occasionally interrupted by the sound of roosters crowing in the background), Neftali talks about the challenges of working in tobacco, her plans for the future, and how her activism has transformed her from a shy girl into a gregarious teenager who enjoys addressing large crowds.

Back Then, All the Kids Slept Together in One Room

People say that it's dead in Pink Hill because nothing goes on here.* But it's not dead—it's just peaceful. People don't really notice the beauty of nature. I live in a trailer park, and outside my house I am surrounded by fields. From the trailer park you can drive three minutes and be in the town. You know how a teenager is like, "I'm gonna go play video games or watch TV"? Well, for me it's a little bit different. I'll go and get one of my friends, a neighbor—the other trailer houses are filled with migrant farmworker families—and we'll walk around, see the birds, play with my dogs and cats. And we got a duck. It adopted itself onto our porch, so I feed it.

I was born in Los Angeles. That's where my parents met. My mom is from Cuernavaca, Mexico.** My dad is from the Dominican Republic. I was one when my parents separated and we moved from Los Angeles to North Carolina—it was me, my mom, and my two older sisters and brother. I don't remember anything about Los Angeles, but I want to visit.

When we first got to Pink Hill we lived right across the street from the school, but my brother and sisters would still be late. I would be like, "Wake up! Wake up!"—just jumping on the couch. I wasn't even a kindergartner then. Then I started school, and my mom would walk me over. My mom had to go to work, so we'd have to get ready ourselves.

Back then, all the kids slept together in one room. It was the four of us. We'd just cuddle up together and go to sleep. We were living in

---

* Pink Hill is a town of about five hundred in southeast North Carolina.

** Cuernavaca is a city of 350,000 in the state of Morelos, about sixty miles south of Mexico City.

a trailer with a kitchen, a very small living room, and two bedrooms. We still live there—our house is homey.

My mom would wake us up at five thirty in the morning and before she left she'd make sure we all had a shower and that our clothes were prepared and our shoes were tied. And she would always do little hairdos on us girls.

That was when she worked in pig farms. She told us why she had to stop working there. A pig was giving birth so she needed gloves, but her employers didn't provide them. She said, "No, I can't do this," and they pretty much fired her. That's when she started working in tobacco.

I Thought it Was Gonna Be Easy-Peasy

My older brother, Henry, was the first to go into the tobacco fields. He was eleven when he went with my mom. He has pale skin, and when he got home that day he was bright red! It took maybe two days for him to get over that because he was so badly sunburned. He didn't go back to the fields after that.

Growing up, we would see our mom go to work in the tobacco fields and get home really tired. And she still had a lot of work to do around the house. When I was about ten, me and my two older sisters agreed to go talk to her, to tell her we had decided to work in the fields. At first she said, "No, you are so not working." We were like, "You know what, we're gonna go to work. We're gonna help you out." She said we were too young. But later she let us go to work in the summers, because she couldn't take care of us all and pay the bills.*

I was twelve when I began working in tobacco. My sister Kimberly was thirteen or fourteen. My oldest sister, Yesenia, was fifteen. We wanted to be independent and to help Mom out. By that time she had another two kids with her boyfriend—my three-year-old brother and seven-year-old sister. My mom said that she'd rather work three jobs than see her kids working out in the fields. She told us that we broke her heart when we decided to work. We didn't exactly understand what she meant, but we understand now.

---

* In the United States, children as young as twelve are permitted to work on large, commercial farms and children of any age can work on small-scale farms.

That first experience in the fields—oof! I didn't wake up that first day. My mom had to wake me up. It was five in the morning. I would guess that it was July. She said, "You only have twenty minutes to get ready." It was dark that first morning, but not a bad dark. I didn't see stars, but I could see the first little ray of sunlight.

I put on a t-shirt and shorts, 'cause it was gonna be hot. My mom said, "Go back into your room." She told me to put on some long sleeves, a sweatshirt, pants, and old shoes. "Clothes that you don't care about," she said. When I asked why, she said, "You'll see."

So my sisters and I climbed into the car and my mom drove. We were driving what we always called our little gray car. I don't know exactly what model it is because I suck at describing cars. I was sitting in the back seat. Driving to the field I was thinking, *It's gonna be really good to be outside.* Like I said, I really like nature. I was thinking, *The sun's gonna be hitting me; it's gonna be nice just to be around plants and walking.* I had always looked at tobacco plants and thought they were pretty. I was thinking, *I'm gonna see that my mom was worrying over nothing.* I thought it was gonna be easy-peasy.

We drove to a designated spot that my mom knew and stopped to wait for other people driving to the fields. A group of a few cars drove by and honked their horns, and we rushed to catch up to them in our car. My mom explained that if we couldn't catch up to them, we'd have to go to another contractor and try to find work.*

After a while, I noticed that the ride starts to get really, really bumpy. The roads that lead to tobacco fields weren't paved. They're dirt roads with huge holes, and I was being thrown around, and I'm like, *What the heck?* And then as we get out, I'm thinking, *Oh my God, the clothes I'm wearing look ridiculous. I don't even want to get out.* Me and my sisters were laughing about it. And we got out and saw dozens of people wearing most of the same things we were. Then we saw the field, just rows and rows of tobacco. And I thought, *We're not gonna get out of here. They're gonna keep us here forever.*

My mom went and talked to the contractor. There were seven or eight other people in our crew. They were all Hispanic. I've always

---

* To ensure a steady workforce, many farmers pay a fee to labor contractors, who are responsible for recruiting and supervising crews of seasonal farmworkers. As a result, many farmworkers have little idea who owns the fields they are harvesting.

only seen Mexicans and African Americans in the fields. I was probably the youngest, though there were at least two or three other young people I recognized from my school.

If you tell the contractor you have work experience, they don't really care what your age is. They showed us how to sucker. Suckers are these little lime-green tobacco shoots growing in between the leaves. They're curvy, fuzzy, and pointy at the very beginning of the stem. They're like another branch growing, and you have to tear them off with your hands and nails.* But they're hard to tear off. And they can look just like a leaf. It's really hard to distinguish sometimes.

I was this short little girl. The tobacco plants were bigger than me; they were huge and would loom over you like crazy. The leaves spread out so far that you have to squeeze your way through the rows. And the suckers aren't just on the top—they're also at the very bottom of the plants. You have to go around the whole tobacco plant. How are you supposed to do that, especially when you're little?

We started at 6 a.m. In ten minutes I was drenched from head to toe in dew. I thought I was going fast, but I got left behind at least twice. Yesenia helped me and then my mom came over and helped me. The contractor said, "She needs to speed up." I was running—struggling with having to be the best, although I knew I never was, like at school and stuff. So I felt really bad when I heard the contractor say that.

Within two to three hours I was feeling nauseous. But I thought it was just me—that I hadn't drunk any water. It was too far back to go and get water, and I thought, *They're probably gonna yell at me if I go.* I was this really shy girl: I didn't want to get in trouble and get fired the first day.

Then I got really sluggish. I was thinking: *Okay, I need to sit down.* But I couldn't sit down, because everybody's gonna move up ahead and I'm gonna get fired, I'm gonna get everybody fired. So I kept going.

I was seeing little circles. I had to take a rest. But I saw the contractor walking by. When I got up and pretended I was working, I felt

---

* When "suckering," tobacco harvesters often use their hands to remove the small shoots (though machines are sometimes available for the job). The removal of these shoots forces the tobacco plant to focus its energy on producing large leaves.

like I was going to faint. The sky started to get blurry and my head literally turned sideways. It's really hard to explain: it's like when you're trying to focus on something and just can't. My mom came over to me and said, "Sit down—I'm gonna get you some water." She went and got me some water and ice; I got back to work. I still felt sluggish, and I remember that within two hours my mom actually had to sit me down again and tell me to take a break.

Kimberly was working fast. She was taking the pace that my mom was. At maybe two or three in the afternoon, I could hear somebody vomiting really loudly—it sounded like she was throwing up her lungs. I couldn't see over the tobacco plants. I was like, *What the heck?* It was Kimberly. Then she stopped and we thought she was okay. We told her to sit down, take a break, go sit in the car. But she wanted to go on, even though she kept throwing up at the same time. It was because of the nicotine.* The leaves would get sticky with nicotine when they were wet. Also, I think the plants had been sprayed with pesticides, like maybe a couple hours before, or the day before. You could really smell it.

At around six or seven that night they said we could go home. We were like, "Okay, yeah!" But then I thought, *Oh God, we have to walk all through the field just to get to the car.* It was muddy, and our mom told us to kick our shoes before we got in. But I couldn't do it. I was too tired. I just got in the seat and by the time we got home I was asleep. There were four of us that needed to take showers. I said, "You all just go ahead." I sat on the steps and fell asleep.

That night when I was asleep, I had strange dreams. It wasn't like I was having nightmares—it was like I was still working in tobacco. I could see myself, my hands cutting suckers, rows of tobacco. It's so dizzying, it'll literally wake you up out of nowhere. It was really hard to sleep afterwards. This happens if you work in tobacco. I couldn't go to sleep till three thirty in the morning. I think it has to do with

---

* Workers absorb nicotine from tobacco plants through their skin, and one in four every harvesting season suffers from acute nicotine poisoning, also known as green tobacco sickness. The symptoms of GTS can include dizziness, vomiting, headaches, abdominal pain, and fluctuations in blood pressure and heart rate. Researchers at Wake Forest University have found that, by the end of the season, "nonsmoking workers had nicotine levels equivalent to regular smokers."

the stuff that was on the leaves, the nicotine and pesticides. Eventually you just get used to it.

My Mom Tends to Everybody

When me and my sisters got that first paycheck, we were like, "We're gonna give it to our mom." She said, "No. Keep it for yourself. Buy whatever you need."

My mom tends to everybody. With me, I don't really like to go shopping, to buy clothes or whatever. So I followed her around whenever she went shopping. I'd look at her and if she really looked at something, like she wanted to buy it, I'd buy it for her. Like stuff for the bathroom—curtains for the tub and a hairbrush. I would stay behind and grab it and put it under the cart and pay for it myself. She was happy!

One time for Mother's Day I got her a red basket with a white bear holding a red rose, with a bag of red candies. She still has it— she loved that one. She hasn't opened it. She hung it on the wall and made sure it was very noticeable.

It was really hard for her. By the time I was twelve and started working she had six kids and she was trying to raise them all. She'd come home red from the fields and take a shower and start cooking. Then she would say, "Neftali, my feet hurt so bad. Can you please rub them for a moment so I can fall asleep?" She had issues falling asleep.

There were moments where we didn't have money, but the thing is my mom always made sure we had everything we needed. Not stuff that we wanted—wants were never really allowed. You could always think about them but never actually get them.

Out of Nowhere, I'd Start Singing

By now I've worked five summers in tobacco. We're usually paid in cash. We're paid the minimum wage, $7.25 or $8.00 an hour, whatever it is at the time, but it should be more.

Every year it gets hotter. It'll get to one hundred degrees, but what people don't know is that if you're working in a field of tobacco, the leaves reflect the sun, so it's ten to fifteen degrees hotter in the fields. Unless there are trees at the very end of the field, the only shade you get is if you sit under the tobacco leaves. But there's hardly ever a moment that you can actually take a rest, because the minute you finish a row you have to go to another row. What I've noticed is that for contractors it's all about the money. You have to work as fast as possible. When she was younger, my sister Yesenia was working and all of a sudden she got really cool. She thought she was okay. But she was experiencing heat stress, where her body suddenly starts to heat up a lot inside, even if it felt to her like she was cold. It was actually a very dangerous thing.*

No one ever addressed any of this stuff. They didn't hand out any instructions about heat stress or nicotine poisoning. No safety lessons. We didn't always have helpful equipment like gloves or anything—we just had to make do. I remember one time I worked without gloves because my sister had our only pair. When I got done my whole arm was pure black—it was covered with tar from the plants. I went home and tried to wash it but it didn't work.

I've seen pesticides being sprayed maybe two fields over, and I've seen pesticides being sprayed in front of our house, over cotton fields. When that happened I told everybody, "Don't go outside. Make sure nothing's outside that you gotta bring inside later."**

Every day me and my sisters try to make a happy moment, even if we're feeling really down. So I'll cut off a really big sucker when I'm working in the field and toss it at Kimberly. I'll be like, "Oh no, it was Yesenia!" Or there were days when everything was really quiet, so I'd find the weirdest, most obnoxious song and out of nowhere just start singing it. And I know that my sisters know practically every song, so they would join in and the other workers would be like, "Oh my God." They'd just start laughing.

We never find out about the cigarette companies we're working

---

* North Carolina farmworkers suffer the highest rate of heat-related fatalities in the nation.

** A study in the *American Journal of Industrial Medicine* of 287 farmworkers—the majority of whom worked in tobacco—from forty-four different farmworker camps in eleven eastern North Carolina counties found that the workers were exposed to a large number of pesticides, and exposed to the same pesticides multiple times.

for. You try to talk to the contractor and he just says, "Get to work." This year we actually saw a farmer—the guy who actually owns the farm. He came up and he talked to my mom and then he talked to me, just to greet us. Afterwards, the contractor said we're not supposed to talk to the farmers.

I Expect to See Young People

I expect to see young people in the fields nowadays. I saw eight- and nine-year-olds working in sweet potatoes. They were getting paid 40 cents a bucket. They had to dig around and pick the sweet potatoes up, clean 'em and put 'em in the bucket. They carried the bucket until it was full, then somebody else would carry it and throw it in the truck. That was in Greenville, South Carolina. We don't really see sweet potatoes in Pink Hill.

My friends, right after school they go to work, and they'll be talking about how they feel bad the next morning. It's actually very common for people working in tobacco to feel sick and dizzy. It wasn't just that first day—I always got sick. One time I got sick for two days. I felt bad throughout the day in the fields. The next morning I had a huge headache and I felt like I wanted to vomit. I don't know exactly what's being sprayed, or if it was just the nicotine. It absorbs into your skin—it's just awful, the way you feel. Last year a friend of mine got green tobacco sickness. He was fourteen or fifteen. His family took him to the hospital and he was there for six days, maybe.

When I was thirteen or fourteen, I was having a bunch of problems. Teenager problems. I was really antisocial, like this emo chick. I liked to walk around outside at one o'clock in the morning, like I wasn't scared of anything, like I was practically already on my own. If somebody tried to be nice to me I would flip out. I'm telling you, I had issues. I don't exactly know what I was so angry about. I guess it was because I wasn't letting my emotions out.

In the ninth grade I had surgery on my tonsils and they gave me painkillers. Me being all depressed, I started taking a lot of them. I was gonna take a bunch at once—seven pills—and I looked at them and said, "Nope," and I closed the bottle and walked away from it.

Afterwards I started talking to my Spanish teacher. I met her in tenth grade. She's kind of like how a therapist is—you know, they don't tell anybody your secrets. I'd go see her every other day. And if I could sneak out of the cafeteria during lunch, I'd visit her in her class. They don't let us, but she always told me, "Definitely come over for lunch." I would tell her some of the stuff that was going on with me, and then I wouldn't feel like doing any of the bad stuff, like cutting classes.

Some Changes Are Being Made

One day when I was fourteen, my sister Yesenia told me she was having a meeting with Miss Melissa, a woman who worked as an activist for farmworkers, and asked if I wanted to go.* I said sure, if it'll get me out of the house! That's how I got involved in Rural Youth Power. It's a group of young people. We talk about working in the fields, the education we've received, or haven't received, and the difficulties of moving around. We've stayed in Pink Hill the whole time because my mom put her mind to it: when she wants to stay somewhere, she stays somewhere. But a lot of families never settle down because they keep moving to find work. One kid, Eddie, I think he's thirteen or fourteen, he had to move six different times. And we have so many at-risk kids. Two farmworker friends who went to school with us died last year in a shooting. They weren't in a gang but they hung around with people who were. They were supposed to graduate with us.

We don't have a lot of opportunities where we're living. I want my family to be able to start off again. Hopefully I can do something to help my mom. I don't want her to have to keep focusing on the rent and everything by herself. My hope is to get into a college this year and get started working on my major. I definitely want to work in agriculture, keep advocating. Farmworkers need better wages. We asked to take the kids out of the fields, but it's kinda hard because sometimes it's the kids who are working to help the family. And we want to reduce the spraying of pesticides.

Some changes are being made. Last year we held an event called

---

* "Miss Melissa" is Melissa Bailey, a farmworker advocate in North Carolina. In 2010 she formed NC FIELD (North Carolina Focus on Increasing Leadership Education and Dignity), which provides leadership training to young farmworkers like Neftali.

YouthSpeak in Kinston, North Carolina. I was a panelist and I did a spoken word; everybody liked it. You get to express yourself and how you feel. You don't have to rhyme, but I like rhyming all the time. We talked about how we wanted to see a change in the minimum wage and how we wanted to give out materials and equipment to the people working in the fields. Educate them so they know the rules—that we're supposed to get a break, for example, and that we should have better bathrooms, with soap, so we can actually clean our hands. One of the people at the YouthSpeak event was from the North Carolina Department of Labor, and he said, "All the stuff you asked for is pretty easy. I think we can actually change it. I think that's really possible." When the Department of Labor guy was speaking, we were all really hopeful. It seemed like all these little things that could make our work bearable were possible. Then a little later at the meeting, Miss Melissa gets a call, and somebody's telling her that a farmworker was behind a truck in the sweet potatoes that day and it went over him. He just got crushed and died. We got really quiet and gave a moment to him.

They Can't Get Me to Stop Talking

Right now school is going really well. This year I think I have all As. And I won an award—the national art and essay contest.* I had always been hearing about the contest, and one day I said to myself, "Okay, I'll do it."

The topic of the essay was "The Rhythm of the Harvest." I got two pages done, but it wasn't a lot. On the last day I started working on it at eleven and it was due at twelve o'clock at night. I was like, *Just think about how it is.* Out of nowhere I finished it and turned it in one minute before it was due.

I wrote first about how at nighttime you hear the slithers of a snake, the flaps of a bat, and in the morning you hear the frogs croaking, the crickets chirping. When you get into the fields you hear the screech of a truck stopping and, as you're working, the noise from

---

* Officially the "Association of Farmworker Opportunity Programs' (AFOP) Migrant and Seasonal Farmworker Children Essay and Art Contest." AFOP is a non-profit that seeks to address the safety and wellbeing of farmworkers, including children.

pulling your boots out of mud. Just the different sounds that go on while you're in the field. So I turned in the essay on time and I got first place for fourteen- to eighteen-year-olds. I got to go to Boston for the award ceremony.

I like to dye my hair different colors: I've dyed it purple and two or three shades of blue. When I won the award my hair was red. One lady who was on the award staff, Norma Flores, was like, "You have to dye your hair black for the trip." I said, "Okay, I'll dye it black, but when I get back I'm dyeing it blond and pink."

There were at least two hundred people at the ceremony in Boston, and I was just freaking out. I'm supposed to go up there and I'm supposed to read my essay. I have stage fright—I've always had it. And I felt really awkward. I was thinking, *Something's gonna happen, I'm gonna embarrass myself.* But I got up there and I started reading. I was very awkward at first but then I just thought, *You know what, it's all good. I'm calm, I'm good.* I read it and at the end I got this whole standing ovation. People came up to me saying they were in tears from my story.

At Rural Youth Power, we're planning on showing kids how to speak up, to not be afraid, to speak for your rights—'cause you do have them. One of my friends was gonna get paid $6.25 an hour to work in tobacco. I was like, "Boy, you do not even need to go there." You should be getting paid the minimum wage at least. That is a right, right there. They can't just fire you.

I'm one of those people to step in. I've become less scared since I got involved. Now I can actually have a phone conversation. Before I was practically antisocial. And then I started talking, but I couldn't get serious. But now Miss Melissa says I've changed. Before it was like, "Speak up, Neftali." Now it's like they can't get me to stop talking.

BOX BROWN

■

Andre the Giant

FROM *Andre the Giant: Life and Legend*

BEGINNING ON THE *following page are a series of excerpts from Box Brown's graphic novel* Andre the Giant. *Andre was a 7'4", 500-pound professional wrestler from France who, we learn in the early chapters of Brown's book, once got a ride home from school from Samuel Beckett. It's a strange world, this one.*

In his introduction to the book, Brown explains that it is important to understand that professional wrestling is built on a foundation of deception. Its outcomes are fixed and most people in the audience know this. That being said, there are still real rivalries and conflicts and moments of improvisation. As Brown says, "the idea of truth in professional wrestling is certainly elastic. . ." And there were few figures in wrestling who were more elastic and enigmatic than Andre the Giant. He was a hero to some and a villain to others, and Brown's book does a wonderful job exploring his complex legacy. This excerpt focuses on the end of Andre's career, as his body is deteriorating and he is preparing to cede his throne to the next great wrestler, a young man named Hulk Hogan.

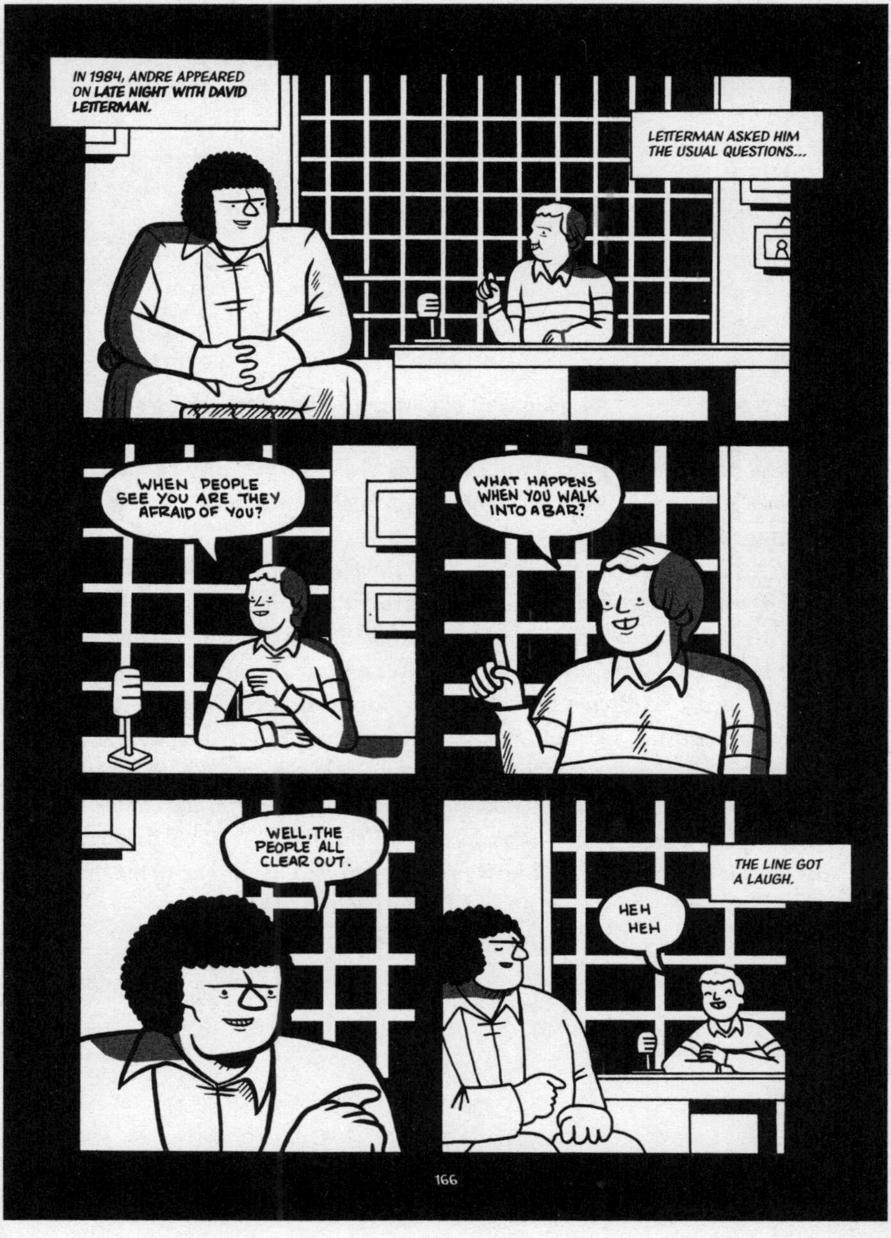
IN 1984, ANDRE APPEARED ON LATE NIGHT WITH DAVID LETTERMAN.
LETTERMAN ASKED HIM THE USUAL QUESTIONS...
WHEN PEOPLE SEE YOU ARE THEY AFRAID OF YOU?
WHAT HAPPENS WHEN YOU WALK INTO A BAR?
WELL, THE PEOPLE ALL CLEAR OUT.
THE LINE GOT A LAUGH.
HEH HEH
166

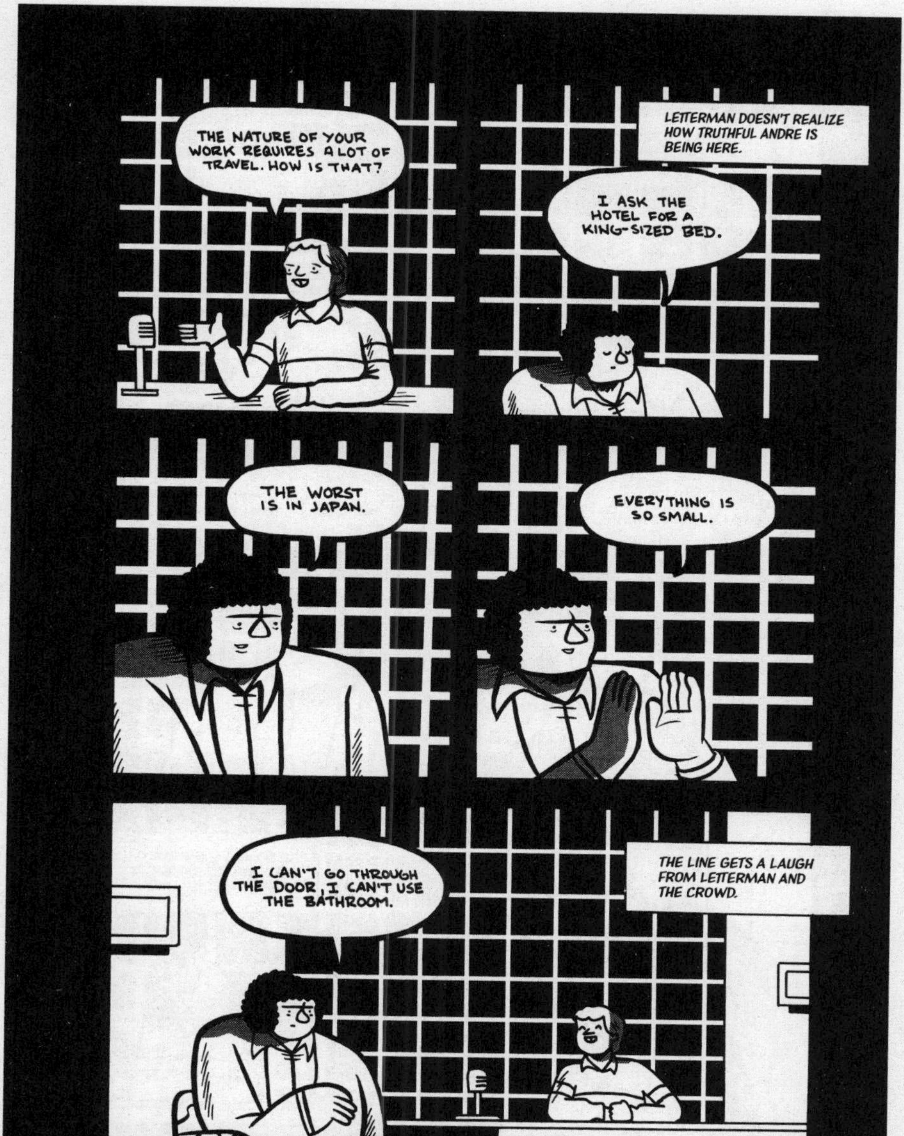
THE NATURE OF YOUR WORK REQUIRES A LOT OF TRAVEL. HOW IS THAT?
LETTERMAN DOESN'T REALIZE HOW TRUTHFUL ANDRE IS BEING HERE.
I ASK THE HOTEL FOR A KING-SIZED BED.
THE WORST IS IN JAPAN.
EVERYTHING IS SO SMALL.
I CAN'T GO THROUGH THE DOOR, I CAN'T USE THE BATHROOM.
THE LINE GETS A LAUGH FROM LETTERMAN AND THE CROWD.
167

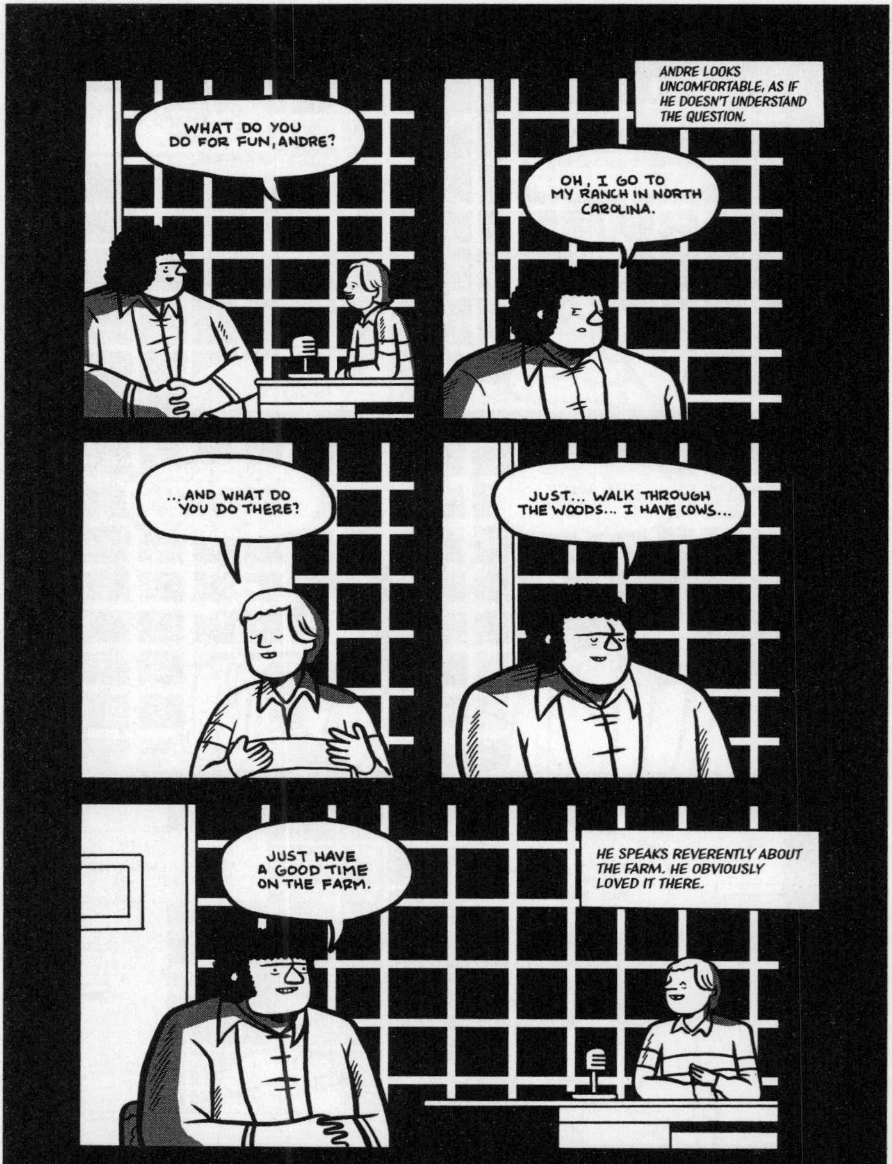
WHAT DO YOU DO FOR FUN, ANDRE?
ANDRE LOOKS UNCOMFORTABLE, AS IF HE DOESN'T UNDERSTAND THE QUESTION.
OH, I GO TO MY RANCH IN NORTH CAROLINA.
...AND WHAT DO YOU DO THERE?
JUST... WALK THROUGH THE WOODS... I HAVE COWS...
JUST HAVE A GOOD TIME ON THE FARM.
HE SPEAKS REVERENTLY ABOUT THE FARM. HE OBVIOUSLY LOVED IT THERE.
168

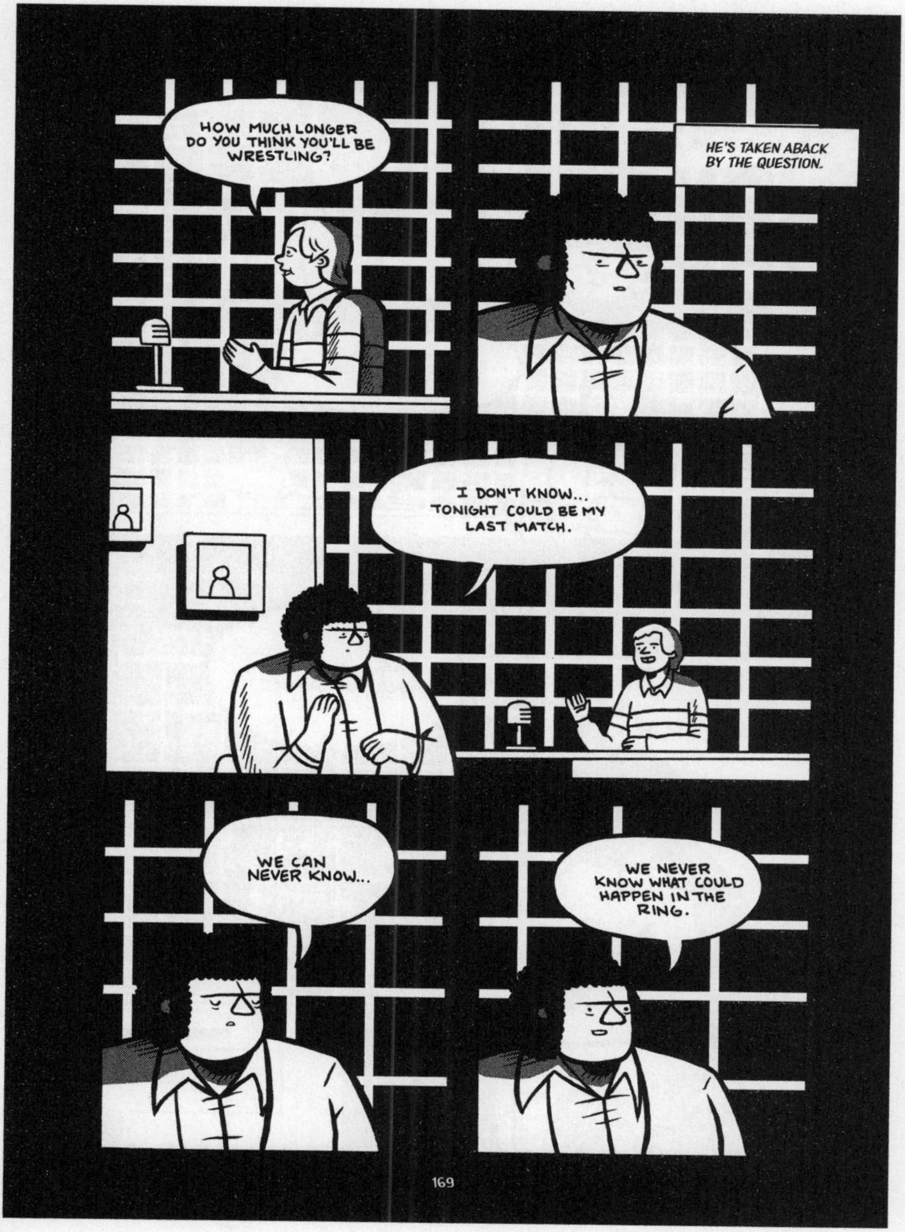
HOW MUCH LONGER DO YOU THINK YOU'LL BE WRESTLING?
HE'S TAKEN ABACK BY THE QUESTION.
I DON'T KNOW... TONIGHT COULD BE MY LAST MATCH.
WE CAN NEVER KNOW...
WE NEVER KNOW WHAT COULD HAPPEN IN THE RING.
169

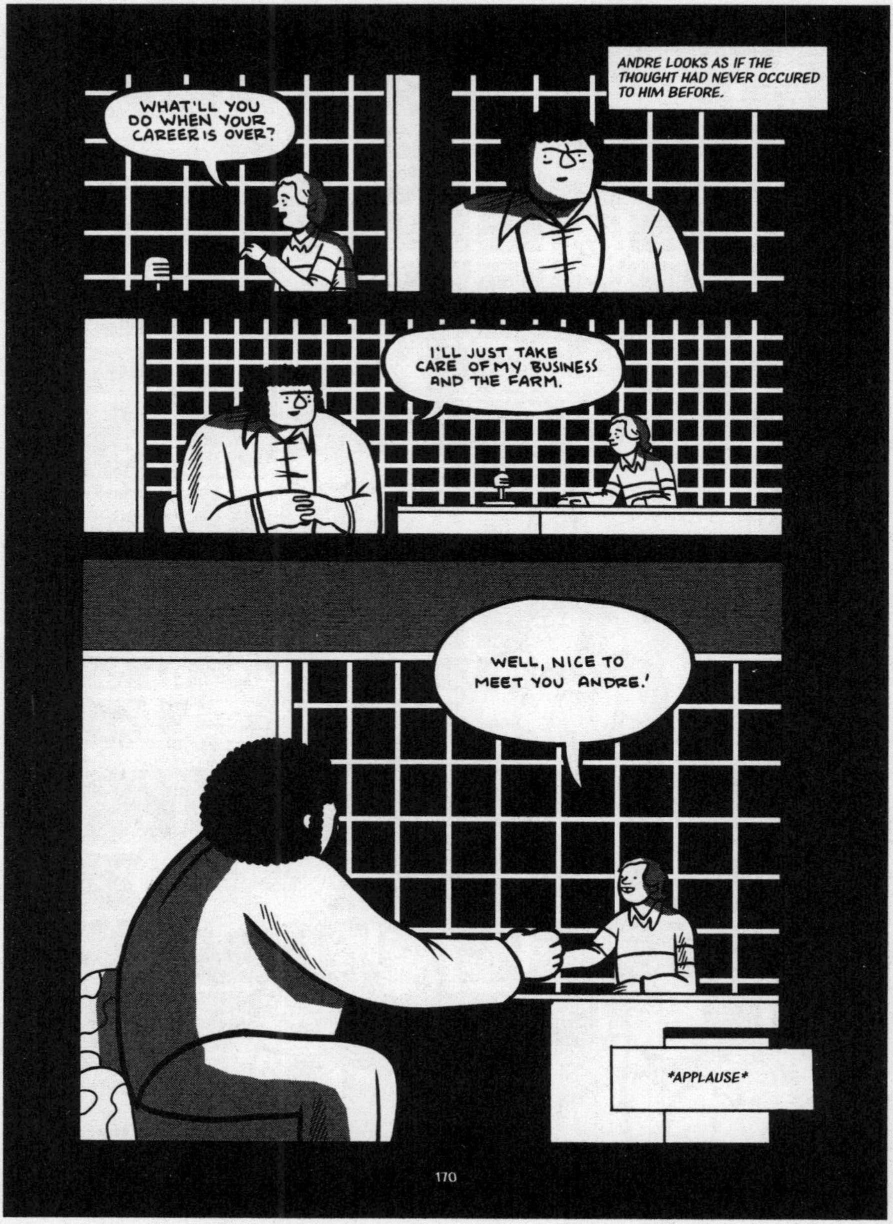
WHAT'LL YOU DO WHEN YOUR CAREER IS OVER?
ANDRE LOOKS AS IF THE THOUGHT HAD NEVER OCCURED TO HIM BEFORE.
I'LL JUST TAKE CARE OF MY BUSINESS AND THE FARM.
WELL, NICE TO MEET YOU ANDRE.'
APPLAUSE
170

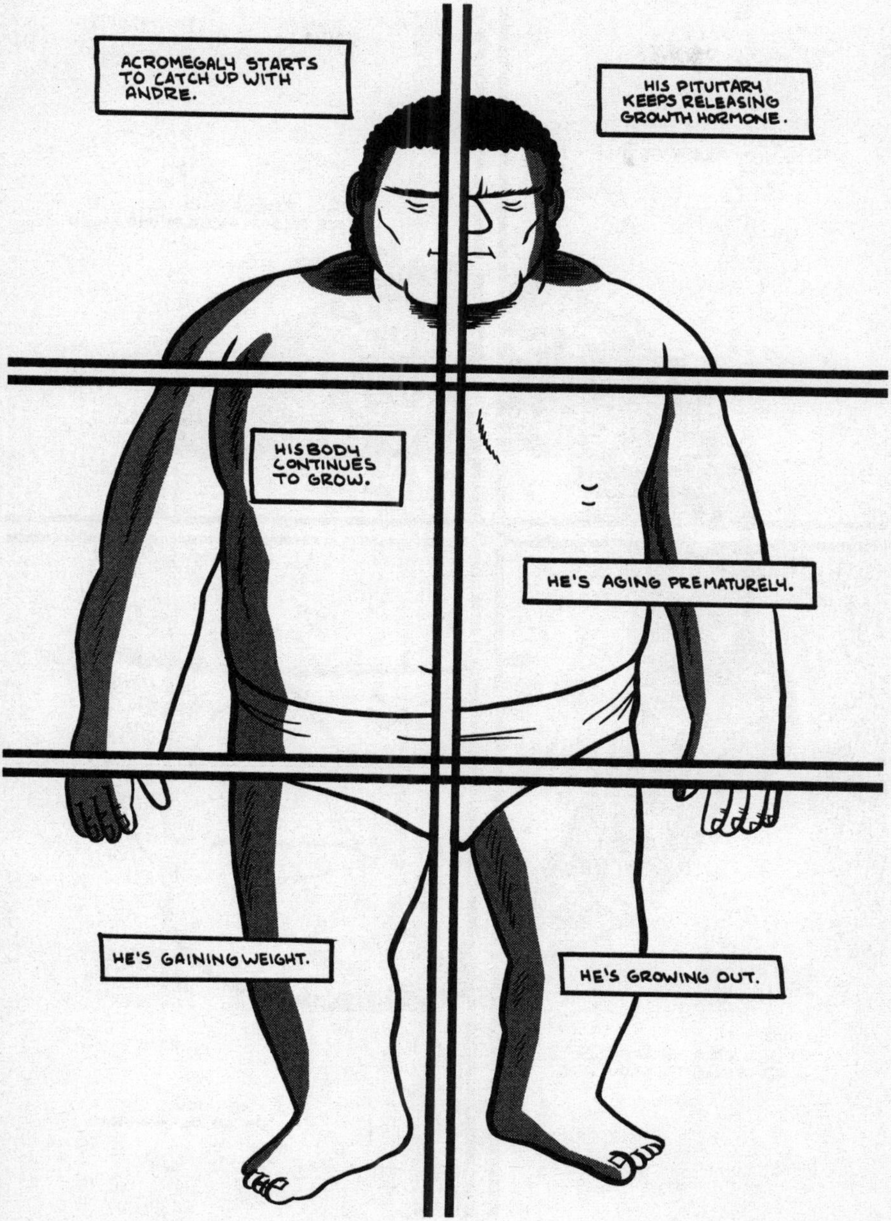
ACROMEGALY STARTS TO CATCH UP WITH ANDRE.
HIS PITUITARY KEEPS RELEASING GROWTH HORMONE.
HIS BODY CONTINUES TO GROW.
HE'S AGING PREMATURELY.
HE'S GAINING WEIGHT.
HE'S GROWING OUT.

HE'S THIRTY-NINE.
THEY TOLD HIM HE
WOULDN'T SEE FORTY.

HIS BROW AND JAW
HAVE GROWN MORE PRONOUNCED.

HIS FACE IS RAPIDLY
STARTING TO SHOW AGE.

HE LOOKS LIKE A
MUCH OLDER MAN.

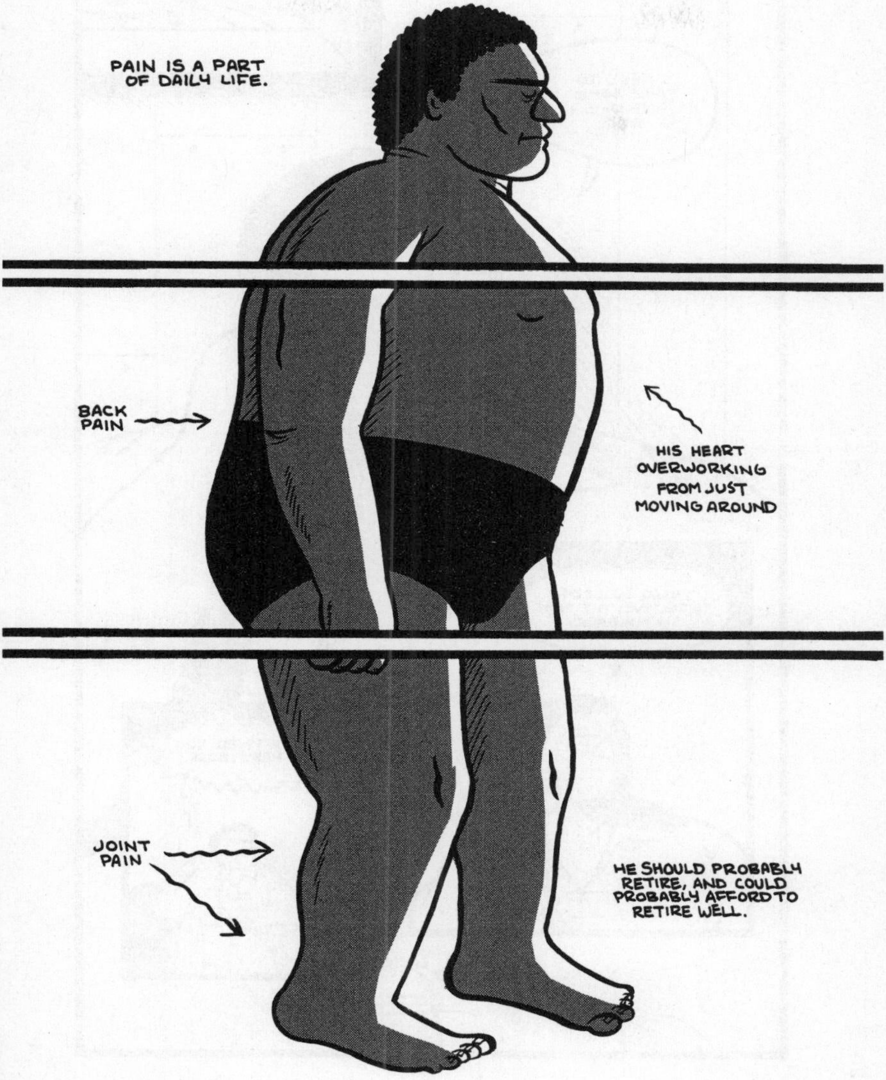
PAIN IS A PART OF DAILY LIFE.
BACK PAIN
HIS HEART OVERWORKING FROM JUST MOVING AROUND
JOINT PAIN
HE SHOULD PROBABLY RETIRE, AND COULD PROBABLY AFFORD TO RETIRE WELL.

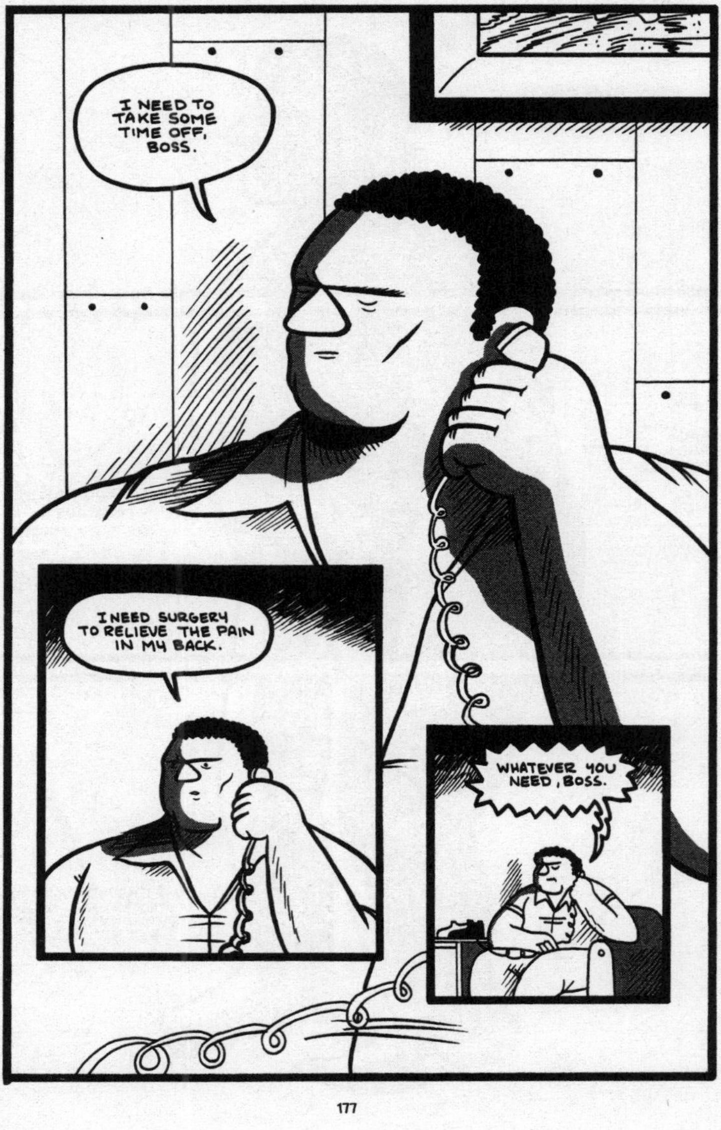
I NEED TO TAKE SOME TIME OFF, BOSS.
I NEED SURGERY TO RELIEVE THE PAIN IN MY BACK.
WHATEVER YOU NEED, BOSS.

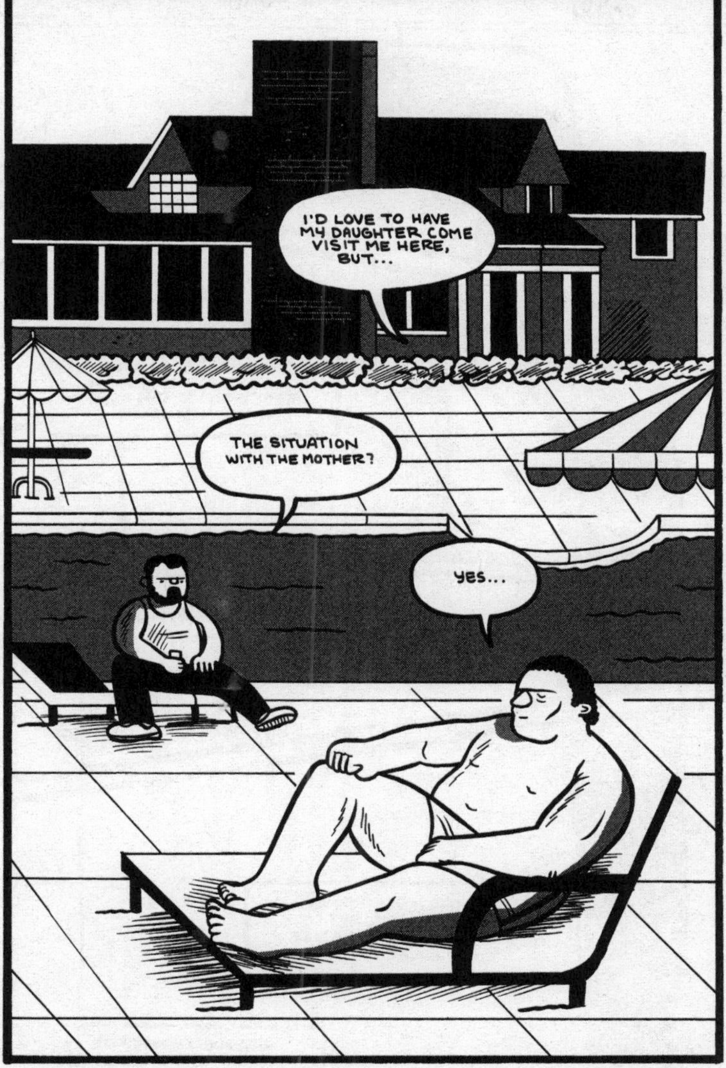
I'D LOVE TO HAVE MY DAUGHTER COME VISIT ME HERE, BUT...
THE SITUATION WITH THE MOTHER?
YES...

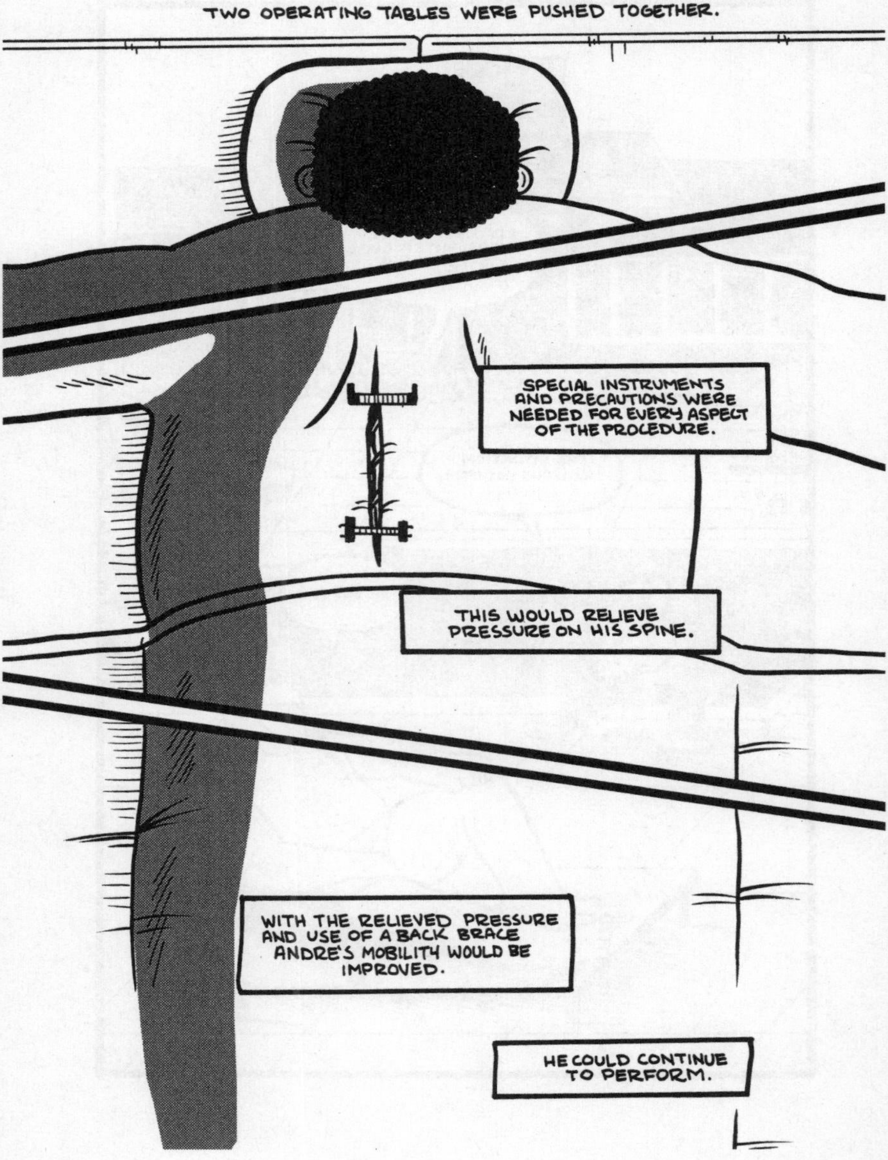
TWO OPERATING TABLES WERE PUSHED TOGETHER.
SPECIAL INSTRUMENTS AND PRECAUTIONS WERE NEEDED FOR EVERY ASPECT OF THE PROCEDURE.
THIS WOULD RELIEVE PRESSURE ON HIS SPINE.
WITH THE RELIEVED PRESSURE AND USE OF A BACK BRACE ANDRE'S MOBILITY WOULD BE IMPROVED.
HE COULD CONTINUE TO PERFORM.

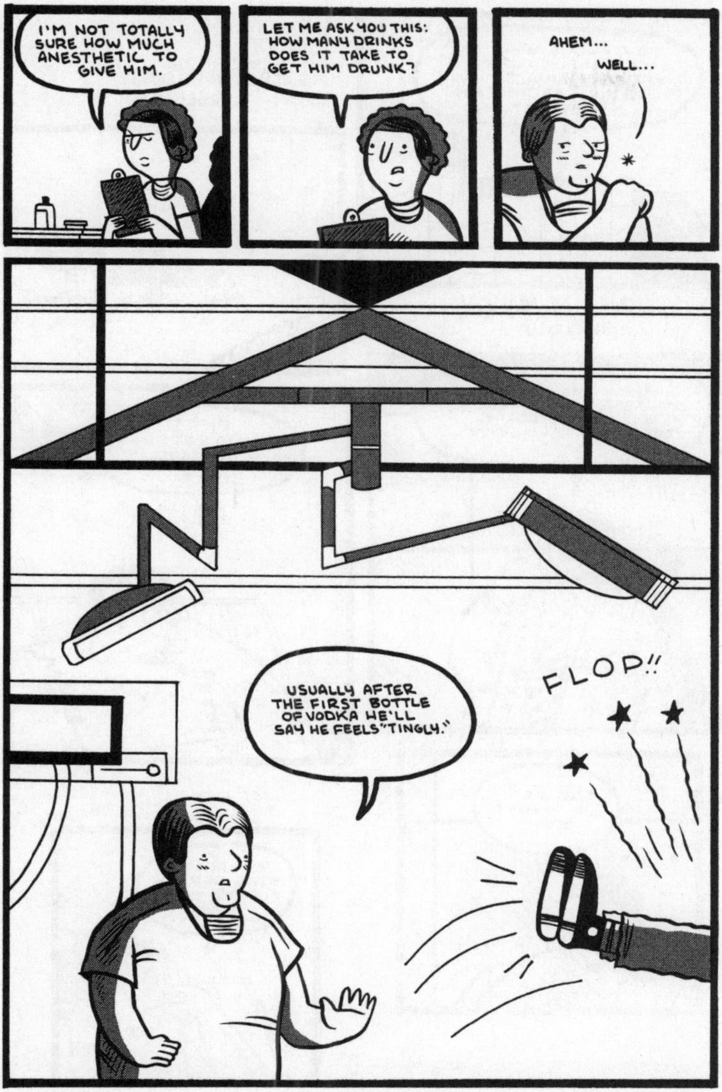
I'M NOT TOTALLY SURE HOW MUCH ANESTHETIC TO GIVE HIM.
LET ME ASK YOU THIS: HOW MANY DRINKS DOES IT TAKE TO GET HIM DRUNK?
AHEM...
WELL...
USUALLY AFTER THE FIRST BOTTLE OF VODKA HE'LL SAY HE FEELS "TINGLY."
FLOP!!

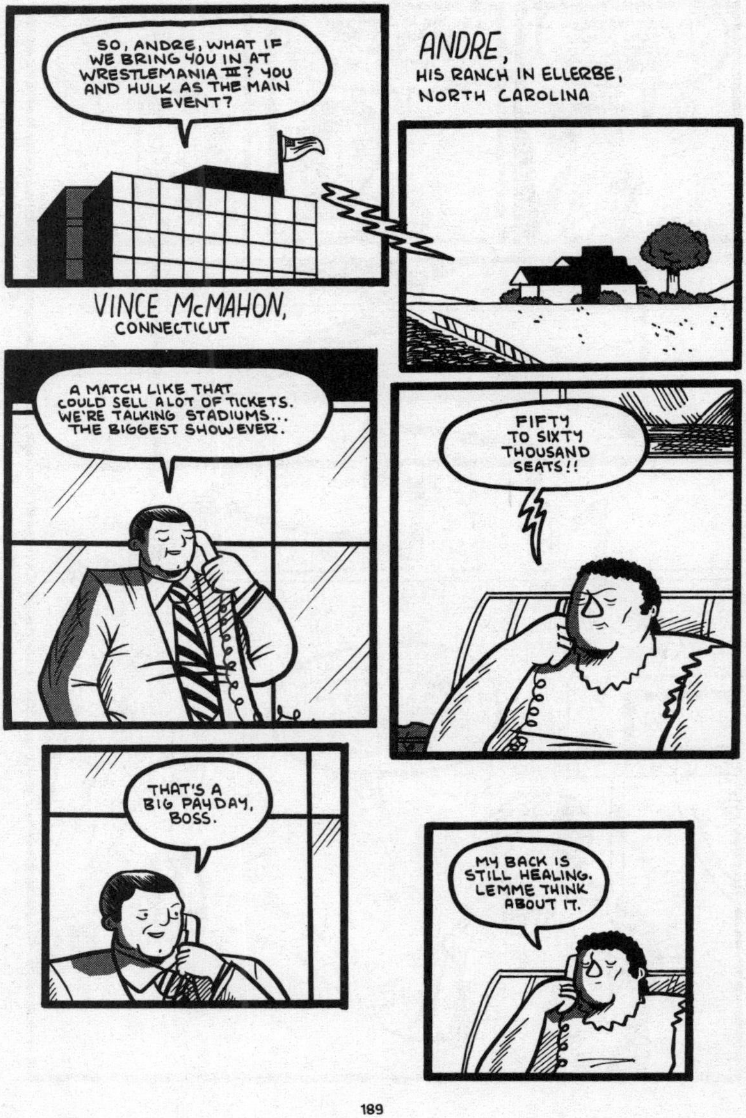
SO, ANDRE, WHAT IF WE BRING YOU IN AT WRESTLEMANIA III? YOU AND HULK AS THE MAIN EVENT?
VINCE McMAHON, CONNECTICUT
ANDRE, HIS RANCH IN ELLERBE, NORTH CAROLINA
A MATCH LIKE THAT COULD SELL A LOT OF TICKETS. WE'RE TALKING STADIUMS... THE BIGGEST SHOW EVER.
FIFTY TO SIXTY THOUSAND SEATS!!
THAT'S A BIG PAYDAY, BOSS.
MY BACK IS STILL HEALING. LEMME THINK ABOUT IT.

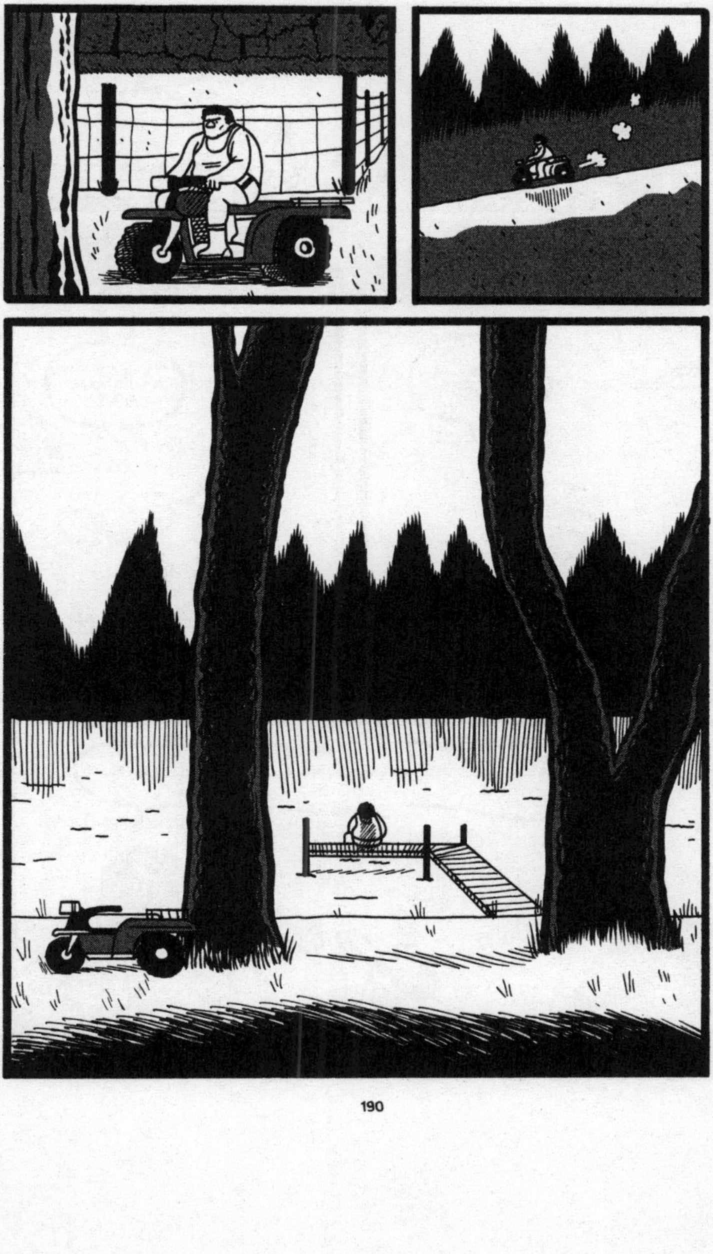

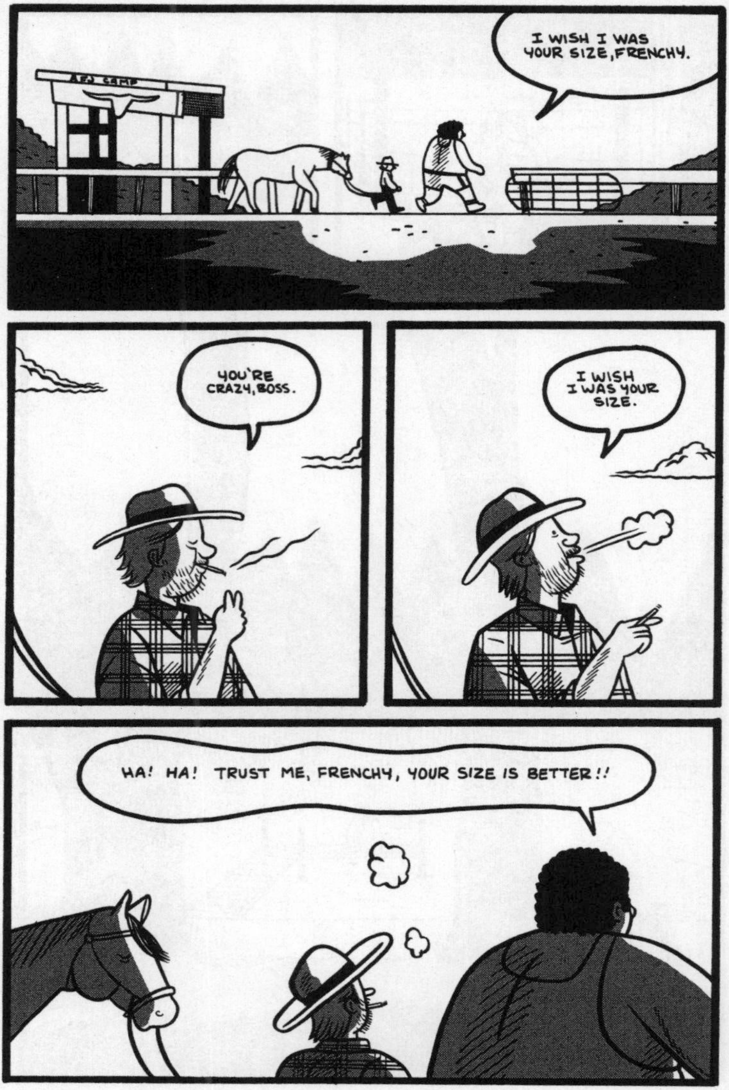
I WISH I WAS YOUR SIZE, FRENCHY.
YOU'RE CRAZY, BOSS.
I WISH I WAS YOUR SIZE.
HA! HA! TRUST ME, FRENCHY, YOUR SIZE IS BETTER!!

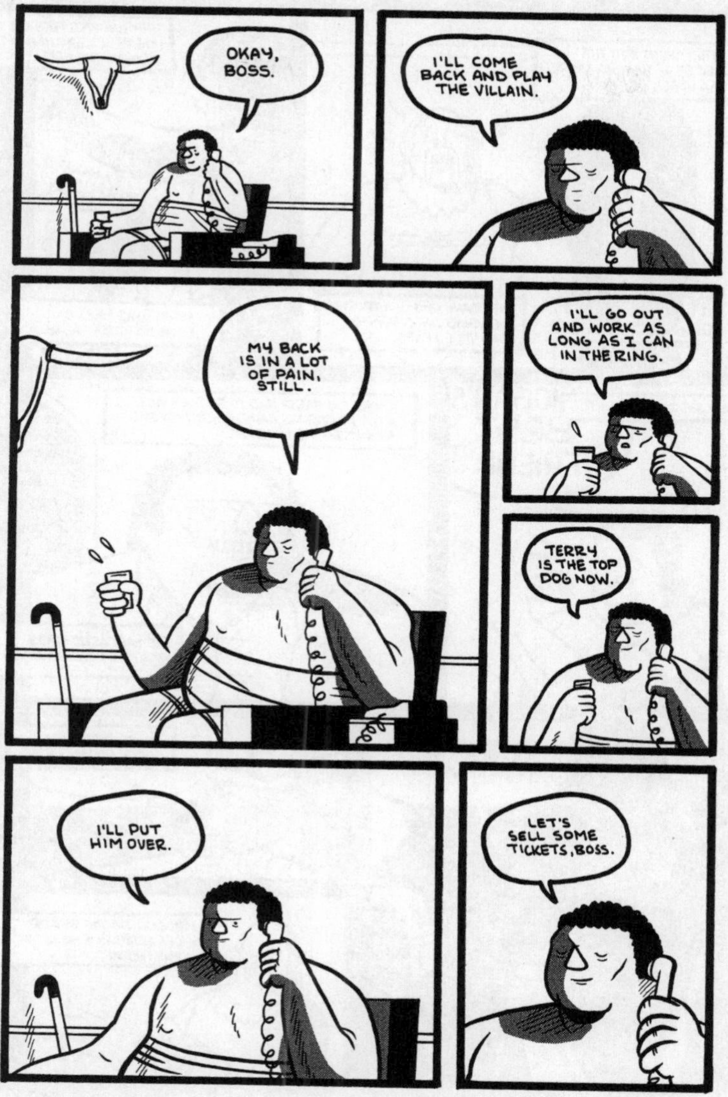
OKAY, BOSS.
I'LL COME BACK AND PLAY THE VILLAIN.
MY BACK IS IN A LOT OF PAIN, STILL.
I'LL GO OUT AND WORK AS LONG AS I CAN IN THE RING.
TERRY IS THE TOP DOG NOW.
I'LL PUT HIM OVER.
LET'S SELL SOME TICKETS, BOSS.

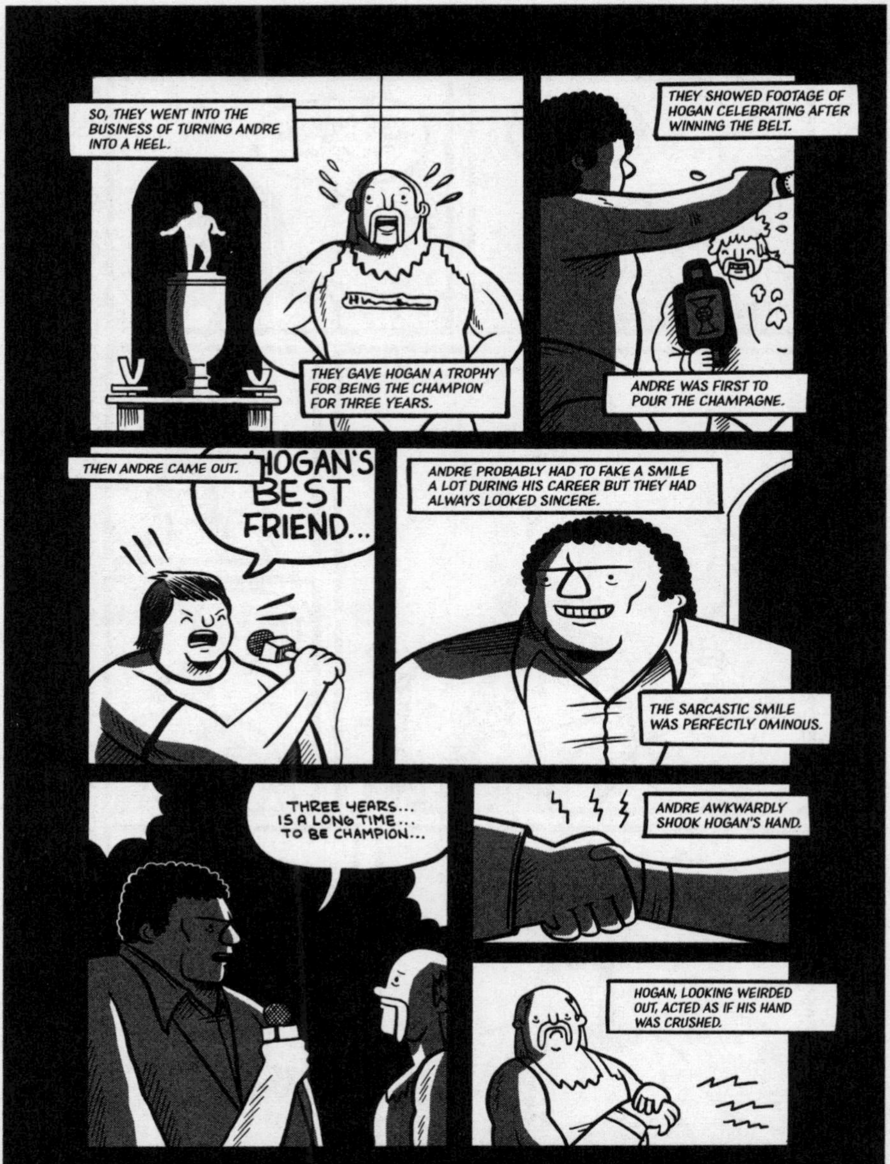
SO, THEY WENT INTO THE BUSINESS OF TURNING ANDRE INTO A HEEL.
THEY GAVE HOGAN A TROPHY FOR BEING THE CHAMPION FOR THREE YEARS.
THEY SHOWED FOOTAGE OF HOGAN CELEBRATING AFTER WINNING THE BELT.
ANDRE WAS FIRST TO POUR THE CHAMPAGNE.
THEN ANDRE CAME OUT.
HOGAN'S BEST FRIEND...
ANDRE PROBABLY HAD TO FAKE A SMILE A LOT DURING HIS CAREER BUT THEY HAD ALWAYS LOOKED SINCERE.
THE SARCASTIC SMILE WAS PERFECTLY OMINOUS.
THREE YEARS... IS A LONG TIME... TO BE CHAMPION...
ANDRE AWKWARDLY SHOOK HOGAN'S HAND.
HOGAN, LOOKING WEIRDED OUT, ACTED AS IF HIS HAND WAS CRUSHED.
193

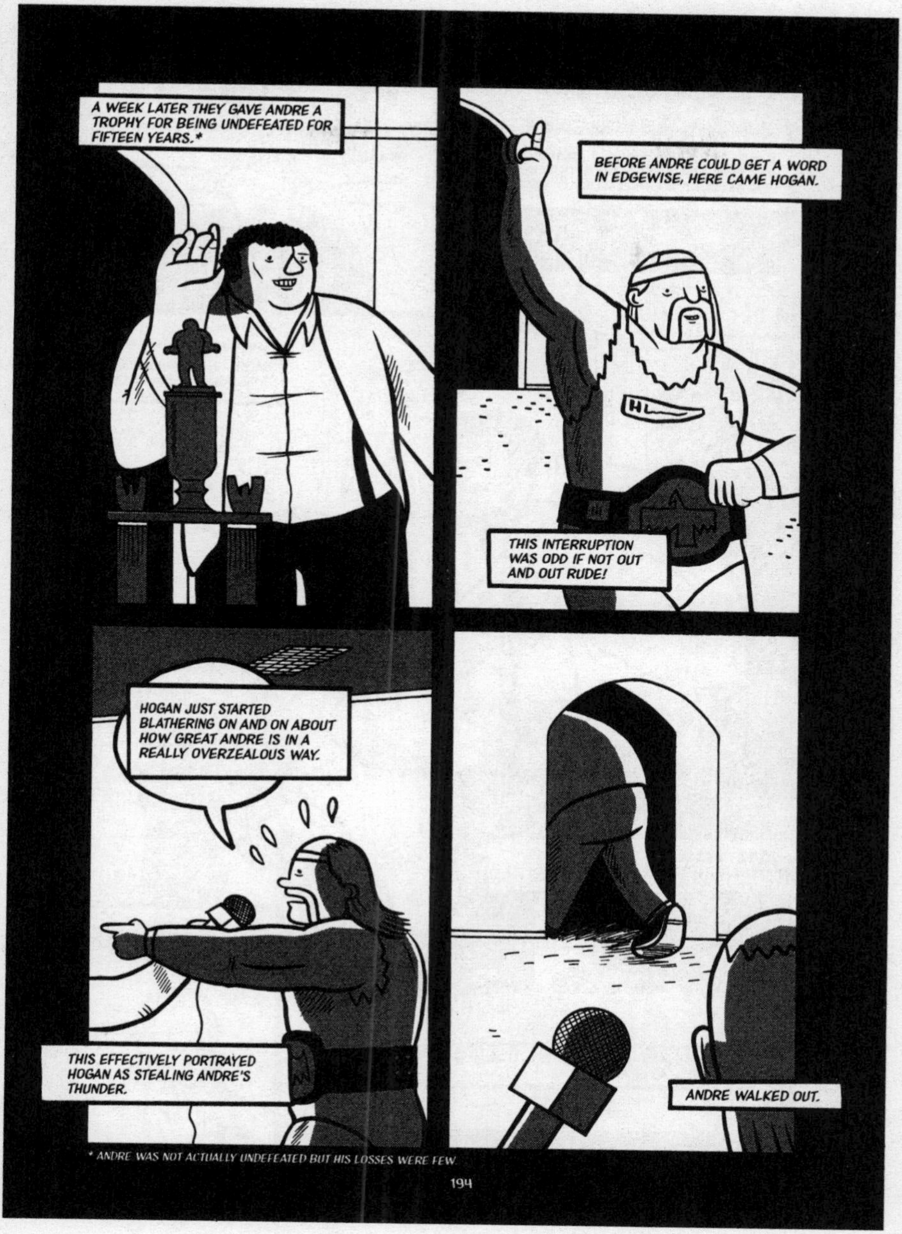
A WEEK LATER THEY GAVE ANDRE A TROPHY FOR BEING UNDEFEATED FOR FIFTEEN YEARS.*
BEFORE ANDRE COULD GET A WORD IN EDGEWISE, HERE CAME HOGAN.
THIS INTERRUPTION WAS ODD IF NOT OUT AND OUT RUDE!
HOGAN JUST STARTED BLATHERING ON AND ON ABOUT HOW GREAT ANDRE IS IN A REALLY OVERZEALOUS WAY.
THIS EFFECTIVELY PORTRAYED HOGAN AS STEALING ANDRE'S THUNDER.
ANDRE WALKED OUT.
* ANDRE WAS NOT ACTUALLY UNDEFEATED BUT HIS LOSSES WERE FEW.
194

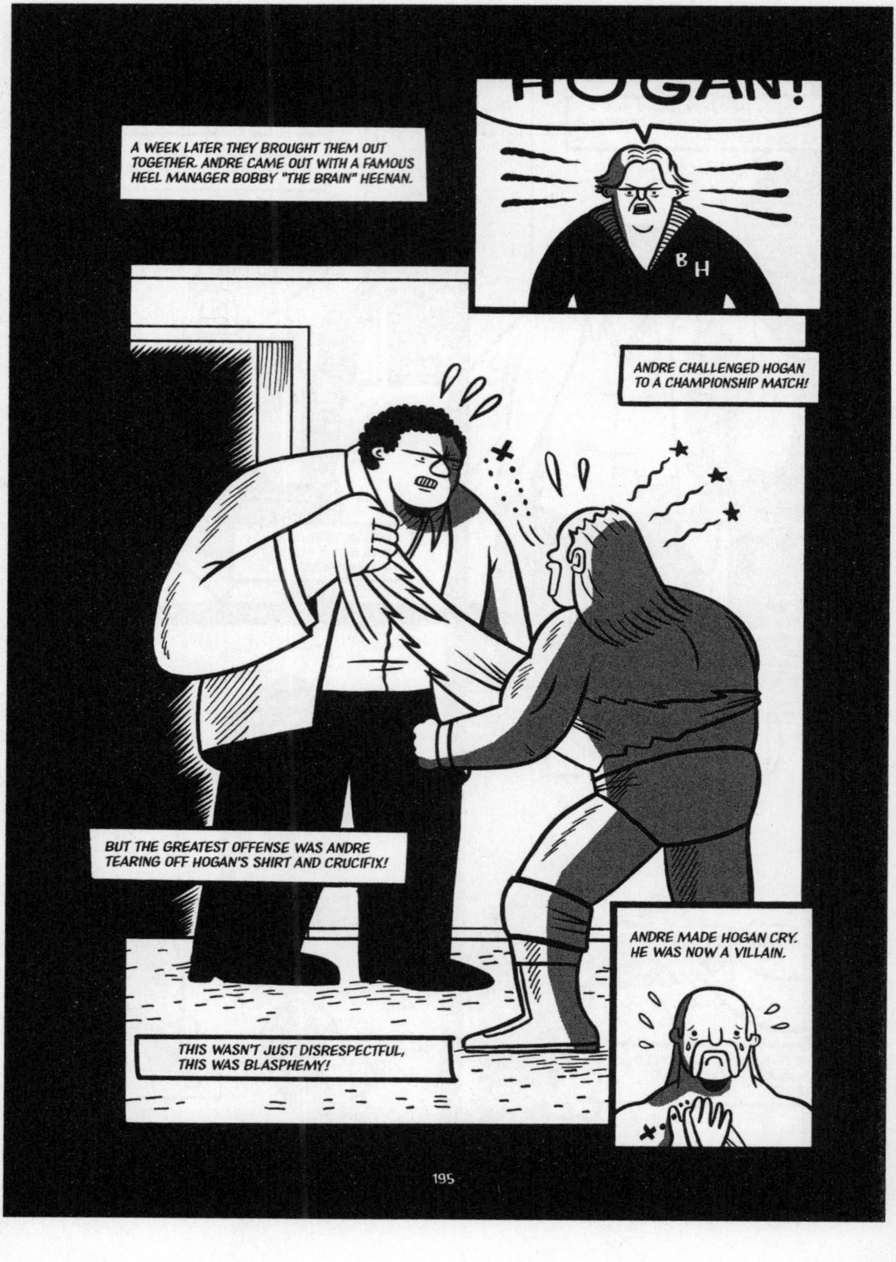
A WEEK LATER THEY BROUGHT THEM OUT TOGETHER. ANDRE CAME OUT WITH A FAMOUS HEEL MANAGER BOBBY "THE BRAIN" HEENAN.
HOGAN!
B H
ANDRE CHALLENGED HOGAN TO A CHAMPIONSHIP MATCH!
BUT THE GREATEST OFFENSE WAS ANDRE TEARING OFF HOGAN'S SHIRT AND CRUCIFIX!
THIS WASN'T JUST DISRESPECTFUL, THIS WAS BLASPHEMY!
ANDRE MADE HOGAN CRY. HE WAS NOW A VILLAIN.

FIGHT OF THE CENTURY

MARCH 29, 1987
PONTIAC SILVERDOME

Silverdome

THEY SOLD OVER 90,000 TICKETS
AND BROKE THE NORTH AMERICAN
INDOOR ATTENDANCE RECORD.

SOLD OUT

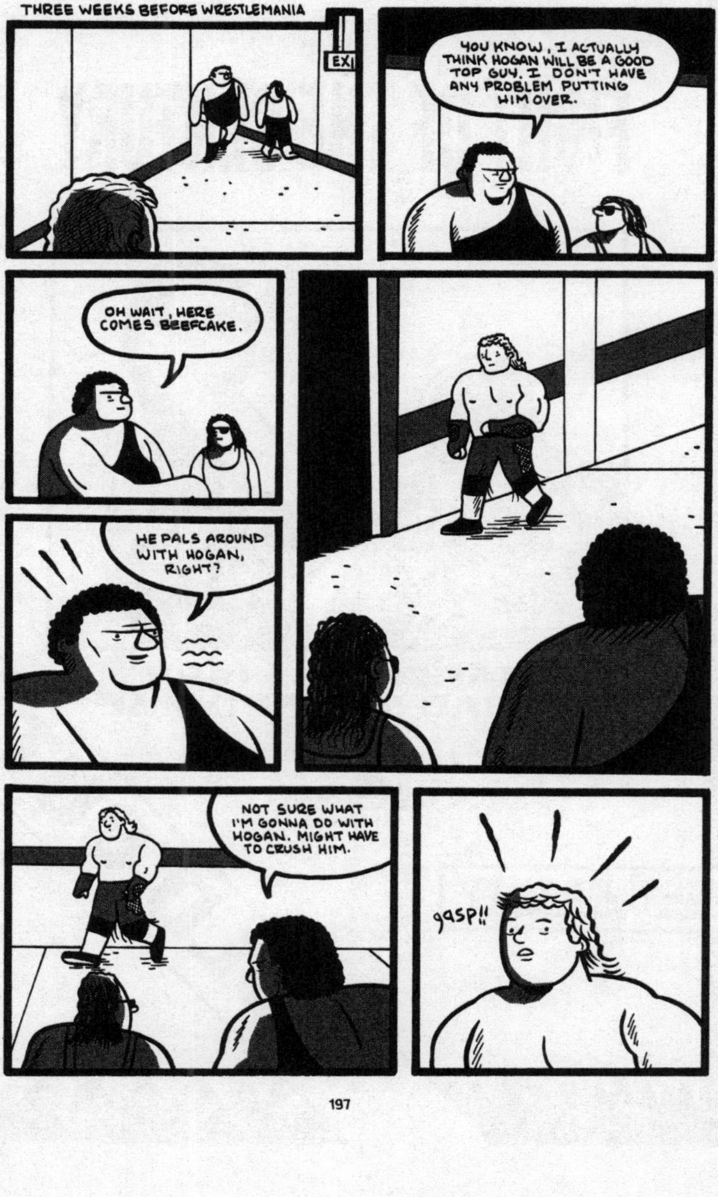
THREE WEEKS BEFORE WRESTLEMANIA
EXI
YOU KNOW, I ACTUALLY THINK HOGAN WILL BE A GOOD TOP GUY. I DON'T HAVE ANY PROBLEM PUTTING HIM OVER.
OH WAIT, HERE COMES BEEFCAKE.
HE PALS AROUND WITH HOGAN, RIGHT?
NOT SURE WHAT I'M GONNA DO WITH HOGAN. MIGHT HAVE TO CRUSH HIM.
gasp!!

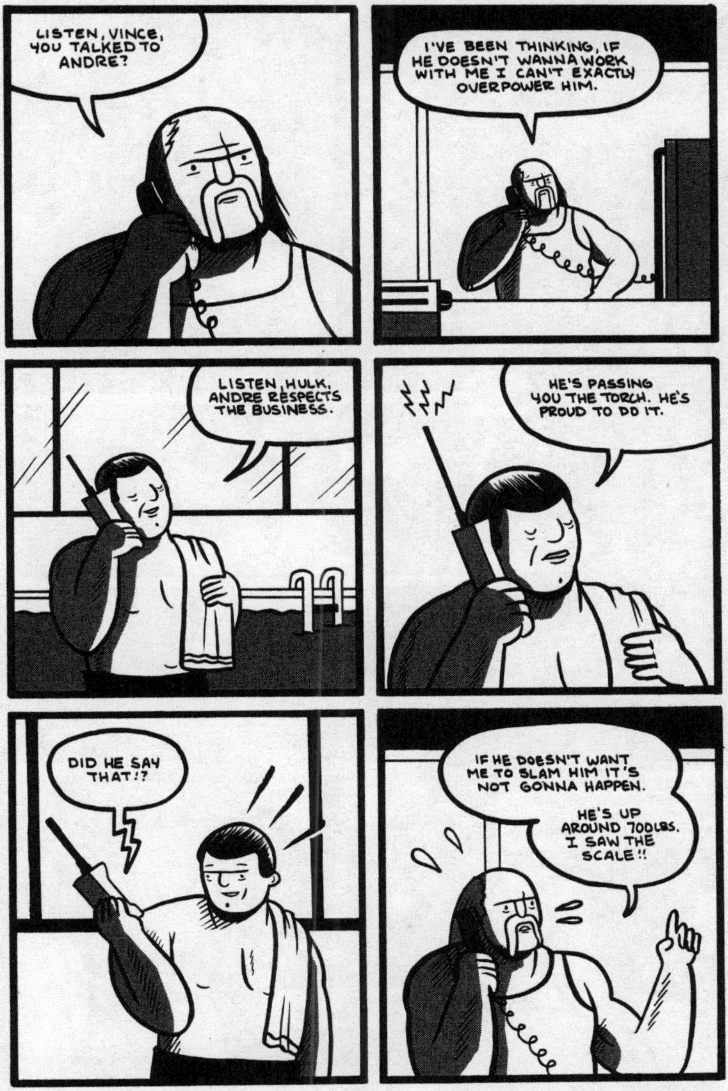
LISTEN, VINCE, YOU TALKED TO ANDRE?
I'VE BEEN THINKING, IF HE DOESN'T WANNA WORK WITH ME I CAN'T EXACTLY OVERPOWER HIM.
LISTEN, HULK, ANDRE RESPECTS THE BUSINESS.
HE'S PASSING YOU THE TORCH. HE'S PROUD TO DO IT.
DID HE SAY THAT!?
IF HE DOESN'T WANT ME TO SLAM HIM IT'S NOT GONNA HAPPEN.
HE'S UP AROUND 700LBS. I SAW THE SCALE!!

THE MATCH ITSELF WAS AN EPIC EXAMPLE OF THE MAGIC OF PRO-WRESTLING STORYTELLING.

HULK HOGAN WAS THE EMBODIMENT OF THE SUPERMAN IN THE EYES OF THE FANS; THE ULTIMATE HERO, THE ÜBERMENSCH.

AND ANDRE WAS A LIVING MONSTER.

199

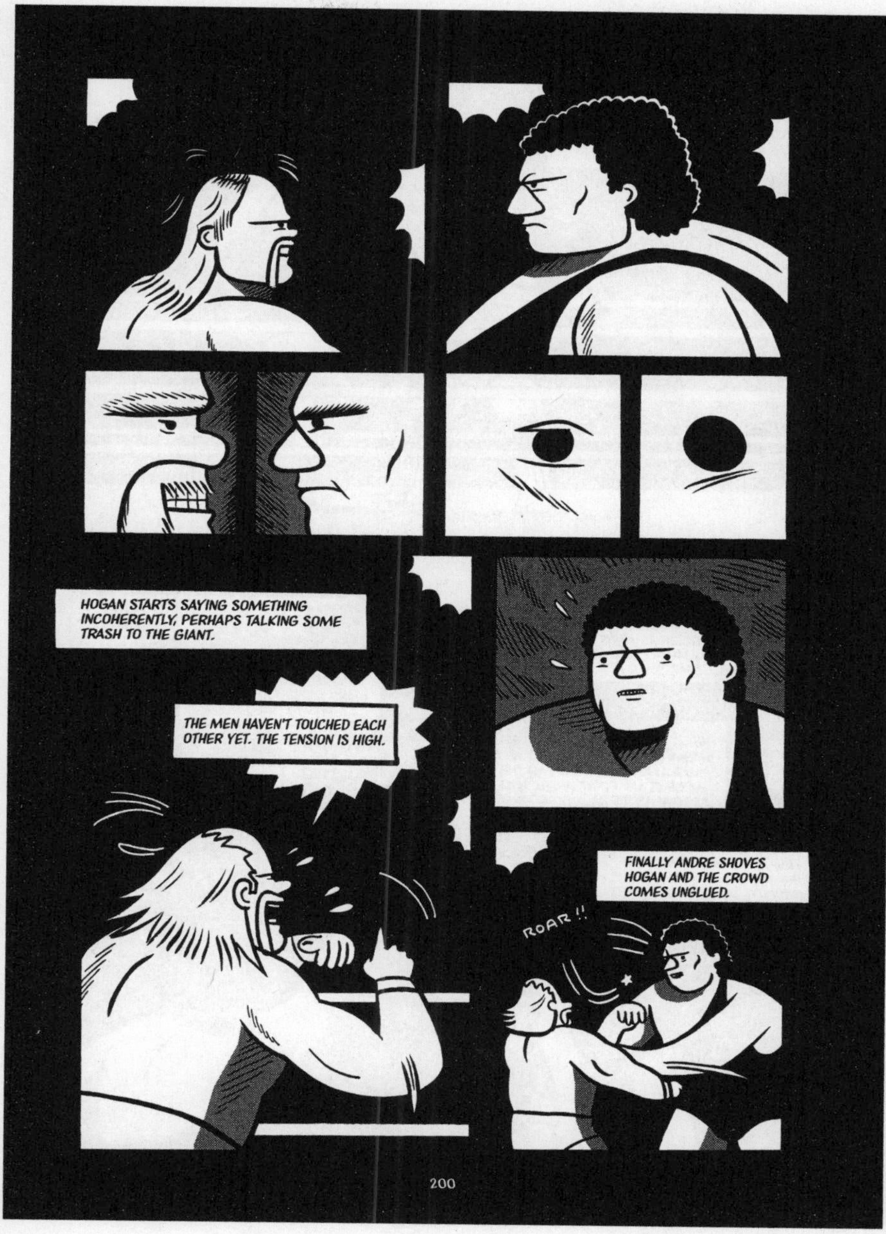
HOGAN STARTS SAYING SOMETHING INCOHERENTLY, PERHAPS TALKING SOME TRASH TO THE GIANT.
THE MEN HAVEN'T TOUCHED EACH OTHER YET. THE TENSION IS HIGH.
FINALLY ANDRE SHOVES HOGAN AND THE CROWD COMES UNGLUED.
ROAR!!
200

A SCUFFLE BREAKS OUT AND HOGAN GETS A FEW SHOTS IN ON ANDRE.

THIRTY SECONDS INTO THE MATCH HOGAN GOES FOR A BODYSLAM AND FAILS.

THIS LITTLE TEASER REMINDS THE FANS THAT SLAMMING ANDRE IS AN IMPOSSIBLE FEAT.

ANDRE FALLS ON HOGAN AND THE REF ALMOST COUNTS TO THREE!

BUT IT IS ALSO IMPORTANT TO GET HOGAN DOWN FAST. THAT WAY HE CAN MAKE A COMEBACK AND END THE MATCH AT ANY POINT. ANDRE WILL GO AS LONG AS HIS BACK COULD HOLD OUT.

MILLIONS OF FANS' HEARTS AT ONCE LEAP INTO THEIR COLLECTIVE THROATS.

THIS ALSO HEIGHTENS THE IMPACT OF THE SLAM THAT HAPPENS LATER IN THE MATCH.

That was three!!

201

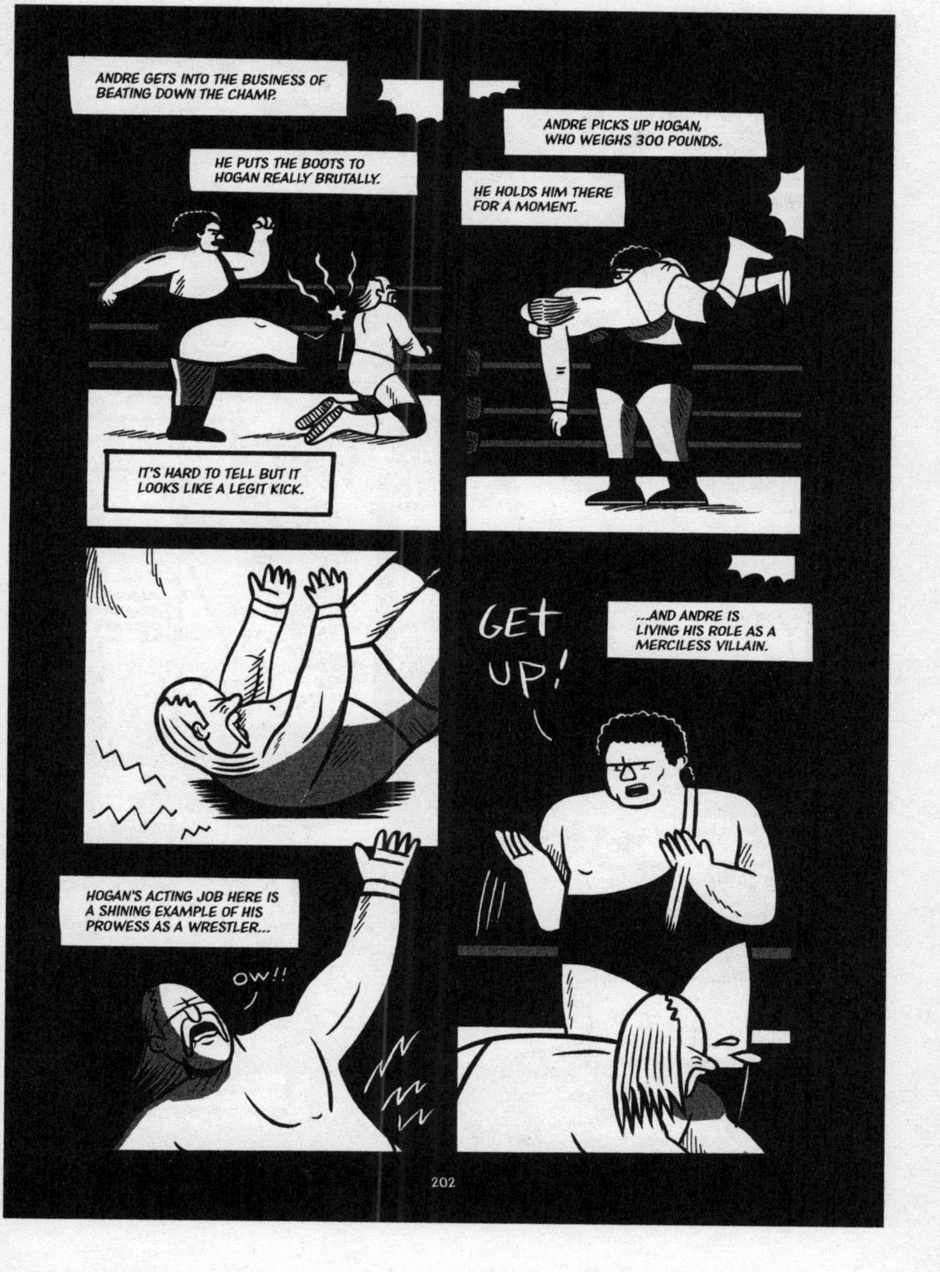
ANDRE GETS INTO THE BUSINESS OF BEATING DOWN THE CHAMP.
HE PUTS THE BOOTS TO HOGAN REALLY BRUTALLY.
IT'S HARD TO TELL BUT IT LOOKS LIKE A LEGIT KICK.
ANDRE PICKS UP HOGAN, WHO WEIGHS 300 POUNDS.
HE HOLDS HIM THERE FOR A MOMENT.
HOGAN'S ACTING JOB HERE IS A SHINING EXAMPLE OF HIS PROWESS AS A WRESTLER...
OW!!
...AND ANDRE IS LIVING HIS ROLE AS A MERCILESS VILLAIN.
GET UP!

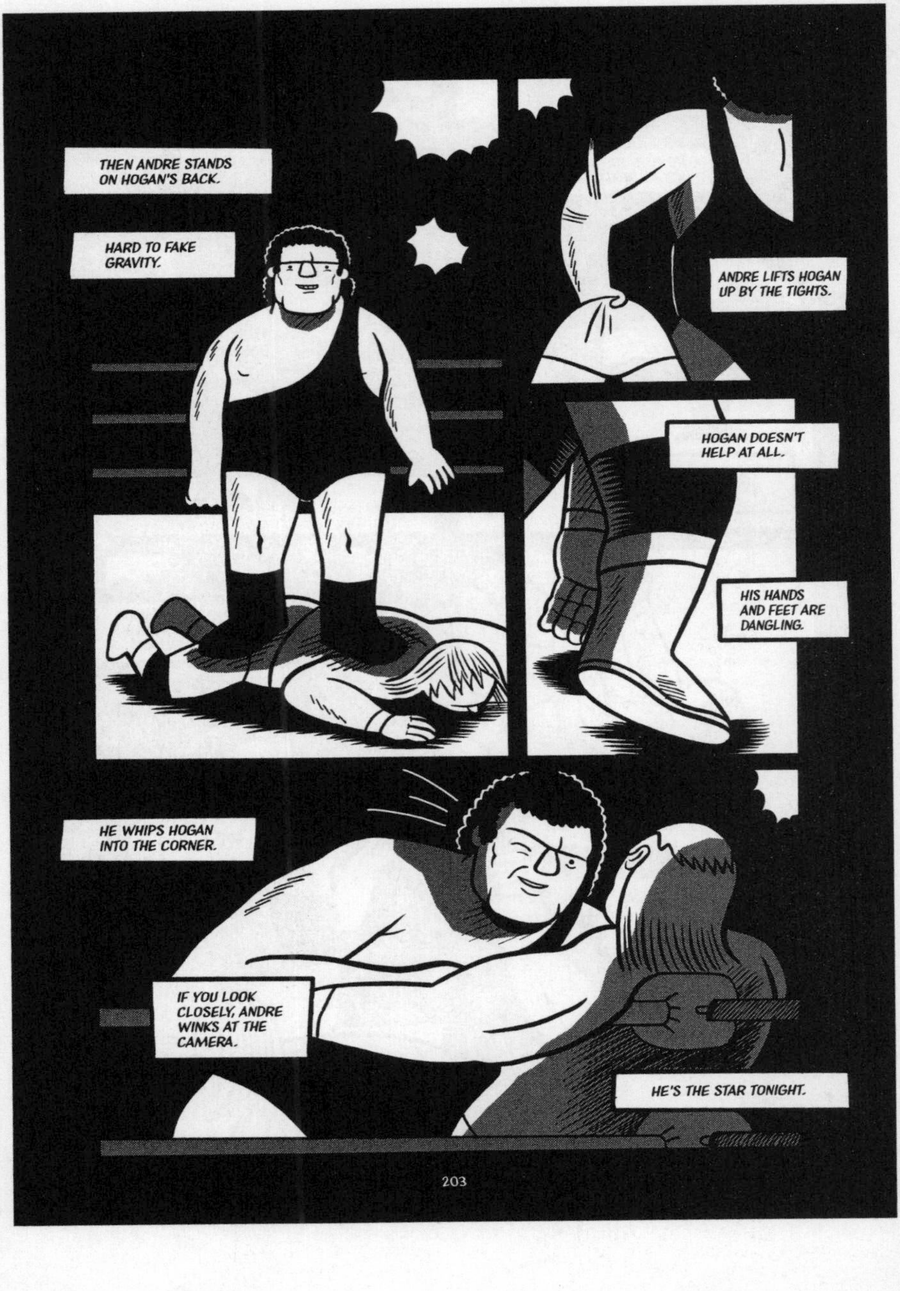
THEN ANDRE STANDS ON HOGAN'S BACK.
HARD TO FAKE GRAVITY.
ANDRE LIFTS HOGAN UP BY THE TIGHTS.
HOGAN DOESN'T HELP AT ALL.
HIS HANDS AND FEET ARE DANGLING.
HE WHIPS HOGAN INTO THE CORNER.
IF YOU LOOK CLOSELY, ANDRE WINKS AT THE CAMERA.
HE'S THE STAR TONIGHT.
203

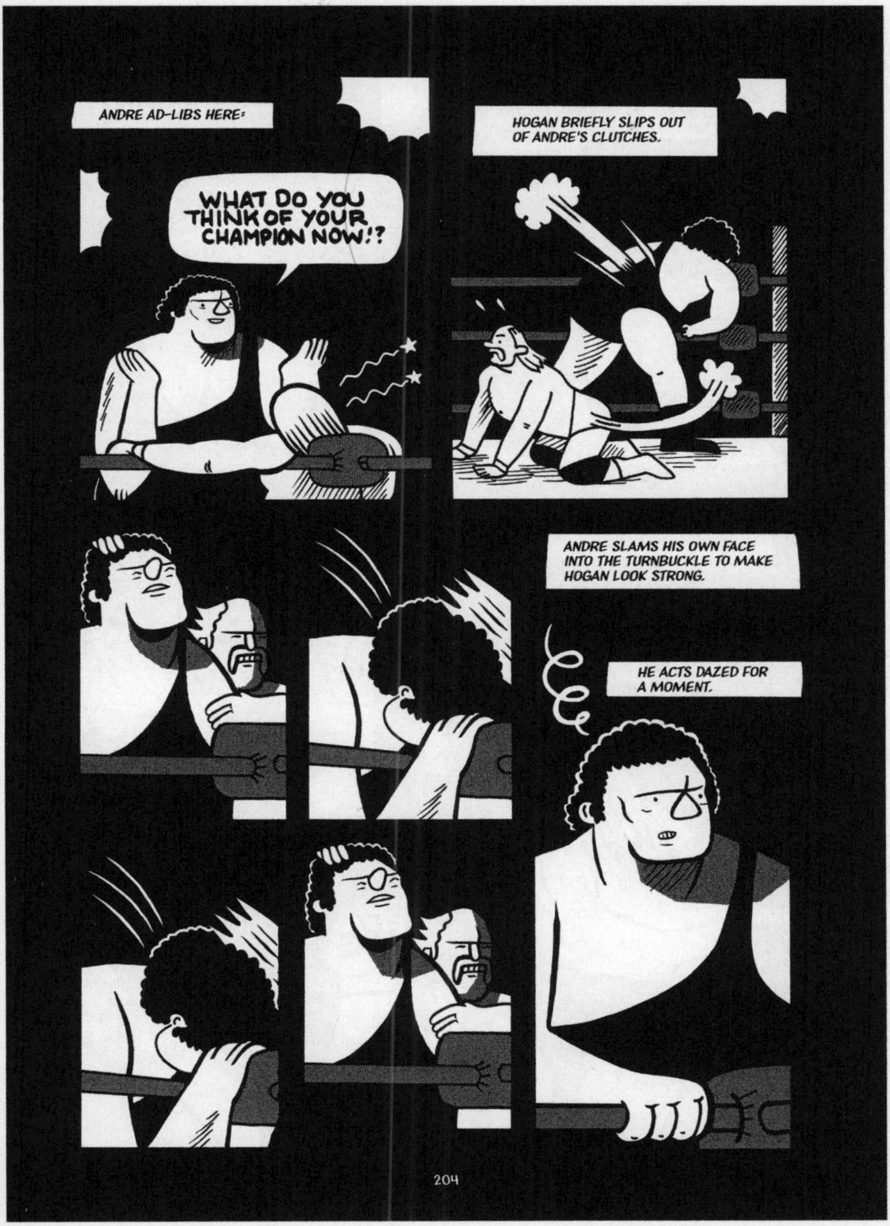
ANDRE AD-LIBS HERE:
WHAT DO YOU THINK OF YOUR CHAMPION NOW!?
HOGAN BRIEFLY SLIPS OUT OF ANDRE'S CLUTCHES.
ANDRE SLAMS HIS OWN FACE INTO THE TURNBUCKLE TO MAKE HOGAN LOOK STRONG.
HE ACTS DAZED FOR A MOMENT.
204

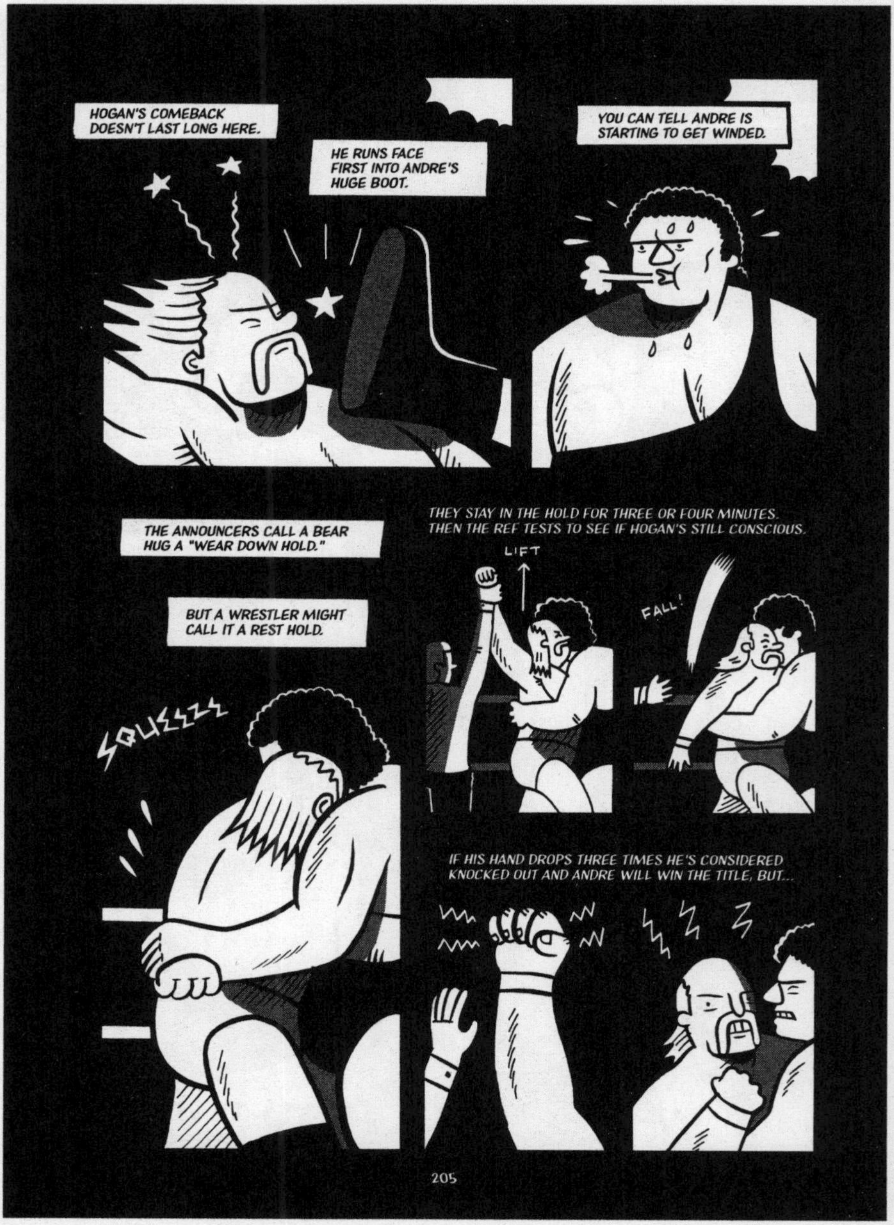
HOGAN'S COMEBACK DOESN'T LAST LONG HERE.
HE RUNS FACE FIRST INTO ANDRE'S HUGE BOOT.
YOU CAN TELL ANDRE IS STARTING TO GET WINDED.
THE ANNOUNCERS CALL A BEAR HUG A "WEAR DOWN HOLD."
BUT A WRESTLER MIGHT CALL IT A REST HOLD.
SQUEEZE
THEY STAY IN THE HOLD FOR THREE OR FOUR MINUTES. THEN THE REF TESTS TO SEE IF HOGAN'S STILL CONSCIOUS.
LIFT
FALL!
IF HIS HAND DROPS THREE TIMES HE'S CONSIDERED KNOCKED OUT AND ANDRE WILL WIN THE TITLE, BUT...
205

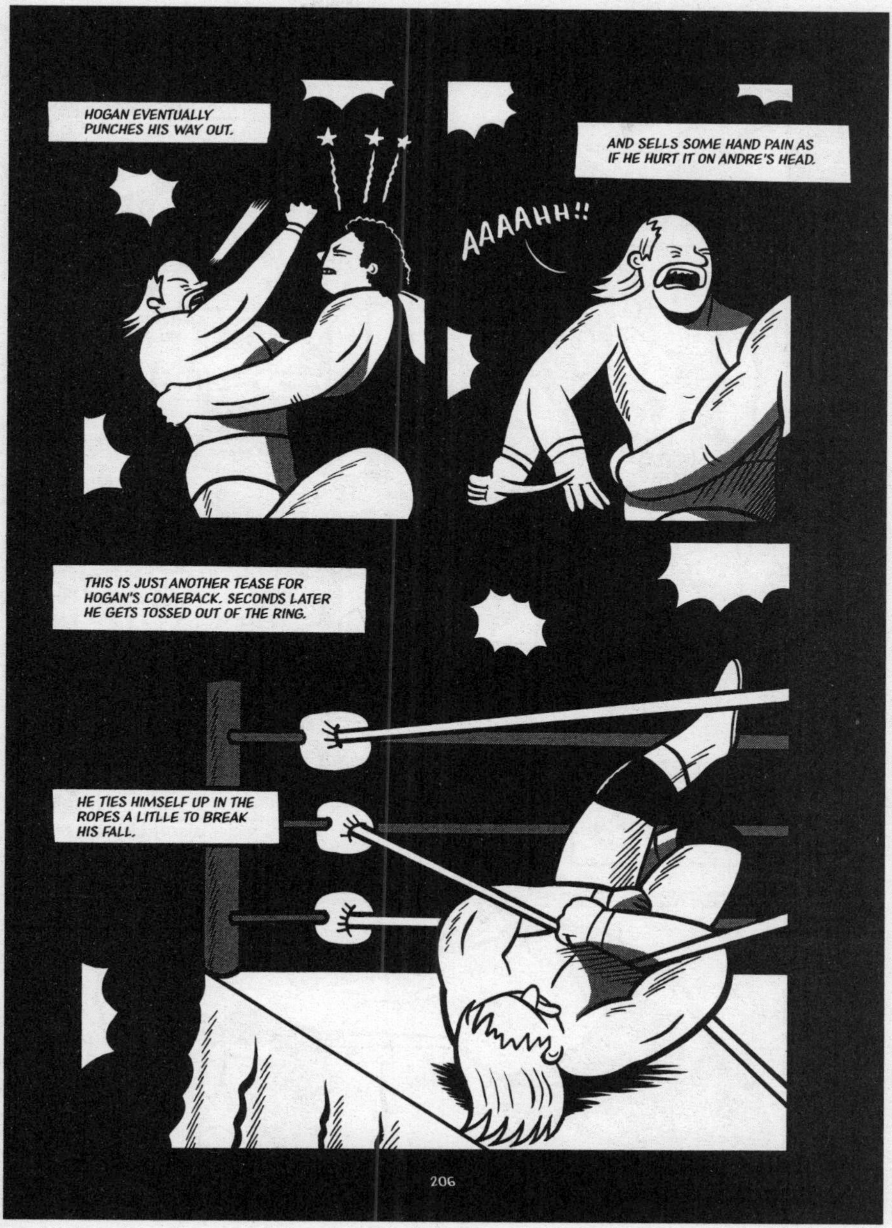
HOGAN EVENTUALLY PUNCHES HIS WAY OUT.
AND SELLS SOME HAND PAIN AS IF HE HURT IT ON ANDRE'S HEAD.
AAAAHH!!
THIS IS JUST ANOTHER TEASE FOR HOGAN'S COMEBACK. SECONDS LATER HE GETS TOSSED OUT OF THE RING.
HE TIES HIMSELF UP IN THE ROPES A LITLLE TO BREAK HIS FALL.
206

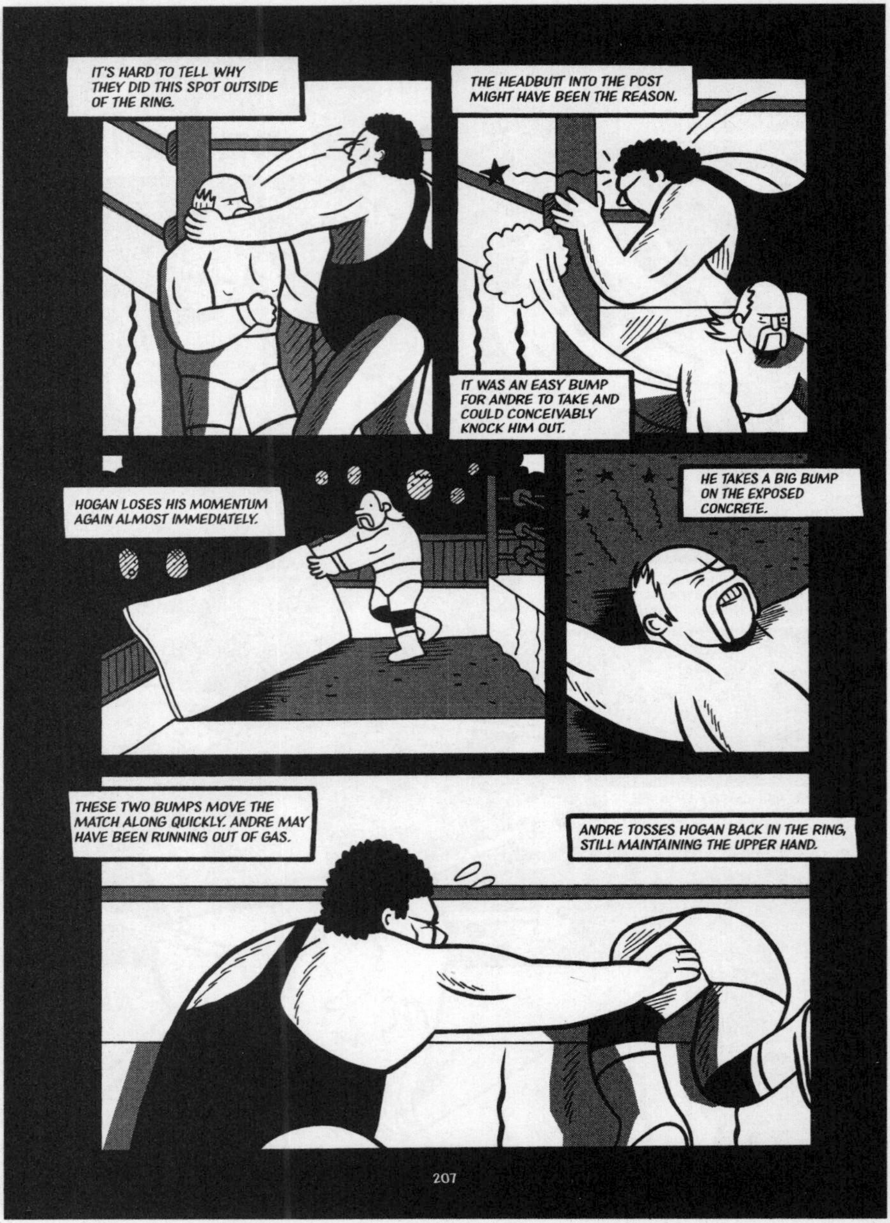
IT'S HARD TO TELL WHY THEY DID THIS SPOT OUTSIDE OF THE RING.
THE HEADBUTT INTO THE POST MIGHT HAVE BEEN THE REASON.
IT WAS AN EASY BUMP FOR ANDRE TO TAKE AND COULD CONCEIVABLY KNOCK HIM OUT.
HOGAN LOSES HIS MOMENTUM AGAIN ALMOST IMMEDIATELY.
HE TAKES A BIG BUMP ON THE EXPOSED CONCRETE.
THESE TWO BUMPS MOVE THE MATCH ALONG QUICKLY. ANDRE MAY HAVE BEEN RUNNING OUT OF GAS.
ANDRE TOSSES HOGAN BACK IN THE RING, STILL MAINTAINING THE UPPER HAND.
207

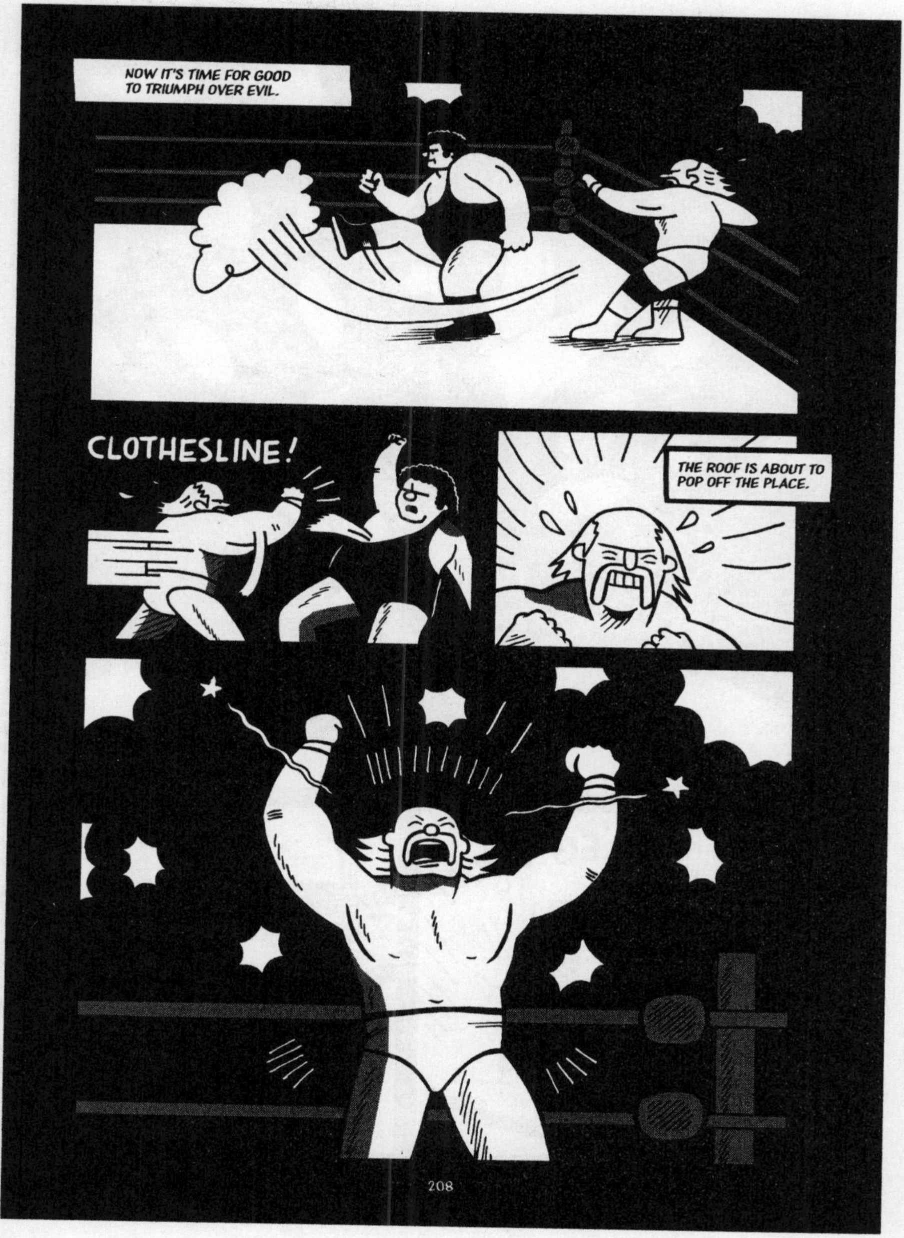
NOW IT'S TIME FOR GOOD
TO TRIUMPH OVER EVIL.
CLOTHESLINE!
THE ROOF IS ABOUT TO
POP OFF THE PLACE.

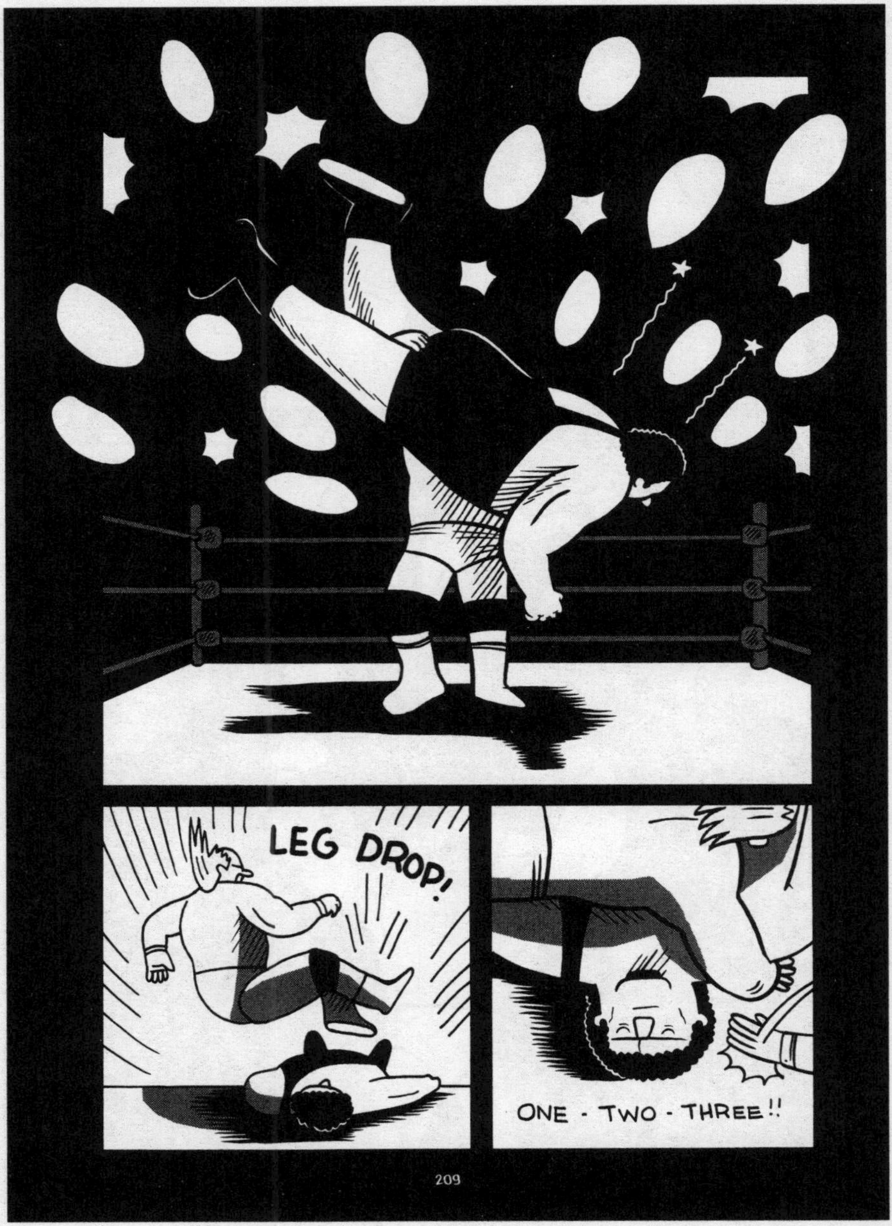
LEG DROP!
ONE - TWO - THREE!!

AFTER THE MATCH ANDRE RODE A MOTORIZED RING CART BACK TO THE DRESSING ROOM AS 93,000 FANS THREW GARBAGE AT HIM.

THE CART WAS THERE BECAUSE THERE WAS CONCERN FOR ANDRE'S ABILITY TO WALK TO THE RING.

STILL, THERE WAS ANDRE SCREAMING HIS HEAD OFF AS IF HE WAS ROBBED, LIKE A TRUE HEEL.

ANDRE IMMORTALIZED HULK HOGAN AND SENT THE WRESTLING BUSINESS INTO ORBIT.

THAT NIGHT, HOGAN BECAME A GOD...

...AND ANDRE MADE IT HAPPEN.

■

Remote Control

FROM *The Believer*

YOU DON'T HAVE to listen very closely to realize we've been wrong for all these years. It's not a difficult phrase to remember, and she repeats it again and again and again, clutching her knee as she rocks back and forth like a child hurt on a playground. It is, in fact, not a phrase at all, but a word—just one—and though we hear it mostly as a keening, inarticulate wail, it's also impossible to mishear. The word is *why*.

In the video—which will be shown on the news again and again in the weeks that follow the incident—she says the word three times, stopping only when she is spirited away from the cameras in her father's arms, her face pressed fearfully against his. She looks, in her lacy white costume, like nothing so much as an anxious young bride being carried over a threshold she isn't quite sure she's ready to cross.

For all the hours she has spent in the public eye prior to this moment, and for the many more hours she will spend there yet, she has been stoic, strong, reserved. She was famous before, for her skills as an athlete and as a performer, but this moment of anguish will make her an icon. Newspaper headlines and magazine covers and reporters and talk-show hosts and families joking in the car and around the breakfast table and on the couch as they watch her on TV will quote her, now and for years to come—or at least they will think they are quoting her. But they will say, without fail, the one thing she didn't say: "Why me?"

Twenty years later, we are still trying to answer this question. And if we have been mishearing something so simple for so long, we have to wonder what else we have been mistaken about.

First, the facts: on January 6, 1994, Nancy Kerrigan left the ice after a public practice session in Detroit's Cobo Arena, where she was to compete in the US Figure Skating Championships the following day. "I was walking toward the locker rooms, away from the ice," she said later, "and someone was running behind me. I started to turn, and all I could see was this guy swinging something . . . I don't know what it was." The man had been aiming for her left knee, but missed, instead hitting her on the lower thigh. Later, in an exclusive interview with Jane Pauley, Nancy put a brave face on the assault, reassuring Americans that she knew how lucky she was, because if the man had *actually* hit her knee she would undoubtedly have been unable to skate at the Olympics. She had to feel thankful, she said in a moment of good-natured wit, for his poor aim. By then, however, it didn't really matter what she had to say. To the public, her injury had already been transformed into a gangland kneecapping, while the assailant's weapon, revealed soon after the assault to have been a collapsible police baton, was routinely characterized as everything but—a crowbar, a wrench, a lead pipe—in an ongoing public game of Clue. Nancy, meanwhile, would be remembered not for anything she was doing now, but for the way she had acted immediately following the assault. There was room for only one image of Nancy in the public's memory, and it had already been chosen.

By the time the cameras caught up with Nancy, her attacker had fled into the parking lot, and was visible on the film played on the news that night—and endlessly replayed, reproduced, referenced, and eventually parodied over the next six weeks—as a blurry black splotch about to disappear through the arena's Plexiglas doors. The assailant lost, the camera then turned to his victim, who had collapsed on the ground, sobbing, as medical personnel tended to her injured leg. The camera zoomed in on her as closely as possible as she wailed, "Why? Why? Why?" When asked what she had been hit with, she responded: "I don't know, some hard, hard black stick. Something really, really hard. Help me. I can't move. I'm so scared. I'm so scared. It hurts so bad."

The next day, Nancy, unable to skate, watched as Tonya Harding became the national champion for the second time. Tonya had won the title for the first time in 1991, and in the process had also become the first American woman to land a triple axel in competition. She never regained the success she had enjoyed that year, and her career had been on the decline since her disappointing performance at the 1992 Olympics, when she began losing the ability to land her famous triple axel in competition. Since then, she had come in sixth at the 1992 World Championships, and fourth at the 1993 US Championships, not even managing to make the American team at Worlds. Her only successes, including a bronze medal at Skate America a few months before, seemed to take place when Nancy wasn't around, and this time was no different: with Nancy out of contention, Tonya delivered a stronger performance than she had in recent memory. "I know there are a lot of people out there who think I'm a has-been," she had told the press. "I have something to prove tonight."

Tonya still didn't have her triple axel, but she landed a spectacular triple lutz. Her spiral sequence—the move Nancy was famous for—displayed more flexibility and grace than it ever had before. After turning up at too many competitions looking exhausted and out of shape, Tonya was dynamic and disciplined again, showing her strength in the deep edges that had wowed judges since she made her senior debut in the mid-'80s. Yet Tonya's skating showed not just a return to form but a maturation. It seemed as if she had finally stopped fighting against her sport, and, remembering her old love for it, was again greeting it as a friend. "For all the skeptics who felt Tonya's peak had passed," commentator Peggy Fleming said, "I think she has proved she still is a winner even without that triple axel."

She was also, notably, a winner without Nancy Kerrigan, though anyone who watched Tonya skate that night would have a hard time believing that she couldn't perform just as well as Nancy. At the time, figure skaters were scored by nine judges, who each awarded two scores, one for technical merit and one for artistic impression, with 6.0 representing a perfect mark. Tonya had been awarded 6.0s in the past, and at her career peak, when she was able to land axel after axel, both her technical and her artistic scores had been dominated by 5.9s and 5.8s. Tonight she earned those scores again. At the end of the evening, Tonya's marks were even higher than the ones that had allowed Nancy to win the national title the year before.

Was Tonya able to pull out a better skate simply because she wasn't sharing the ice with Nancy that night? Perhaps. In the few years they had occupied the spotlight together, Nancy had gradually come to embody all the qualities that Tonya, it seemed, would never quite be able to grasp. Nancy's presence was elegant and patrician despite her working-class background; her skating was as graceful and dancerly as Tonya's was explosive and athletic. Audiences and commentators wanted elegance and grace; they wanted Nancy, and as good as Tonya was—as great as Tonya was—it had become painfully clear, over the last few years, that she would never quite be *right*. With Nancy out of sight, perhaps Tonya could for once remember all she was, rather than all she wasn't, and deliver the skate of a lifetime.

And perhaps, too, the judges had something to do with it. Audience members weren't the only ones who liked Nancy: the judges liked her, too, and had ways of showing it. When it came to the technical merit score, with its necessary deductions for errors and falls, judges' rankings were more or less objective; artistic impressions left a little more room for interpretation. Despite its specific list of requirements—for musicality, use of the rink, deportment, and other qualities—"artistic impression" was a far more elastic score. Judges could allow their scores to be influenced by a skater's costume, or by a skater's appearance, or simply by some ineffable quality that struck them, somehow, as "right"—right for the moment, right for the event, right for the sport. Many judges saw these qualities in Nancy. "She's a lovely lady," an Olympic judge, who preferred to remain anonymous, told sports writer Christine Brennan. "She was raised as a lady. We all notice that."

At the time, judges' opinions were also far less reliable—and far more malleable—than many outside the sport would have imagined. Working without the aid of instant replay or slow-motion analysis, judges—some of whom were former skaters, many of whom had simply devoted their careers to the sport—had to judge a program as it happened, with no opportunity to take a second look at a skater's performance. Judges were all too likely to miss skaters' errors on the ice—and at times did—making even the most objective portion of the score surprisingly unreliable. It was standard practice for judges to "leave room" in their scores, meaning that if a skater performed phenomenally at the beginning of the evening, they would be likely to receive a lower score than if they had performed at the end of the night, so that later and potentially better skaters might have a chance to win. Judges sat in on practice sessions, and scored skaters not just on their performance on the night of the competition but on the skill they displayed over a period of time. And judges were also likely to prop up the scores of skaters they knew to be solid competitors, even if the performance they were actually scoring was mediocre.

If Nancy Kerrigan had skated in the US Championships that night, and had skated just as well as or even somewhat worse than Tonya Harding, she likely would have beaten her, not because of the quality of her performance but because she was more consistent, more admired, more in keeping with the sport's ideals, and, above all, because she was the American skater who seemed the likeliest to bring home Olympic gold. The judges knew it. Nancy knew it. Tonya knew it. The only thing that remained a mystery was just who had taken Nancy Kerrigan out of contention, and why.

But that night, none of those questions mattered, and none of the unspoken rules of judging held true. Tonya won the gold by a generous margin. She would be going to the Olympics, but so would Nancy, who, even injured, was still more valuable to her country than any other skater in good health, and was given a bye despite her inability to compete at the US Championships. Unlike Tonya, Nancy didn't need to prove her worth.

Nancy Kerrigan may not have had the protection she needed to ward off an assault at the US Championships, but Tonya Harding did: namely, a man named Shawn Eckhardt, who at the tender age of twenty-six boasted an Errol Flynn mustache, a three-hundred-pound girth, an ambitiously fabricated résumé studded with counterterrorism and espionage, and a company called World Bodyguard Services, whose headquarters occupied a spare room in his parents' home. Though he described himself as Tonya's bodyguard, he entered her life as a high-school friend of Tonya's ex-husband, Jeff Gillooly. According to Shawn, it had been upon Tonya's return from the NHK Trophy the previous December that Jeff, believing the judges had shafted her, suggested they might find a way to keep Nancy out of contention for the Games.

Later, Tonya would claim that the plot had been motivated completely by Jeff's greed, that she had been aware of it only after the fact, and that she had failed to come forward only because she feared Jeff would kill her if she tried. Jeff would claim it was Tonya's idea from the beginning, and that he had merely gone along with her wishes so he could help make her dreams come true. The public, given the opportunity to select one story as the more plausible—and juicier—version, overwhelmingly chose the latter. It seemed there was nothing more enjoyable, in prime time or real life, than a devious plot with a manipulative woman at the top.

In his search for someone to carry out the assault, Shawn called his friend Derrick Smith, a Phoenix man who aspired to open a paramilitary survival school in the Arizona desert, and who in turn suggested his twenty-two-year-old nephew, a weightlifter, steroid enthusiast, and aspiring martial artist named Shane Stant. Shortly after Christmas the two arrived at World Bodyguard Services headquarters for a meeting with Jeff and Shawn. The tape that Shawn secretly made of the meeting that night recorded both his suggestion that they hire a sniper to murder Nancy, and Jeff responding, "What can we do less than that?" Figure-skating insider that Jeff was, it was his idea to break her landing leg. Shane would do the job for the bargain price of $6,500, and Derrick would drive the getaway car.

What happened next was soon known to the world, even if the identity of the assailant was not. But Smith's anonymity wouldn't last long. The Detroit police—and, to an increasing degree, the public—immediately began suspecting that Tonya and Jeff were involved, but they didn't have much to go on until an anonymous woman called the Detroit police and voiced her suspicions that Tonya, Jeff, Shawn, and some other men in their employ were behind the attack. She also sent unsigned letters to the FBI, and to KOIN-TV and the Multnomah County DA's office (both in Portland, Oregon, where Tonya lived) detailing the same suspicions. Later, she would be identified as Patty May Cook, an acquaintance of Shawn Eckhardt's father, Ron, who called Patty up every few weeks to tell her about his problems and occasionally tried to initiate phone sex. She had barely listened to him as he bragged about his son's espionage career one night, but she was horrified when, the following day, she turned on the TV and realized Shawn's plans had come to fruition.

After the attack, though, the gang began to fall apart. Shawn, his initial excitement perhaps turning to guilt, played his tape of the planning meeting for Eugene Saunders, a classmate in his community college paralegal class. Saunders, a twenty-four-year-old pastor, came forward with what he had heard, speaking to both the FBI and the *Oregonian*. As the story gained notice, reporters started hounding Tonya and Jeff, and Tonya's practice sessions became jammed with nearly as many TV cameras as the Olympics would be in a few weeks' time. The FBI also began monitoring their house, and the evidence began mounting against them, though not quite as quickly as the public's opinion.

Finally, on January 18, 1994, Tonya came forward to the FBI, saying she was frightened of Jeff, and telling them everything she felt she could. Jeff was arrested. The US Olympic Committee notified Tonya that it was reviewing her status, and Tonya secured the services of her coach's husband, a prominent Portland lawyer, who filed a lawsuit for twenty million dollars in damages in the event that Tonya was kept from going to the Games. On February 13, the USOC announced its controversial decision to keep Tonya on the Olympic team. On the morning after Valentine's Day, Tonya left for Lillehammer. Before she even landed in Norway, she began the endless round of press appearances that would take up much of her time at the Games, granting an in-flight interview to Connie Chung somewhere over the Atlantic. "I feel really lucky," she said. For perhaps the first time in her life, Tonya Harding was flying first class.

In 1991, when Tonya Harding became the second woman in the world to land a triple axel in competition and became the US champion in the process, Nancy Kerrigan was standing beneath her on the podium, her crooked teeth hidden beneath a shy smile, and a bronze medal hanging around her neck. A few weeks later, Nancy would win bronze again at the World Championships as Tonya Harding and Kristi Yamaguchi, who had medaled silver at the US Championships, again stood above her. This time, their roles were switched: Kristi won the gold, and Tonya, even after landing a more impressive axel than she had at the US Championships, took home the silver. Despite whatever disappointment Tonya may have felt, it was a landmark moment for American ladies' figure skating, marking the first time a single nation had so dominated the podium at the World Championships. It also gave each of the podium's proud young occupants her first true taste of fame—and prepared them, however inadequately, for the pressure and scrutiny they would experience at the Olympics the following year. For Tonya, the 1992 Olympics would seem to mark the beginning of a baffling career decline. For Nancy, they would mark the beginning of an equally swift—and perhaps equally terrifying—rise to fame and fortune.

At that year's Games, Nancy's skating was flawed, but her image wasn't. Though her imperfect performance was good enough to keep her in the medals on a night when not even Kristi Yamaguchi managed a clean skate, the solid and ambitious jumps Nancy did land attracted considerably less attention than her costume: an unadorned white leotard whose elegant lines matched her own, and whose sweetheart neckline seemed to echo all too aptly the role she had begun to play in American life. By this time, the promise Nancy had displayed in 1991 had attracted the attention of some key individuals, including Vera Wang, a former figure skater who designed Nancy's costumes pro bono. Nancy got her teeth fixed, and began to get acquainted with the feel of the cameras following her every move, though she never grew to like it. Her performance at the 1992 Games was not a triumph of athleticism—though even then Nancy was a far more formidable athlete than anyone gave her credit for—but it was a triumph of image-making. To the commentators, she was "lovely," "ladylike," "elegant," and "sophisticated," and the audience agreed. Vera Wang had based the design for Nancy's costume on a dress from her bridal boutique, and as Nancy took the ice in Albertville, France, skating to the theme from *Born on the Fourth of July*, she seemed to be presenting herself as America's hopeful young bride. Even her lack of competitive savvy gave her an air of innocence and sincerity: she was radiant when she landed a difficult jump, and appeared near tears after making a mistake. She had the style and grace of a woman, but the bashfulness and sincerity of a girl. She was beautiful without being sexual, strong without being intimidating, and vulnerable without being weak, and in the end she embodied no quality quite so perfectly as she did the set of draconian contradictions that dictated a female athlete's success. Once again, Nancy went home with the bronze. Tonya, who had finished narrowly behind her, in fourth place, went home with nothing.

As the 1994 Games drew closer, and as Tonya's skating grew weaker and Nancy's stronger, singling her out as America's only serious contender in ladies' figure skating following Kristi Yamaguchi's retirement, Nancy signed endorsement deals with Campbell's Soup, Reebok, Northwest Airlines, Seiko, and Ray-Ban. It was as if the rewards for Olympic championship had already been bestowed on her: she was sure to win, and even if she hadn't yet, she *looked* like a winner. Somehow, she had broken the rules that for so long had dictated the shape of a skater's career: years if not decades of penury and toil, and a reward if and only if you won the gold. Those rules had applied to everyone else, but they didn't apply to Nancy. She didn't need the gold medal around her neck so long as she had a neck lovely enough to deserve it.

It was a new variation on an old theme, and one perhaps best exemplified by Peggy Fleming, whose Olympic victory had set the standard for the career—and the fame, and the wealth—a female figure skater might aspire to. Not quite twenty-five years before, at the 1968 Grenoble Olympics, Peggy, coltish and wide-eyed as a young Audrey Hepburn, had become the only American athlete to win a gold medal at the games. Upon her return home, she had been crowned America's sweetheart.

Her subsequent fame was unprecedented, even if her victory was not. Tenley Albright, who in 1956 became the first American ladies' skater to win an Olympic gold medal, left the sport altogether after her win, attended Harvard Medical School, and became a surgeon. Following her victory at the 1960 Games, Carol Heiss had skated in a few ice shows and appeared in a Three Stooges movie, then retired from skating altogether in 1962, quietly returning to the sport in the 1970s to work behind the scenes as a coach. But Peggy would never have to attempt such strenuous work, or aspire to such anonymity. Her job now was to make a living being—and selling—herself. Over the years, she appeared in ads for L'eggs and Hanes pantyhose, Concord Mariner and Rolex watches, Halo shampoo, Colorado Interstate

Gas, Trident gum, Bell Telephone, the United States Postal Service, Kellogg's cereal, and Equitable Life ("Maybe your girl won't become a sports star like Peggy Fleming. But every youngster—including yours—can be as physically fit as the most talented athlete"). She met Lyndon Johnson on a trip to the White House, visited Vietnam veterans in the hospital, was named the Associated Press Athlete of the Year, and rode through her homecoming parade perched on the back of a convertible, clad in a smart double-breasted skirt suit, cradling a drift of red roses, and looking as dewily innocent as Jackie Kennedy had, sitting in the Dallas sunshine, before the first shot cracked through the air.

In 1973, after Janet Lynn had tried for both the gold medal and the position of America's sweetheart at the 1972 Sapporo Olympics and finished with a disappointing bronze, Peggy, title still intact, appeared in an hour-long special titled—rather unimaginatively but nonetheless intriguingly—*Peggy Fleming Visits the Soviet Union*. (Only Nixon could go to China, but only Peggy Fleming could go to the USSR.) Peggy's career had spanned some of the most frightening years in the United States' recent memory: the issue of *Life* magazine on whose cover she appeared, rosy-cheeked and radiant after her gold-medal win, advertised itself with two headlines, schizophrenically promising stories of both OLYMPIC CHARMER PEGGY FLEMING and KHE SANH. Some Americans might have needed the magazine to remind them just who this Olympic charmer was, but the Vietnam combat base required no introduction. But there were no images of the Battle of Khe Sanh on the cover of *Life* that week, or of the ongoing Tet Offensive, or the recent attack on the American embassy in Saigon, or of Kosygin or Brezhnev or McNamara or Johnson, or of any of the other people and events weighing so heavily on the minds of Americans that winter: there was only a beautiful young girl making her country proud. It was a feat for which she would be handsomely rewarded for the rest of her life.

Now Nancy seemed poised to inherit her crown. She was just as elegant, just as humble, just as stylish, and just as graceful. She was also just as steely a competitor as Peggy had once been, and concealed the same athletic rigor beneath the same veneer of girlish charm, but that was, perhaps, best left unexamined. More important than her skill or her strength or her contributions to the sport, Nancy could make Olympic audiences feel good about being American. Nancy Kerrigan was growing more and more famous simply for being Nancy Kerrigan. And she was also coming to learn, just as Tonya was, that there were certain exceptions to the sport's rules. Being a winner could make you lovable, but being lovable, it seemed, might also be enough to make you a winner.

Nancy's family—her gruff but devoted father; her blind mother, whose tough-as-nails and Southie-inflected voice softened only when she spoke of her daughter; and her two boisterous, hockey-playing older brothers—was just as easy to love. When Nancy went to Albertville, all the Kerrigans went with her. Interviewed for the *New York Times*, Nancy's mother, Brenda, recalled her daughter's reluctance to go back to the Olympic Village with the other athletes: "She asked if it was OK. Of course it was OK; this is her time to be with the other kids. Nancy is always so apologetic. I don't want to say she's a perfect child . . . but she's a caring child who loves family." Nancy, the twenty-two-year-old baby of the family, still lived with her parents in the same modest green house in which she had grown up. When she traveled to competitions, she shared a hotel room with her parents. She didn't have much time for friends or dating, and didn't seem to have much interest in either, describing her mother as her best friend. Nancy's mounting success was a victory not just for her, or even for the Kerrigans, but for a way of life Americans feared was fast shrinking: that of the wholesome, hardscrabble working-class clan. One network profile showed Nancy brushing her mother's hair. Another showed the Kerrigan family seated around the dinner table, toasting each other with glasses of milk.

But if Nancy got to be a working-class hero worthy of a Horatio Alger story, Tonya had to be pressed into service as her counterpart, and as one of America's most reviled demographics: white trash. In the weeks and months following the scandal, a new variety of sports journalism emerged that could perhaps most aptly be called the Tonya-bash. It was an easy form to learn, about as simple as a Mad Lib, but far more enjoyable, and almost impossible to avoid. Once an author set down one anecdote or piece of biographical information, he had to add one more, and then another. There seemed to be a greasy, eventually shameful pleasure that came with both writing and reading about not just Tonya's gaffes or problems but the basic facts of her existence. Her mother had been married six times to six different men, or maybe seven, depending on the journalist's sources. Tonya owned her first rifle, a .22, when she was still in kindergarten, and had moved thirteen times by fifth grade. She dropped out of high school at fifteen. (In fact, she later obtained a GED.) She drank beer and played pool and smoked even though she had asthma. She raced cars at Portland International Raceway, and was involved in a much-hyped traffic altercation in 1992, when she brandished a Wiffle-ball bat at another driver (reported, inevitably, as a Louisville Slugger). She skated to songs like Tone Lóc's "Wild Thing" and LaTour's "People Are Still Having Sex." She was ordered to change her free-skate costume at the 1994 Nationals because the judges deemed it too risqué. Her sister was a prostitute. Her father was largely unemployed, as was her mother, as was her ex-husband. No matter how journalists added up the details, however, they all seemed to reveal the same motive: Tonya was going nowhere fast, and she had decided to take Nancy with her.

Somehow, in the scandal's aftermath, the form of the Tonya-bash was able to alchemize even the most chilling details of Tonya's life into tabloid gold. In a *Rolling Stone* article published shortly after the scandal, Randall Sullivan chronicled a visit to the Tonya Harding Fan Club, where he met "the [club] newsletter's editor, Joe Haran, a puffy Vietnam vet with white hair and spooky eyes, [who] said he identified with Tonya through his memories of abuse and poverty suffered as a child. Haran was someone for whom it was not inconceivable that a world-class figure skater might phone the police, as Tonya Harding did in March of 1993, to report that her husband, Jeff Gillooly, had emphasized himself during an argument by slamming her head into the bathroom floor." More than anything, it seemed, Tonya's history of abuse proved that she didn't belong in the world whose acceptance she so craved.

Yet her biography was nothing if not malleable. When Tonya first rocketed to fame by landing the triple axel in 1991, the media had tried to put a more positive—and more salable—slant on her lifestyle, using the same information, which they would later call in as proof of her trashiness, to paint a picture of a spunky, all-American tomboy. In the words of one profile piece, "She's only five feet one inch . . . and weighs only ninety-five pounds. But as petite as she is, there's a tomboy streak in her that she's proud of. She drives a truck and tinkers with her car . . . Yet there's clearly a young lady coming through in her skating, and her personality." In 1991, the skating world had no choice but to try to love Tonya: she had done what no other American woman could, and if she continued to grow as a skater—and continued to act more and more like "a young lady"—she could make her country proud at the Olympics, and earn both its love and its money.

Back then, she also didn't need stories of ladylike behavior and quirky tomboyishness to convince her audience that she was worth believing in. At the pinnacle of her career, Tonya was, in a word, spectacular. At the time, the only other woman who had landed the axel was Midori Ito of Japan. Midori was a remarkable jumper, and she made the axel look effortless: launching all four feet nine inches of herself into the air, her body seemed light, buoyant, and meant for flight. Tonya's axel did not look effortless. It did not even look beautiful. It looked difficult—which, of course, it was.

The axel is the only jump that a skater executes by facing forward and taking off from the front of the skate, but like all other jumps it is landed backward. The skater, having taken off from a position that makes gaining the necessary height that much harder, must also somehow squeeze out another half rotation while she's in the air. Then she has to land it. Completing three and a half rotations in midair is far from easy, but even more difficult is coming back to the ice with all the speed, power, and momentum you need in order to leave it, to somehow land steadily, and to continue with your routine.

Tonya was tiny, but her presence on the ice was powerful, undeniably muscular, and impossible to ignore. Commentators like to talk about skaters "fighting for each jump"; Tonya seemed to fight the jumps themselves. Later, much would be made in both the press and in parody about Tonya's thighs: they were *huge!* They were so *fat!* How could she pretend to be pretty, or even feminine? But they were, at the end of the day, nothing more or less than the thighs of an athlete.

They were thick and powerful because she needed them to be that way to launch herself into the air. When Midori jumped, she seemed to float like a leaf borne on the wind. Tonya, *Time* magazine wrote during the scandal, "bullies gravity." They meant it as a criticism of her skating, and, by extension, of her, but one wonders: did this have to be a bad thing? What was inherently wrong with a spectacle of female power in which you could almost taste the athlete's sweat, and feel her desire, her soreness, and her determination to leave the ground? She wasn't artful, but it wasn't her job to make art; she wasn't soft and feminine, but it wasn't her job to be those things, to sit still, or to smile passively while the cameras lingered on her face. It was her job to jump and spin, to tear the ice with her speed, to fight and fall and get up and fight again. And for a while—when the axel was a novelty and her country needed a skater who could challenge the Japanese, when the old narrative of American spunk versus a foreign juggernaut was ready to be dusted off for yet another Olympic year, and when Tonya could be counted on to win—the axel was enough to make Tonya enough. For a moment, everything seemed within her reach.

When Tonya took off, you were never sure if she was going to make it as far as she needed to: she struggled for every inch of clearance, and as she completed her rotations her body often tilted in the air, her physical power overwhelming her attempts to control it. Sometimes she seemed impossibly tilted, and still, somehow, she was able to dig her skate in and swing her free leg as hard as she could as a counterbalance, saving her landing and skating on. Sometimes she wasn't. Increasingly, she wasn't. And eventually it seemed she had lost the ability to land the jump at all.

After the 1992 Olympics, at which Tonya had fallen on both her axel attempts—sliding painfully across the ice and receiving a 0.5 deduction from each judge—she stopped constructing her programs around the jump and began working on the kind of elegance and artistry that had eluded her for so long. In an interview later that year, she suggested, hopefully, that this would be enough: "I still have all the jumps without the triple axel right now, and I have more style . . . I mean, if other people can do it without a triple axel, why can't I?"

But if Tonya couldn't bring the axel, we weren't interested. She wasn't rewarded for working on her artistic impression, and no one cared if she landed a triple lutz or a triple-triple combination that would have garnered high praise for any other competitor. She tried to remake herself as a skater, and perhaps it was when it became clear to her that this wasn't enough—that it was the axel, and not Tonya herself, that the people loved—that she began to have real trouble competing. It was all too easy for the skating community to write her off as a once-promising has-been: the sport, after all, was littered with them. Tonya gained weight, and began replacing even her easiest triple jumps with doubles. She started competing under the name Tonya Harding-Gillooly, then divorced her husband in 1993, only to reconcile with him soon after. Later, when it came time to fit her life story into the scandal's narrative, journalists delighted in using this detail as proof of Tonya's tackiness. Despite her allegations of abuse, despite the restraining orders and 911 calls she placed, and despite her claims that she feared for her life both before and after the assault on Nancy, few phrases had quite the same cachet, or were quite so gleefully suggestive as *white-trash lifestyle*, as *live-in ex-husband*.

As the quickly accepted press narrative also had it, the assault on Nancy Kerrigan was only a hop, skip, and a failed jump away from Tonya's disappointment at the 1992 Games and her growing frustration thereafter. She was trash: trash cheats. Trash wants reward without working. Trash is dangerous. Trash doesn't care about other people's dreams. Why question a story that made such easy sense, and provided so much to laugh at along the way?

The only thing missing from the media accounts of Tonya's life was her own version of the story, and it would remain missing for a very long time. For a period in the late '90s, Tonya worked with ghostwriter Lynda Prouse on a memoir, but for various reasons the project fell apart and wasn't released until 2008, when a small press published a collection of the interviews that were to have formed the basis of the book. The collection, titled *The Tonya Tapes*, met with very little fanfare and even less in the way of sales, despite the fact that it provided something the public had been missing for nearly fifteen years: Tonya's own detailed account of her life and her role in the scandal. The picture she painted of her role in the assault— or rather, her lack thereof—was shocking not so much for its deviations from the publicly accepted image of her as for its unsettling plausibility.

In the interviews, Tonya described her mother using her skating trophies to store loose change, calling her fat and ugly, gulping down a thermos full of brandy as she drove Tonya to the rink in the morning, and hitting her or sending her to her room without dinner as punishment for a bad skate, preparing Tonya for the relationship she would eventually have with her husband. "My mom hit me, and she loved me," Tonya recalled thinking. "[Jeff] hits me, he loves me. It's just the way life goes." She described marrying Jeff—at the time the only man she had ever dated—at nineteen, largely because she was so desperate to get out of her mother's house. She described her half brother—who was later arrested for child molestation—attempting to rape her when she was fifteen, and how her mother refused to let her testify against him. She described Jeff's abuse—abuse that was corroborated by her friends and by police reports available to the press at the time of the scandal, but generally utilized only as proof of Tonya's trashiness—and how neither her family nor her coach was willing to believe her claims. She described leaving Jeff and coming back to him, leaving him again and coming back again, because he was "always saying the right things to get me back, and I'd be stupid enough to go back and get beat up again." As with so many other women at the center of a scandal, the media did an exceptionally good job of selling Tonya as an extraordinary specimen, a woman unique in her shamelessness, greed, and brutality. Her talent aside, however, she was not unusual at all, but merely one of the countless American women attempting to escape, or at least endure, an abusive marriage. Her relationship with Jeff may have become famous for its explosive ending, but it was identical to millions of others unfolding without the aid of tabloid headlines or prime-time specials.

In the book, Tonya also maintained her innocence in the scandal's planning, telling a version of the story that seemed just as plausible as the one that had quickly gained acceptance during the event's coverage. She said she had attempted reconciliation with Jeff following their divorce, in 1993, because a representative from the United States Figure Skating Association told her to do so "unless I didn't want the marks. If I wanted to make the Olympic team, I need to make myself a stable life . . . They said I had a stable life when I was with him—married, settled down . . . And they wanted to make sure I was still going to be that way to go to the Olympic Games."

In a sport where judges routinely give skaters criticism on their hairdos and costumes and earrings and eye makeup and teeth (and suggest that failing to change such details might well result in lowered scores); in a sport where, to this day, very few gay male skaters can afford to be openly gay and deal with inevitable backlash not just in the media but in their scores; in a sport where women are sometimes rewarded more for salability than skill; in a sport where gender roles are policed so rigidly, on and off the ice, that Tonya Harding, a petite, blond, white woman, was somehow butch enough to register as a threat to skating's femininity—in a sport where all this went on, and was in fact common knowledge, the idea that the USFSA would attempt to control a skater's marital status is hardly implausible. It wanted Tonya to be proper, or at least as proper as she could be. They wanted her to train hard and skate reliably so she could compete well at the Olympics if she remained the only American skater who could match Nancy's maturity and skill—a very plausible prospect at the time, even if the USFSA didn't want to admit it. If the representative Tonya says she spoke to had been aware of Jeff's abuse, there must have seemed too much at stake to give Tonya's claims much credence. Tonya was abused by her mother, her husband, and finally her sport, whose criticisms of her—she wasn't pretty; she was too fat; she didn't deserve to be here; why couldn't she do anything *right?*—savagely echoed the criticism she had been enduring for her entire life.

In discussing her failure to come forward upon finding out about Jeff's role in the assault after the fact—the only crime of which she was eventually convicted—Tonya said that Jeff's abuse had only grown more severe following the attack on Nancy. He had put the plot in motion, she believed, because he was angry that she had reunited with him only at the USFSA's request, and that she planned to leave him as soon as she had competed at the Games. "When he found out," she said, "he came unglued . . . He told me he'd ruin me." If this really was his plan, he could hardly have been more successful.

After the attack, Tonya told her interviewer, Jeff decided to threaten her by holding a gun to her head, letting two other men rape her, and then raping her himself, telling her he would kill her if she took her story to the FBI. Even if one finds reason to disbelieve this claim, Tonya's history of abuse, her justifiable lack of trust in authority figures, and her equally justifiable fear of how the public might treat her if she came forward with what she knew all make her failure to act seem perfectly fathomable.

As for Tonya's claims about her own innocence in the plot itself, any attempt to dismiss her version out of hand somewhat falls apart once one realizes that the dominant version of the story—the story the press picked up and popularized, and the story that endured largely for that reason—was Jeff's. Tonya's version of events is implausible only because it contradicts the story we've been familiar with for the last twenty years. Telling it nearly fifteen years after the scandal took place, she also had far less of a reason to lie than Jeff did while he was still trying to strike a deal with the prosecution. Eugene Saunders, the pastor to whom Shawn Eckhardt confessed his role in the plot, told the press that Shawn made it seem as if Tonya had been uninvolved in planning the assault. Shawn had said the same when he was first interviewed by the FBI, and though he changed his story later, the backpedaling testimony of a scared would-be hit man hardly seems as unimpeachable as the public made it out to be.

Beyond Jeff's, and, eventually, Shawn's testimony, there was relatively little to link Tonya to the attack's planning at all. The only involvement Tonya had that could be corroborated by any witnesses beyond Jeff, Shawn, Shane, and Derrick was insignificant: she called a friend who wrote for *American Skating World* to find out where Nancy practiced, saying she had a bet with Jeff; she went along to Shawn's house when Jeff delivered the information on Nancy and the up-front pay Shawn had requested before the attack, but stayed downstairs, making small talk with Shawn's mother; and she asked for Nancy's room number from the desk clerk at the Detroit Westin where she and Nancy were both staying during the US Championships. These instances were enough to arouse suspicion, but were hardly damning. Jeff could, in fact, have made a bet with Tonya as to where Nancy skated, and she could have found out what he needed without suspecting he planned to put the information to such a use. She was also likely used to waiting around at Shawn's house while he and

Jeff played at being assassins, and when questioned as to why she had asked for Nancy's room number, she later claimed that she had wanted to slip a poster under the door so Nancy could autograph it for Tonya's friend and fan-club founder, Elaine Stamm. This wasn't especially unlikely behavior for Tonya, who, despite the press's seemingly endless reports of her anger issues, tantrums, and ruthless competitiveness, had always been friendly with Nancy, and made an effort to keep things that way even as the scandal progressed.

She was also remarkably good-natured in her dealings with the press for the weeks leading up to the Olympics, but even her politeness and positive attitude could easily be used against her: saying it had always been "her dream" to return to the Olympics meant she didn't care whom she had to step on to get there, or at the very least that she was deeply delusional. Being kind to the press meant she craved its attention no matter what the cost. And attempting to show kindness to Nancy, as she did when she said she wanted to give her a hug on her arrival at the Olympic Village, was the worst of all. The media had a field day with the statement, suggesting it was further proof of Tonya's cold-blooded intimidation tactics—a hug from Tonya, the newscasters' arch tones suggested, would no doubt have involved a knife between the ribs—but it could also be read as the well-meaning suggestion of a woman who desperately wanted to act as if nothing was wrong, and who believed, more than a little naively, that she might still be able to convince the world, or at least her alleged victim, of her innocence. By then, however, it was far too late. Nancy declined the offer, and the two women never actually spoke for the duration of the Games.

Tonya had famously arrived late to the 1992 Olympics, but she was right on time in 1994. Her ability to compete at the Games despite the mounting suspicions against her seemed, to viewers, both an affront to decency and sportsmanship and an unimaginable boon. Something was coming—something *good*. In the six weeks since the attack, media coverage of the scandal had built Tonya up from a somewhat tactless young woman into a bloodthirsty fiend; when she and Nancy appeared together on the ice for the first time after the assault, their practice session was glutted with reporters, the constant snapping of the cameras' shutters sounding like nothing so much as the shuffling and reshuffling of a deck of cards.

But whatever reporters had been hoping for—accusations, hair-pulling, a bloodbath right there on the ice—didn't happen. The conflict, it seemed, could be resolved only through competition, a belief widespread enough to make the ladies' short program the fifth most watched television broadcast of all time. Forty-five million viewers in the United States alone tuned in to watch Tonya deliver a lackluster skate, seeming strained and exhausted in a glittery red costume. She was in tenth place at the end of the night, while Nancy, skating cleanly, and looking calm and happy to be on the ice, easily glided into first place. Anyone who wasn't on tenterhooks as they waited for a confrontation between Tonya and Nancy may have noticed an impossibly polished performance turned in by an impossibly young skater named Oksana Baiul. But forty-five million Americans didn't sit through a ladies' figure skating competition just to watch some ladies figure skate. They wanted anger, screaming, tears. And if an actual fight was impossible, they at least wanted more of what had made the scandal itself so compelling: the spectacle of female pain.

Three days later, when Tonya's name appeared on the marquee to announce the beginning of her free skate, her audience was ready for her, but Tonya wasn't ready for them. Her lace had broken during the warm-up, and now she couldn't find a replacement: because of her jumps, Tonya's skates were specially designed, and required longer laces than those other female skaters used. As Tonya tried to make do with a regular lace, the clock ticked down the seconds she had to appear on the ice before being automatically disqualified. The arena audience waited, confused, while the audience at home watched Tonya backstage, the cluster of people around her growing, her expression inscrutable in the murky light.

Tonya made it onto the ice with seconds to spare, went into her opening jump—a triple lutz—and completed only a single rotation. Not just her jump but her body seemed to come apart in the air, her legs and arms splaying toward opposite points as she froze for a moment above the ice, looking almost as if she was about to be drawn and quartered—which, in a very real sense, she was. She landed, looked down at her skate, and attempted to continue, but a few seconds later, as her music came to a fluttering crescendo, she dropped her head and began to sob. After making her way over to the judges' table, she lifted her skate up to show them her lace, her lucky gold skate blades glinting in the stadium lights.

Tonya had done everything the protocol demanded: in such an event it was a skater's job to go to the judges, tell them what was wrong, and get permission to fix it. Later, her problems would be overwhelmingly presented as a last-minute ploy for attention and the second chance she didn't deserve. Anyone who had watched her historic performance at Skate America in 1991, however—the event at which she had landed two of the best triple axels of her career—would know she had dealt with the same issues years before. Leaving the ice after her flawless free program at Skate America, Tonya, screaming with joy, plowed into her coach's arms. The last words the cameras picked up from her before the commercial break were the untroubled afterthoughts of a girl too flush with good fortune and newfound evidence of her own invincibility to think of anything else. "You know what?" she told her coach as she relaxed her embrace. "I broke my boot again."

It was clear the problem was one she had dealt with for years, and that she had long ago come to realize that her sport's equipment simply wasn't designed to contain her strength. But that night at Skate America it didn't matter. Despite the fact that she had broken an eyelet—and her fears that her boot wouldn't hold her during her triples—she had skated a perfect program, and ended the night with two 6.0s for technical merit and a gold medal for the event. But on that night, the whole world was behind her, urging her to land the axel, urging her to win. Little more than two years later, Tonya took to the ice knowing that the world now wished just as fervently for her failure.

After Tonya explained that her skate lace was too short to hold her on her jumps, the judges allowed her to go backstage and fix her skate with the longer lace her coach had finally found for her, while Canadian skater Josée Chouinard took Tonya's place in the lineup. She was a beautiful skater in all the ways Tonya wasn't—graceful, stylish, and stunning in a Fosse-esque ensemble of pink leotard and gloves—but that night she had a hard time dragging the cameras away from Tonya as she sat backstage, coughing and staring numbly at her skate. Tonya moved several spots down in the lineup, and was greeted by more than a few jeers when she finally took to the ice. Yet anyone who had come to the stadium or turned on their TV hoping to witness one more night of Tonya performing the role of Tonya— trashy, shameless, greedy, lazy, and above all entertaining—couldn't help feeling their appetite had only been whetted by her earlier problems. That had been the appetizer; now for the entrée. Would she try to find another excuse to get off the ice? Would she cry again? Would she fall—again, and again, and again? Would she hurt herself? Something would happen—something *had* to happen.

Tonya had disappointed her audience before. She had given lackluster skates, sometimes disastrous ones. She had fallen while attempting her axel or left it out entirely. She knew what it was like to let people down by skating badly. This time, though, she had let the world down by skating well. She had given them their drama for the evening, had let all the confusion and fear and anger of the last six weeks get to her when she should have been most impervious, and had let herself become, for the briefest moment, a spectacle of pain, just as Nancy had six weeks before. But now, like Nancy, she pulled herself together and faced the crowd. This time, she landed as flawless a triple lutz as she had at the US Championships, and skated with some of the same newfound grace and maturity she had displayed there not so long ago. Her triple axel was gone: she would never land it in competition again, would never compete again, and she knew it. But she took her time, seeming to savor the feeling of being out there, of having made it to the Olympic ice at all, and of being able to do, just one last time, the only thing she had ever been great at, and the only thing she had ever loved that had loved her equally in return.

Writing about Tonya's insistence on skating, Christine Brennan argued that "she had every right under US law to skate in Norway. But the responsible thing would have been for Harding to gracefully withdraw." Yet if Tonya had to be painted as shameless—and after the last six weeks there was no other role she could play—she could at least put her supposed shamelessness to good use. If the judges she had tried so hard to please had never been able to find any gracefulness in her skating, then why did she have to conduct herself gracefully now? And why—at the end of a career in which everything she did, every role she was allowed to play, and every achievement she was considered capable of was dependent on other skaters—did this moment have to be about anyone but her? She had refused to slink away when the public wanted her to buckle under the pressure not of competition but of humiliation. She had spent her entire life struggling to deliver the performance that was expected of her. Now, expected to do the easiest thing there was—to fall apart on the ice, to be weak, punished, and ashamed—she rebelled, and did the hardest thing that not just she but any woman performing that night could have: she skated the way she wanted to. She finished the Games in eighth place, but in her own way, and on her own terms, she had won.

Reporting from the wreckage of the scandal's aftermath, journalists would make much of the fact that Tonya had skated her free program to the theme from *Jurassic Park*. The *New York Times* suggested she may have felt "that if fictional dinosaurs can be resurrected, so can her career." Extinction jokes abounded. Beyond the subject matter, authors implied, it was the sort of tacky and unfeminine choice one could expect from Tonya. (Meanwhile, former Olympic champion Katarina Witt didn't seem to inspire any flak for skating to the theme from *Robin Hood: Prince of Thieves*, clad in a tunic and breeches and including a mimed bow and arrow in her choreography.) In *Women on Ice*, an anthology on the scandal released the following year, Stacey D'Erasmo took a more sympathetic approach, writing that "watching Tonya walk barefoot up and down that long, dark corridor Friday night as the other women in their shiny little outfits passed her by, then watching her skate to the music of *Jurassic Park*, a movie about extinct animals, I felt that I was witnessing the final act of an American tragedy."

Yet D'Erasmo, for her embrace of the moment's pathos, still somewhat missed the point. Watching the Olympics that night, viewers witnessed not just the end of Tonya's career but the extinction of a whole era of ladies' figure skating. If Tonya was a T. Rex, lumbering out of her enclosure and bringing chaos to the night's well-ordered spectacle of heavily regulated female strength, then

Nancy was a velociraptor, hissing with stifled aggression as her turf was overrun by tiny, quick-blooded mammals. As Nancy warmed up with the final group, she found herself surrounded by teenagers: Tonya may have famously trained in a mall, but Nancy had to compete against girls who looked like they would have been more at home shopping in one. Nancy delivered a beautiful routine that night, elegant, nervy, and technically flawless. But it was also the skating of a grown woman, and she narrowly lost both the gold medal and the crowd's favor to Oksana Baiul, the bubbly, crowd-pleasing sixteen-year-old orphan in pink marabou. However much the public had tried to situate Tonya and Nancy as enemies, they remained united, if only in their representation of the sport's old guard, and of the last gasp of a period during which skaters could just possibly be seen as women and not as girls.

After the Games, Nancy lingered in the spotlight just long enough to see public opinion turn incongruously against her, a phenomenon that might have seemed no stranger to her than the sudden adulation she had recently been the subject of. The process began mere minutes after Nancy skated, as she waited to take her place on the podium. She was ready to receive her medal, and most likely to go home and turn her back on the events of both that night and the previous six weeks, but Oksana was still backstage. As it turned out later, no one could find the copy of the Ukrainian National Anthem they would need to play during the medal ceremony, but at the time Nancy was misinformed that Oksana was having her makeup done, to which she groused, "Oh, come on. So she's going to get out here and cry again. What's the difference? It's stupid." Was Nancy—radiant Nancy, good Nancy, Nancy who just wanted to go out and skate for herself—being *competitive*? Was it possible that she was being not just competitive but *bitter*?

It was. In fact, Nancy seemed to be irritated not just about her loss to Oksana but about—well—us. Soon after the Games, in a homecoming parade at Disney World in which Nancy stood on a float with a Mickey Mouse–costumed employee, wearing her silver medal and a weary smile, she complained: "This is so corny. This is so dumb. I hate it. This is the most corny thing I've ever done." Mickey shrugged mutely. The rules he obeyed while wearing his costume didn't allow him to say anything, but the rules Nancy had to follow didn't let her say much more.

Yet the public had an even stronger motivation for its newfound distaste: Nancy had failed. She hadn't won the silver. She had lost the gold. How, after miraculously recovering from her injuries (which were in fact relatively minor), after training harder than she ever had before, and after gaining the adoration of her country, if not the world—how, after all this, could she fail? She was skating not just for herself but for us, for middle America, for goodness, for sportsmanship, for proper femininity, and she was propelled by the strength of our needs and desires. Wasn't that enough?

But Nancy's lack of adherence to her role soon faded into memory: someone had to play the victim, and television abhors a void. Tonya and Nancy reverted back to their old roles within the public eye, and for the next few years wandered in and out of newspaper and tabloid pages with declining frequency. Whenever they turned up, however, they were considerate enough to do what was expected of them. Nancy continued to perform in ice shows and TV specials; Tonya was banned from the sport. Nancy married and had two children; Tonya married her second husband, then had her second divorce. Nancy started the Nancy Kerrigan Foundation and was named as the spokesperson for the Foundation Fighting Blindness; Tonya completed a court-ordered five hundred hours of community service. Their sport went on without them, and teenagers continued to flood the rinks.

Shortly after the Olympics, in the kind of surreal moment Tonya's career would contain far too many of, Woody Allen briefly considered her for a role in *Mighty Aphrodite*, but gave up on the idea when he learned that her probation prohibited her from leaving the West Coast. Instead, Tonya made her film debut alongside Joe Estevez in a low-budget 1996 thriller called *Breakaway*, which earned her ten thousand dollars and a lot of ribbing from the press. The gimmick casting didn't sell many tickets, but Bill Higgins, the film's unofficial Tonya-sitter, was still able to sell the story to *Premiere* magazine. He recalled Tonya's on-set diet of fifty-nine-cent Taco Bell bean burritos, orange soda, and Benson & Hedges 100s; her wonder at the sight of Aaron Spelling's fifty-four-thousand-square-foot mansion ("Now

that's cool"); her requests to go to Disneyland; and her state of denial, well after her lifelong ban from competitive figure skating and
her unofficial ban from exhibition skating and ice shows, as to what
life held for her. Acting, she said, was "really fun," and "the action
part," when she got to beat up a man twice her size, "was really cool,"
but as a career it wasn't for her: "I had, and still have, my career," she
said, "and that's skating." Then, scaling back her ambition a bit, she
added, "If they do a movie of my life, I would just like to do the skating. Nobody skates like I do."

She was right. No one did, and in the last twenty years, no one
has. Since Tonya became the second woman in the world to land a
triple axel in competition, only four others have managed to follow
her: Ludmila Nelidina of Russia, Yukari Nakano and Mao Asada of
Japan, and Kimmie Meissner of the United States, who landed a triple axel for the first time at the 2005 US Championships, which were
held that year, coincidentally, in Portland, Oregon. The women who
came after Tonya struggled, much as their predecessor had, to understand how best to use their strength in a sport that had never quite
learned what to make of it, let alone whether or not to reward them
for it. Neither Yukari Nakano nor Ludmila Nelidina ever medaled
at Worlds or made it onto an Olympic team, nor did they rocket to
the sort of fame they might have imagined would accompany such
a feat. Kimmie Meissner came in sixth at the 2006 Olympics and
won a gold medal in the World Championships a few weeks later,
but, like Tonya, she had trouble hanging on to her axel, and she was
forced into retirement by a string of injuries before she had a chance
to compete at another Games. Present at the 2010 Olympics, however, was Mao Asada, who planned—and gorgeously executed—a
record-setting two triple axels in her free skate. She had hoped that
they would help her to beat Yuna Kim, whose elegance and beauty
on and off the ice had made her a favorite for the gold and a mil-
lionaire in her native South Korea before the games had even begun.
They weren't. Mao Asada came in second, but anyone familiar with
the narratives of figure skating knew what had really happened: she
hadn't won the silver. She had lost the gold.

* * *

Clackamas County, Oregon, the roughshod collection of edge cities, mini-malls, and farmland whose communities Tonya shuttled between throughout much of her life—Happy Valley to Milwaukie, Lents to Beavercreek, Oak Grove to Estacada—hasn't changed much since its fabled daughter's girlhood. The areas closest to Portland have seen the crowding and expansion that came with the city's growth into a legitimate metropolitan area: driving from the city center into Clackamas County, you will pass the new-car dealerships and strip malls and condo developments whose signs promise if you lived here, you'd be home by now. But you don't have to drive far to get beyond the suburban sprawl and into the past. There, as in 1994, you will find ranches and ranch houses; towns with names like Boring and Needy, which don't so much invite mockery as head it off at the first pass; and roadside farm stands and U-Pick outfits that, in the summertime, erect signs telling motorists WE HAVE BERRIES: BLACKS AND BLUES.

It is a place of freeway exits and depressed communities and temporary living, but it is also a place filled with surprising beauty, home to protected rivers and forests, and so close to Mount Hood that the snow visible on the face of the mountain seems capable of falling straight into people's yards. It is the sort of place where a young girl whose early life has conspired to make her feel worthless might find comfort and happiness fishing and hunting, splitting wood and fixing cars, and proving that she can be as strong as any boy. It is a place where a girl might learn to rely on her talent and determination rather than her looks, and in that sense it is not an unlikely breeding ground for an Olympic athlete, but it is, perhaps, the most natural place in the world for one to grow up. And if another such athlete comes from this place, and has less experience than her competitors at posing for the cameras, smiling for the crowd, and learning to hide all the desire and effort that go into her sport, one can only hope that she will not be punished quite so harshly as her predecessor.

The rink at Clackamas Town Center, where Tonya Harding learned to skate—and which, Susan Orlean wrote during the scandal, was "the only place in America where an Olympic contender trains within sight of the Steak Escape, Let's Talk Turkey, Hot Dog on a Stick, and Chick-fil-A"—is now long gone, and the Town Center, once the headquarters of the Tonya Harding Fan Club, has removed all traces of its famous former tenant. But if you venture into Portland's Lloyd Center mall, you can still find the rink where Tonya skated for the first time. She was not quite three years old. "They had this archway with bars in it," she recalled fondly, nearly thirty years later, "and there was an ice rink down below. We were walking across it—my mom and me and her son, and I said I wanted to do that, and she said no . . . I sat down and started screaming . . . I had a fit. And I guess they said, 'OK, fine.' Went down, put some skates on me, and I sat down on the ice, and I kicked at it and picked it up and was eating it. They told me not to do that because it was bad for me and that I had to get up and do what everybody else was doing. And so I did. I got up and skated around. After that, I told them I liked it and wanted to do it more . . . I told them this was what I wanted to do." And so she did. Tonya had her first skating lesson on her third birthday, and didn't stop skating for the next twenty years. And though in that time she would spend thousands of hours learning to do what everybody else was doing— executing pretty spiral sequences and ornate choreography, doing her best to hide her strength and her sweat, smiling for the cameras and the crowds—her instincts would never really change. For the next twenty years, every time Tonya entered the rink, she was guided by the same desire she had felt that first time: to tear the ice's perfect, shining surface apart, and make her presence known.

RACHEL ZUCKER

■

wish you were here you are

FROM *The Pedestrians*

time isn't the same for everyone there is
science behind this when you fly into space
you're not experiencing time at the same rate
as someone tethered to Earth & someone
moving quickly experiences time at a slower rate
even on Earth so as I run through Central Park
at a speed not much faster than walking but slightly
I am shattering fields of time around me
& experiencing time differently from those I pass
last night I saw my son's adult self &
in the same moment toddler self this really
happened he was playing "Wish You Were Here"
by Pink Floyd on his electric guitar & feeling it
he's 11 & in between 2 kinds of time on the verge
of worlds I think we are too you & I who are old
young women it's not all 'downhill from here' we are
here you are & I am & this beautiful moment our sons

The Future Looks Good

FROM *PANK*

EZINMA FUMBLES THE KEYS against the lock and doesn't see what came behind her: her father as a boy when he was still tender, vying for his mother's affections. Her grandmother, overworked to the bone by the women whose houses she dusted, whose laundry she washed, whose children's asses she scrubbed clean; overworked by the bones of a husband who wanted many sons and the men she entertained to give them to him, sees her son to his thirteenth year with the perfunction of a nurse and dies in her bed with a long, weary sigh.

His step mother regards him as one would a stray dog that came by often enough that she knew its face, but she'd be damned if she'd let him in. They dance around each other, boy waltzing forward with want, woman pirouetting away. She'd grown up the eldest daughter of too many and knew how the needs of a child can drown out a girl's dreams. The boy sees only the turned back, the dismissal, and the father ignores it all, blinded by the delight of an old man with a young wife still fresh between her legs. This one he won't share. And when the boy is fifteen and returns from the market where he sold metal scraps to find his possessions in two plastic bags on the front doorstep, he doesn't even knock to find out why or ask where he's supposed to go, but squats in an abandoned half built bungalow he shares with other unmothered boys where his two best shirts are stolen and he learns to carry his money with him at all times. He begs, he sells scrap metal, he steals and the third comes so easy to him it becomes his way out. He starts small, with picked pockets and goods snatched from poorly tended market stalls. He learns to pick locks, to hotwire cars and finesses his sleight of hand.

When he is twenty-one, the war comes and while people are cheering in the streets and shouting "Biafra! Biafra!" he begins to stockpile goods. When goods become scarce, he makes his fortune. When food becomes scarce, he raids farms in the dead of night which is where he will meet his wife, and why Ezinma, fumbling the keys against the lock doesn't see what came behind her: her mother at age twenty-two, not beautiful, but with the fresh look of a person who has never been hungry.

She is a brash girl who takes more than is offered. It's 1966, months before everything changes and she is at a party hosted by friends of her parents and there is a man there, yellow-skinned like a mango and square-jawed and bodied like the statue of David, wealthy; the unmarried women strap on their weaponry (winsome smiles, robust cleavage, accommodating personalities) and go to war over him. When she comes out the victor, she takes it as her due.

Almost a year into their courting, the war comes. Her people are Biafra loyalists, his people think Ojukwu is a fool. On the night of their engagement party only her people attend. And when she goes by his house the next day she discovers he has left the country.

Her family is soon forced to flee the city, soon forced to barter what they have been able to carry, soon forced to near begging and for the first time in her life, food is so scarce she slips into farms at night and harvests tender tubes of half-grown corn in stealth and they boil so soft she eats the inner core and fibrous husk, too. One night, she finds a small farm tucked behind a hill and there she encounters a man stealing the new yams that would have been hers. There is no competition, he is well-fed and strong and even if she tries to raise an alarm out of spite, he could silence her. But he puts his finger to his lips and he gives her a yam. And being her, she gestures for two more. He gives her another one and she scurries away. The next night when she returns to the farm he is waiting for her. She sits by him and they listen to crickets and each other's breathing. When he puts his arm around her she leans into him and cries for the first time since her engagement party many months ago. When he puts a yam in her lap, she laughs. And when he takes her hand, she thinks, I am worth three yams. She will have two daughters, the first she names Biafra out of spite, as though to say "look mother, pin your hopes onto another fragile thing" and the second is named after her mother, who has since died and doesn't know that her daughter will forgive her for choosing the losing side and name her youngest child Ezinma, who fumbles the key against the lock and doesn't see what came behind her: her sister whom everyone has taken to calling Bibi because what nonsense to name a child after a country that doesn't exist.

Bibi, who is beautiful in a way her mother never was. Bibi, stubborn like her mother was always. They've fought since Bibi was in the womb, lying so heavy in her mother's cervix a light jog could have jostled her out. Bedridden, Bibi's mother grew to resent her and stewed so hot the child should have boiled in her belly. And three years later, Ezinma, pretty, yes, but in that manageable way that causes little offense. She is a ghost of Bibi, paler in tone and personality, but sweet in the way Bibi can be when Bibi wants something. Bibi loathes her. No, Ezinma can't play with Bibi's toys; no Ezinma can't walk with Bibi and her friends to school; no Ezinma can't have a pad, she'll just have to wad up tissues and deal with it. Ezinma grows up yearning for her sister's affection.

When Bibi is twenty-one and in the university and her parents are struggling to pay the school fees, Bibi meets Godwin, yellow-skinned and square-jawed, like his father, and falls in love. She falls harder when her mother warns her away. And when her mother presses, saying you don't know what his people are like, I do, Bibi responds you're just angry and bitter that I have a better man than you and her mother slaps her and that's the end of that conversation. Ezinma serves as go-between, a role she's been shanghaied into since her youth, and keeps Bibi apprised of all the family news, despite her mother's demands to cut her off.

And Godwin is a better provider than Bibi's father, now a modest trader. He rents her a flat. He lends her a car. He blinds her with a constellation of gifts, things she's never had before, like spending money and orgasms. The one time she brings up marriage, he walks out and she can't reach him for twelve days. Twelve days that put the contents of her bank account in stark relief; twelve days where she sits in the flat that's in his name, drives the car also in his name and wonders what is so precious about this name he won't give to her. And when he finally returns to see her packing and grabs her hair, pulling, screaming that even this is his, she is struck ... by his fist, yes, but also by the realization that maybe her mother was right.

The reunion isn't tender. Bibi's right eye is almost swollen shut and her mother's mouth is pressed shut and they neither look at or speak to each other. Her father, who could never bear the tension between the two women, the memories of his turbulent childhood brought back, squeezes Bibi's shoulder then leaves and it is that gentle pressure that starts her tears. Soon she is sobbing and her mother is still stone-faced, but it's a wet face that she turns away so no one can see. Ezinma takes Bibi to the bathroom, the one they have shared and fought over since they were old enough to speak. She sits her on the toilet lid and begins to clean around her bruises. When she is done, it still looks terrible. When Bibi stands to examine her face, they are both in the mirror. I still look terrible, Bibi says. Yes you do, Ezinma replies and they are soon laughing and in their reflection they notice for the first time that they have the exact same smile. How have they gone this long without seeing that? Neither knows. Bibi worries about her things that are still in the flat. Ezinma says not to worry that she will get them. Why are you still nice to me? Bibi wants to know. Habit, Ezinma says. Bibi thinks about it for a moment and says something she has never said to her sister. Thank you.

Which is why Ezinma, fumbling the keys against the lock doesn't see what came behind her: Godwin, who grew up under his father's corrosive indulgence. Godwin, so unused to hearing "no" it hit him like a wave of acid, dissolving the superficial decency that accompanies a person who always gets his way. Godwin, who broke his cello when he discovered his younger brother could play it better, which is why he came to be there, watching Ezinma, looking so much like her sister from behind, fumbling the unfamiliar keys against the lock of Bibi's apartment so she doesn't see who comes behind her: Godwin, with a gun he fires into her back.

PAUL CRENSHAW

■

Chainsaw Fingers

FROM *Jelly Bucket*

WHEN MILLS LOST HIS FOOT in Afghanistan, no one was able to help him find it. They had been traveling in convoy from Kabul when the IED went off and the lead Humvee flipped and the howling men appeared from among the rocks and began shooting. The windshield splintered. Then an RPG flew toward the Humvee and Mills went black. When he woke up his foot was missing, and his leg from the knee down. Fire rose white-hot all around him and he could hear Skeeter screaming and Johnson or Johnson moaning, though he couldn't tell which Johnson it was.

When he was finally found, the doctors could not reattach his foot so they gave him a prosthetic limb. After the initial soreness went away and the stitches were pulled and all the swelling went down, he found himself walking lop-sided, never quite balanced. He tilted sideways in the wind and walked like a young child pretending to be an airplane.

When he came home from Afghanistan he stood in his house turning in circles. He did not recognize the room. Everything seemed to have been moved a few inches to one side or another: the leather chair with the knife rip in it, the ugly lamp that had been here when he moved in, sitting in the middle of the floor like a forgotten statue, the refrigerator that stayed warm enough to grow mold. He walked lop-sided down the hallway and decided it was his real foot that made him feel off-kilter, like the world was constantly spinning. He went around the house with his arms out but kept tilting into walls and chairs and hallway pictures that had been here when he moved in, gray-faced people he had never met. He went out in the yard and ran around the house trying to get acclimated to the new leg but pitched into the bushes. When he came back in he sat staring at his legs, remembering rocket fire and black smoke, Skeeter crying out for his mother, Harris saying Oh fuck, oh fuck, oh fuck, Johnson or Johnson moaning. He opened the bottle of whisky he had saved for the day he returned and late at night he took out his gun and put the barrel against his shin bone and when he pulled the trigger the bone shattered. He took a long drink of whisky against the pain and shot his instep. When the red wave of blind pain wrapped itself around him, he covered his leg with a tablecloth and drove to the hospital.

At the hospital the doctor ran his hands over the leg and watched it through the X-ray machine. Then he brought out a saw and cut through the bone and sawed the leg off. He said, You are a lucky man, Mr. Mills, but Mills was unconscious.

With two prosthetic limbs he was no longer unbalanced, and he found he could run twice as fast. He could leap onto the house and stand there looking around the neighborhood. He raced cars up and down the street. The neighborhood kids came by all day every day. Jump on the house, they would say, then clap when Mills did it. Jump up in that tree. Catch that car. Catch that stray cat. Chase that wino until he throws up wine that looks like blood. Most of the time he enjoyed it. But sometimes he got angry standing on the roof. Jump down, the kids said. Now jump back up. Run to the far hills and back. Let us see your gun. Let us touch your fake legs. They shouted in unison like they were calling cadence or pledging allegiance and when they did this he wanted them to go away so he roared and threw pine cones and shingles and forgotten frisbees at them, but they only ran off a little ways and soon came back. Run a marathon, they said, standing in his yard. Do a backflip. Now do two.

To keep from staring at the walls all day, Mills started running. He ran up and down the street like a bullet with the neighborhood kids watching. His prosthetic legs flexed and bent with his body's rhythm and he flew like an aircraft streaking toward Baghdad. He was disqualified from his first 5k. He ran it in just under ten minutes. That's gotta be a New World Record! a man with a bullhorn said. The race was for charity. But they took the medal away because some people complained about Mills's prosthetic legs.

He started running because a lot of his friends did: Skeeter and Harris and one of the Johnsons. They came back from the war with drinking problems. They passed out in the front yard at two in the afternoon. They got roaring drunk and climbed trees and howled at the moon. They got in bar fights and got thrown in jail and when they went before the judge the judge said, I appreciate your service, but you need to find a new hobby.

So they woke in the morning before dawn and splashed cold water on their faces and lit out the door before the world etched itself into shape. They ran in long lines like trains heading east, little reflectors on their clothing catching headlights of passing cars. Sometimes they mumbled cadences under their breath, though they never sang loud enough for anyone to hear.

When Mills ran with them the first time they tried to keep up with him, but none of them could. They ran until their eyes were bulging and their tongues had turned black and their hearts felt like rockets soaring skyward but they could not keep up.

Mills, old buddy, Skeeter said after Mills had been running with them for a few days. It was just dawn. The sun rose like a bomb. Mills, what Skeeter means is, Johnson said. What he means is. They stood in a circle with their hands on their knees, panting for air. Mills bounced lightly on his prosthetic legs.

Mills, you're too goddamn fast, Harris said. We can't keep up with you.

Mills stopped bouncing. What are you saying? His voice rose at the end.

So Mills started running by himself. He woke before dawn and lay in bed until he heard his old friends laboring past and then he ran out the front door and whizzed by them. Sometimes he circled them two or three times before running on. They waved to Mills and said Hey, old buddy, but secretly they cursed under their breath.

The neighborhood kids began following him on their bicycles. When they couldn't keep up they got their mothers or fathers to wake before dawn and drive them, so that Mills often had a long line of cars with their parking lights on swinging through the neighborhood after him, fathers balancing cups of coffee on their knees as they drove with the window down. At first the fathers yawned sleepily into the headlights of coming cars and wondered aloud why they were up this early in the morning to watch a man run, even if he did have two fake legs. But after a while they leaned forward and peered at the speedometer and said Holy shit that's thirty miles an hour! Thirty-four! Thirty-six! Forty!

There was a long line following him the morning the car hit him. He had forgotten to put on his little reflectors and the car came screaming around the corner and clipped him, knocking him backward, where one of the cars following him crushed all the bones in his right hand. He was still lying with the tire on top of his hand when his old friends from the Army came running by. At first he thought they were going to pretend not to see him. Like it was really dark. But he called to them, and they came, kneeling around him in a circle. They picked the car up off his hand. Skeeter had been a medic, and he had seen some nasty shit, some really nasty shit, he told Mills once, back when they were both drinking, you don't even fucking want to know. Little kids with their guts ripped out. Dead dogs swollen and bloated in the streets, then dead dogs rupturing in the streets, the smell, Jesus fucking Christ, Mills, you can't imagine. He didn't vomit when he looked at Mills's hand, though Mills could see him thinking about it really hard.

What do you think they will put on him now? one of the kids said.

At the hospital it was the same doctor. He said, You are a, but Mills cut in.

Please don't tell me how lucky I am, he said.

We're going to have to operate, the doctor said, clearing his throat.

Mills waved his good hand.

Is there anything, you, aah, want? the doctor said, clearing his throat. He made a point of looking at Mills's prosthetic legs. Anything you, aah, need?

What can you do?

We've done guns, knives, billy clubs. A shotgun. A grenade launcher. A samurai sword.

I want a saw, Mills said.

A saw?

A saw.

The doctor cleared his throat. He was a champion at clearing his throat. Later in the night he would go home and take so many Vicodin his heart would stutter and skip as he staggered around the house yelling the name of a woman he had once known. May I ask why? he said.

So when whatever happens next happens I won't have to come back here. I can saw on my own body.

Well, I don't know how well that would work, the doctor said, but we'll see. He lowered the mask over Mills's face. The anesthetic smelled like mouthwash. The lights dimmed. Mills tried to stay awake but the lights kept dimming. It was like driving through tunnels in the mountains, or when landmines went off too close to the vehicle you were driving and the ringing in your ears lasts for months.

When he woke the doctor was gone and a nurse sat in the chair next to his bed reading *Soldier of Fortune* magazine. She had huge breasts, Mills noticed right away, and her uniform was unbuttoned enough he could see her red bra, nipples poking through the satin. His mouth was dry and the world swam dizzily. He said, You're a nurse? She had long blond hair and lips that reminded him of apples.

She said, I welcome patients back.

I went somewhere?

She held a glass of water to his lips. She smelled like apples too. You did indeed. How do you feel?

Mills held up his arm. His hand was gone, cut off a few inches above where his wrist used to be. A metal exoskeleton was attached to his flesh. His fingers were tiny little chainsaws. He said, How does this work?

She said, Pretend you are flexing your fingers.

He pretended he was flexing his fingers. The little chainsaws roared to life. They sounded like bees on his arm. The little chains spun and a pall of blue smoke came out of them. He straightened his fingers and they shut off. Then he did them one at a time.

This is amazing, he said.

The nurse put a hand on his arm. I'm glad you like them.

Am I the first?

She thought for a moment. For the chainsaws, yes. But we've done shovel-hands for people who like to garden. And gun hands for hunters. You must like trees?

Not really, he said.

Then why the chainsaws?

He was still examining them and didn't answer. The finger-saws came to life one by one, all he had to do was think about it. You guys can do anything, he said.

We've had lots of practice.

He slept with the nurse later in the afternoon. She straddled him on the hospital bed and lowered herself down. He watched the door, afraid someone would walk in.

Have you ever done this before? he said.

I am not a virgin, if that's what you mean, she said.

That is not, he started to say, but then could not finish. He gritted his teeth. When he came the chainsaw fingers fired up accidentally and tore the sheet.

Afterward she lay on his chest, breathing. Her skin smelled like sunlight in winter. She punched her number into his cell phone. She said, Call me. Take me to dinner.

He said, You won't be embarrassed of me?

No, she said. I am not embarrassed easily.

He stroked her nipples with his other hand. I have found one thing these are not very good for, he said, and she laughed into his chest.

When he got home the neighborhood kids were waiting on his front lawn.

Show us the chainsaws, they said.

Mills wondered how they already knew. He fired one of the chainsaws.

Do them all, they shouted.

He had to walk sideways to get through them. He said, Excuse me. He said, Move please.

Do them all, they shouted. Cut something down. Cut up that tree.

Mills made it to the door and closed it behind him. When he looked out the window the children were standing silently in his yard, waiting. When they saw him peeking they yelled Come back out and cut something.

His Army buddies came by later in the afternoon with a case of beer and some whisky. There were more of them now. The other Johnson had come back. He had a shotgun for a right arm, and Greggs had a wheel for a right foot. He could turn it on and go whizzing down the street on one leg.

We are through with running, they said, and have started drinking again. Mills looked at Johnson's shotgun arm, double-barrel. He wondered how Johnson loaded it, how he took a shower. It was because of the car, Davids said. He was the tallest of them all but he looked short standing there, like he was shrinking. One of his fingers was a butter knife. Seeing you lying there like that reminded us of too many things we hoped were forgotten but really weren't. The others stood in a circle nodding. Johnson was rubbing his shotgun arm with an oiled cloth. They gave Mills a beer. Now show us how those things work.

Mills spent the evening sawing off the tops of beer cans. He sawed pencils into smaller and smaller sections. He sawed his name into the front door and the neighborhood kids cheered. He sat in the front room with the summer light fading and fireflies hitting all up and down the street and the neighborhood kids standing on the sidewalk in front of his house trying to see his chainsaw fingers. Skeeter nicknamed him Cutty McCutter. They talked about Afghanistan, where it was not uncommon to see someone missing an arm or leg from an IED detonation or an errant bullet or bombs. They saw people missing eyes and ears and noses, people with burns all over them, women wailing over the body of a dead child in the streets, dogs slinking through alleyways, cowering at explosions in the distance.

I suppose, Mills said, waggling his fingers, that there are worse things than having chainsaw fingers.

Dead would be one of those things, Johnson said, but Mills was still inspecting his hand. He had not yet grown used to having chainsaw fingers. He still smelled like the apple nurse.

They do not have this technology, Mills said, turning his chain-saws off and on. They do not have the ability to replace hands with chainsaws, or to bring people back from the edge of death, so they just die. His head felt like a balloon, floating slightly above him. How many people dead did you see? Mills said. Because I for one saw far too many and hope that I do not ever see another unless it is myself when I am rising upward toward wherever it is we go when the spirit leaves the flesh. When he crossed the room to get another beer his prosthetic legs were wobbly.

At some point they went out in the yard and Johnson fired his shotgun into the air and the children screamed. Greggs went roaring down the street and ran over a mailbox and the children clapped and shouted and hooked their fingers into the corners of their mouths and whistled. Mills tried to jump on top of the house but he sprung awry and ended up in a tree. Cut it down, cut it down, the children screamed. Mills turned on his chainsaw fingers and started sawing away until all the limbs but the one he was standing on were gone, and when he swung himself down the children yelled for him to cut that one too. When he had cut the last limb they wanted him to cut the tree down and when it fell the children scattered, screaming timber at the top of their lungs, all of them cheering and taking pictures with their phones. When he had cut it all up into small pieces they told him to cut the neighbor's tree down as well but he was getting tired of them telling him what to do so he waved his chainsaw fingers at them crazily and went inside.

In the morning all the limbs from the tree he had cut were gone and the neighborhood kids were still outside his house. He pulled the blinds and went back to sleep.

He woke when the nurse knocked on the door. She said, You didn't call me.

The sun stabbed into his forehead. He smelled like alcohol, he could feel it still swimming in his blood.

Some friends came over, he said.

It looks like it, she said. He turned and looked at the room. There were beer cans and whiskey bottles all over the living room. At some point he had sawed up the furniture and it lay in little piles. There was a hole in the floor. He held up his hand and little wood chips were stuck in the teeth of his chainsaws.

Outside, the children were standing in rows, waiting. Go away, he yelled, but they only stared at him until he pulled the nurse in and closed the door.

He took a hot shower and let the water run over his head. He held his chainsaw fingers out of the shower. When he turned them on the sound echoed off the tile walls like he was in the bottom of a well. Walking to the showers in Afghanistan you could hear distant explosions. Walking back the sand blew all over you and you were dirtier than before because the sand stuck to you when you were wet.

He got out of the shower and wiped off the mirror with his good hand. He fired up his index finger and cut his hair, occasionally scraping his scalp, bright bits of blood springing up. When he looked out the window he could see faces pressed against the glass.

When he came out of the bathroom she was cleaning up the living room, picking up the beer cans and whiskey bottles and trying to piece the furniture back together. She had raised the blinds and the light was too bright and on the sidewalk were more kids, dozens now, and a few adults too, sitting in lawn chairs like it was right field at a baseball game. He closed the blinds.

I can't see, she said. It's too dark in here.

It's perfectly fine. Even through the blinds he could imagine the kids standing out there. It reminded him of the circus, the strong man, the bearded lady, the mermaid. Chainsaw Fingers! the sign would read. Watch Him Slice and Dice!

You could throw apples at me, he said, and I could cut them in half in mid-air.

She was scrubbing at the floor. What?

In the circus, he said. We'd make a hell of a team.

Are you still drunk?

I am not, he said, although I wish I was. Drunk, or dreaming.

She stood up. Let's go dancing. Or get dinner. You need to get out of this house.

I am not going out there, he said.

She peered through a slit in the blinds. This has happened before, she said. The guy with shovel hands threw dirt at them. The one with guns used to walk outside and fire up into the air to make them run, but they only cheered. But they're only kids, and they will go away. Probably.

I don't think so, he said.

They made love in his bedroom but he could not finish because he could hear the crowd outside. Occasionally someone would yell for him to come out and cut something in half and that, combined with constantly having to remember not to turn on his chainsaw fingers and slice through her flesh kept him from it. He lay on his back while she went down on him, her tongue caressing him as she moved her head gently, but it did not work. When she left in the morning the children cheered as the door opened, but the cheer turned into a sigh of disappointment when they saw it wasn't him. One of the children threw a rock that struck her on the forehead and Mills ran out and screamed at them, his fingers roaring to life in little palls of blue smoke. The children screamed. Cut something down they said. Cut a car in half. Cut the nurse in half. The nurse put a hand to her head and came away with blood. Mills led her to the car. He waved his chainsaws at the kids to keep them back but they were chanting Cut her up, cut her up.

The neighbors started charging for parking. People set up across the street with video cameras. Mills stayed in his bedroom. He put blankets over the windows. When the nurse called he did not answer the phone. The kids took turns running up to the house and ringing the doorbell. When the nurse came over and rang the doorbell he thought it was the children again, so he did not answer. The neighborhood kids, thinking the nurse might be let inside when they were not, threw rocks at her, and she ran screaming back to her car.

His army buddies tried to come by but the children would not let them through either. Johnson aimed his shotgun arm at them but they only smiled. When Greggs tried to roll through them they held him down and took his wheel off and he hopped back to the car and Johnson drove away with his arm out the window. The army sent a chaplain from Bragg and the children let him through, but Mills did not answer the door. The children rang the bell all day and night now. It got into his teeth, the constant rattle, so he cut through the wall and ripped out the wires. The chaplain stood on the front porch pressing the button for a long time, but Mills did not hear because there was no sound.

When the chaplain quit ringing the bell and knocked, Mills peered through the peephole.

Let me in, Sergeant Mills.

I am not a sergeant anymore, Mills said through the door. My fighting days are done.

I would like to speak with you.

You are speaking with me.

The chaplain looked over his shoulder at the children. There were hundreds of them now, watching silently with long drawn faces like melted wax.

Are they always here? the chaplain asked.

Always, Mills said.

That must get tiresome, the chaplain said.

After the chaplain left the kids chanted for hours, keeping Mills awake. He finally drifted off but woke in the green glow of the alarm clock to hear them screaming Cut it down, cut it down and Do them all, do them all. Then they said, Cut her up, cut her up and after that it was Cut yourself, cut yourself. It sounded like the crowds at professional wrestling chanting USA, USA when a bad guy came into the ring.

Some mornings, if the kids weren't chanting Cut it Down or Do them all or USA, he could hear his army buddies calling cadence a few streets over. It reminded him of army bases he'd been on, platoons running in formation before first light. From a distance they sounded like hound dogs crying out for quarry, or men pinned down in the rocks by sniper fire. He'd sit in the living room with the lights off and listen to them circling and circling, voices growing strained and weary, and sometimes he would think they were drawing nearer, they were coming to save him while the neighbors in lawn chairs slept with their chins on their chests and the kids sprawled out asleep in the dew-wet grass, but always the kids woke when the voices drew too near, and the kids swarmed out into the street to chase Johnson, yelling at him to fire his shotgun, for Greggs to ramp something with his wheel-leg. When his army buddies saw the children coming for them, they turned and ran back the other way, their red-hooded flashlights bobbing into the tops of trees, and the kids assembled themselves in formation in his front yard.

He caught the first intruder early in the morning. He had not slept. He was waiting to hear his army buddies running in the early hours before dawn, but had heard nothing, and he wondered if they were out boozing somewhere, pissing in the middle of the road and wrestling each other and firing their shotgun arms into the air and whizzing around on their one wheel and only occasionally slumping over with their arms around their insides as if something had come loose and saying Oh Dear Fucking God in Heaven why does it have to hurt so much? and Why can I not get these images of people with missing limbs out of my mind, the dead dogs in the streets, the streets themselves, long and silent and filled with rubble while glassless windows stare like silent eyes.

He was lying there in his bed trying to remember what the nurse smelled like when one of the neighborhood kids came crawling through the bedroom window. The kid pushed the blanket and blinds aside and fell onto the floor and lay there looking at Mills.

Mills sat up in bed. He raised his hand and turned on all the saws at once and the kid crawled quickly back out the window. Through the walls Mills could hear the children cheering.

Another one came just after dawn, and another in the afternoon. Mills spent the day nailing the windows shut. He called the nurse and asked her how long until they left the shovel guy and the gun guy alone and she said I'll let you know when it happens.

You mean it hasn't happened yet?

I was trying to make you feel better.

You didn't.

I assumed they would. Leave them alone. Leave you alone. Eventually. But they are drawn to you. To all of you. You have gone some place they do not understand. They cannot help but look. You are something more.

More than what?

Than they are, she said.

In the night they broke out his windows with rocks and he woke with his bedroom full of people watching him sleep.

Turn on your fingers, one of them said. Cut something in half.

Jump on the house, another one told him. We want to see it.

Could you kill people with those? another one said.

Where's the nurse, one of them said. Have you fucked her yet?

Get out, he said. Get the fuck out of my house.

But there were too many of them. They picked him up. Turn them on, they said, and pulled his hair until he did. Then they worked through the night, holding him, a dozen of them at a time, all of them taking turns, their parents sitting in the yard in lawnchairs watching as the kids used his hand to cut away the walls of his house. They started in the corner, holding Mills like he was made of cardboard, his arm extended, chainsaw fingers roaring as they cut a vertical line at the corner and then a horizontal line across the top of the wall and then down the other corner and then the kids all together pushed and the wall tilted outward and landed with a loud cough like a landmine going off. Then they did the next wall and the next until all sides of the house were peeled away. They threw the TV in the front yard and cheered as the glass exploded. They cut up his favorite chair. They threw the pictures like frisbees. Mills struggled and kicked and tried to rake them with his chainsaws but there were far too many. Mills was screaming and crying, yelling for someone to help him but there was no one to help. When they finished and only the roof and a few supports were left standing, they gently deposited him in his bed and went back and stood in the front yard again. All the walls had been cut away. Everyone could see inside now.

ALEX MAR

■

Sky Burial

FROM *Oxford American*

IN FEBRUARY OF 2002, Patricia Robinson wrote to her daughter, the third of her five grown children, about a hospital appointment for her broken wrist.

> Mary, I was wearing your hat—the purple & green & other colors one—to keep me warm & cover up my bad hair which was uncombed. Picture the old lady in gray sweatsuit, in jaunty hat with sprigs sticking out, shawl-wrapped wrist clutched to breast, shod in fat socks & men's slippers—what a mess! And I had NO underwear, let alone clean. No pocket handkerchief. Dreadful! But they were nice to me anyway.

Patty was sixty-nine then—she would live seven more years—and she'd long ago developed a cavalier attitude toward her aging body, and her mortality, as one of many strategies for shrugging off disappointments. She told Mary that she'd turned down the doctor's recommended surgery because "I'm betting on my body to repair itself as always." She wrote, "I really do think *my* bones know who's the boss, and I have spoken to them."

Now it is May of 2014, and I am removing Patty's bones from a long cardboard box. Here are the pieces that made up her arms: the humerus, the ulna, the radius that was fractured. Here are the halves of her pelvic bone, each ilium curved like a dish. Her vertebrae have been collected in a pile; her individual ribs are banded together with a Velcro tie. I remove her skull and cradle it, upside down, in the palm of my hand, where it fits perfectly. Without the jawbone, I can see her dental work clearly: two large gold molars, a bridge, and two porcelain crowns. When she's turned upright to face me, I can also see the markings in her orbital bones, around her sockets.

I lay my fingertip there, just inside the socket, where some of the bone is chipped away: it was pecked out, by the beaks of vultures. These are the markings the huge black birds made when they consumed her eyes, with the permission of her family.

The few thousand acres of Freeman Ranch in San Marcos, Texas, include a working farm; fields studded with black-eyed Susans; and a population of white-tailed deer, Rio Grande turkeys, and brawny Gelbvieh bulls. But there's more nested here: if, on your way from town, you turn off at the sign onto dirt road, and if your vehicle can handle the jerky, winding drive five miles deeper into the property, you will come across two tiers of chain-link fence. Behind this double barrier, accessed by key card, sixteen acres of land have been secured for a special purpose: at this place, settled in the grasses or tucked under clusters of oak trees, about seventy recently dead humans have been laid out in cages, naked, to decompose.

Just beyond the gates is where I meet Kate Spradley, a youthful, petite, and unfailingly polite woman of forty. She has short, mousy hair that's often clipped in place with a barrette, and dresses in yoga-studio t-shirts that explain her slim, almost boyish figure. Kate is so utterly normal that it takes a moment to register the peculiarity of her life's work: she spends her days handling and cataloguing human remains.

Kate, an associate professor at Texas State University in San Marcos, does most of her work at their Forensic Anthropology Center (FACTS)—the centerpiece of which is the Forensic Anthropology Research Facility (FARF), the largest of America's five "body farms." Including Kate, FACTS has three full-time researchers, a rotating crew of anthropology graduate students and undergraduate volunteers, and a steady influx of cadaver donations from both individuals and their next of kin—brought in from Texas hospitals, hospices, medical examiners' offices, and funeral homes. When I arrive, Kate is helping lead a weeklong forensics workshop for undergrads, spread out across five excavation sites where skeletal remains have been buried to simulate "crime scenes." Under a camping shelter, out of the intense sun, she stands before a carefully delineated pit that contains one such skeleton: jaws agape, rib cage slightly collapsed, leg bones bent in a half-plié. In the time since it was hidden here, a small animal has built a nest in the hollow of its pelvis.

Over a year ago, back when he was "fully fleshed" (as they say), this donor was placed out in the field under a two-foot-high cage and exposed to the elements, his steady decomposition religiously photographed and recorded for science. Across the property are dozens of cadavers in various stages of rot and mummification, each with its purpose, each with its expanding file of data: the inevitable changes to the body that the rest of us willfully ignore are here obsessively documented. For the past six years, FACTS has been collecting data on human "decomp" while steadily amassing a contemporary skeletal collection (about 150 individuals now) to update our understanding of human anatomy. More specifically, for the forensic sciences, FACTS works to improve methods of determining time since death, as well as the environmental impact on a corpse—particularly in the harsh Texan climate. Texas Rangers consult with them, and law enforcement officers from around the state come to train here each summer, much like this collection of nineteen- and twenty-year-olds.

While her students continue brushing dirt from bone, Kate offers to take me on a walking tour of the cages. Or, as she gently puts it: "I'll show you some things."

As we wander down the grassy path in the late spring heat, the first thing I encounter is the smell. "Is that nature or human?" I ask.

"Oh, I can't smell anything right now—sometimes it depends on what direction the wind is blowing. But probably human."

The smell of rotting human corpses is unique and uniquely efficient. You need never have experienced the scent before, but the moment you do, you recognize it: the stench of something gone horribly wrong. It reeks of rotten milk and wet leather.

As I struggle to adjust to the odor, I see, from a distance, the rows of cages, staggered on either side of a rough path in a grassy, overgrown field. As we approach, the bodies begin to come into focus, each with the wet, tan look of wax paper. As we come closer still—and though I'd like to slow down, I keep pace with Kate—I also see how they're deflated now: the viscera have collapsed into the cavities, and the limbs have withered.

"You can see a theme here," Kate says with professional calm. "They're a dark, leathery color: it's a type of mummification." This climate mummifies, and what's most shocking is how this warps each body's skin into a puckered, leathery casing, raised up just enough you can imagine peeling it off in one go. Then there's the shriveling, the wasting away. Kate points out one man who was four hundred pounds when he came in. He's now emaciated, drained into the earth, browning the grasses beneath him. "He took a long time to reach that state." A shock of short hair still clings to his skull. Sometimes the scalp remains fastened indefinitely, and sometimes "it just melts right off with the skin." Another body, a woman's, has a chest that's puffed up like a massive balloon but almost no stomach left. In spite of the cage, built to prevent scavenging by animals and birds, she has patches of tissue damage by foxes—maybe a small one managed to slip through the wire. "I don't know how they do it," Kate says.

After enough time has passed (often a year), the students dismantle the remains with medical scissors, place the thoroughly decayed parts in bright red biohazard bags, and take them into the lab to be "processed." Then the bones, finally clean, are labeled and boxed and added to the collection.

The odor is strong as I walk among the cages, the air redolent with the heavy, sour-wet scent of these bodies letting go of their bile, staining the grasses all around them. I look at the sprawl, each individual in its strange shelter, shriveled and shocked-looking; each with more or less of its flesh and insides; each, in its post-person state, given a new name: a number. They died quietly, in an old-age home; they died painfully, of cancer; they died suddenly, in some violent accident; they died deliberately, a suicide. In spite of how little they had in common in life, they now lie exposed alongside one another, their very own enzymes propelling them toward the same final state. Here, in death, unintentionally, they have formed a community of equals.

An Army brat, born in the Philippines in 1932, Patty Robinson grew up all over the world, wherever her father was stationed—a life she briefly replicated with her husband, moving to Berlin when he was posted there early in their marriage. Even as a teenager, she knew she wanted more than to be defined by a domestic life. "Mother undertook my training to be a wife and mother," she wrote in another letter to her daughter, Mary. "I was NOT interested." She managed to graduate from high school early and head to college at Louisiana State University—to the dismay of her conservative father, who had plans for her to marry as soon as possible. "Her father came to LSU to drag her out!" Mary says—to no avail.

Patty met DJ when her father was transferred to a base on Long Island. DJ was the duty officer the night she arrived and, unlike her father, he had a sense of humor and seemed attracted to her independent streak and creative mind.

Patty gave birth to five children in seven years—a feat that every one of them mentions when I talk to them. Today, Jim, the oldest, works in tech management in San Francisco; Mary, the only daughter, teaches special-needs kids at an elementary school in Connecticut; and Carl, John, and Ted all live in Austin and work as arborists for electrical companies. But back in the '60s, after an Army stint in Berlin, where the first two boys were born, the family settled in Westfield, New Jersey, and Patty was expected to oversee the entire brood single-handedly. "If they'd invented the phrase 'free-range parenting' then," Jim says, "that would have been what to call her style." Theirs was the house other parents on the block might be scared to let their children play at—"because we were the ones climbing curtains and bookshelves," says Ted.

She was just as instinctive and free-form with their education: when she saw how bored Jim was with his classes, she gave him an encyclopedia set, and would let him take apart and reassemble any gadgets in the house. And when Ted was unusually slow learning how to read in school, Patty refused to make a fuss: she saw how easily he read the cookbooks when he was at home with her, helping in the kitchen. In this way, learning at home was just as important as anything that might happen in a classroom. Mary remembers how, when she was five, her mother woke the kids so they could watch the moon landing; and again when their cat Thomas had kittens, using the occasion to explain how animals give birth. In a way the kids were her great project: creating a clan of clever, progressive, fearless little people. "She loved us unreservedly, I never doubted that," says Carl. "She wanted us to grow up to be her friends, to get to a point where we could talk like adults with each other. She told me on a few occasions that she never felt she had a lot of peers, people she could talk to about things—and that's where the kids came in."

Although she converted to Catholicism as an adult, Patty's spin on the religion was unorthodox. She was staunchly pro–birth control—in her later years, she kept Plan B stocked in her guest bathroom, in case any woman in the neighborhood might need it—and, says Jim, she was very much against the "punitive, go-to-hell parts" of the church. "Patty's belief in religion was 'God is love' and 'Be nice,'" Carl says. She took the kids to services when they were very young— a lover of gospel music, she sang in the choir of every church she attended—but, in the late '60s, mass was informal, often led by a young priest with an acoustic guitar. Once the kids started to put up resistance, she simply attended on her own: no big deal. And so it came as a surprise that, when Patty knew the marriage had soured for her (by then her oldest was twelve), she chose not to file for divorce from DJ: instead, embracing her technically Catholic status, she had the marriage annulled. Mary says their staunchly atheist father "had a field day. It was 'Okay, you're all bastards now!'"

One might assume it would be difficult to annul a marriage that produced five kids, but Mary says her mother reasoned their father had "tricked" her. "When she met him she thought, 'Oh my God, I've met my intellectual equal, and he's fun!' And then they got married, and before they even had the first baby he had towels made up that said *boss* and *slave*—and he thought that was hilarious. But she thought, 'Oh no, no, that's not funny.'" Or, as Jim puts it, "Mom thought, 'I'm getting away from my stifling family, and we're going to do things the way we want to'—and then he was like, 'Well, I worked all day, and you can take care of everything.'"

Meanwhile, Patty, though very proud of her children, was aching to go back to work herself. She filled the free time she didn't have with constant volunteering: for community theater, for public-television pledge drives. "She felt like her brain was turning into a marshmallow when she was staying at home," Mary says—she wanted to make as much use of herself as she could. And so when Ted, the youngest, went off to kindergarten, she found a job, becoming one of the first generation of women to work for Xerox. Not long afterward, the marriage ended.

In spite of the loaded logistics of rotating five kids through the separate homes of two estranged adults, Patty was finally free of an unsatisfying relationship, and the newly single working mom decided to grant herself a whim: after one too many snowstorms in New Jersey, she pulled out a map, drew a line, and announced to the kids "I will live north of this latitude no more!" She convinced Xerox to transfer her, and she moved her little crew out of a New Jersey suburb and into a life by the beach in Corpus Christi, Texas. And all the while, Patty continued singing in choirs, and amassing a library of titles she let the local kids borrow—from Agatha Christie mysteries to science fiction by Harlan Ellison. She had stage-managed for local opera productions in Princeton, New Jersey, and now she worked with an amateur theater group in Texas. "Theater was her sanity," Mary says: her own social sphere and a way of holding onto her sense of humor. Not long after the split, she donated her wedding dress to be dyed and used as a costume.

The first thing Elaine Johnson tells me about her fiancé, Bill, is that he is intensely private. "He flat-out doesn't trust anybody." She has a habit of using the present tense when talking about Bill, though they took him off life support two months ago.

Now fifty-six, Elaine grew up in San Marcos—her father taught biology at the university for decades—while Bill grew up in Fort Lauderdale and rural Missouri. (He was fifty-two when he died.) A career Army man, Bill spent twenty-six years in the service, including work as a technician for Hawk air and missile defense systems and a tour in Iraq as a truck driver, training others to avoid land mines while transporting supplies.

She and Bill knew each other for four years before he died. They'd met on a biker dating website in the fall of 2009: he'd been riding motorcycles "forever," while she'd started just the year before—the only good habit to come out of a short-lived affair. A devoted Harley rider, Bill was often in Harley tees and owned mugs and caps in Arabic, from their dealership in Kuwait. He wore a long ponytail and a series of black do-rags, sometimes sporting a POW MIA patch or one that read *Live to Ride, and Ride to Live*. He rode an Ultra Classic and a Heritage Softail, and under his watch Elaine graduated from a Honda Shadow to her own Fat Boy, with a comfy custom seat for the thirteen-hour days Bill liked to pull on the road. Out of character for Elaine, Bill loved to take off on a trip at a moment's notice. "To be more spontaneous, I bought myself a little bitty bag I put overnight stuff in, so anytime he wanted to hop on the bike and ride down to Corpus I'd be ready," she says. "I didn't even get to use it."

Bill retired as a sergeant first class a few years before Elaine met him. After that, he was hired to do IT work at the Guantánamo base for a year and a half, and then for the military hospital in San Antonio. He was on VA disability for various health issues, including knee and neck problems, but the deepest damage was psychological: his endemic lack of trust, his fight-first instincts, the nightmares that redeployed him to Iraq whenever he fell asleep. Sometimes the dreams were particularly bad: "He'd be shaking real hard with his fists tight, like he was having convulsions. I couldn't *touch* him because he would think he needed to fight, but I would call his name until he would calm down." Sometimes Bill would prod Elaine and ask if she'd heard something, maybe people talking outside the house, and she'd say, "No, I didn't hear anything, honey." Other times he'd need to sleep on the sofa in order to keep his back against a wall, like his cot in Iraq, and she'd be awakened by the sound of Bill shouting her name from the living room, making sure she was there. He kept loaded guns in every room of the house.

He was often on edge, and often combative. Elaine's nickname for Bill was "Central Texas Weather," because his moods were always changing: you never knew what you were going to get. "He was extremely direct in an in-your-face kind of way. You never had to guess what was on his mind: he'd come right out and say it, no matter how non-diplomatic it was. He and I were totally different: he's not worried about hurting feelings, and I don't *like* hurting feelings. And he was always ready for a fight." In his dating profile, he'd posted (to women hoping for a wealthier man, Elaine guesses) "You think you're too good for a simple guy?" Unimpressed by his presumptuousness, she'd blasted right back: "Every woman who doesn't want to go out with you doesn't think they're 'too good.' Maybe you're not their type!" Bill had been waiting for someone to challenge him, it seems, because he asked her out right away.

As untrusting of the world as he was, once he partnered with Elaine, that was it: he was with her completely. Once Elaine told him, during his night panics, that there was no danger, he could fall back asleep: some primal, half-asleep part of him thought that if she said so, it must be true. Estranged from much of his family, while working at Guantánamo he gave Elaine power of attorney so she could handle all his affairs back home—including the house he'd bought. And when he realized he wanted someone to leave his possessions to, he drew up a will and named Elaine his sole beneficiary. "He did everything to make sure that if anything ever happened to him, I'd be taken care of." They moved in together on his property, a six-acre, 1940s military house that had been relocated out to Guadalupe County. Within two months of Bill's death, Elaine was able to make the last mortgage payment.

He was generous in other ways as well, quietly. While working at a mental hospital in San Antonio, he'd take clothes to the teenagers who were inpatients there. And, never having had a father figure himself, he always made an effort with Elaine's father, nearing eighty and a little overwhelmed by the work needed on his land. Whenever he and Elaine planned to visit, Bill would tell him, "You have a project planned and we're gonna do it. Be waiting for me in the driveway with your tool belt on."

"Bill is such a contradiction," Elaine says (again in the present tense). "He's serious a lot, pissy and pissed off. He calls himself an asshole, which he can be. So when he does something funny, it totally catches the guys by surprise." She shows me photos: Bill striking a pose outside Disney World with a woman done up as Snow White; Bill and his best buddy, Joe, a motorcycle mechanic, standing in their helmets in a cotton field, a grinning Bill holding a jumbo cotton puff over Joe's head; Bill in wire-rimmed glasses and salt-and-pepper beard, his eyes soft and smiling as he grips a black cat to his chest a little too tightly. "He says he doesn't like animals, but he really does," Elaine says. "You don't think he likes *anything* when you talk to him, besides riding, cutting wood, and mowing grass—but you just have to watch him."

Doing just that, his friends quickly saw a change after he met Elaine: Bill was happier and more stable than he'd ever been. Plus, she was okay with managing his anger—though sometimes, she says, "it sapped my energy." While he never got into a fistfight in front of her, twice—at a gas station, and at an electronics store—Elaine had to talk Bill down from a confrontation "because if he would've started, he wouldn't have been able to quit before someone was really hurt. The vein would be popping out of his neck and he would be fuming—you could see it in his eyes. He was a real all-or-nothing kind of guy. His mind was his own worst enemy. I just told him, 'It's not worth it. It's not worth it, man, let's go.'" He'd think of that phrase, he told her, whenever he felt himself on the verge of losing his temper.

Elaine says she stayed with Bill through these episodes, and the difficult nights, because "you could see he was worth it, the person in there. It was hard, but he was doing a lot of things to show me he really cared—and I don't mean buying me shit, because I can buy my own stuff. Even being the hardass that he was, he was *trying*."

Nearby on Freeman Ranch, Kate takes me into the processing lab, a room with the white-tiled walls and easy-mop floor of a high school cafeteria kitchen—as well as some of the very same equipment. Industrial-size pots are stacked on the floor, and two large aluminum kettles stand against the wall, the kind used for bulk food prep. These are "where we do the de-fleshing," says Kate, "where we put whole bodies," once they've been brought in from the field. She lifts the lid of one kettle, which should be clean, and finds some dark brown sediment at its bottom. "Sometimes the decomp just settles down there." This, she explains, is mummified tissue that's been sloughed off. "Like when you boil a pot of soup with meat in it or something."

I ask about the crock pots on an adjacent shelf, each decorated with a friendly floral design: these are for smaller animals, "or if you've just got a hand." There's also an incubator, where particularly delicate remains are placed for a slow hot-water bath so they won't damage while being de-fleshed. "We had a stillborn come in—" She stops, anticipating a reaction. "I know. I can't believe it: somebody do-nated their infant. Which is *great*."

She points out the red plastic bags on the floor: they may look like garbage bags tied to be taken out, but these are remains recently brought inside, now ready to be processed. In other words, these are fleshy bones in a pile. At just this moment, a kind of fly lands on my left cheek, and for the first time I notice: large black insects are touching down on surfaces throughout the room.

While grad students carry out the "intake" and "placement" of the bodies outdoors, about twenty-five undergrads volunteer to process the remains for free, from disarticulating the sun-dried cadavers to soaking them in the kettles to scrubbing the last bits of cartilage off with their gloved hands. They remove tendons with hemostats and toothbrushes, then they wash the bones again by hand, adding Dawn if still greasy. Finally, they leave them out on countertops to dry.

I can imagine rushing to volunteer at a crime scene, I tell Kate, but it seems another thing entirely to hand-wash decomposition off the bones of dead strangers. "I know," she says. "This is really the worst, most difficult part of the whole process, this room right here. But I think these students realize that they wouldn't otherwise get a chance to handle actual human remains. And so they do the work. We're really grateful."

Kate did plenty of processing herself as a PhD student in the an-thropology department of the University of Tennessee, home to the first body farm in this country, opened in 1980. One major difference between the two facilities is the climate: the dry weather and the Cen-tral Texas sun combine to guarantee mummification, rather than the thorough skeletonization that naturally occurs in humid Tennessee. Another is also a function of location: Texas is at the center of what Kate calls "a mass disaster," with hundreds of undocumented im-migrants dying each year as they attempt to cross the southwestern border with Mexico. In the "dry" lab, they store and analyze migrant remains, hoping to lead to positive identifications (the long-term project is dubbed Operation ID). Most of these bodies were exhumed in Brooks County, where last year a colleague of Kate's from Baylor University delivered sixty body bags in a single day. Those remains, kept separate from the donations, are still being processed, and the personal items and clothes sorted and hand-washed by volunteers. (They recently discovered one young woman's ID card in the shoes she'd been buried in.) Some law enforcement divisions, aware of the work being done, now bring bodies directly to FACTS, rather than burying them where they were discovered.

While FACTS had only three cadavers donated in 2008 (its first year), by 2012 that number was up to fifty new donations, and then sixty-six last year. Thirty-six have been placed since January. Unlike medical schools, FACTS has no restrictions: the only disqualifiers for donation are communicable disease or extreme obesity; people can donate their organs and tissue before being brought in. Plus, they try to accommodate any specific requests: one person wanted his cellphone and charger to be stored with his bones in perpetuity; another wanted a photo of himself included, so that researchers would see his face while working with his remains; one woman wanted to have a hummingbird feeder installed above her decomposing cadaver; and another woman, in perhaps the most eccentric request of all, wanted to be laid out to rot in eighteenth-century colonial dress. "As long as they can provide the outfit," Kate says.

Kate, like most of the people who work here, plans to donate herself—though with the stipulation that she be buried for three years before her remains are handled. "When *I* donate, I don't want people that I know looking at me. Even if I go to Tennessee, people know me there. I want to be a nice skeleton when they excavate me. I figure three years will be enough time for that, under any soil conditions."

In her later years, Patty moved to Austin, closer to Carl and John and Ted, to finish her PhD in Psychology (the career she'd quietly dreamt of). But, having expended huge reserves of energy on raising her brood and somehow, miraculously, paying the bills—after Xerox she'd tried real estate (bad market), work on an oil rig, then a series of bookkeeping jobs—Patty had already begun to adjust her ambitions. Now that she finally had a chance to complete her degree, she found she no longer had the flexibility it required: her ego could not stand the condescension of her much younger grad-student advisors. And so this was her last hurrah. "She wasn't going to be able to accept the situation, so she bailed out," says Jim. "She figured out how to live on lower wages. She found a condo on terms that let her afford the mortgage, figured out what her means were, and learned to live within them, and stayed out of stores so she wouldn't be tempted to buy things."

In her condo, says Carl, "she had a pool, she had a yard she never had to cut, she had plenty of space to spread her books out and do her crossword puzzles"—and that was that. She wore a bathing suit, says Ted, "ninety percent of the time," with "the little muumuu thing to put over it." In her final months, when she wasn't working odd jobs, you'd find her at choir practice at St. James Episcopal (they were chosen to sing at Lady Bird Johnson's funeral). Otherwise she was out by the pool with a paperback, drinking her coffee and relishing a cigarette. "She went from being a fairly successful businesswoman," says Carl, "to not really caring about materialistic things." Jim tells me, "She was happy with what her kids were doing, by and large—that was a big one. She thought she had done it well enough—and for a while there, she wondered if she'd be able to."

Patty died with the kind of stubborn independence that marked her life. Her children had no idea just how ill she'd been, and they agree she must have feared needing to restructure her life around her health, being defined by rounds and rounds of hospital appointments—something she had no patience for. A couple weeks before she died, she sent an email to her kids: "They did an x-ray, and I've got a hernia, and I'm naming the hernia Penelope." Penelope had long been her play name for moments of denial, moments when she wanted to be free and invisible: whenever she'd found herself in a houseful of kids calling for her, she'd call back "My name is not Mom, it's Penelope!" In hindsight, Mary thinks, the so-called "hernia" was "a huge growth in her intestines, and she didn't want to put it out there because people would try to boss her around." As the daughter of such an independent woman, Mary is sympathetic. "That's the greatest thing that you fear, that you won't have say over your life anymore."

Patty was rushed to the hospital with severe abdominal pains, and soon after her arrival the stress induced a heart attack. In examining her, they discovered a mass in her intestines large enough that nothing could be done. Long ago, when the kids were still young,

Patty had made absolutely clear to her children that she did not want to be kept alive on machines or through extreme surgical measures. "There was no doubt in anyone's mind," John says. "She wanted it *her* way. That was her iron will, one last time." In brief moments of lucidity, through the haze of morphine, Patty saw her sons John and Carl and Ted. She died a few hours later.

Then came the question of what to do with her body. Again, Patty's children had long known her wishes: while she'd considered herself a Catholic, she'd often spoken about her faith in science, and she'd seen no need for her body to be pumped full of chemicals and sealed into an expensive coffin after death—Patty would much rather her remains be put to use in a cool experiment, part of discovering new terrain. And while they range in spiritual leanings from improvised New Age (Mary) to "your most straight-up Richard Dawkins athe-ist" (Jim), her children all share Patty's view of her physical self. "She would mock the foolishness of thinking that there was anything go-ing on with your body after you died," says Jim. "The special part is the alive person."

"Her body was whatever carried her spirit and her brain around," says Carl, "and in the end it was just a bag of meat when she was done with it. Whatever happened after that, that could be useful, was a good thing." If in life she hadn't become a psychologist, at least in death, perhaps, her pieces could be put to work for science.

Once all the Robinson siblings were gathered in Austin, they dis-cussed how best to put Patty to use at such sudden notice. Without advance arrangements, options were limited. Searching online, Jim soon encountered FACTS—and Carl recalled Patty mentioning to them that a body farm was being built in San Marcos. For the Robin-sons, this was the perfect way to satisfy their mother's wishes.

Her choir had a memorial for Patty at the church, which her kids dutifully attended—except Jim ("I didn't want to see her church la-dies, and I don't feel bad about it"). As for the siblings themselves, in lieu of a traditional funeral, they gathered friends and family at John's house. "There was a tremendous amount of sadness," Ted says—and then corrects himself. "Not really sadness: a *release*. But it wasn't that movie scene where everyone's wailing and wearing black and just *acting*." Everyone drank and told stories about Patty. And, sometime in the middle of all this, the morgue handed the remains of Patricia Robinson off to the body farm.

Years before there was a forensic research facility in San Marcos, Elaine's father, an entomologist and parasitologist, staked out a pig to observe the process of decomposition and which insects arrived first. He worked on a couple of cases with the Austin PD and DPS, collecting maggots and flies from bodies at crime scenes, and helped train law enforcement to do the same. He never had to explain his work to Elaine and her two younger sisters, she says, "because we were biologists' kids! We were always camping in the hill country, picking up fossils or arrowheads. Mom and Dad had us making plaster casts of animal footprints we found." They collected tadpoles, snakes, and horned toads. As a family, says Elaine, "we don't shy away from things. We don't get the *ooh gross* syndrome so many people have."

Elaine had always been fascinated with science herself, but because of "how life shook out," she took a very winding road through employment, from waitressing gigs to a stint operating a wastewater treatment plant. There was also a year and a half, in her early twenties, as a gravedigger. "Needless to say, death does not bother me a whole lot. To work in the cemetery, you've got to not be thinking about it too much." Now, mostly retired, she does ornamental ironwork in her own blacksmithing shop.

The combination of her reptile- and insect-friendly childhood and her time spent interring the dead made Elaine a very un-squeamish individual, and one with a clear understanding of the inevitable progression of the human body. And so when Bill announced that, when the time came, he wanted to be donated to science, she was instantly comfortable with the idea. Watching local TV one night, he saw a news item about the body farm, and he told Elaine "That's where I want to go. I want to write it down and notarize it."

This was two days before the accident.

That morning, they woke up at 4:45 as usual—Bill started work in San Antonio at 6 a.m.—but Elaine remembers him being out of sync. "He did say that he just couldn't get it together." It was in the forties that day, so he needed his leathers, but he took a long time finding his gear. And though the cold meant taking his Ultra Classic was the best idea (it blocked more wind), at the last minute he decided on his Softail. "Before we met, he had three wrecks on a red Softail just like that," says Elaine. Then Bill rode off down the same winding route he'd taken every day for years.

Elaine watched the morning news with her coffee and saw that there'd been an accident on their road, way out in the country. "I was listening for the word 'motorcycle'—and then I heard it. Crap, it's him! I called his work: he hadn't gotten there. I called again, and now it's a quarter after six. I threw on clothes, no jacket—it was cold, but I didn't care—and I raced over there." The road was blocked by a fire truck, but the volunteer firefighters (her neighbors) told her the bike was red. She knew it was Bill. He'd run off the road. "We just really don't know what happened," Elaine says, "but he ended up flipping." The helicopter had already transported him to the hospital, leaving the sheriff's department there to survey the scene. They gave her Bill's wallet, and the leathers they'd cut off him, and she cleared out his saddle bags "because he had made himself a special lunch the night before, something from Germany that he was used to eating"—he'd been stationed there early on in the Army—"and I got it out of his bag because it would've been no good."

At the hospital, the trauma team was hard at work: on the surface, Bill had merely fractured a tooth and scraped his nose, but internally, the damage was much more serious. Because his neck had already been broken twice—once at seventeen, in a car accident, and fractured again in the military—Bill could only wear a lightweight helmet: a standard helmet would put too much pressure on his neck. And so he'd suffered extensive brain trauma and re-broken his neck, leaving him unconscious, in need of a breathing tube, and paralyzed from the throat down. "He was one of those few cases that would have had zero chance at recovery," says Elaine. "So, you know, it sucked big-time."

During that week, friends took turns being on call, sitting in the waiting room, rotating through visiting hours. "He didn't think the guys liked him that much, because he thought he was so different," Elaine says. "But he had friends that were there for him every single minute he was in the hospital. He was a hard character, but he really doesn't know the effect he had on people."

For Elaine, someone who had never witnessed her partner sleep through the night, "Those days were the calmest I'd ever seen him." He was admitted on February 28 and never regained consciousness. On March 6, a decision was made, and Elaine left the hospital room as they took him off the respirator.

When they first met in person, on a date at a friend's dairy farm, Bill's hair hung to his shoulders, and Elaine can still go on and on about his black locks. "He had thick, thick hair, super-wavy and curly, and when it was wet, it was total ringlets. It was so pretty! He always kept it in a braid or tucked down his shirt in the back, because he didn't want anybody to be able to grab it—he's always thinking *fight*, right? It had to be wet for me to be able to braid it because it would puff. It was luxurious, man." Bill let his hair grow throughout the four years they spent together, with the idea of donating it someday to make hairpieces for sick children. "When we ended up cutting it off, at the hospital, it was down to his butt crack! It was so thick, we had to snip a little bit at a time. They had to go get a bigger pair of scissors." She gave his ponytail to Locks of Love.

Then, as happens, came the question of the body. Once they knew he would not recover, Elaine looked into donating Bill's remains to a medical school—but, as is usually the case, they were unable to take him because he had died in an accident. So she made arrangements with FACTS, and on the day of his death they sent a pair of graduate students to pick the body up from the morgue.

"People know that he donated his body to science," Elaine says. "*Some* know it was to FACTS, but they don't know what that means— I don't call it 'the body farm' because most people would not be able to deal with it. But Bill would never have wanted to be in a hole in the ground." Respecting his contempt for traditional funerals, Elaine held a "memorial barbecue" for Bill. "He's not social, but he always wanted to have friends over for barbecue: he just grills and lets them talk with each other." And since Bill was a Mason and a Shriner—he often wore his Shriner patch on his biker vest—she followed instructions and cremated his white sheepskin Masonic apron on the grill, sprinkling the ashes around their yard.

I ask Elaine how she can handle the idea of her fiancé being at the facility right now, the "details" of it. She hasn't had to handle the thought, she says, "because for some reason I'm able to block out the part where they're actually doing the initial research. I *know* what it's all about, but my brain doesn't even focus on that side of it"—the body of someone she loves laid out to rot—"not even when I'm talking about it. I don't think of him being outside in this situation, going through the steps we go through after death. I'm able to totally separate myself from that." Instead, she tries to think about "what people might learn from him that will identify somebody or save somebody or whatever might come of it."

She and her two sisters are all considering donating. The application sits on Elaine's desk.

In the 2012 issue of *Forensic Science International*, an article entitled "Spatial Patterning of Vulture Scavenged Human Remains" appeared. It featured computerized maps and tables of data, as well as a series of color photos taken outdoors, over a twenty-five-hour period, with a motion-sensitive game camera. The sequence of images went as follows:

December 26, 2009, 11:16 a.m.: A deceased woman's fully fleshed body is laid out in a dry field, the belly extremely bloated, in stark contrast to the arms and breasts and legs, now withered. The head is turned over the right shoulder, facing the camera, but she remains anonymous, a thin black bar Photoshopped over her eyes. An American black vulture stands by the left leg, peering at the body.

12:06 p.m.: A swarm of vultures, over two dozen of them, have descended on the body. Only the distended belly is visible above the fray.

3:39 p.m.: The body, still covered in its outer casing of skin, is now deflated entirely, all viscera removed. The skull looks as if it's been stripped, but the right hand, stretched above its head, is still mostly intact. A cluster of birds lingers.

The next day, 12:12 p.m.: The body is finally de-fleshed, mostly skeleton, and in an entirely different position. Turned completely around by the frenzy of vultures, its head now rests at the opposite, right-hand edge of the frame, turned upright; its right arm bones are stretched out above the shoulder; its right leg is no longer visible. One bird remains at work on what little might be left inside the rib cage.

The article, the result of a FACTS study, was coauthored by Kate, her fellow researcher Michelle Hamilton, and Texas State geographer Alberto Giordano, who tracked the impact of vulture scavenging patterns on one human body over a seven-month period.

Things we know about New World vultures: They soar when the air heats up, sniffing out their meals from on high. Their heads can be as red as flayed skin (the turkey vulture), or as gray and cracked as dry earth (the black vulture). They're literally repulsive: they urinate on themselves, vomit when threatened, and feed on carcasses. But as far as *how* they scavenge remains—and human remains in particular—our knowledge is only anecdotal, based on research done with pig cadavers. Using photography and GPS mapping to track even the smaller bones, this FACTS study provided new information that impacted forensic work in the vulture-friendly Southwest: the birds are capable of de-fleshing a human body in as little as five hours; they cause signature damage to the orbital bones (around the eyes) and the rib cage; they dramatically disturb the positioning of the body (within two more days, they would drag the subject out of the camera's range).

As a result, when this paper was published, a short related article ran in the Associated Press and spread around the Internet. The AP story included a slide show set at FACTS, featuring images of Kate standing in the field with the anonymous woman's now-skeletal remains. But this time the subject of the study, the woman in the journal, was no longer anonymous: she was identified as Patricia Robinson, placed on-site at FACTS on November 19, 2009. In the first week after being placed, deliberately without a cage, two vultures had been spotted consuming her eyes; thirty-seven days after placement, the day after Christmas, the swarm arrived; by December 27, she had been skeletonized.

Her children recognized her skull by its gold teeth.

It was Jim, in San Francisco, who'd spoken briefly on the phone with the AP reporter and, perhaps not realizing the quick turnaround of the piece, did not tell his siblings about the article before its publication, or the fact that he'd given the writer permission to identify their mother's remains by name. So when Ted, in Austin, was scanning headlines online one morning, he came across an item about the San Marcos facility and discovered the slide show. He saw a photo of a skull in the grass and he knew, before reading the captions, that this was his mother: he could see one of her gold molars.

Perhaps surprisingly, his immediate reaction to the photos, and the details of the research—scientists "captured the vultures jumping up and down on the woman's body, breaking some of her ribs"—was one of pride. "Just the amount of damage done to the body—it was hours, literally *hours*, and it was clean," he says. "It was just this huge amount of unthought-of information." In his enthusiasm, Ted posted a link on Facebook saying, "Hey, look! Mom got eaten by vultures! Awesome!"

In a third-grade classroom at her elementary school, Mary was online and saw the note from her youngest brother. She clicked on the link—and had a typical Robinson family reaction: "I was like 'Oh, cool! They're *talking* about her!'" Then she saw the pictures. "And it was 'Oh, there's Mom's face! There's her teeth! Oh, there's her ribs! Oh, wow.'"

Mary was deeply hurt when her friends and colleagues at work were unable to relate to her excitement at the news. "I have just hit revulsion, revulsion, revulsion—and it's very lonely and hard. This is *awesome*—but it's so out-of-the-box, there's no paradigm. *That's your mom? What?*"

As the link spread to the rest of the siblings, their experience was the same: the painful feeling that, outside of the family, there weren't many people they could share their decision with. "The people that I know," says Carl, "most of them were like, 'That's really weird,' and 'That's just gross. How could you leave your mother to lie out in the cold rain?' So I didn't talk to a whole lot of people about it." In the middle of a culture that is in denial of aging, never mind *death*, the body farm at San Marcos is one of the only places in America where death is literally splayed out in front of us, laid bare in a field, undeniable—and it makes most people very uneasy.

However shocking it is to the mainstream American sensibility, deliberate excarnation (or de-fleshing) is also a practice with a history—a *spiritual* practice sometimes referred to as "sky burial." After death, the bodies of many Tibetan Buddhists are partially flayed and left exposed on a mountaintop for birds and animals to consume. The Parsis of India, a Zoroastrian population clustered around Mumbai, place their dead atop Towers of Silence to be picked clean by vultures. And certain Native American tribes once left their dead on elevated platforms to be excarnated. While the AP article revealed that many Americans are deeply unsettled by body-farm donation (no great surprise), its outing of the vulture study also exposed an unexpected, if rarefied, desire in *this* country: FACTS began receiving calls from potential donors *requesting* to be consumed by vultures. It made religion-specific sense when a little-known Zoroastrian group in Texas reached out, proposing that FACTS build a similar facility on *their* property. (The researchers politely declined.) But at this point, more than two years later, these inquiries make up about one in three of the calls FACTS receives about donation. "They usually say, flat-out, 'I want to be eaten by vultures,'" says Sophia Mavroudas, who coordinates with donors. "Some are interested in Tibetan sky burial—but we're *here*, in this country," so the body farm is the next best thing.

Within a week of Patty's "placement," the sprawling Robinson clan—four of the five siblings, along with their spouses and girlfriends and some of the kids—decided to drive to San Marcos to visit Patty. "It was not a sad trip for any of us," says Jim. "The kids ran around looking at stuff. It was more of a celebration than anything else."

Michelle gave them a tour of the lab, showing them how the skeletons are filed and stored in boxes. She told them their mother's number (D10-2009), and pointed out the pin designating her placement in the field on an aerial map. "So when your mom's done, we'll bring her in," she said. The outdoor facility, with its rows of cages, remained off-limits. "There was no desire, either," Mary says, "to go out to look at that."

I see what the Robinsons did not: how a body, like their mother's, is received and placed on the grounds. It happens unexpectedly, on Wednesday morning. "There's going to be an intake," Kate announces—and the group is ushered into the lab by a grad student named Hailey. Looking around, I now notice that nearly the entire class is female, in ponytails and college-casual clothes that give a person the look of having just rolled out of bed or off an elliptical machine. In spite of their age, they seem mostly un-phased by the events about to take place. I, on the other hand, feel legitimately un-prepared.

Hailey, in signature forensics cargo pants, her brown hair tied back, leads us to the intake area: an open space by a rolling service door where another student will soon pull up in the "body truck" with the latest donation. "Just to warn you guys," she says, "this person has started to marble—I don't know to what extent."

"And for those of you who have not seen a body except in decom-position, prepare yourself," Michelle adds. "You've all worked on graves with a person in it, but this is a very fresh person." "One thing I always keep in mind," says Kate, "is that this person donated them-selves, or their family donated them—so it's a nice thing."

The truck arrives, someone opens its back doors, and we see it: the white plastic body bag. Since FACTS receives remains before the official medical examiner's report is completed, there's often a de-lay between the donation and a complete understanding of cause and circumstances of death—meaning that each body bag may con-tain some very real surprises. All we know at the moment is that this specimen was just retrieved, in its immediate post-mortem state, from a funeral home in Houston.

Now clad in blue surgical gloves, booties, and plastic smocks, four grad students load the heavy cargo onto a collapsed gurney in the center of the space. The undergrads readjust their position in the room, clustering and re-clustering according to their individual levels of bravery.

"This is D25-2014," Hailey announces. "Our twenty-fifth donation this year." She turns to the others: "Okay, go for it."

They unzip the bag.

D25-2014, it turns out, is a fifty-seven-year-old white man with a handsome, grizzled, mountain-man sort of face. He has curly white hair and a beard, an oversized belly, and skin that has started to turn an oxidized green around his neck and along his right side. Some reddish "purge" fluid has pooled at the bottom of the bag, having leaked from the body. Hailey, pretty cool and no-nonsense, talks the first-timers through this: "Sometimes, when they die and they're kept in a cooler for a long time, they start to turn green. He's starting to change, to decompose. The cooler slows down the process, but it doesn't halt it."

While the others position and measure the body, Hailey takes the standard photos—of each limb and the face, including a shot with the lips pried open to display the teeth. They check for any medical devices to remove, from catheters to colostomy bags. They take nail and hair samples, allotting clippings to other research institutions, and a DNA sample from the purge by his feet. When one woman adjusts his head, a red trickle runs from his nose and mouth, and I can see her tense up for a moment: the unexpected movement is a reminder of just how recently he was alive. Finally, they tag each arm and wrist with the assigned donation number: from this moment on, D25-2014 will no longer be referred to by his name in life.

At this point, I realize how quickly I've already adjusted to the shock of the dead: the trembling I felt in my stomach when they unzipped the bag has now mostly left me, and I've almost, *almost* stopped noticing the smell of cadaver. Though I'm not easily unsettled, to learn this about myself must count as a minor revelation: how rapidly I can recalibrate what repulses me—an ability taken for granted as a basic skill by many of the people in this room. I also realize that I've drawn a large measure of my comfort, my staving-off of total, primal panic, from the group reaction to rotting human flesh—which *here*, in this very particular place, remains one of calm appraisal.

In the parking lot, the students reorganize and hop into various pickups and SUVs, creating a caravan to follow the body truck out into the field. D25-2014 will be placed in a newly cleared area under some trees, to see what different results the shade might produce. The bag is unloaded, buckled to the gurney, and rolled over bumpy terrain to the designated spot: a bed of dry leaves under a cluster of oaks, where the students set down the bare corpse. The sight of a man laid out so neatly on his back, naked, in nature, makes me feel as if we're sneaking up on an older hippie taking a nap—until, of course, the volunteers step forward, in their gloves and booties, and flip him onto his stomach, planting his face in the leafy dirt. Hailey now photographs him again from this angle: too tricky to pull off indoors without a mess.

Once he's turned onto his back again, leaves still clinging to his body (Hailey asks a volunteer to wipe off his face), we can see the flies converge. One of the older male students decides to explain this to me. "What they're doing is they're laying eggs: they're going to the mucous membranes—the nose, the mouth, the genitals—or where there's a cut or an open wound. We can come back tomorrow and you'll see: on the eyes, the mouth, and so forth, there will probably be maggots. It's amazing."

Someone hammers a wooden stake into the ground close to the head, with his number written on it in thick magic marker, and a cage is placed over him, granting some order to his new natural state. Then we simply walk away, leaving D25-2014 in the clearing, a palace for the flies.

Nearly the same things happen to the human body during decomposition, whether in the open or underground in a carefully sealed box: variables aside, we *decay*. But perhaps what prevents some of us, given the choice, from excarnating the body of a loved one, rather than embalming and sealing her in a casket, is how human decay plays out in our minds. In one scenario, total chaos, the elements allowed their full range, scavengers allowed to freely tear and consume and toss things around; and in the other, an elegant, abstract box, a theater, a contained stage on which decomposition can take place, allowing us the illusion of some control. The results may be the same, but the decision hinges on how well those of us left behind can live with the *imagining* of it all.

Two months after his death, I meet Bill.

He lies on his back, under his cage, in the rough and weedy grass, his head turned over his right shoulder—probably turned that way by the natural course of events, the flow of his bodily fluids, the movement of the large families of maggots that would have taken up residence there in his first few days outside. Right away, I notice his salt-and-pepper beard, and his hair: long for a man, but cut blunt at the ends, with a practical purpose—not to be worn that way. It's stained with his body's enzymes: the strands are now as rust-colored as the grass beneath them, the color of damp earth. While most of him has thoroughly browned, the warped, wrinkly skin of his chest and his sunken abdomen have turned a golden, buttery color from their own fat. Each arm and thigh, now tough as leather, is collapsed like an accordion; and his genitals are gone. Strangely, but typical here, his feet are almost completely intact, and it seems unusually intimate, even under the circumstances, to see them bare without his knowledge—like catching a glimpse of the fleshy underside of someone's feet when they've yanked the sheets up in their sleep.

The anger that had defined Bill, and the night terrors, and the strain held in his body from years spent weaving through land mines, and the necessity of sitting with his back to the wall wherever he went—all that is gone, has leaked (or so it seems) from his guts and innards, through his back and his buttocks and the backs of his thighs, into the grasses, and the tension of living has stunted the plant life. The only taut thing left of him now is his casing of skin, mummified by the Texas sun into a husk shaped like a man, and the shape of his skull, just starting to peek out from where the skin has split open at the back of his head. The body itself, the core of it, is deflated, like all the others here, making it easy to imagine that the essential soul stuff has escaped, leaked out or drifted upward. And maybe it has. But what becomes certain here is this: that weeks ago the flies arrived and laid their eggs, and the maggots were hatched and began to feed, and ants and beetles arrived to feed on the larvae, and the blood decomposed, marbling the skin, and decay bloated the belly, only to puncture it. And now, two months into the inevitable, the remaining skin has hardened, making a shell for the continuing rot inside.

I can say that I've met Bill—but this is *not* Bill. It is no longer him. This is the remainder of the man, the epilogue we usually cut from the hero's narrative, the precise stuff Elaine's brain does not let her imagine. But on these sixteen acres in San Marcos, this process is laid out in the open, observed and annotated calmly by a rotating cast of young students, people just beginning their adult lives. In driving through five miles of ranchland and swiping a card to pass through the fences, you enter a world in which the naked dead are accepted, and rot is all right, and the only ceremonies needed to protect us from the fact of death are those provided by science.

Of course, there is a limit to what any of us can handle—including the Robinsons, who all plan to donate themselves. Seeing their mother's completely de-fleshed skull online was okay for them, something they could digest. It was even exciting. But clicking through to the journal article itself, complete with photos of her recently dead body being scavenged by vultures, was more than they could, or wanted to, endure. This is the line they must draw to prevent themselves from losing their minds. Mary wishes she could un-see it.

"I don't believe it hurt her, my mom, when vultures were eating her body. I don't believe she was *in* there—I believe more that she's kind of floating around." But in seeing the time-lapse photos, she says, "It was, 'Oh, that's Mom's body.' And it wasn't bones. And that was very, very, very hard. Traumatic. Like, I can freak myself out if I flash back on that picture in my head. Seeing her *bones* just filled me with love. Seeing her *body*, in the field, with the necrosis starting on the arms, and her midsection bloated, and her double chin, and her long, lanky legs—that is a haunting image. I don't *believe* she is still in that body, but she *looked* like my mom. So I never went back to that link again." To see someone you know intimately in a state of rot, that prolonged, viscous disappearing act after death, is too much— but somehow their *bones* are easier to handle, once the memory of decay has been rubbed out of them with a toothbrush.

Mary holds onto the notion that her mother is, in some ways, still around. "Because I think that we are energy. And when we die, our souls go up and they get mixed up up there. Ted said, 'Oh, you mean like a soul soup?' Yes! I believe in soul soup! We die and our soul, our spirit, our energy, is just mixing around up there, and then a handful comes out and goes into a new person. So I definitely feel her around. And talking about these things that were found out because of her, she's out in the world again." When her mother died, Mary says, "I wailed on my hands and knees, banging the floor and saying 'No, no, no!' I cry easily—all the kids at school are used to it." Back home from Austin, "it sounds silly, but I danced in the yard and I prayed. I pushed energy out my chest."

When Mary tells me this, I am struck again by the nature of mourn-

ing: no matter what kind of rituals we subscribe to, it's an improvisation, an aid, a brace. Most people find some consolation in knowing
that others in their culture take part in the same rites when someone
they love dies—but it's only a small comfort. And what we're left with
is the stubborn sense of how *peculiar* mourning is, how little we know
about what we'll need when a parent or brother or fiancé dies. And
sometimes what's needed most of all, to make the loss less vivid, is
the passage of time, like the blanching of bone. In a letter that Mary
makes sure to copy and send to me, Patty herself wrote:

> For some reason, knowing tomorrow won't be so bad doesn't make to-
> day pass any faster. In my experience. But that awful day was Monday,
> and now it's Friday and I don't remember how bad I felt. Now *that* is a
> genuine blessing, because I do remember how bad I hated all the mis-
> ery I can't remember.

Kate and I sit at the glossy black tabletop, the long cardboard storage
box of D10-2009 open, its contents now in makeshift rows before us.
Sitting here with Patty spread out in front of me, I know that I will
not be able to tell the Robinsons that I handled their mother's bones,
that I have done what they may never choose to do. That I've held
their mother's skull in my hands. That I've lined up the pieces that
make up her fingers, and held the halves of her pelvis. That Kate and
I assessed her remains, remarked on how diminutive her frame was,
for a 5'10" woman. "You can see she's very petite," says Kate. "She
had a very narrow face."

She *did* have a narrow face, her jaw especially long and lean, with
apple cheeks set round and high above her long grin. I know this
from the photographs—not the ones published in that forensic journal (her face was hidden then, having become both Patty and *not-*
Patty) but the family photos Mary sent me. There's teenaged fan-girl
Patty, in gingham and librarian's glasses, standing next to Bob Hope;
twenty-something Patty, visibly pleased to be at work on a theater
fundraiser at some Baton Rouge Holiday Inn; Patty, now married
and in feathered hair, watching Carl and Jim play in their Berlin living room; Patty on the rocks by the water in Corpus Christi, beaming
in one of her signature bathing suits; Patty mid-laugh as she watches
her barely-adult kids build a human pyramid on her fiftieth birthday.

Each of these is a piece of her, not unlike the slivers she tried to piece together of her own family—her parents, her grandparents—in her letters to Mary. Patty wrote about her mother Ruth's memory of a one-armed Civil War vet coming to visit when she was a little girl, and how he helped sweep the house with "the broom handle in his armpit." And how her stern father, while a student in Maine, had "stoked people's coal furnaces to put himself through school." She wrote of how Ruth, in "long sausage curls and flowers," had won a Mary Pickford look-alike contest while also playing on her high school basketball team. And how Ruth had somehow carved out a career in the 1930s as a nurse—but that later, at home raising her daughter in lean times during the war, she "took out her official nurse's cape, navy blue wool with a red wool lining, and cut it up to make clothes for both of us." Patty wrote of summers by the sea in Islesboro with her Grammy, in a cabin that had an old water pump in the kitchen sink, and an outhouse, and how they "dug clams and baked them in a sand pit, with seaweed to make steam." She tells Mary that years later, while she was at college against her father's wishes, Grammy would mail her money so she could eat.

These are fragments—less tangible than bone, but of stronger substance, perhaps. Taken together, they make up a kind of catalogue, a measuring-up of the past.

When a researcher, with gloved hands, peels the last vestiges of mummified flesh off the donor, and with a toothbrush scrapes away the most stubborn tendons clinging to the joints and soaks each of the bones in dishwashing liquid, down to the smallest segments that make up each finger and toe, what is *she* cataloguing? There is data to measure and chart, to scan and upload—but no matter how carefully each of her phalanges is collected from the grasses beyond the locked gates, Patty Robinson remains scattered. You can never gather up all of her.

In a later letter to her daughter, Patty wrote of their relationship as adults, which had been strained when Mary was a teenager.

I love you so much more now that you're YOU, instead of Mary-in-training. I have loved you from the time you were on the way—I never would have guessed how much bigger love can stretch to encompass the well-grown woman. Now that I know, I predict my love bubble with your name on it will be visible from Connecticut. Keep an eye on the sky—it will look like a giant purple balloon.

Whether as a balloon or lifted up by God or an "energy" or a gross, red-headed bird, Patty believed the best part of her would be airborne.

■

Four Poems

FROM *Zion*

Meridian, MS 1958: My Grandmother Meditates on the Miracles of the Christ

In the world we knew, what went blind stayed blind.
What was laid low, languished. The world we knew was dark

but manageable. The world we knew favored speed
or steel. Or both. We could run when they took up arms or

we could square the body against the pain we each would know.
The world revealed itself in this way, the choice it offered.

Hard then, to pray for more than this. But we did pray. Oh,
how we prayed. We prayed to the river to spare us flood. To the trees

and their turning. To the wind and its lamentation. If you know
nothing of prayer, know this: to pray is to ask—*Lord, will we be delivered?*

The world we knew said *no*. Said *wait*. Said *no* again. To pray is to ask—
Lord, have mercy. The world we knew said *no*, said *wait*, said *wait*.

And the Lord said unto us: *You ask not for My mercy; go forth
and ask your brethren*. And we were sore and right afraid.

Meridian, MS 1963: My Mother Considers the Mechanics of Flight

I want to save you, dark girl of thunderhead, dark girl falling upward.
I want to tell you the voices fluttering in the dark of your body are all true:

you will leave this place, and those who would harm you will pass over.
   Dark Girl,
even now you cannot be held within your soft, slight bones—synapses

firing all at once—first the aura, then borealis of red and yellow light
sparking your firmament—your body thundering, writhing, thundering

against the ground. What did you find in those liminal places? Consider
the jewel-throated hummingbird; keep your wings by beating them faster

than the human eye can see. Did you return to your mother standing guard,
gently thrusting a stick into your mouth to hold the tongue, to save it?

Kyrie: Notes to the God I Cannot See

When you consider creation, Lord—think of me:
this misfiring body, this broken machine.

We die here on earth, spinning like a child's top—
spin and gyre then falling down. Have mercy.

This may not be of much import, Lord—there is so much
wind and distance. So many birds and stars. There are those

who know not of their suffering. Knowledge of suffering
is amplitude. Lord, have mercy. Is this what is meant

to clothe a man in thunder? I know I suffer, Lord
and I am afraid. Have mercy. Shall I praise this body?

What can I praise when all You have done

may be undone? Have mercy. Have mercy.

We Are Soldiers in the Army of the Lord

The old gods are falling. So are we all.
Citizen, they will not tell you that falling

can be forward motion, or that freedom is less
being broken than will to rise. Go, my dark sweet girl.

Praise our fresh dead. Raise them up—
Call each by rightful name.

Citizen. Citizen.

Have they called you animal, Citizen?
You are bone and spirit too.

Rise, girl, for we are soldiers.
This earth is littered with our fallen.

Weep not. The ground shifts
with the ghosts of the fallen. Rise.

KATIE COYLE

■

Fear Itself

FROM *One Story*

ON A TRIP with their U.S. History class to a presidential wax museum in a nearby city, three girls make up a game they call Categories, the rules of which are perfectly simple. First, one girl suggests a type of person or thing—Beatle Wife, *Pride and Prejudice* Sister, Greek Goddess, Mode of Fortune Telling. Second, each girl tries to identify one another within said category. That's it. That's the extent of the game. As they play, one girl feels like crying and another feels like screaming and another wants to stop playing Categories altogether, because no one wants to be the Yoko Ono, and no one wants to be the Mary Bennett. But they never officially quit. They are sixteen. They've been best friends since grade school. They are Kara (The Mean One), Ruthie (The Funny One), and Olive (The Smart One). All three are mean and funny and smart, but Kara is probably the most of each.

By noon, their classmates have scattered across the museum to smoke and take inappropriate pictures of themselves with Millard Fillmore. The girls, cursed with a sense of moral superiority correlating directly to their social inferiority, find a corner of the lobby in which to become invisible. After an hour, they've exhausted ideas for Categories, even Alcoholic Beverages (which none of them have drunk) and Women of the Bible (which none of them have read).

"What else, what else," says Kara.

"Maybe we should walk around the museum for a little while?" says Olive, Old-Fashioned and John the Baptist's Mom. Olive can tell Kara's getting bored, and when Kara gets bored, she gets nasty. "We *do* have to write a response paper . . ."

"We could write it in haiku and Olsen would accept it," says Kara. Their teacher, Mr. Olsen, is fresh from college, bright-eyed and weirdly-bearded. He has a habit of rewarding substandard effort with high grades for the sake of irony.

Ruthie laughs a bit too loudly at this. "Imagine him reading the haikus out loud to Cassidy Fontana. 'Listen to *this* one, honey. I think I'm really getting through to them.' And she's all, 'You're so *Mr. Holland's Opus*, baby. Take me now."

Cassidy Fontana is a creation of the girls' collective imagination: Mr. Olsen's beautiful, hypothetical girlfriend, the primary audience for his sardonic puns and excessive interest in mumbly indie rock bands. At the beginning of the school year, all three indulged in fantasizing about Cassidy, who, if the Category was Girlfriends, would be the coolest possible option, the one none of them would feel confident enough to claim. But now it's November, and Ruthie alone won't let it go. While Mr. Olsen reads *A People's History of the United States* out loud to their class, Ruthie writes awkward erotica about his afterschool trysts with this imaginary woman. *'You be the robber baron and I'll be the anarchist,' Cassidy moaned in ecstasy as Mr. Olsen slid himself inside her.* She passes one fevered page at a time to Kara and Olive, and though the dread that Mr. Olsen will one day notice is a constant sickness in her stomach, she can't stop.

Kara was the one who came up with the name "Cassidy Fontana"—alluring and perfectly unreal—but now she stares at Ruthie through half-closed eyes, sleepy with disdain. "Sometimes it feels like Cassidy Fontana is just an excuse for you to think about Olsen's dick."

Ruthie's mouth pops open in protest, but Olive, the oldest of four sisters and a natural diffuser of conflict, quickly rattles off a list of prospective Categories before the argument can snowball. "Sandwiches? European Cities? Pink Ladies?"

There's a pause. Then Ruthie's eyes widen; she points. In the center of the lobby is a reproduction of LBJ taking the Oath of Office, one hand raised beside a wax ear, the other resting on an invisible Bible. Beside him is Jackie O., blank-eyed in her bloodstained pink suit.

"First Ladies!" cries Kara.

"No good," says Olive. "By default I'm Michelle Obama. Or Sally Hemings."

"Laura Bush," says Ruthie. "*Black* Laura Bush. Do you accept?"

Olive thinks this over. "Laura Bush is a librarian. And possibly a secret feminist. I'll consider it."

"Ruthie should be Jackie O., since she's the most virginal," says Kara. Kara always makes Ruthie the most virginal one—Joan of Arc when the Category was Historical Figures, and "Only the Good Die Young" when it was Billy Joel Songs. It doesn't matter that, as Ruthie constantly reminds her, all three of the girls are virgins—that none of them have so much as kissed a boy.

"What about Kara?" Olive prompts, before Ruthie can object.

There's a beat of silence, and then Ruthie says, "Eleanor Roosevelt."

"What does *that* mean?" Kara cries. Ruthie always identifies Kara as the ugliest thing in any given Category. Kara has already been named Ursula (Disney Villainesses), *Rocky* (Oscar-Winning Films of the 1970s), and Tugboat (Modes of Transportation).

Ruthie sighs. "Eleanor Roosevelt helped write the Universal Declaration of Human Rights. She practically *was* president. Easily the best First Lady."

"Right," Kara says. "It has nothing to do with the fact that bitch was horse-faced as fuck."

"Eleanor Roosevelt is a compliment. It means you're strong," Olive says. "And by the way? I find it upsetting that you can dismiss a woman's entire body of work just because she didn't fit a patriarchal society's definition of beautiful."

Kara snorts. "God, Olive. You sound like a lesbian."

Olive's stammering retort ("And what exactly does a lesbian *sound* like, Kara?") is interrupted by a man clearing his throat nearby. Mr. Olsen stands beside them in his jeans and tweed blazer, twisting a strand of beard between two fingers, watching them with eyebrows raised.

"Hey, dudes," he says.

"Hey," say Kara and Ruthie and Olive.

"This museum's pretty cool, huh?" He takes a step. "I mean, in a totally lame way."

Ruthie shoots Kara a quick, smiling glance—a peace offering that lasts no longer than a second. Though Kara can feel her friend's eyes on her, she does not turn her head.

"Still." Mr. Olsen puts his hands in his pockets. "Maybe you should walk around a bit? Take some notes? You might learn something! Probably not, though."

Kara and Ruthie and Olive begin to shuffle away in a tight pack—staying, even during an altercation, no more than an arm's span apart. They stop when Mr. Olsen clears his throat again.

"Separately," he says.

Olive looks to Ruthie who looks to Kara. If anyone could challenge Mr. Olsen's authority at this moment, it would be Kara, who regularly calls him a "man-child" to his face, in front of other students. Each time she does it, a shivery thrill goes up the spines of Ruthie and Olive—they know it's mean, but they love watching their fierce friend make this tiny man squirm. Even Ruthie, who—it must be said—continues to talk about Cassidy Fontana as an excuse to think about Mr. Olsen's dick, gets off on how cruel Kara is to him. They wait for it now, the delicious snap of Kara's retort. But Kara has already begun to stalk away, down a corridor over which hangs a sign reading *In Times of War* . . . Ruthie and Olive have no choice. They separate.

The war corridor holds Dolley Madison in flight, a portrait of Washington held tight to her wax breast; Abraham Lincoln at a podium, the Gettysburg Address crackling through a speaker behind him; and Kara's huge, insurmountable anger. She is sick to death of her only two friends. She used to have more; they used to be a group of six or seven. But when high school started, the other girls drifted away to drink beers in the basements of thick-necked football players, to give blowjobs in the backs of mini-vans. They didn't invite Kara or Ruthie or Olive to join and the remaining three never figured out how to invite themselves. Now they're stuck with each other.

Kara never actually forgets that she's a virgin; she just believes that the larger she makes Ruthie's virginity, the more impossible it is to miss, and the smaller her own becomes. The problem is that Ruthie and Olive carry their virginity around as if it is a gift, a choice, whereas for Kara it is an impossible oppression, so much dead weight. Kara is not as skinny as Ruthie and Olive, not as take-off-your-glasses-and-let-down-your-hair secretly beautiful as Ruthie and

Olive. And every time Ruthie compares her to Eleanor Roosevelt, to a tugboat, it's as if she is saying, *No one will ever love you.*

"Fuck!" Kara shouts into the abandoned corridor.

She hears a laugh just beyond Woodrow Wilson. She imagines one of her asshole classmates, Rob Rafi or Andrew Atwell or somebody, hiding and watching and laughing at her.

"Fuck *you!*" she calls out.

"That's not very ladylike," says the laugher, and Kara knows she does not know him. A figure in a wheelchair moves out of the line of presidents and towards her. She's embarrassed by the wheelchair, the expletive.

"Sorry!" she calls before she can see his face. "I thought you were someone I knew."

"You usually scream 'fuck you' at people you know?" asks the figure. He's directly in front of her now, illuminated by the spotlight hanging over Lincoln. The funny thing is, he looks like Franklin Delano Roosevelt. Same jaw, same hairline, same round glasses perched on the same strong nose. Between his teeth is a long black cigarette holder. Kara does not recognize the look the man gives her. His mouth grins but his eyes are dead, two expressionless blue glass beads. She feels a wave of cold spread from her center, some combination of curiosity and fear.

"Are you an actor?" asks Kara. "I didn't know they had actors here."

"Sure, honey," says the man who looks like Roosevelt. "Let's call me an actor."

Kara thinks this is a weird answer, but the fact that he's called her 'honey' keeps her from caring. No one has ever called her 'honey' before, not in the smirking way FDR just did. Kara thinks she likes it. "How long have you worked here?"

"Hell, I don't know," FDR replies. He tugs at a gold chain attached to his vest and opens the watch hanging at its end. Kara notices that inside there's just a blank white face, no numbers. "Five years? Ten? However long this wing has been open."

"Well," says Kara. "It's a great museum."

"Yeah, you really seem to love it." FDR's voice gets flinty but he never stops smiling. "Such a filthy little mouth on such a pretty little girl."

"Oh!" Kara is flustered. "It's not the museum. I got in a fight with my friends. It's no big deal. Just girl stuff."

FDR nods once. "Human stuff."

"Human stuff," Kara agrees. "You're right. I never thought of it that way. Not just girl stuff. Everyone can be unhappy."

"Are you unhappy, honey?"

It's an easy question, but to answer it truthfully is difficult. Kara takes a moment to evaluate what she thinks of as her life— her parents and school, but mostly Ruthie and Olive, her own fat face in an endless stream of mirrors. Whiskey Sour, Lot's Wife. Tugboat. Eleanor Roosevelt.

"I'm lonely," she says.

FDR reaches out and takes Kara's hand. Immediately she knows something is wrong. His skin is neither warm nor cold. It feels nothing like skin. It feels slippery and malleable, like a melted candle.

"I'm lonely, too," he says.

At two p.m., the class boards the bus for the trip back to Meadow Ridge. Mr. Olsen stands at the door, making checkmarks next to the names of students as they enter. Ruthie stumbles as she and Olive climb aboard, but Olsen doesn't notice—he's too busy perfecting a casual slouch.

"Basically," Ruthie hisses to Olive, continuing a conversation they never stop having, "Kara is toxic." She likes the feel of the word in her mouth. It sounds spiky and diseased. Here on the bus, though, where Kara already sits by herself near the back, staring out the window pensively, Ruthie has to admit she looks pretty harmless.

"Where've you been?" Ruthie asks, sliding into the seat beside Kara. She doesn't apologize, and neither will Kara. The girls let the moments where they hate each other happen, and once they've happened, they don't remark on them again.

"We looked everywhere for you," Olive lies, sitting in front of them. Actually, she and Ruthie went to the museum cafeteria and ate hot dogs.

Kara turns her head from the window slowly, as if she doesn't want to tear herself from the view. She looks at Olive's affable face, framed between the two gray seats, and Ruthie's, frowning and still hungry. Kara appears utterly at peace, and the sunlight that streams into the window behind her lights up her head like a halo.

"I *met* someone," she says.

That afternoon is play practice. Mr. Olsen is directing *The Crucible*, and because their school lists 'all-inclusiveness' in its mission statement, everyone who auditioned got a part. Kara and Ruthie and Olive were cast with twenty others as "Hysterical Village Girls." They have one big scene, where they wail and claw at one another in the courtroom and scream the same words: "Begone! Begone!" They don't particularly like acting, but they do like this scene—how loud they're allowed to be, how frightening. Waiting in the wings for their cue, Kara and Ruthie and Olive inhale the sawdusty backstage smell and let their brains go fuzzy; they wake up to their open mouths and sore throats when Olsen bounds onstage with some new direction.

When the girls are not needed onstage, which is most of the time, they help build the sets. They paint backdrops, cut plywood with a buzz-saw, and construct John Proctor's jail cell, using a blow-torch to bend the metal bars. When there's no work for them, they sit in the lobby outside the auditorium and play Categories. But today they talk about FDR.

"So he's made of wax?" asks Ruthie. On the bus ride home she got swept up in Kara's exhilaration and managed to momentarily forget her toxicity—at one point Kara squealed, made a prolonged "Eeee!" sound, and Ruthie couldn't help but join in.

"Yes," says Kara. "At least, I think so. It doesn't seem like the kind of thing you can *ask* a person, you know?"

"Remember those candy wax lips we used to get on Halloween?" Ruthie says. "Do you think that's what kissing him would be like?"

"I'm not going to take a bite out of his lips."

Ruthie giggles. Kara's mouth is a prim line but her eyes beam. Everything looks beautiful to her right now: the fluorescently lit lobby, the red-leaved branches scraping the window, her friends in their starchy costume bonnets.

"Listen." Olive has been quiet a while. "Are we going to pretend this is normal? I'm sorry," she says, because Kara instantly gets that look in her eye, the murderous one, "but there's nothing sexy to me about a wax figurine. This isn't a supernatural romance novel. In real life, people don't have relationships with vampires and zombies."

"Maybe you don't think it sounds sexy, but you weren't there," says Kara. "And anyway, no offense? But you don't always have the best judgment about these things."

Olive bites the inside of her cheek. Last year, she had a crush on Nicholas Dawkins, a gawky, big-eared junior. Kara and Ruthie teased her, but they couldn't ignore the nods he'd give Olive in hallways, the way he'd linger by her locker on Fridays to talk A.P. Chemistry. Olive asked him to homecoming and he said maybe—shyly, she thinks, like he was really going to think about it—but after a week with no answer, Kara told her she was being played and confronted him in the cafeteria with Ruthie, saying if he didn't treat Olive right he'd have to answer to them. Nicholas never spoke to Olive again, and Kara and Ruthie still consider this their finest, bravest, most legendary act of friendship.

"I'm just saying," Olive says. "You barely know him."

Kara rolls her eyes. "I know plenty."

"Like?"

"Polio? The New Deal? 'The only thing we have to fear'?"

"But is it *actually* Franklin Delano Roosevelt?" asks Olive.

"Are you even listening?" Kara snaps.

"I was *listening*," Olive snaps back. "What I'm asking is—is it the spirit of Franklin Delano Roosevelt imbued in this wax figurine? Or is it just a wax figurine that's come to life?"

Kara thinks. Besides his admission of loneliness—the thought of which, and the memory of his hand touching hers, sends something soaring in her stomach—she can't recall many specifics. She remembers the hack of his laugh in the empty corridor; the blue blankness of his eyes. The way he appeared there at exactly the right moment, to her and her alone. Kara has a prickly awareness that Olive's trying to take something away from her by asking the question. Kara won't let her: she remembers FDR's sweetness, and something else, too—some force of character emanating from him as he sat in front of her. Massively confident. Sexy/dangerous. She feels it now. Whatever it is, she thinks, it's presidential.

"It was him," says Kara confidently. "It was FDR."

* * *

It's easy to be happy with Kara, when Kara is happy. Ruthie and Olive are at first devoted listeners to their friend's smitten wonders: do they think FDR would come to homecoming? Do they think he'd like her hair up or down? Do they think he minds that she can walk, that she's not made of wax? The details of Kara's infatuation become more and more minute as the days pass. But her moods swing less violently now, and her wax president boyfriend proves a more fascinating topic of conversation than endless rounds of Categories. By Wednesday, something has shifted in Kara—she walks taller, spaces out during class and conversation, wears an infuriatingly permanent half-smile. When Ruthie passes her a page of Olsen-Fontana smut in History, Kara writes a note at the top: *Can you write one about me and FDR?* It's an alarming request Ruthie pretends not to have noticed. She itches to diagnose Kara with something awful—Narcissistic Personality Disorder? Borderline?—but it seems possible all Kara suffers from is love.

Olive worries that love gives Kara a sense of authority she does not deserve. On Wednesday, when the three of them walk out into the cold sunshine after school and see Nicholas Dawkins driving by in his beat-up station wagon, and Olive's hand raises involuntarily in a wave that's really more of a Nazi salute, and they all see Nicholas cringe as he passes, Kara turns to Olive with a look of sympathy.

"You guys never really had that *spark*, did you?" she says.

And Olive wants to retort. She wants to say, "At least Nicholas Dawkins has *bones*." But what's the point? Kara's thing with FDR is bigger than a high school crush. It gives her an otherworldly sheen, a glamour. It turns her into an adult. It turns her, Olive realizes with dawning horror, into Cassidy Fontana.

For months, the girls have waited for a movie that opens on Friday. It's a revamp of *The Castle of Otranto* set in high school, starring an actor whose prominent cheekbones and long eyelashes render him androgynous enough to be attractive to them. "Opening night," Kara and Ruthie and Olive confirm every time they see the trailers on TV. They'll love every second of it, and at the end they'll pretend they were only loving it ironically. Ruthie went so far as to order tickets in advance.

"*Otranto High*, 7:50," she reminds Kara on Thursday afternoon.

"*Otranto High*, 7:50," Kara repeats. The girls sit outside the auditorium—Ruthie and Olive with their homework, Kara with an issue of *The Economist* she is reading to impress FDR. They are waiting to be called to the stage when Kara glances at her cell phone, and sees a text message from a number she doesn't recognize:

i miss u

Who is this? she replies.

Ten minutes later, a response arrives: *lol ur crazy*

Normally, Kara would obliterate this digital stranger for having wasted her time—even now, she imagines the rude things she could say. *Eat a dick, moron. Leave me alone.* But loving FDR has softened her. *I think you have the wrong number,* she texts back, adding a smiley face. Then she puts down her phone and tries to get Ruthie and Olive to help her analyze everything FDR said to her as well as the way he said it—she imitates for her friends his gently teasing tone.

Olive focuses on her textbook, and after a while Ruthie's eyes glaze over. "Why don't we go watch rehearsal?" she finally suggests, cutting Kara off mid-sentence. The girls move to the dark auditorium; they watch Abigail Williams and John Proctor read from scripts.

"I have once or twice played the shovelboard," says the dark-eyed senior playing Abigail, "but I have no joy in it."

The buzz from Kara's phone is so loud, Proctor stumbles over his line at the sound.

y r u mad?

I'm not, Kara texts back. *I just don't know who this is.*

This time the answer comes quickly: *met u at the museum, kara.*

If Kara had to visualize the effect this message has on her, she'd picture her heart ripping itself from the veins that hold it steady to hammer alarmingly at her ribcage. *I didn't know you had a phone,* she texts.

got it from the lost n found, FDR replies. *when do i c u next.*

Kara puts the phone down and tries to concentrate on the play, to pretend everything is normal, as though she does not have to remind herself to breathe. She wipes her sweating palms on the legs of her jeans. She's trying to think of a good response, but the only flirtatious banter she's had with the opposite sex has run a little too heavy on banter. She wants to do this right. Something is happening, finally, to her. Her phone buzzes again.

kara r u there kara? i need to c u kara when do i c u

Tomorrow! Kara sends back, and she nearly laughs out loud.

When she looks up, her face lit white by the glow of her phone, Ruthie and Olive are watching. She sees identical concern in her two friends' faces, twin grimaces of love and frustration furrowing their brows, and hates them for it.

On Friday Kara Googles "Franklin Delano Roosevelt favorite drink" and finds a page that claims it's Scotch, but when she surveys her parents' liquor cabinet she's so nervous she grabs a half-empty bottle of coconut rum instead. She stops at a convenience store before getting on the parkway and buys a disposable lighter, Diet Coke, and trail mix. Her eyes graze over the colorful boxes of condoms hanging in rows behind the cashier's head, but she cannot work up the nerve to ask for one. It needs to happen sooner rather than later, but she can't make her mouth say the words. In the car, she feels like laughing and crying. "This is only a first date," she tells herself.

She arrives at eight p.m. The museum has been closed for hours and the janitors have already made their rounds. Kara parks in the employee lot. She pushes open the unlocked back door FDR texted her about. She turns on her flashlight and makes her way through a hallway that opens up into the lobby. Kara is the best kind of nervous. What she's doing feels utterly surreal, partly because she's told no one else she's doing it. She considered telling Ruthie and Olive, of course, but in the end it seemed sweeter to hold the plan inside her, secret and safe and all her own. Still, she pictures her friends now, glancing at the time on their phones, waiting for her outside the movie theater, wondering how much of *Otranto High* they've already missed, and Kara regrets not telling them. Not because she's stood them up, but because she wants someone to call later to describe how good she's feeling.

In the *In Times of War* . . . corridor, the lights are on, and FDR is waiting.

"Hi," says Kara.

"Right on time!" FDR marvels. "So you're not one of those dummies who's always getting herself lost."

"Ha ha," says Kara as she comes closer, and then, "What?"

In the last week, she's almost forgotten what FDR looks like. He wears the same dark suit he wore when they first met, the same red tie. He has the bright white rectangular grin of a wind-up monkey. For days she's scoured the internet for pictures of the thirty-second president, but none of them capture him exactly as he looks now. The pictures show a man tall but bowed, with weak-looking legs and liver-spotted skin. This FDR has those, but also glossy blue eyes, and thick black lines etched into his face. He looks older than Kara remembered. Less real, too. She doesn't quite know how to proceed. Should she kiss him? She thinks it might be too soon to kiss him.

"Pull up a seat," says FDR. "Get comfortable."

Kara looks around for a chair, but there are none. She sits at his feet and opens her backpack. She pulls out two red plastic cups and the bottle of coconut rum. "I know you like Scotch, but this was all my parents had."

FDR just grins. "I can't drink. I don't have a throat."

"Oh, my God," says Kara. "I feel so dumb. I didn't even think of that."

"That's okay," FDR says.

Embarrassed, Kara fills her cup, half rum and half Diet Coke. The result tastes like sunscreen. FDR watches her sip.

"I've never really been on a date," says Kara. "I know how pathetic that sounds. But I've never met anyone like you before." She waits for FDR to respond, but he doesn't. "I guess this isn't new for you."

"No," says FDR, "it isn't. There was another girl a few years ago. She went to school in Cherry Hill. I can't remember her name. Maybe Tina?"

"Another high school girl?" Kara is surprised, but she tries to play it cool. She knows Roosevelt had affairs when he was alive— she's spent lots of time on Wikipedia this week.

"Now that I think about it, there was another one before that. Cute," he says, inspecting Kara. "Thinner than you. But they both went to college. You won't do that, will you, Kara? You won't go away and leave me?"

Kara is confused. "I've already started looking at schools."

"Well, stop," says FDR.

They're silent a while. Kara can hear the buzz of electricity from the spotlights over each president. She stares at the MISSION ACCOMPLISHED banner hanging behind George W. Bush at the end of the hall. She stares at the open door.

"What are you looking at?" FDR snaps. "Are you looking at Lincoln?"

Kara shakes her head. "No, I—"

"If you're here for Lincoln, you can get up and go. I don't appreciate having my time wasted by dummies who just want a shot at boning Lincoln."

"I'm not here for Lincoln," Kara says. "I'm here for you."

The muscles in FDR's face relax. He hasn't stopped smiling. "Damn right you are."

Kara watches him a long moment, waiting for him to blink. He never does. She tries to remember that she's having a good time.

"Hey!" she says suddenly, happy to remember her surprise. She reaches into the convenience store bag and pulls out the lighter, flicking it until a flame appears. Kara moves the flame toward the cigarette at the end of FDR's holder, but FDR quickly rolls away.

"What the hell do you think you're doing?" he shouts. "Are you some kind of an idiot? I'm made of wax, retard!"

"Oh, God!" Kara drops the lighter and starts to cry. "Oh, God, I'm so sorry. I wasn't even thinking. I just thought you might miss cigarettes."

She's kneeling in a wax museum on her first date, crying in front of the only man who has ever called her pretty. She is sixteen—too old for this to be happening this badly. *You are a tugboat*, Kara thinks. She wipes her nose on her sleeve and FDR wheels towards her again.

"Hey," he says. "Hey, dummy. Calm down. I'm not mad anymore." He puts his wax hand on her shoulder and whistles through his square teeth. "Boy oh boy, are you lucky you found me. Other guys wouldn't put up with that kind of crap, you know. But I love you, Kara. Even though you are a dummy."

"You love me?" Kara looks up into his beady eyes. "Oh, FDR."

FDR grins down at her. "What's an 'FDR'?" he asks.

* * *

The next day, Saturday, is dress rehearsal for *The Crucible*. Kara walks into school a little past noon to find Ruthie and Olive sitting on the floor, waiting. Ruthie's dour-faced under her white bonnet, makeup-less, her eyes ringed and tired. She scrambles to her feet when she sees Kara. Olive's expression is stony; she takes her time. Kara pretends she hasn't noticed them and slips into the drama classroom, but her friends are on her heels.

"Are you okay?" asks Ruthie. "Why didn't you meet us at the movies last night?"

"Did you have *sex*?" asks Olive.

Kara shushes her. The classroom is filled with their co-stars—stretching, doing vocal warm-ups, buckling their pilgrim shoes, paying no particular attention to the girls. They step into the large closet where Kara's costume hangs, and Ruthie closes the door behind them.

"Well?" Olive asks.

"I don't see how it's any of your business," says Kara.

Ruthie sighs in relief. She can tell by Kara's tone—quiet and strange, not clipped and smug—that she didn't. Olive only gets angrier—all morning she's imagined, in gory detail, the things that could have happened to Kara last night, and now it burns to see her in one piece and still a virgin.

"What happened?" Olive asks.

"Nothing," Kara shrugs. "He asked me to visit him. We just hung out and talked." She ignores the look Ruthie and Olive exchange. "It was, if you must know, really nice."

"How did you even get in?" Ruthie asks.

"There's a back door near the employee parking lot they always forget to lock. FDR told me about it. He knows everything that goes on in there."

"Are you, like, boyfriend and girlfriend now?" asks Olive.

Kara says nothing. She slips the scratchy brown Puritan dress off its hanger, and struggles to pull it over her head.

"Why didn't you tell us?" Ruthie asks. "We could have come with you."

"Oh, yeah," said Kara. "That would have been great. 'Hey, FDR, I'm so excited for our date; by the way, my friends think I'm a child so they've come, too.'"

"It's just moving so fast," Ruthie says. "We don't even know the guy."

"Maybe it would be easier for you if he wasn't a former president of the United States?" Kara's smile is frosty. "Maybe you'd prefer him to be, like, a History teacher or something?"

Ruthie feels her face go hot. Earlier that day—as inspired by Kara's new boldness as she was itchy not to be left behind—she had stepped into Mr. Olsen's classroom wearing a clingy blue dress she didn't have the nerve to wear to homecoming. Ruthie had planned what to do the night before, re-reading key sections of the 254 pages she'd written about Mr. Olsen and Cassidy Fontana. She was going to touch his face and whisper, "You dumb hipster fuck" and then he was going to lay her flat and do things to her, more explicit versions of things she wrote about him doing. But Mr. Olsen only looked up from his laptop and said, "What's up, Rachel?" She could smell the coffee on his breath. She could see a little white glob of donut frosting caught in his mangy beard. "My name is *Cassidy*," she'd said, before stumbling out of the room.

Ruthie felt stupid then but now she feels even stupider. She looks to Olive—this is the part where Olive usually intercedes, changes the subject, protects them both from themselves—but Olive stares pointedly in another direction, her jaw clamped shut. She looks like she has given up. She looks like she is going to burn down the school.

Kara's phone buzzes then, and when she takes it out of her bag, she watches three texts arrive from FDR in rapid succession:

Miss you, says the first.

C u soon, says the second.

Send me a pic of ur boobs, says the third.

Kara quickly shuts off her phone. "Well," she says at last. "We can't share FDR, if that's what you're thinking."

"What?" Ruthie exclaims. "What's *wrong* with you?"

"I don't know what to tell you." Kara laughs a high, mean laugh, a laugh with no laughter in it. "Maybe you're happy being best friends with people you hate. Maybe you're happy being alone. But I'm not."

She ties her costume apron around her waist. Ruthie and Olive stare at her.

"I don't hate you," says Olive.

"We're not worried because we *hate* you," Ruthie says.

Kara shrugs, reaching into the cubby where her bonnet sits. She pulls out the bonnet, and something falls out of it and onto the floor. Ruthie glances down and screams.

"What is that?" she shrieks. "Is that a finger?"

Kara looks. At her feet is a man's ring finger, still circled by a gold wedding band. She can tell instantly that it's wax. It's fallen out of her bonnet along with a couple of roses. The roses are dead. Ruthie's still screaming. Olive grips Ruthie's arm, her face furrowed in disgust. Kara swallows. She crouches to sweep the items back into her bonnet, murmuring, "It's just a gift, it's just how he shows he cares," as the rose petals come loose and crumble in her hands.

Mr. Olsen has them run through all of Act Three. For once the girls are onstage for most of rehearsal, writhing and screaming "Begone!" and beating their breasts. But they're distracted. Kara stands as far away from her friends as Mr. Olsen's blocking will allow. She ignores the exhortations they hiss at her. The finger has terrified Ruthie and Olive so much that Ruthie can ignore her discomfort in Mr. Olsen's presence, and Olive can stop pretending she doesn't care. Kara's relationship with FDR is, clearly, flipping weird as all get out. She can't accuse her friends of being jealous now, because they aren't. Kara is gray-faced and jumpy the whole rehearsal, and once when Olsen snaps at her for being distracted, she *apologizes*. When it's over, she runs for her car, still in costume, clutching the wax finger to her chest.

"She's going to go see him," says Olive, as they watch Kara drive away.

"You know what we have to do, right?" Ruthie says. "We have to go to the museum and confront FDR. Like when me and Kara talked to Nicholas."

"You think?" Olive's face goes sour, as it always does when she remembers the incident.

"Absolutely. He needs to know what he's dealing with— otherwise he'll do whatever he wants to her. That's how older guys are," Ruthie explains with a sigh. "They underestimate you. They assume you've got no one looking out for you. They assume you're nothing."

Olive thinks Ruthie is full of shit, but she knows they need to save Kara. Olive has always been the responsible one, unfailingly good and self-sacrificing. In *Little Women* Characters, Olive was Marmee. In Articles of Clothing, she was Mom Jeans. It's far preferable to being the ugly one or the prude, but it's boring, too—nobody falls in love with the mom. Olive stares after Kara and raises two fingers to her mouth. She sucks on the imaginary cigarette she holds there.

"Okay," Olive says. "Let's roll."

It is a rush—making the plan, telling the necessary lies, taking the train into the city that night. The girls stow two weapons in Ruthie's bag—a hammer Ruthie finds in her dad's toolbox, and a blowtorch stolen from *The Crucible*'s tech crew. "Just in case," Ruthie says, and Olive begins to understand why her friends took down Nicholas Dawkins: this act, this rescue mission, is the most powerful performance of love Olive has ever attempted.

The night is especially dark, the moon obscured by clouds. Ruthie and Olive realize—once they push open the same unlocked door through which Kara entered the museum—that they haven't brought a flashlight. Ruthie grasps Olive's hand. Olive takes her phone out of her pocket and turns it on; it casts a short span of blue light in front of them, enough to make their way down the back hallway. They don't know where in the museum they are until the clouds shift outside and moonlight pours in through the large front windows of the lobby. Jackie O. looms up in front of them, gaunt and widowed and waxen.

Olive nods at the *In Times of War . . .* sign, visible for only a second before the moon goes dark again. "In there," she says.

They creep through the corridor, Olive shining light on the faces of the presidents they pass. She stops at Lincoln. His hands are frozen in some eternal gesticulation.

"Wait," says Ruthie. "Look at his hand!"

Olive looks. Lincoln's left ring finger has been cleanly lobbed off. "It wasn't even *his*," Olive says. The girls exchange a look of disgust. They keep moving.

When they finally reach FDR, they're surprised by how old he seems. He's perched in his chair like a grandfather, and far from life-like. He looks more like the Penguin from *Batman* than a former president of the United States.

"Um," says Olive. "Excuse me, sir?"

FDR doesn't move. His gaze fixes on some point beyond them.

"Is he asleep?" Ruthie whispers. "Does he sleep with his eyes open?"

"I can't tell." Olive stretches a tentative hand forward, waves it in front of FDR's blank eyes. Nothing happens.

The girls hear a shuddering noise, like a door opening—it's distant, but the silence around them has been so tense that Ruthie, startled, drops her bag at FDR's feet. The hammer clonks to the floor. Olive shut her phone off quickly, snuffing out their only light.

"What was that?" she hisses.

"I don't know!" Ruthie inches her way down the corridor, arms outstretched in front of her, shaking for fear she'll actually brush against someone. She doesn't. Her eyes adjust to the dark lobby, and when she discerns nobody moving within it, she turns on her heel and wanders back to Olive, using the sound of her friend's nervous ragged breathing to guide her.

"I don't see anybody," she says to Olive.

"Okay," Olive says. She turns on her phone again, casting its blue light. She and Ruthie take in each other's alarmed faces. Then they look at FDR.

His grinning head is tilted upwards. He's looking at them; there is no mistaking this. And in his left hand, he is holding Ruthie's hammer.

Ruthie's scream is something low and gurgling and feral. She pulls at Olive's arm, trying to drag her away, but Olive can't move. Her mouth is open and her eyes are perfect circles. Suddenly, the lights come on. Ruthie's scream dies in her throat. She and Olive turn to the opening of the corridor, where Kara stands, hand poised over the light switch, her *Crucible* bonnet askew.

"What the hell is going on?" Kara says.

FDR places the hammer calmly in his lap. "Friends of yours, dummy?" he asks.

It's shocking for Ruthie and Olive to hear this wax figurine speak, but it's even stranger to hear someone call Kara "dummy." They see their friend's face flush as she approaches.

"Not anymore," says Kara.

FDR sizes the two girls up, gazing at them for a moment too long. His expression never changes, yet both Ruthie and Olive feel a strange wave pass over them, a sense that their own bodies no longer belong to them.

"Pretty," he grins at Kara. "Why hasn't any of that pretty rubbed off on you?"

Kara's hand is wrapped around Lincoln's severed finger. She's holding it so tightly that her arm trembles.

"Hey," says Ruthie faintly, in protest.

The girls had assumed FDR would be handsome, or magnetic—at the very least, kind of nice. But it's beginning to dawn on them that he's completely horrible. That whatever Kara has with him is nothing they want.

"You guys should probably go," Kara says after a moment, not looking at them.

"Don't be like that," FDR says. "I thought we could play your game. Categories, right? You want to play Categories with me? Kara told me the rules—you're each a different thing in the category, and Kara's always the Ugly One. Isn't that right?" His eyes shift to Kara. "You're the Ugly One. Right, dummy?"

"Hey!" says Olive this time. "You can't talk to her like that."

FDR's head begins to bob, the cigarette holder between his teeth bouncing up and down. It's as if he's laughing, but they don't hear any laughter. "Oh, little girl. Of course I can."

Olive and Ruthie look at Kara.

Kara tries to smile. She tugs at the string of her bonnet. "It's okay," she tells them. "He's just joking around. I'll call you tomorrow."

Olive sucks her teeth a moment, then shakes her head. She picks Ruthie's bag up off the floor. Ruthie's so embarrassed for Kara she can't quite look at her. Plus, she needs to retrieve the hammer from FDR's lap; it's her dad's only hammer. But she doesn't want to ask. She leans in as quickly as she can and takes the hammer by the handle, but FDR grabs her around the wrist before she can pull back. Ruthie whimpers. FDR laughs again.

"Little girl," FDR taunts softly. He lets go.

Olive takes the hammer from Ruthie and drops it in the bag,

where it clangs against the blowtorch. She and Ruthie begin to walk down the corridor, but they haven't gotten very far—only to a bemused William McKinley, shrugging over the Spanish-American war—before Olive stops, and turns.

"Kara," she says. "Come with us. We'll get pizza or something."

Olive sounds gentle, but firm. Her voice makes Ruthie's courage return. Ruthie remembers how she felt, standing beside Kara in the cafeteria last year, shouting at Nicholas Dawkins— strong. Bigger than human. Like if she wanted, she could breathe fire. She stares at Kara now, mortified in her bonnet, and thinks of Mr. Olsen calling her 'Rachel.'

"Come on, Kara," Ruthie says. "Let's go." And then she adds: "What would Cassidy Fontana do?"

But it's the wrong question, because all three know what Cassidy Fontana would do. Cassidy Fontana would stay at home in slinky clothes, laughing and sighing and waiting to be fucked. Cassidy Fontana would do what she has always done. She would do exactly what Kara is doing.

"No," says Olive. She takes a few hesitant steps toward FDR's wheelchair. Kara is wild-eyed and frightened. But Olive keeps moving toward them. "Don't be Cassidy Fontana." She reaches into Ruthie's bag and pulls out the blowtorch. "Be Eleanor Roosevelt."

The girls don't know whether FDR doesn't understand what they're saying or just doesn't care; he continues to chomp down on his cigarette holder without expression. But Kara takes the blowtorch and turns it over in her hands, gazing at it like it's some kind of a talisman. She looks at Ruthie. She looks at Olive.

"Begone!" Olive screams suddenly.

And Ruthie joins in. "Begone! Begone! Begone!"

They use their loud, screechy stage voices. Olive stomps and Ruthie waves her fists wildly. Both of them have their teeth bared, and they wear the exact expressions they get right before Kara says something awful to Mr. Olsen, something she should really get detention for but somehow never does; they look at her like she's the most powerful creature in the world. Kara loves that look. She drinks it in now.

Kara adjusts the blowtorch and stands up straight. Then she extends one arm and releases the trigger, and with her other hand she pulls the plastic lighter from her pocket and flicks the wheel in front of the gas. A line of blue fire emerges, melting the tip of FDR's cigarette. Fat white drops of melted wax spill onto FDR's lap and he starts to yell through his teeth, rolling his wheelchair backwards, but whether it is from fear or basic anatomical inability, he can't turn his head. He backs into the wall. Kara follows until FDR's cigarette holder has melted down, then his teeth, then his lips. She holds the blowtorch steady until FDR no longer has a mouth, just a smooth seal of white wax across the bottom of his face. She drops Lincoln's finger, which she's been squeezing so tightly it's now misshapen, to the floor, and she turns the torch on that, too.

"What kind of a gift is a *finger*, you freak?" Kara yells at FDR as it turns into a small, flesh-colored puddle. Ruthie and Olive stand behind her and cheer.

Outside the museum, Kara hands Ruthie the keys to her car and crawls into her own backseat. When Olive gave her the blowtorch every nerve in her body went wild with adrenaline; she could feel the blood coursing through her veins. But now she's tired and her head hurts. The three girls are silent as they drive.

Olive and Ruthie are stunned by what they've done. Olive touches her imaginary cigarette to the end of the blowtorch, then lifts it to her lips. *Begone*, she thinks, blowing imaginary smoke out the open window. Ruthie has already started re-writing Cassidy Fontana in her mind. Now Cassidy Fontana smears on poison lip gloss and kisses Mr. Olsen until his mouth burns away; she takes off on the back of an eagle to become an avenging Amazon, a terrifying virgin princess. As they hit the parkway, Olive turns on the radio and Ruthie picks up speed and they let the cold wind whip around their faces as they sing along to the worst pop song they have ever heard, their favorite.

When they played the Category of Musical Components, Olive was a drumbeat, Ruthie was a synthesizer, and Kara— the loudest, the only one they'd ever want to speak for them— was vocals. Now Olive and Ruthie bounce and shimmy, approximating dancing as closely as they can without unbuckling their seatbelts, and Kara leans her head back. She can feel Ruthie's eyes on her in the rearview mirror, so she mouths along with the lyrics. But she doesn't sing. She doesn't make a sound.

KAWAI STRONG WASHBURN

■

What the Ocean Eats

FROM *McSweeney's*

JANUARY, THE NEW YEAR passed at last, and Pomai will soon be gone. She sits at her large desk, large room in her mother's large house, reading the buoy reports on the internet. An eel of fear squirts up her throat. A savage swell has arrived on the coast, north-north-west, waves hitting at twelve to fifteen feet, the edge of her ability. The whiteblue light of the computer screen is on her face. She closes her eyes and hopes for bravery, but finally it doesn't matter, the fear; she can't stop herself, knowing this is her last weekend in Hawai'i. The truck is packed. She's going direct into the teeth.

Pomai had shot her last three teenage years up as a signal flare to her parents—her father busy playing freedom fighter with the *Kanaka Maoli*, her mother nose-deep in legal briefs; dad with his weekends gathering signatures at endless rallies, mom with her thin-lipped smile and another delivery dinner night at the office, and in between Pomai, losing her schoolbooks, quietly seething at the cliquey cunts in her gym class, burning enough blunts to get a whale stoned, dropping from prep school to public school to home school in less than five semesters—but swiping through the ashes, she'd found a direction of sorts. California calling, USC. She's headed there two years late, a twenty-year-old freshman only starting to get things straight.

But this first: the weekend, the surf, the long, humming drive from Niu Valley to the North Shore.

The sun has just begun to burn the bottom of the sky when Pomai arrives at the beach parking lot and hops from her truck. Her bare feet grind against the sand-dusted blacktop. A boom sounds off, just over the ridge of the lot, the way Pomai imagines a bomb drop: round and sudden and knotted with violence. She clamps her board against her ribs. All across the lot, car roofs are racked—rhino chasers, fish tails, old-school longboards—the fins inverted and pointing heaven-wards, the surfboards sharp as spears and ghostly white in the low morning. The booming sounds again, followed by the sizzle of the ocean sliding up the beach.

Pomai is at the edge of the lot, about to crest the hill, when she sees her father approaching: his stubbled chin; his shallow brown chest and paunched stomach; those round Hawaiian eyes, foggy red from the sea. Pomai feels a flare of frustration at her temples. She'd been hoping not to see anybody she knew, even in the crowded waters of winter, but he's seen her, now, and anyway, there's nowhere to go. Pomai raises her chin and sets her face like concrete.

"Po-Po," Rylan says. "It's been a while."

Pomai leans away, spits into the bushes. "Come on," she says. "Don't call me that."

"I forgot," Rylan says. He closes one eye, as if appraising her. "How's it?"

"You forgot I don't like to be called something that sounds like a cop or baby shit?"

Pomai shakes her head, then nods towards the ridge, the surf they can't see. "Were you out?" Another wave hits. Pomai feels goose bumps coast up her forearms. "Sounds hectic."

"It's not too bad, if you know how for ride it. How you been?"

"Everything's fine," Pomai says.

"How's your mother?"

Pomai shrugs. "Busy."

Rylan blows out a long breath. Pomai's heard the breath before, cool with his disapproval, longer every time he judges her.

"I gotta piss," Rylan says.

"Take your time," Pomai says, and starts walking towards the sand.

"You going to wait for me?" Rylan asks to her back.

She throws a hand up, over her shoulder, without turning. "Maybe if you hurry back."

Pomai crests the hill. The surf is firing. Stretching out in front of her, beyond the beach—its cool bright sand dotted with lumps of clothing and half-empty backpacks—dark swells of ocean roll in from the deep, walls of water that mist at their peak then wallop the reef below. A cluster of surfers float at Second Break. Their bodies look tiny against the swells.

A moment later Rylan has returned, and from the top of the ridge he sees his daughter in her final preparations. Pomai is crouched, combing the wax on her six-six, the board dirty with other sessions. Her shoulders are brawny and run through as much with hula as with surfing, and when he sees her like that he sees the blood of Hawai'i and knows Pomai's mother hasn't spoiled all of her.

In their early days everything was different. Rylan and Keala had just had Pomai—she was maybe three, four?—when Hi'ilawe was found noosed with electrical cord, creaking from a rafter in his house with eviction notices stacked on the counter, food-stamp card taped to his note. *I don't know why it's so hard*, it said. *But I'm not going to fail anymore.* Rylan and Keala had always talked about the Sovereignty Movement, how and where it made sense to try and reclaim their annexed kingdom. But the way Hi'ilawe had left, coupled with that week's evening news of the *Kanaka Maoli*—their *malo* loincloths and *pa'u* skirts, standing together in front of the black breath and industrial blades of the government—was all the convincing they'd needed. Within a month, Rylan and Keala were out on the street, brown and gleaming with the work of the Movement, dancing and chanting at the capitol, picketing at the Modern Community Development Sites, marching at the Highway Construction Zones. Their eyes burned with the fluorescent light of late-night strategy sessions, debates over how to beat gerrymandering and push another petition through to the ballot.

The years went, the years were hard, but there were little victories, and then bigger ones–first official US apologies for the annexation, then the return of Kaho'olawe. Rylan was flush with the possibility, their small ax chopping at the big tree of the state, but something had changed in Keala.

"I don't think I can do this anymore," she said one night. "The military bases aren't going anywhere, neither are the hotels. Who owns all the factories? Who has all the good jobs?"

"Thanks so much, Miss Attorney," Rylan said.

"But don't you see?" Keala said. "It's only because I went to Berkeley that I'm a lawyer now."

She could list a litany of *Maoli* failures: its leaders had been bought out by the state, it was disorganized, it was male dominated. Rylan always told her these were just the growing pains of any movement, but in private, he thought she was looking for a way out. She was *hapa-haole* anyway, half her family from Arizona. He'd been blind to it because he was young and stupid but now he could see she'd always been using the Movement as a chance to pretend she was full Hawaiian and not just an approximation. And so she slowly began to break away, to poison his daughter's mind with talk of opportunity on the mainland, of how much more efficient it was, how much cheaper, that you could get in a car and drive from one state to another, and that somehow, when you were more American, everything got easier.

But she hadn't gotten all of his daughter. Rylan had kept just enough of Pomai. She'd learned from Rylan and there was *mana* in her yet, the flex and pump of *hula*, and surfing, and she knew plenty of their language, could hold whole conversations in their real tongue. He sees this while he stands above, watching her finish the wax combing and then heft the board under her arm. Now he grabs his board and joins her on the beach.

Rylan can hear the way Pomai is breathing. "You ready for this?" "Of course," Pomai says. "I've ridden bigger than you think."

Then they're in the water, at their knees, and Pomai has stopped to watch again the cracking surf. She's nervous, Rylan thinks.

"Every time before I get in," Rylan says, "I think about where surfing came from. Our *ali'i*. Our blood, you know? Our kings."

Pomai's still watching the surf. "There were queens, too," she says. "Everyone seems to forget that." From Second Break comes a faint whooping, like a war cry. A double overhead wave assaults the lineup, tossing a late-dropping surfer. He disappears into the white water. "Anyway, it's just a history lesson," Pomai says. "It's not going to keep me floating out there."

She swipes at her forehead, her eyes, with the palm of her free hand. "Rip looks strong today." Pomai pulls herself up onto her board. "Hope you're ready to paddle."

In the water Pomai surges ahead and arrives at the lineup far before her father. All the surfers are floating together, sit-straddling their boards, waiting for the next set. Pomai sees her father, far back and coming on slowly, each arm rising and slapping down to pull the water. All around, the ocean rises and falls beneath them, the slow-breathing lungs of an animal. Water gurgles and chuffs against the boards. Smaller swells roll under, breaking far closer to shore; then a set rises, the dark of new waves headed to Second Break, to the lineup of waiting surfers. It's what she came for.

Pomai and three others leave the lineup. Almost immediately Pomai sees it's a mistake. The wave is close to fifteen feet at the peak; she's ridden maybe ten feet, twelve at the biggest. She and the others are quiet, each paddling for the deepest spot, jockeying for calling rights. Pomai pulls across the group, into the deepest position—she's surfed this break so many times it's automatic, the way a person can forget their commute even as they're driving it—so she's the first to feel the lunge of the surf, the wave rising behind and hollowing out below. The others pull up. She strokes hard and presses down on the board and slides into the wave and the ocean spits at her all over as she launches, and for the first few feet it is exactly like jumping off a cliff. But then the rail of her board catches smooth and she leans into the curling face and glides down into the blue cave of glass, the mouth closing even as she chases, and then it is farther ahead, and smaller even, and just as the cave collapses around her, she shoots through the spume and into the sun, the wave thundering its last into foam. She slides to the mushy shoulder of the surf, where onlookers *chee-hoo* and her blood bangs in her throat with joy.

Out in the channel, Rylan has arrived, and he's watching it all. She's so angry, Rylan thinks. He'd believed they were removed from the era when Pomai had found a new way to ruin every opportunity she was given, when she'd spent her nights at friends' houses and in their cars, at beaches and parking lots and streets, bludgeoning herself with chemicals and—although Rylan has no proof—sex. The fights with other girls, the pathetic grades, again and again, Rylan remembers all of this. Much of that was Keala, he knows it now.

You take his daughter away and leave her with a tired, compromised mother . . . Pomai had never been so angry when they were all together. And after the divorce, when Pomai was acting up the most, impossible to find, sharp-tongued when available, there were still times she'd snuck into *his* apartment when she could've gone anywhere, even back to her mother.

The anger, then, Rylan tells himself, didn't come from him.

And look at Pomai now. Strongest surfer in the water, liquid hips and quick feet, so much of that from him. She'd finished school and had a job. Things would get better for her, things would get better for them. He just had to say the right words now and she'd soften up.

Pomai has paddled back to the channel, starts to pass him for the lineup.

"Hey, not bad," Rylan calls out. Pomai keeps paddling. "Pretty good for your biggest wave ever, yeah?"

Pomai pulls up now, turns towards him. Rylan sees eyes that are bright, like she's swallowed electricity. "It's unreal out here today," she says. "But I'm just getting started." She nods towards the inside break, where five-foot waves are wrecking ten-year-olds and Occasionals. "You been sticking to the inside?"

Rylan laughs off the insult. "I was riding out here when you was still in *hana-bata* days. When you was trying to take off your diapers and run around naked."

"Those days are long gone," Pomai says.

"Ah, come on," Rylan says. "Loosen up a little, okay? We don't see each other so much, we might as well make it fun." But she doesn't smile when he says it.

"No," she says. "We're not going to make this fun. You don't get to do this. You don't get the easy, happy day."

"Damn," he says. "I was just trying for enjoy the surf."

Yes, Dad, there you go, turn it to me, Pomai thinks. She knows what comes next: *I didn't raise you to be this way.* It was always his favorite, an easy way to extraction, and she'd always wanted to say: *right, you didn't raise me to be this way. You didn't raise me to be any way at all.* Pomai wants to ask Rylan where he was when it was after midnight on a Saturday and she needed someone to be waiting up for her, refusing to turn out the lights. Or when she'd seen in the mirror that swimming and surfing were thickening her back into a slab of muscle that strained against the seams of her blouses and she'd panicked that she'd never turn herself into a ribbon of sex like Nicky and all the girls in Aloha Club—where was he then? Or when she'd pulled back from Hana in his bedroom, slipped her hand from his erection and said she wasn't ready, and a week later she was a slut somehow, the label echoing around her in the long empty shines of recess halls, where was her father then?

For a moment Pomai is fourteen again and in the *halau*, practice before the Merrie Monarch, locked in line with the other girls and boys, all moving their feet and arms and hips in time to the rolling bump and tap of the *ipu*, the chants of the *kumu*, the dancers bouncing and turning on their knees, flipping and sweeping their arms, the *kumu* telling of the life of the gods, the dancers calling back when the kumu asked, and all of it she can feel running like water from her into the same river that her father draws from, the place where he talks of the old Hawai'i. Pomai had been proud then and heated in her heart for being a part of the same place as her father, and she'd waited for him the next day at the airport, ready for him to join her at the competition. Surely he wouldn't miss this, the Merrie Monarch tickets sold out for months ahead, the stadium seating filled. But Rylan never showed. It was just her and her mother, and by the time Pomai had taken stage with her *halau*, when they were supposed to answer the *kumu*, Pomai found she no longer had the voice, and she failed, the *halau* failed, and when she left the stage she knew it. If she could go back, the girl she was would still be up there onstage, waiting for the father who would never show.

"I don't want to pretend," Pomai says, "that we're a happy family."

Rylan blows again, that long sigh Pomai's heard so many times. "So start in, then," he says. "Gimme all the words your mom been giving you, about how I'm this or that."

"I don't need Mom's words. I've got my own."

"Do you?"

"Dad—" Pomai starts. But then she stops. "You know what, fuck it, I'm leaving for California next week."

She sees the words bolt through Rylan's spine. "What?"

"USC," Pomai says.

"I don't understand."

"Everyone's gone," Pomai says. "Tracy's gone, Nicky-them, they're all doing something with themselves. And here I am."

"You can do plenty with yourself here," Rylan says.

"What, like you did?"

Rylan clamps his jaw shut. Pomai can see the flex of his cheek. She notices, too, how far they've drifted in the ocean. It's not just the tide on top, but something deeper and more insistent that's steadily taking them away. "I done plenty good here," Rylan says.

"Look around you," Pomai says. "You're a part-time electrician. You only get paid if some *haole* lets you work on his house. I'm no better. You should see me smile at Sunset's: another burger for you, sir, your joke about my ass is so funny, let me make sure I wear my V-neck—"

"I know," Rylan says. "I know it's like that. What do you think I'm fighting with the *Maoli* for?"

"So you can hide from me and Mom."

"Who told you that? You don't know nothing," Rylan says. "Who was there when you first walked? Who's the one who took you up at night when you was crying, who didn't always have to work in the morning? Shit." He raises his arms to encompass everything around them, "Who taught you to *surf*?"

"I taught myself," Pomai says. "You were gone more than you were around."

"That's your mom telling you that," Rylan says. "That's school counselors and state workers—"

"There's no one else, Dad," Pomai says. "Not this time. Only me. God," Pomai says, gritting her teeth.

And then she paddles away.

Rylan sits and stares after Pomai, rage thudding through his skull. She's moving strong to the waves and he's slowly sliding away. Her words are still there in his head. Something in him closes on itself and falls like a runaway elevator.

No, he thinks. You're wrong.

This island. This damn island. Is still taking from me.

Rylan lies chest-down and paddles after Pomai. The water is cold and heavy through his hands. A herd of clouds rushes by, shadows sliding over the waves. He paddles. She's there, flattened on her board, the white bottoms of her feet bobbing in and out of the water. A set is rolling in and he can see his daughter going for the third wave back. Rylan follows, closer with every pull of his hands through the water.

The wave approaches. Wind ripples across the face as it curves and rises, dark and massive, one of the biggest waves yet. Pomai is positioning for it, and Rylan's only a few strokes behind. Yes, he thinks. He wants it to crush them both. He wants it to pound the whole island and drag it away: all the white hotels on the coast; all the State Department buildings; all the freeways, the traffic lights; all the *haole* houses, big and elegant as palaces; the hundreds of carpenters he'd met from Ohio or Arizona who'd moved on a whim and banked more in their first year than he had in ten; all the clean smiles and dirty cash and stupid *lu'aus*, as if Hawai'i was a casino and not a kingdom. It had taken so much from him. Now his daughter, too, had lost sight of the real islands, the ones underneath. Pain flames through the muscles at the base of Rylan's neck, goes to the skeleton, to the nerves. He's up next to Pomai, the noses of both their boards lunging forward with each stroke. He's beaten her to the lane.

"This one's not yours," Rylan calls out.

"The hell it's not," Pomai responds. "You're too late."

The wave has arrived. It rolls into them and they turn for the drop zone.

Pomai is panting with exertion. She's been under few waves this gigantic. But there is her father, pulling for the wave so hard his shoulders are striating through his skin. He's beaten her, now she sees it. He's made it to the deeper section before her and now it's too late, the wave is forming, he's in the proper place, already posturing up for the drop. The wave is his; she should leave off paddling and let him take his ride.

But instead Pomai paddles and kicks and pulls with her fingers through the water, even as the wave peaks. She'll cut him off if she has to.

The drop takes her breath away.

She's shooting down the face. Rylan has already dropped and established, he's turning toward her and tucking and sliding for the curl of the coming barrel. And as Pomai drops in and cuts him off, she sees his face. Her drop forces him off the line and the wave detonates on top of him. He's gone instantly in the churn.

For a moment Pomai feels the sneering joy of revenge. But the feeling is hollowed out almost as soon as it arrives. The way her father's face was before he went under, the eyes of surprise and pain—Pomai knows she's broken something big, bigger than she'd meant to. There is a shift in her weight and her rail catches in the streaking water. The nose of the board dips, yanks out from under Pomai's feet. She pitches forward into the air. Through the wave she sees the throwing-star shaped *vana*, the knuckles of green reef, rushing up. Her body puckers and she slaps into the ocean.

The wave breaks like a truck accident. The air blasts from Pomai's nose. She's down and up and twisting. The porous reef smacks her shoulder and scrapes skin away. Her ears are full of the white noise of churning water; her chest aches; she's rolled again. The last of her breath leaks from her lungs and her head begins to fill with brainy light.

On the beach, far from the accident, Rylan surfaces. He's rolled into shore by the last of the rip, and he crawls on his hands and knees in the fringe of the tidewater, his board sliding up and down the shore with each wash of waves. He stops and belches up a sheet of prickling salt water. Gasps. The oxygen is cool and sweet in Rylan's lungs. He rolls onto his back and opens his eyes against the sky.

"Goddamn, Rylan, you okay bruddah?"

It's Kui, one of the lifeguards, standing above him. Rylan knows Kui. They've surfed together before, been to the same barbecues at the same houses. Kui bends to inspect Rylan, his shadow falling across Rylan's chest.

"I'm fine," Rylan says.

"Just give me a second," Kui says, and he puts his hands on Rylan, starting a basic trauma examination.

"No." Rylan bats off Kui's hands, then lurches to his feet. Water drips from his nose, slick and warm with his own snot. "Did she make it?"

"Air drop," Kui says. "She went under right after you. Howard-them are going for her."

Rylan looks out at the sea. "But did she make it back up?" he asks. "After?"

Kui does not respond; he's looking down the beach. Rylan follows his gaze and sees the thrashing, sees the two lifeguards and then, surfacing, his daughter. The lifeguards start swimming her to shore, holding her on her back with her head up. Her board's been snapped in half and both pieces are tumbling through the white water, bobbing and tucking like kites as surges of water bat against them. As the lifeguards stand Pomai up, Rylan sees her back, the blue rash guard, shredded open from the reef and red with blood.

Rylan starts jogging towards her, dragging his board behind. He rips the leash strap free from his ankle and keeps going.

In the medical tent they treat Pomai, staunch her gashed back with bandages and wrap her torso with medical tape. She raises her arms as they wrap, her skull twirling inside itself from the fall, made worse by the tang of antiseptic. She's sitting in an open-air tent, a flat green tarp they've staked high with poles and tied deep and locked with boulders, so that sun and air run through the tent and the patients can sit as Pomai does, on a folding metal chair with her feet in the cool grains of sand. The slick tatters of her rash guard are pooled at her feet. Pomai sees her father out along the shore. He's loping towards her, his shorts floppy and soaked and slapping against themselves.

"He looks okay," Pomai says, to no one in particular. The ocean rips and booms. "It looks like I didn't hurt him."

She sits still and watches her father come toward her.

Sometimes Pomai's mother would say to her: *You're just doing this to piss me off. Why don't you act right?* And she would say, *Because dad. Because you.* And maybe at the start that was true. But soon enough the friction—chain-swearing at counselors, padding through midnight Honolulu with a stolen bottle in her hand, talking down her mother, her father, bitches in their makeup, tourists at her first restaurant job—it became the because. She was tired of these choices: Hawai'i or the mainland, his version of the divorce or hers, a house in Niu Valley or a brick apartment on the fringe of Kaneohe. Pomai wanted none of it. *I choose the land out in front of me and a million ways to go,* she wanted to say. *I'll go any way, I'll go all ways, and feel the white blast of the world filling me up.*

But now Pomai thinks of everything her father told her in the water. There are pictures in her mind she hadn't wanted to remember: The two of them at 'Ehukai beach, bucketing sand into the shape of a turtle; the first time she'd stood on a board, he *was* pushing her from behind; during the hard years, after screaming matches with her mother, she'd snuck into his house, coming down off a glassy high and crashing on his couch. He'd laid a blanket on her and never said a word and she was gone in the blue-black morning, long before he'd stirred. She wonders how it must have felt to him to see the wormed blanket, empty when he woke.

Her father has stopped walking towards her. Pomai stands and moves to where she can see him better, into the sun.

Out on the sand, Rylan sees his daughter come to the edge of the tent. She shades her face with the blade of her hand. Rylan hears a soft thump; Pomai's accidentally kicked one of the halves of her board, lying in the sand. She's looking down at the shards now, then back up at him. Do her eyes brighten? Please. Just once more. She used to be that way, five years old, arms thrust up towards him, begging with her shining eyes for a pick-up-and-spin. "You're home," she'd say, like it was a reward, "You're home!" He feels himself about to split open with words. He wants to say about the board, that it shouldn't be the only one she breaks; he wants to say again about the *ali'i*, the kingdom, about her people, what they were and what they can be again. But she's still so far away.

He raises his hand to wave to her. The grit falls from his fingers. Pomai's still looking at him, but she hasn't moved. Another set arrives at Second Break. A wave booms down. Rylan looks to the surf, his hand still raised to his daughter. You don't even have to move for it to happen, he thinks. It makes no difference. The waves keep coming. Here the ocean is big and blue but Rylan knows if he could see it from above—from an airplane, say, flying away—he'd see it as a scribble of white, rolling in again, battering the island into something smaller.

BRYAN STEVENSON

■

The High Road

FROM *The New York Times Magazine*

THE VISITATION ROOM was 100 feet square, with a few stools bolted to the floor and wire mesh running across the room. For family visits, inmates and visitors had to be on opposite sides of the mesh. Legal visits, on the other hand, were "contact visits"—the two of us would be on the same side of the room to permit more privacy. I began worrying about my lack of preparation. I had scheduled to meet with the client for one hour, but I wasn't sure how I would fill even fifteen minutes with what I knew. I sat down on a stool and waited until I heard the clanging of chains on the other side of the door.

The man who walked in seemed even more nervous than I was. He glanced at me and quickly averted his gaze when I looked back. He was a young, neatly groomed African-American man with short hair—clean-shaven, medium build—wearing bright, clean prison whites. He looked immediately familiar, like everyone I grew up with, friends from school, people I played sports or music with, someone I'd talk to on the street. As the guard left, the metal door banged loudly behind him.

I walked over and offered my hand. The man, who had been convicted of murder, shook it cautiously. We sat down.

"I'm very sorry," I blurted out. "I'm really sorry, I'm really sorry, uh, okay, I don't really know, uh, I'm just a law student, I'm not a real lawyer." Despite all my preparations and rehearsed remarks, I couldn't stop myself from apologizing repeatedly. "I'm so sorry I can't tell you very much, but I don't know very much."

He looked at me, worried. "Is everything all right with my case?"

"Oh, yes, sir. The lawyers at S.P.D.C. sent me down to tell you that they don't have a lawyer yet," I said. "But you're not at risk of execution anytime in the next year. We're working on finding you a lawyer, a real lawyer."

He interrupted my chatter by grabbing my hands. "I'm not going to have an execution date anytime in the next year?"

"No, sir. They said it would be at least a year." Those words didn't sound very comforting to me. But he just squeezed my hands tighter.

"Thank you, man," he said. "I mean, really, thank you! I've been talking to my wife on the phone, but I haven't wanted her to come and visit me or bring the kids because I was afraid they'd show up and I'd have an execution date. Now I'm going to tell them they can come and visit. Thank you!"

I was astonished. We began to talk. It turned out that he and I were exactly the same age. He told me about his family and his trial. He asked me about law school and my family. We talked about music and about prison. We kept talking and talking, and it was only when I heard a loud bang on the door that I realized I had stayed long past my allotted time. I looked at my watch. I had been there three hours.

The guard came in and began handcuffing him; I could see the prisoner grimacing. "I think those cuffs are on too tight," I said.

"It's Okay, Bryan," he said. "Don't worry about this. Just come back and see me again, Okay?"

I struggled to say something appropriate, something reassuring. He looked at me and smiled. Then he did something completely unexpected. He closed his eyes and tilted his head back. I was confused, but then he opened his mouth, and I understood. He had a tremendous baritone that was strong and clear.

> Lord, lift me up and let me stand,
> By faith, on heaven's tableland;
> A higher plane than I have found,
> Lord, plant my feet on higher ground.

It was an old hymn they used to sing all the time in church where I grew up. I hadn't heard it in years. Because his ankles were shackled and his hands were locked behind his back, he almost stumbled when the guard shoved him forward. But he kept on singing.

His voice was filled with desire. I had come into the prison with such anxiety and fear about his willingness to tolerate my inadequacy. I didn't expect him to be compassionate or generous. I had no right to expect anything from a condemned man on death row. But that day, I could hear him as he went down the hall, until the echo of his earnest, soaring voice faded. When it had gone, the still silence of that space sounded different from when I entered. Even today, after thirty years of defending death-row prisoners, I still hear him.

CONTRIBUTORS' NOTES

Daniel Alarcón is a novelist, journalist, and radio producer. His most recent novel, *At Night We Walk in Circles*, was a finalist for the 2014 PEN Faulkner Award. He is Executive Producer of Radio Ambulante, a Spanish language audio journalism podcast, and teaches at the Columbia University Graduate School of Journalism in New York.

Shane Bauer is an award-winning journalist and senior reporter at *Mother Jones* magazine. His work on the criminal justice system and the Middle East has appeared in *The Nation*, *Salon*, the *Los Angeles Times*, the *Guardian*, and many other publications. He lives in Oakland with his wife, Sarah Shourd.

Box Brown is an Ignatz Award-winning American cartoonist best known for the comic *Bellen!* In 2008 he was awarded a Xeric Grant for the comic *Love Is a Peculiar Type of Thing*. A passionate proponent of the serial comics format, Brown runs the micropress Retrofit, which is dedicated to supporting independent serial comics work. He is also a lifelong professional wrestling fan. His next graphic novel will be about Tetris.

Anders Carlson-Wee is a 2015 NEA Fellow, 2015 Bread Loaf Bakeless Camargo Fellow and the author of *Dynamite*, winner of the 2015 Frost Place Chapbook Contest (Bull City Press). His work has appeared in the *New England Review,* the *Missouri Review,* the *Southern Review, Prairie Schooner, Blackbird, Best New Poets,* and elsewhere. Winner of the Ninth Letter Poetry Award and the New Delta Review's Editors' Choice Prize, he holds an MFA in poetry from Vanderbilt University and certificates in wilderness survival from the Tracker School.

Emily Carroll was born in London, Ontario in 1983. In addition to the many short comics found at her website, her work has been featured in numerous print anthologies. She currently lives with her wife Kate and their large orange cat in Stratford, Ontario.

Katie Coyle grew up in Fair Haven, New Jersey, and has an MFA from the University of Pittsburgh. Her debut novel, *Vivian Apple at the End of the World* (Houghton Mifflin Harcourt, 2015), was named one of the forty best YA novels of all time by *Rolling Stone,* and was followed by a sequel, *Vivian Apple Needs a Miracle.* Her short fiction has won the Pushcart Prize and been featured in *One Story,* the *Southeast Review,* and *Critical Quarterly,* among others. She lives in San Francisco with her husband, and blogs at katiecoyle.com.

Paul Crenshaw's stories and essays have appeared or are forthcoming in *Best American Essays 2005* and *2011, Ecotone, Glimmer Train, Brevity, The Rumpus,* the *North American Review,* and the *Texas Review,* among others. "Chainsaw Fingers" is drawn from a collection of stories about characters that have been affected by the wars in Iraq and Afghanistan.

Neftali Cuello has been a farmworker in North Carolina since age twelve. Today, she is also a worker rights activist who has served with organizations such as Poder Juvenil Campesino and NC FIELD. She lives in Pink Hill, North Carolina.

Rebecca Curtis received a B.A. from Pomona College, an M.A. in English from New York University, and an M.F.A from Syracuse University. Her first book, *Twenty Grand and Other Tales of Love & Money* (Harpercollins, 2007) was a New York Times Notable Book of 2007, a San Francisco Chronicle Notable Book of 2007, and an L.A. Times Best Book of 2007. It was also a finalist for the PEN Hemingway

Award and the Los Angeles Times Art Seidenbaum Award for Best First Fiction, and it won the New Hampshire Literary Award for Outstanding Work of Fiction 2006 & 2007. Curtis' fiction and essays have appeared in *The New Yorker*, *Harper's*, *Esquire*, *Harper's Bazaar*, *McSweeney's*, *N+1*, and elsewhere.

Joshua Fattal is a historian of twentieth century United States and the Middle East. He is coauthor of *A Sliver of Light* and has written for the *New York Times* and *Los Angeles Times*. He believes the world is round. He lives in New York City with his partner and child.

Corinne Goria is a writer and immigration attorney. Her fiction has been featured in *The Silent History* and she is the editor of *Invisible Hands: Voices from the Global Economy*, which is part of the Voice of Witness (VOW) book series. For more information, visit www.voiceofwitness.org

Sheila Heti is the author of six books, including *How Should a Person Be?* and an illustrated book for children, *We Need a Horse*. She is also one of the editors of the anthology, *Women in Clothes* and frequently collaborates with other artists and writers.

TJ Jarrett is a writer and software developer in Nashville, Tennessee. Her recent work has been published or is forthcoming in *Poetry*, *African American Review*, *Boston Review*, *Beloit Poetry Journal*, *VQR*, and *West Branch*, among others. She has earned scholarships and fellowships from Colrain Manuscript Conference, Vermont Studio Center, Sewanee Writer's Conference, and the Summer Literary Seminars. She was a runner-up for the 2012 Marsh Hawk Poetry Prize and 2012 New Issues Poetry Prize, and the winner of VQR's Emily Clark Balch Prize for Poetry 2014.

Heidi Julavits is the author of four novels, including most recently *The Vanishers*, along with the memoir *The Folded Clock*. She is the winner of the PEN New England Award, an editor of the anthology *Women in Clothes*, and a founding editor of the *Believer*. She is currently a professor at Columbia University.

Ammi Keller published the zine *Emergency*. She was a Wallace Stegner Fellow at Stanford and now teaches in the Certificate Program in Novel Writing there. Ammi's work appears in *Joyland*, *Bottoms Up*, and *Stories Care Forgot*. She is at work on a novel-in-stories about Hurricane Katrina, sexuality, and disaster capitalism.

Victor Lodato is the author of the novel *Mathilda Savitch*, which won the PEN USA Award for Fiction. His stories and poems have appeared in *The New Yorker*, the *Virginia Quarterly Review*, and the *Southern Review*. He is the recipient of fellowships from the Guggenheim Foundation and the National Endowment for the Arts. His new novel, *Edgar and Lucy*, is forthcoming.

Alex Mar is a non-fiction writer who lives in her hometown of New York City. She has contributed to the *Believer*, the *Oxford American*, *Elle*, the *New York Times Book Review*, *Slate*, *New York*, and other publications. She is also the director of the documentary feature *American Mystic*. Her first book, *Witches of America*, about present-day witchcraft in the United States, is out in October of 2015 through Farrar, Straus and Giroux.

Sarah Marshall grew up in Oregon and now lives in Wisconsin, where she is pursuing a PhD in English at the University of Wisconsin-Madison. Her writing has appeared in *The New Republic*, *Lapham's Quarterly*, *Bitch Magazine*, and the *Toast*, and her writerly obsessions include insects, invasive species, exotic pets, crime, confessions, vampires, vigilantism, sports, masochism, teenagers, witches, Florida, and maligned women.

Tom McAllister is the non-fiction editor at *Barrelhouse* and co-host of the weekly *Book Fight* podcast. His memoir, *Bury Me in My Jersey*, was published by Villard in 2010 and his debut novel, *The Widower's Handbook*, will be published by Algonquin in summer 2016. He teaches in the English department at Temple University. You can find him on Twitter at @t_mcallister.

Richard McGehee is a research fellow in the Teresa Lozano Long Institute of Latin American Studies at the University of Texas at Austin and works in the areas of sport literature and history. His translations of sport-related stories and poetry have appeared in *Aethlon*, the *Southern Review*, and *World Literature Today*.

Inés Fernández Moreno was born in Buenos Aires, Argentina. She has worked as creative director of an advertising agency and written extensively for newspapers and magazines. She is the author of a number of novels and stories, and won the 2014 Sor Juana Inés de la Cruz Prize for her novel *El cielo no existe*. The prize is awarded to the best novel written by a woman in Spanish. She lives in the small Buenos Aires neighborhood of Parque Chas.

Christopher Myers was born and raised in Ohio. He worked in the poker industry in Nevada and later spent several years working in an entomology laboratory in Vermont. He has also been a teacher's assistant and tutor at an adult high school. He is currently serving time in Lovelock, NV. Christopher Myers was awarded third place in Memoir in the 2013 PEN America Prison Writing Contest.

U.S.-based Nigerian writer, **Lesley Nneka Arimah**, has received grants and awards from AWP, the Jerome Foundation, the Elizabeth George Foundation, the Minnesota State Arts Board, and others. Her work has appeared or is forthcoming in *PANK*, *Granta*, *Mid-American Review*, and elsewhere. She is at work on a novel and collection of short stories.

Claudia Rankine is the author of *Citizen: An American Lyric* and four previous books, including *Don't Let Me Be Lonely: An American Lyric*. She is a chancellor of the Academy of American Poets and the winner of the Jackson Poetry Prize, the Los Angeles Times Book Prize in Poetry, and the National Book Critics Circle Award in Poetry.

Paul Salopek crossed his first border at age six when his family moved to central Mexico, where he later worked as a rancher and cowhand. For years he made his living as a commercial fisherman. As a foreign correspondent, he has reported on conflicts in Africa, the Middle East,

Central Asia, and Latin America, as well as on global topics such as oil production, overfishing, and the human genome. His stories have appeared in *National Geographic*, the *Chicago Tribune*, the *Atlantic*, *Foreign Policy*, *The Best American Travel Writing*, and other publications. His reportage has earned many awards in the United States, including two Pulitzer Prizes; the George Polk Award; the National Press Club Award; the Overseas Press Club Award; the Daniel Pearl Award for Courage in Journalism; the Lovejoy Award for defending press freedom; a Princeton Ferris-McGraw Fellowship; and a Nieman Fellowship at Harvard.

Leanne Shapton is a Canadian artist, author, and publisher based in New York City. She is the author of *Important Artifacts . . . and Swimming Studies*, winner of the 2012 National Book Critics Circle Award for autobiography.

Sarah Shourd is journalist, public speaker, playwright, editor, and a Visiting Scholar at UC Berkeley. She is a regular contributor to the *Daily Beast* and focuses primarily on issues pertaining to solitary confinement and the U.S. prison system. Shourd is currently based in Oakland, California and can be reached at sarahshourd.com.

Bryan Stevenson is the founder of the Equal Justice Initiative and the author of *Just Mercy*, from which "The High Road" is adapted.

Paul Tough is the author, most recently, of *How Children Succeed: Grit, Curiosity, and the Hidden Power of Character*. He is a contributing writer to the *New York Times Magazine*, where he writes mostly about education and economic mobility. His writing has also appeared in *The New Yorker*, *Slate*, *GQ*, and *Esquire*. He lives with his family in Montauk, New York.

Wells Tower is the author of *Everything Ravaged, Everything Burned*, a collection of short fiction. His fiction and nonfiction have appeared in *The New Yorker*, *Harper's*, the *Paris Review*, *McSweeney's*, *GQ*, and elsewhere. He lives in North Carolina.

Kawai Strong Washburn was born and raised on the Big Island of Hawai'i. He has since lived, worked, and traveled all over the world, including Sub-Saharan Africa, post-communist Europe, and Central and South America. In addition to his work as a writer, he has been a web developer, systems administrator, microfinance analyst, and English/math/computer science teacher. His fiction has appeared in *McSweeney's*, the *Mid-American Review*, and *Barrelhouse*; he has also written commentary for *Flavorwire* and book reviews for *Publishers Weekly*. He is terrible at surfing, loves his wife and daughter, and is hard at work on a novel and short story collection.

Joan Wickersham's most recent book of fiction is *The News from Spain*. Her memoir *The Suicide Index* was a National Book Award finalist. Her short stories have appeared in many magazines, as well as in *The Best American Short Stories*. She teaches in the Bennington Writing Seminars.

Rachel Zucker is the author of nine books, most recently *The Pedestrians*, a double collection of poetry and prose and *MOTHERs*, a memoir. She teaches at NYU and lives in New York with her husband and their three sons.

THE BEST AMERICAN
NONREQUIRED READING
COMMITTEE

Behold! The bios of the *Best American Nonrequired Reading* (*BANR*) committee. These students meet on a weekly basis at McSweeney's Publishing in San Francisco in order to read and read and then read some more. From all this reading, they select the work that ends up in this book. They are aided by a group of students in Ann Arbor, Michigan at 826 Michigan who do the exact same thing.

Juan Chicas is a student at City College of San Francisco. He enjoyed being on the Best American Committee very much. His favorite comic book characters will always be Shazam and Moon Knight. He is the funniest guy ever to be on the committee. He is also a socialist and hopes that one day this country stops digging its own grave.

 Cosmo Comito-Steller, sixteen years old, Lowell High School: PROS: 1) Always dresses warm, 2) Can differentiate between stalagmite and stalactite, 3) Fuel-efficient, four-wheel drive. CONS: 1) Does not dot i's, cross t's, 2) Has failed Erik Erikson's psychosocial stage of Ego Identity v. Role Confusion, 3) Had trouble thinking of cons. <Expected to proceed to status of senior within the year.>

Milo Comito-Steller, sixteen, student at Balboa High School, is an avid reader and writer of science fiction—and other genres as well, if the mood strikes him. Raised on *Harry Potter* and *The Lord of the Rings*, he now enjoys the works of Joseph Heller and Kurt Vonnegut. When he grows up, he wants to be a writer, or at least someone who writes books in his spare time.

Claire Fishman is a freshman at Brown University in Providence, Rhode Island. This has been her fourth year in *BANR* and she is very grateful for all the enlightening and weird pieces that she has read over the years, and for all the fascinating people with whom she was able to discuss those pieces. Martin Van Buren remains her favorite president.

Sophie Halperin is a freshman at Smith! She's from San Francisco and graduated from Mission High School. She thought *Mad Max: Fury Road* was the best action movie she's ever seen, and it made her believe in Hollywood's potential to make great movies.

Kelly Lee is a senior at George Washington High School. She likes people most of the time, likes math none of the time, and could always go for a burrito. She speaks softly but carries a big stick, and she has a strong desire to travel the world with her friends.

Rita Liu is a junior at Pioneer High School. She can usually be found covered in some sort of paint, trying to coerce her friends into modeling for impromptu photo shoots, or hopped up on coffee. She adores short stories and she sometimes stares dramatically out the car window.

Samantha Ng is a senior at June Jordan School for Equity. It's her second year on the *BANR* committee and she loves reading stories in class. She also likes to practice karate. Even though she is only a yellow belt, her moves are surprisingly butt kicking.

Marco Ponce currently attends George Washington High School where he is a senior. He likes to read and play lacrosse, and he's interested in community organizing. His motto is: "in order to feel good you have to dress good," and he recommends that everyone find their own motto because it's nice to have a motto.

Evelyn Pugh is currently a first-year at Macalester College in St. Paul, Minnesota. In her free time she enjoys drinking mochas, watching sitcoms, and sharing groan-worthy puns. For example, what is Michelle Obama's favorite veggie? Barokoli.

Zola Rosenfeld is currently a sophomore at Jewish Community High School by day and a brooding vigilante by night. When not spending her Monday evenings at McSweeney's with her posse, she protects her great city with pride and explores unmarked Pacific islands. If you should ever see her, be careful not to be blinded by her dazzling smile.

Isaac Schott-Rosenfield is fifteen years of age, and currently majors in creative writing at the Ruth Asawa School of the Arts. He is an upstanding citizen, by which he means he is forced to stand up a lot. Really more than he'd like.

Cynthia Van, seventeen, is a senior at George Washington High School. She is horrified by the inevitable doom of the universe and how it will affect arctic flowers. She is very close to entering the totally not-radical void of adulthood. In order to cope with this, she eats large quantities of potatoes and yam leaves.

Grace VanRenterghem is a senior at Huron High School and has been a committee member for two years. Besides reading, her favorite past times include examining creepy bugs, drinking copious amounts of Yorkshire tea, petting her cats, and trying to sing along to Spanish songs.

Hadley VanRenterghem is a senior at Ann Arbor Huron High School and has participated in *BANR* for two years. She always loves attending *BANR* and looks forward to another year of intriguing reading. As you may have guessed, she and Grace are identical twins, so who knows who is who in these pictures. . .

Very special thanks to Nicole Angeloro, Clara Sankey, Daniel Handler, Mark Robinson, Eric Nyquist, Inez Tan, Nora Byrnes, and Belle Baxley. A bow and a salute for our lovely and talented intern, Taylor Stephens, whose hands played a vital role in the production of this book. And thanks also to 826 National, 826 Valencia, 826 Michigan, Houghton Mifflin Harcourt, Scholar-Match, Laura Howard, Andi Winnette, Jordan Bass, Ruby Perez, Shannon Davis, Ian Delaney, Dan McKinley, Sam Riley, Sunra Thompson, Elizabeth Hanley, Cal Crosby, Casey Jarman, Zoë Kleinfeld, Mara Bandt-Law, Steve Elias, Pete Endicott, Mimi Lok, Cliff Mayotte, Claire Kiefer, Gerald Richards, Molly Parent, Lauren Hall, Olivia White Lopez, Jorge Eduardo Garcia, María Inés Montes, Bita Nazarian, Allyson Halpern, Amy Popovich, Ashley Varady, Emma Peoples, Christina V. Perry, Claudia Sanchez, and Caroline Kangas.

NOTABLE
NONREQUIRED READING
OF 2014

STEVE AMICK
  The Measuring, *Zoetrope*

IAN BASSINGTHWAIGHTE
  When Trains Fall from Space, *Carolina Quarterly*

MATTHEW CLARK
  Shedders, *Ecotone*
LYDIA CONKLIN
  Pioneer, *The Southern Review*
DIANE COOK
  The Mast Year, *Granta*
BILL COTTER
  The Window Lion, *The Paris Review*
MICHELLE CHIHARA
  The Bride Laid Bare by Her Bachelors Even, *Santa Monica Review*
DOUG CRANDELL
  A Murder Remembered, *The Sun Magazine*

SAM DOLNICK
  The Sinaloa Cartel's 90 Year-Old Drug Mule, *The New York Times Magazine*

Ginger Eager
Beyond the Boundaries of Flesh, *Bellevue Literary Review*
Cloe Feldman Emison
US: Deceased Shopping, *Salt Hill Journal*
Brian Evenson
Maternity, *Ploughshares*

Andrés Felipe Solano
Pig Skin, *Granta*

Jim Gavin
The Copy Chief, *Zoetrope*
Aisha Gawad
The Guardians of America, *American Short Fiction*

Laura Hartenberger
The Canvas, *subTerrain*
Ben Hoffman
Reports from a Higher Roof, *Zoetrope*

Geetha Iyer
The Mongerji Letters, *Salt Hill Journal*

Kendall Klym
Pavlova, *Hunger Mountain*

Zachary Lazar
We Forgive Those Who Trespass Against Us, *Brick*
Henry W. Leung
This is Not a Tourist Attraction, *The Asian American Literary Review*
Jill Logan
A Daughter's Letter to Tamsen Donner, *Zyzzyva*

Ben Mauk
Stethoscope, *The Sun Magazine*
Elena Mauli Shapiro
Bank Repos for Sale, *Zyzzyva*

MATTHEW NEILL NULL
   The Island in the Gorge of the Great River, *Ecotone*
ADAM NICOLSON
   Chasing Wolves in the American West, *Granta*

SHELLY ORIA
   My Wife, in Converse, *The Paris Review*

FRANCES DE PONTES PEEBLES
   The Crossing, *Zoetrope*

JOHN PICARD
   The Double, *Hayden's Ferry Review*

JAMIE QUATRO
   Bedtime Story, *Tin House*

ANA MARÍA SHUA
   Circus Freaks, *New Orleans Review*
SARAH MOLLIE SILBERMAN
   Armor, *Booth*

ROBERT UREN
   Omniplanet, *Post Road Magazine*

ABOUT 826 NATIONAL

Proceeds from this book benefit youth literacy

A PERCENTAGE OF the cover price of this book goes to 826 National, a network of seven youth tutoring, writing, and publishing centers in seven cities around the country.

Since the birth of 826 National in 2002, our goal has been to assist students ages 6–18 with their writing skills while helping teachers get their classes passionate about writing. We do this with a vast army of volunteers who donate their time so we can give as much one-on-one attention as possible to the students whose writing needs it. Our mission is based on the understanding that great leaps in learning can happen with one-on-one attention, and that strong writing skills are fundamental to future success.

Through volunteer support, each of the eight 826 chapters—in San Francisco, New York, Los Angeles, Ann Arbor, Chicago, Boston, and Washington, DC—provides drop-in tutoring, class field trips, writing workshops, and in-schools programs, all free of charge, for students, classes, and schools. 826 centers are especially committed to supporting teachers, offering services and resources for English Language Learners, and publishing student work. Each of the 826 chapters works to produce professional-quality publications written entirely by young people, to forge relationships with teachers in order to create innovative workshops and lesson plans, to inspire students to write and appreciate the written word, and to rally thousands of enthusiastic volunteers to make it all happen. By offering all of our programming for free, we aim to serve families who cannot afford to pay for the level of personalized instruction their children receive through 826 chapters.

The demand for 826 National's services is tremendous. Last year we worked with more than 6,000 volunteers and over 32,000 students nationally, hosted 730 field trips, completed 218 major in-schools projects, offered 378 evening and weekend workshops, welcomed over nearly 200 students per day for after-school tutoring, and produced nearly 1,000 student publications. At many of our centers, our field trips are fully booked almost a year in advance, teacher requests for in-school tutor support continue to rise, and the majority of our evening and weekend workshops have waitlists.

826 National volunteers are local community residents, professional writers, teachers, artists, college students, parents, bankers, lawyers, and retirees from a wide range of professions. These passionate individuals can be found at all of our centers after school, sitting side-by-side with our students, providing one-on-one attention. They can be found running our field trips, or helping an entire classroom of local students learn how to write a story, or assisting student writers during one of our Young Authors' Book Programs.

All day and in a variety of ways, our volunteers are actively connecting with youth from the communities we serve.

To learn more or get involved, please visit:

826 National: www.826national.org
826 San Francisco: www.826valencia.org
826 New York: www.826nyc.org
826 Los Angeles: www.826la.org
826 Chicago: www.826chi.org
826 Ann Arbor: www.826mi.org
826 Boston: www.826boston.org
826 Washington, DC: www.826dc.org

826 VALENCIA

Named for the street address of the building it occupies in the heart of San Francisco's Mission District, 826 Valencia opened on April 8, 2002 and consists of a writing lab, a street-front, student-friendly retail pirate store that partially funds its programs, and satellite classrooms in two local middle schools. 826 Valencia has developed programs that reach students at every possible opportunity—in school, after school, in the evenings, or on the weekends. Since its doors opened, over fifteen hundred volunteers—including published authors, magazine founders, SAT course instructors, documentary filmmakers,

and other professionals—have donated their time to work with thousands of students. These volunteers allow the center to offer all of its services for free.

826 NYC

826NYC's writing center opened its doors in September 2004. Since then its programs have offered over one thousand students opportunities to improve their writing and to work side by side with hundreds of community volunteers. 826NYC has also built a satellite tutoring center, created in partnership with the Brooklyn Public Library, which has introduced library programs to an entirely new community of students. The center publishes a handful of books of student writing each year.

826 LA

826LA benefits greatly from the wealth of cultural and artistic resources in the Los Angeles area. The center regularly presents a free workshop at the Armand Hammer Museum in which esteemed artists, writers, and performers teach their craft. 826LA has collaborated with the J. Paul Getty Museum to create Community Photo-

works, a months-long program that
taught seventh-graders the basics of
photographic composition and analysis, sent them into Los Angeles with
cameras, and then helped them polish artist statements. Since opening
in March 2005, 826LA has provided
thousands of hours of free one-on-
one writing instruction, held sum-

mer camps for English language learners, given students sportswrit-
ing training in the Lakers' press room, and published love poems
written from the perspectives of leopards.

826 CHICAGO

826 Chicago opened its writing lab
and after-school tutoring center in
the West Town community of Chicago, in the Wicker Park neighborhood. The setting is both culturally lively and teeming with schools:
within one mile, there are fifteen
public schools serving more than
sixteen thousand students. The center opened in December 2005 and

now has over five hundred volunteers. Its programs, like at all the
826 chapters, are designed to be both challenging and enjoyable. Ultimately, the goal is to strengthen each student's power to express ideas
effectively, creatively, confidently, and in his or her individual voice.

826 MICHIGAN

826 Michigan opened its doors on June 1, 2005, on South State
Street in Ann Arbor. In October of 2007 the operation moved downtown, to a new and improved location on Liberty Street. This move
enabled the opening of Liberty Street Robot Supply & Repair in May
2008. The shop carries everything the robot owner might need, from

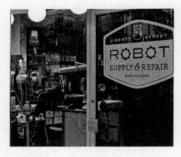

positronic brains to grasping appendages to solar cells. 826 Michigan is the only 826 not named after a city because it serves students all over southeastern Michigan, hosting in-school residencies in Ypsilanti schools, and providing workshops for students in Detroit, Lincoln, and Willow Run school districts. The center also has a packed workshop schedule on site every semester, with offerings on making pop-up books, writing sonnets, creating screenplays, producing infomercials, and more.

826 BOSTON

826 Boston kicked off its programming in the spring of 2007 by inviting authors Junot Díaz, Steve Almond, Holly Black, and Kelly Link to lead writing workshops at the English High School. The visiting writers challenged students to modernize fairy tales, invent their ideal school, and tell their own sto-

ries. Afterward, a handful of dedicated volunteers followed up with weekly visits to help students develop their writing craft. These days, the center has thrown open its doors in Roxbury's Egleston Square— a culturally diverse community south of downtown that stretches into Jamaica Plain, Roxbury, and Dorchester. 826 Boston neighbors more than twenty Boston schools, a dance studio, and the Boston Neighborhood Network (a public-access television station).

826 DC

826DC, opened its doors to the city's Columbia Heights neighborhood in October 2010. 826DC provides after-school tutoring, field trips, after-school workshops, in-school tutoring, help for English language learners, and assistance with the publication of student work. It also offers free admission to the Mu-

seum of Unnatural History, the center's unique storefront. 826DC volunteers recently helped publish a student-authored poetry book project called *Dear Brain*. 826DC's students have also already read poetry for the President and First Lady Obama, participating in the 2011 White House Poetry Student Workshop.

ABOUT SCHOLARMATCH

Founded by author Dave Eggers, ScholarMatch began as a simple crowdfunding platform to help low-income students pay for college. In five short years ScholarMatch has grown into a full service college-access organization, serving more than 500 students each year. We support students at our drop-in center, at local schools and organizations, and online through our crowdfunding platform and innovative resources like the ScholarMatcher—the first free college search tool built specifically with the needs of low-income students in mind.

Our mission is to make college possible for underserved youth by matching students with donors, resources, colleges, and professional networks. More than 80 percent of ScholarMatch students are the first in their families to go to college, and over 50 percent have family incomes of $25,000 or less. ScholarMatch students are bright, resilient young people who have overcome significant challenges, and maintain their determination to seek a better future through college.

With the support of donors, volunteers, schools and community organizations, we ensure that college is possible for underserved students in the San Francisco Bay Area and beyond. To support a student's college journey or learn more, visit scholarmatch.org.

THE BEST AMERICAN SERIES®

FIRST, BEST, AND BEST-SELLING

The Best American series is the premier annual showcase for the country's finest short fiction and nonfiction. Each volume's series editor selects notable works from hundreds of periodicals. A special guest editor, a leading writer in the field, then chooses the best twenty or so pieces to publish. This unique system has made the Best American series the most respected—and most popular—of its kind.

Look for these best-selling titles in the Best American series:

The Best American Comics

The Best American Essays

The Best American Infographics

The Best American Mystery Stories

The Best American Nonrequired Reading

The Best American Science and Nature Writing

The Best American Science Fiction and Fantasy

The Best American Short Stories

The Best American Sports Writing

The Best American Travel Writing

Available in print and e-book wherever books are sold.
Visit our website: *www.hmhco.com/popular-reading/general-interest-books/
by-category/best-american*